SAWMILL ROAD

Other novels by Patrick J. O'Brian include:
The Fallen
Reaper: Book One of the West Baden Murder Series
The Brotherhood
Retribution: Book Two of the West Baden Murder Series
Stolen Time
Sins of the Father: Book Three of the West Baden Murder Series
Six Days
Dysfunction
The Sleeping Phoenix
Snowbound: Book Four of the West Baden Murder Series

Updates and information about the author can be found at:
www.pjobooks.com
or
www.myspace.com/pjobooks

SAWMILL ROAD

A Novel

Patrick J. O'Brian

iUniverse, Inc.

New York Lincoln Shanghai

Sawmill Road

iUniverse books may be ordered through booksellers or by contacting:

iUniverse
2021 Pine Lake Road, Suite 100
Lincoln, NE 68512
www.iuniverse.com
1-800-Authors (1-800-288-4677)

Because of the dynamic nature of the Internet, any Web addresses or links contained in this book may have changed since publication and may no longer be valid.

This is a work of fiction. All of the characters, names, incidents, organizations, and dialogue in this novel are either the products of the author's imagination or are used fictitiously.

ISBN: 978-0-595-47040-2 (pbk)
ISBN: 978-0-595-91323-7 (ebk)

Printed in the United States of America

This is for my grandparents
who all live in New York and
influenced my life for the better
in many ways they may never
know. It's always great to go home
again. Thank you so very much.

Thanks to my "crew" of helpers who do
a fantastic job of making me look good:
Nannette Bell, Carol Pyle, Brad Wiemer,
Joy Winslow, Mark Adams, and Dave
Blackford.

Thanks to Ken "Juddy" Plumb, Jennifer
Delk, Howard Scheetz, and Jason Urwin
for technical assistance.

A special thanks goes out to Sheriff
Timothy Howard in Erie County, New York.
Without him taking time from his busy
schedule to answer my dozens of e-mails
this book wouldn't have nearly the degree
of accuracy or authenticity that is now does.
Thank you very much, Tim.

My other technical source wishes to remain
anonymous, but I owe him a great many
thanks for his insight and input as well.

Thanks to my cover people, including:
David Haines, Kent Chalfant, Rhiannon
O'Dell, James Fullhart, Frank Stapleton II,
Paul Starr, and Aaron Shreves. All of
you were a pleasure to work with.

And thanks as always to Kendrick
Shadoan for putting the cover together.

www.klsdigital.com

CHAPTER 1

▼

Deputy John Hardegen wanted nothing more than to see his wife and two children, but his unyielding sense of duty placed him on a county road east of Buffalo, New York.

Officially assigned to the drug task force unit comprised of local and state police agencies, his work day was over. Driving home in an unmarked Crown Victoria, Hardegen heard his dispatcher call for a unit in the area of Davison Road over the radio. Between the towns of Clarence Center and Newstead, the road ran north to south, dotted with residences.

Though he worked for the Erie County Sheriff's Department, Hardegen had just participated in a tri-county detail three miles northeast of the Tonawanda Indian Reservation.

He decided to take the check of welfare call from his dispatcher for a change of pace, and because it was on the way home. It seemed a family of three had gone several days without calling anyone, or answering phone calls.

While he wasn't a road officer per se, Hardegen decided to save someone else the trouble of checking on the family. For all he knew, they might have gone on a trip without telling anyone, or their phone wasn't working. His car was simply transportation, because the state police provided several confiscated cars for undercover use during the drug sting. Since he wasn't in uniform, he hoped both the car and his badge convinced anyone he encountered that he was indeed a legitimate police officer.

Because he grew up on a farm, Hardegen knew his home county exceptionally well. Weekends in rural New York provided little entertainment to teenagers, so he and his friends usually took to the roads during his high school years.

Few people knew back roads like John Hardegen.

Fully capable of getting lost within Buffalo's city limits, Hardegen could recall nearly every county road from memory. His fellow deputies typically had to refer to a map book to find their way to obscure roads, while his collected dust in his cruiser's back seat. They were the same deputies who stayed close to the cities and towns, rather than patrol the rural areas.

While he didn't know the Wilson family specifically, he found Davison Road rather easily. He turned south from Clarence Center Road, beginning to look for the address his dispatcher provided.

Only thirty-five years old, the deputy had made a name for himself doing undercover work in his department. He worked extensively with the New York State Police, conducting "buy" operations where the officers posed as buyers, arresting drug dealers after they took the bait.

Hardegen loved the position because his hours weren't set, he had very few people to report to, and any dress code was virtually nonexistent. But as much as he loved it, his wife hated his current assignment. She did little to hide her displeasure, making comments during dinner, or over the phone when he called several times a day.

Jamie didn't worry much about the danger, because she knew Hardegen could protect himself as a ten-year veteran of the Erie County Sheriff's Office. She worked a full-time job teaching school, then spent most of her time with the kids at night. He felt bad that she didn't get much of a break, but stayed home with his son and daughter as often as possible.

Reading the mailboxes as he passed them, Hardegen searched for the correct residence. All around him, trees displayed their fall change like peacocks, shedding their orange and red leaves. Several landed on his car, quickly whisked away by the wind as he found a mailbox painted like a red barn with the correct address.

"This figures," he muttered, finding a somewhat lengthy gravel driveway that led to an old barn and a newer modular home.

Aside from the house, the property appeared very much like a fairly traditional farm setting. Animals grazed behind barbed-wire fences, the smell of manure entered the deputy's nose, and two vehicles were visible near the house.

A worn down, white Pontiac Grand Prix and a newer Ford pickup looked good enough to serve as the family's primary vehicles.

Hardegen felt certain he had just wasted a trip.

Jamie was already going to be pissed at him, so he decided to step out of his car to check on the family.

Looking only partly like a cop, Hardegen wore blue jeans, an old button-up shirt, and a brown leather jacket to combat the latest cold front. What started as a warm sunny day turned overcast and chilly by mid-afternoon.

Between his full beard and disheveled hair, Hardegen wondered if the family might mistake him for a neighboring farmer or a vagrant. His position didn't call for him to look like a model member of society.

He stepped from the car, tucking his holstered firearm into his belt behind him.

After pulling his badge from inside one of the jacket pockets, Hardegen hung it around his neck to ensure no one thought he was a trespasser. For once, he wanted people to know he worked for a police agency.

Standing beside his car a moment, he hoped someone might emerge from the house so he could be on his way. A quick survey of the grounds revealed little to him. A large tree in the front yard displayed fall foliage with a blanket of orange leaves at its base. The wind suddenly picked up, causing the tree to sound like a rattlesnake as it sent several leaves seesawing toward the ground.

Pumpkins sat on the front porch steps, reminding him that Halloween was less than a week away. Luckily his children weren't old enough to pick out their own costumes, or he would surely get drafted into taking them to a department store. A cluster of dried leaves tumbled across the driveway as the deputy decided to approach the house to escape the miserable weather.

"Anyone home?" he called as he drew near the front door, finding it closed.

He rapped on the door several times with his knuckles, receiving no answer.

After waiting several seconds he knocked again, wondering if the Wilsons were hermits who hated visitors.

"Sheriff's Department," he announced as he tried the door with his right hand, finding the knob turned without restraint, allowing him access.

He started to take one step inside when his eyes detected blood.

Not just a drop or two, and not even a single source of blood. Along one wall in the living room, he found a projectile mist pattern created by only one type of weapon.

A gun.

Knowing his rung in the investigative ladder rested somewhere near the bottom, Hardegen wanted to step outside immediately to preserve evidence. He wasn't about to report to his dispatcher, however, until he found something more conclusive.

Though highly unlikely, the stain might have come from someone shooting the family dog inside the house for all he knew. Of course the dog would have needed to be standing on its hind legs to place the pattern so high on the wall.

Hardegen stepped fully inside, careful to search for clues and not step onto anything except clean flooring. He searched the house from one end to the other, finding nothing except more trace amounts of blood along the floor, beneath the wall spatter.

Several times over he found family portraits of the three potential victims. Some were framed atop tables or night stands, while a few hung on walls. Nothing about the family appeared the least bit unusual, except that they couldn't be found. Even people who quickly abandoned a property took prized possessions like photographs.

Hardegen suspected the worst concerning this family.

In the back of his mind he didn't want to find bodies, because he knew gunshot corpses were typically messy, as was the paperwork that accompanied any homicide case.

Nothing inside the house appeared ransacked. Every drawer was closed, the beds were made, and most of the house looked tidy.

Stepping outside, the deputy walked around the house, surveying the grounds and any nearby objects as he went. He noticed red speckles dotting the Grand Prix's front left fender as he rounded the corner of the modular home. One look to the ground revealed little, because blood would either soak into the ground, or stick to grass petals.

He refused to step near the car, because doing so might risk destroying delicate evidence. Instead, Hardegen walked toward the barn, feeling his heart thump inside his chest. After the house turned up no bodies, he just *knew* something bad awaited him inside the old barn.

Several animals squawked and cackled at him when he approached the gray structure. At first, he thought they sensed him intruding upon their grounds, but noticed several empty troughs. Not even crumbs remained in the far reaches of the troughs, and the pigs all scurried his way, making a commotion.

These animals hadn't eaten in at least a day.

Hardegen approached the conventional door at one end of the barn, deciding he didn't want to unlock or disturb any more evidence than necessary. While he initially believed the barn's gray color came from paint, it turned out the hue came from a complete lack of paint, or any kind of treatment. The wood had begun deteriorating and splintering in several areas, leading him to believe the Wilson family decided to let God do what he would with the old barn.

Standing outside the door momentarily, Hardegen smelled something odd when the breeze picked up once more. The odor crossed his nose just long enough for him to think he recognized it, but disappeared before he identified what it might be.

Inside, the barn felt even more creepy. Holes in the roof provided just enough light for Hardegen to navigate his way through the place. He checked the cooped chickens, finding them half-starved, then stepped into the workshop, spying undisturbed tools hung along the walls and lying on workbenches.

Over the next few minutes, the deputy climbed a ladder to check the hayloft, then searched around the large farm equipment, including a tractor and hay baler. He found no bodies, and no further evidence of foul play.

He wondered if they might be testing fake blood for some kind of haunted hay ride, or covering their tracks if they wanted to disappear. In his experience, people sometimes did strange things for attention, or to distract others from the truth. For all he knew, they had mounting debts, and wanted out before the bank foreclosed.

Hardegen found a different way out of the old barn, sighing heavily as he looked up to the gloomy sky. Feeling duped, he decided to check around the barn before radioing his dispatcher. He straddled a wooden fence, climbing over to find a few horses in the nearby pasture. Accidentally catching their attention, Hardegen decided to conduct his search quickly before they pestered him for food.

He walked around the barn, jumping two more short fences along the way, before drawing near the area where he first entered the structure. Hardegen had all but given up hope of finding any true evidence of foul play when his eyes spied a manure pile. If not for incredible contrast, he might never have noticed something considerably out of place, sticking out from the pile.

A dirty, otherwise pale human hand with a wedding band on the ring finger hung limply from the mound's center.

CHAPTER 2

▼

Hardegen's day went from bad to worse when he called Jamie to let her know what happened. Instead of being compassionate and understanding, she berated him for taking someone else's call, then finding a body.

He decided she was right in a way. One of the younger officers might have been thrilled about finding a corpse. Most police officers typically feel curious about the idea of seeing a dead person until it becomes a recurrence. Hardegen didn't mind sneaking a peek this time, because this went beyond a typical death scene.

Three people had likely been slaughtered on their own property.

"You okay, son?" Sheriff Paul Gaffney asked when he approached his deputy.

"I'm fine," Hardegen answered, leaning against the unmarked car as several uniformed officers began setting up a perimeter around the property.

A retired state trooper, Gaffney typically made appearances on homicides and major cases, though not because he wanted publicity. A former investigator for the state police, he took an interest in what happened within his territory. Like Hardegen, Gaffney had spent much of his life in the Erie County area.

Gaffney had retired from the state police after winning the election a few years prior. Now in his early fifties, the sheriff found more gray strands in his otherwise dark brown hair almost daily.

A thick mustache resided below the man's nose, while his shrewd blue eyes never missed a beat, like an eagle searching for prey. Remaining in physical condition just short of younger athletes, the sheriff worked out regularly. Today he wore his official departmental uniform, complete with sidearm and insignias, prepared to do battle with the media.

He had traveled from Buffalo where the administration and the jail were housed, while the state police investigators came from Batavia, in the heart of adjacent Genesee County. Dusk was now less than an hour away, because it took everyone nearly an hour to arrive and set up their equipment.

What few investigators the sheriff had available at the moment were busy with a fresh murder-suicide along the northern tip of the county. One was on vacation, and two were out-of-state at a special school, leaving the Erie County Sheriff's Department unusually short-staffed. Putting aside his usual bulldog attitude of keeping cases in his yard, Gaffney asked for assistance from the state police. By no means was he relinquishing the case to them, but his experience told him his people needed additional manpower.

If felt too early to form a task force, but unofficially they were doing just that.

"What were you doing out here?" Gaffney asked his deputy, now that he knew what Hardegen found.

"My team was working outside of Akron. I was on my way home when dispatch asked for one of our units to check on this family. Since I was just a couple miles out, I took the call."

Gaffney looked toward the barn, where several members of the forensic team inspected the manure pile.

No one else would be allowed near the house or barn until they finished combing every square inch of the property for potential evidence.

"Looks like whoever did it got a couple days jump on us," Hardegen stated.

With a displeased expression, the sheriff looked from the death scene to Hardegen, then to the reporters barely standing behind the crime scene tape near the road. At the moment, only a few stood near the driveway's edge, but more were sure to come, like nomadic zombies in a horror movie.

"They want answers I can't give," Gaffney said solemnly. "And we don't have shit to go on."

Hardegen suspected the man planned to give a statement of some sort once more reporters showed up. Gaffney didn't care for the idea of having a public relations specialist, mainly because he spoke very well in front of cameras.

And it *was* an election year.

For the most part, Hardegen had been ignored by the forensic technicians, even the two who worked on his department. He counted at least three so far, but they ducked in and out of the buildings like worker bees, making a headcount difficult. They carefully walked around, dressed like they were ready to perform surgery with disposable gowns across their bodies and foot covers over their shoes.

Hardegen saw the state's forensic people arrive around the same time as the investigative team, and though they all worked under the same roof, and technically as one team, they split up. The investigators cautiously traced the outskirts of the property while the forensics people dove into the heart of the matter.

Gaffney had coordinated his efforts and people with the state police, so the two organizations worked different aspects of the scene simultaneously.

Over the course of just fifteen minutes, the deputy saw the forensic people bag and tag evidence, videotape the scene, swab some fluids, and search for trace evidence with numbed interest. He never had an inclination to take classes in forensic studies, though he understood how it worked hand-in-hand with his duties. As they placed little arrows and markers beside key pieces of evidence, the deputy realized he didn't have the meticulous nature to analyze such things.

He preferred kicking in doors and doing minimal paperwork afterwards.

One of the investigators from the state police finally approached him, holding out his hand to introduce himself, which Hardegen shook.

"Grant Lamoureux," the man said plainly, since he was obviously a member of the state police.

Probably a few years older than Hardegen, Lamoureux kept his head nearly shaved, because most of his hair had gone south permanently. He appeared to have a five o'clock shadow, but Hardegen guessed his brown stubble always showed against his light skin. Wearing khaki slacks and a navy blue sport coat, he looked the part of any standard state police investigator.

"I need to know exactly what you did once you arrived," Lamoureux stated, pulling out a notepad and pen, his deep blue eyes unblinking as he waited for an answer.

Hardegen spent the better part of ten minutes detailing his search of the grounds after the initial call from the dispatcher. He told the investigator exactly where he stepped, what he found, and his assessment of the farm animals.

"How long would you say they've gone without food?" Lamoureux asked, impressed enough by the statement that he pursued it.

"Every trough I saw was bone dry," Hardegen answered. "They've probably been a day or two without."

Lamoureux made a notation on paper, then turned to Gaffney.

"Do you plan on making a statement?"

"Something brief to hold them over until we know more," the sheriff replied, eyeing the reporters. "Anything specific you want said? Or do you trust me to wing it?"

The investigator chuckled, knowing the sheriff asked as a professional courtesy, and not because he planned on relinquishing his throne and scepter to his former organization.

"This is still your baby, Paul. I'm going to have my people talk to neighbors and comb the surrounding area."

"Use anyone from my department you need," the sheriff said.

Hardegen had the impression the sheriff knew the investigator from past experience, which might have explained in part why he requested Lamoureux's team. He knew Gaffney worked in Batavia at some length, so the two probably worked together.

He personally knew only a handful of state troopers, most of whom worked on the drug task force. Assisting on violent crimes wasn't something Hardegen typically dabbled in, because his job seldom got messy.

"Can I borrow Deputy Hardegen?" Lamoureux asked, surprising the deputy.

"Certainly."

At first, the deputy suspected Lamoureux simply wanted to formally interview him, but the investigator motioned for Hardegen to follow him elsewhere.

One look to the sheriff indicated Gaffney had enough faith in him to recommend him for the investigator's use. The sheriff gave him a discreet nod and a wink, though Hardegen wondered what plans Lamoureux had for him.

"Sir?" Hardegen asked Gaffney.

"He's one of the best, John. I want you to work with him as long as he'll have you."

Hardegen's burning question had just been answered, though he wondered why the sheriff threw him to the wolves instead of having him learn from their own investigators who continued to work near the barn. He had his reasons, and since they were obviously working together until they found the killer, Hardegen figured Gaffney wanted him to experience a *real* task force.

Above all, Gaffney was an investigator at heart.

Lamoureux led the way toward his state-owned vehicle, calling over members of his team for a brief meeting.

During the investigator's instructions to his team, Hardegen learned the man was the Senior Investigator of the VCIT (Violent Crimes Investigation Team) and a fairly seasoned investigator from his demeanor. He quickly assigned each of the four people surrounding him tasks, beginning with interviews of all the neighbors.

He then asked them to check friends, family members, financial records, political ties, church affiliations, clubs and organizations, employers, former employees, criminal histories, and phone records. Hardegen figured that covered just about anything the forensic team couldn't cover while they were busy collecting evidence.

From what Hardegen recalled, the VCIT worked with the FIU (Forensic Investigation Unit) often and extensively, but the VCIT and its Senior Investigator called the shots.

Each member of Lamoureux's team paid close attention to him, showing the utmost respect. To the deputy, he treated this homicide much like any other. A standard approach worked in cities like Buffalo, but not rural Erie County where neighbors were few, and witnesses even fewer.

If anyone had known anything about a local shooting, the case would have started two days sooner.

Within a minute, a state trooper cleared the media from the driveway's edge so the three investigators could depart to carry out their tasks. Lamoureux was about to speak with the deputy when one of the forensic technicians approached him after stepping from the modular home.

Lamoureux quickly introduced the man as Steve Nelson, describing the man as his most trusted resource at a crime scene. Not an overly handsome man, Nelson had acne scars on his cheeks and neck, while his black hair desperately needed a trim.

"I'm flattered," Nelson said, producing a brief smile.

"What have you got for me, Steve?"

"We're still collecting evidence inside the home, but the answering machine had a few pretty standard messages on it. Mostly worried friends and family members."

"Any prints?" Lamoureux inquired.

"Quite a few fingerprints. It'll take some time to draw comparisons, so I'm focusing on any footprints we produce for more immediate gratification. The blood spatter looks consistent with a small firearm, and there weren't any shells or casings, so we're looking at a small revolver, or someone who picked up after themselves."

Hardegen didn't feel quite so ignorant, considering the experts couldn't pinpoint the weapon used, or exactly what happened inside.

"We did find something kind of strange in a closet," Nelson added, directing his statement at Lamoureux. "There were two family albums with photos removed."

Hardegen didn't recall seeing the photo albums, but his search was for bodies and anything highly unusual. He didn't have the luxury of looking through every cupboard, drawer, and shelf like the forensic team.

"Do you think the killer took some souvenirs?" Lamoureux asked.

Nelson nodded affirmatively.

"It looks like he searched all of them, but his focus was on two of the earlier books."

"Earlier books?" Hardegen inquired.

"The books that had photos of the daughter when she was real young."

A strange look crossed Lamoureux's face as he turned in thought a moment.

"See if you can dig up any negatives," he told Nelson. "I want to know what our guy was after."

Nelson gave a confirming nod.

"The boys are still digging the body, or bodies, from the shit pile back there," he said, nodding toward the barn. "This is already a cold case, and we ain't finding much in the house to help."

Lamoureux gave an understanding sigh, though Hardegen wondered if the family albums might lead to some answers. Perhaps the photos were somehow incriminating to the killer, or just personal.

"Check everything. Recent cell phone calls, the computer, and especially their paperwork. I've got my people talking to neighbors and checking the family history. Right now, this could be any number of things. They might have pissed someone off, or maybe gotten in the middle of some drug or gang activity."

Hardegen glanced his way, wanting to double-check if the investigator was being serious or not. After all, this wasn't anything like the big city, or the people the deputy busted on a regular basis.

"Seriously," Lamoureux assured him. "We have to look at every angle."

Thinking it over, Hardegen realized he had just come from a drug-related scenario in a small town, so why should the rural parts of the state be exempt?

Before either investigator said another word, one of the forensic team members approached them from the backyard. He had a strange look on his face, like someone who had just found a cockroach beside his porterhouse steak at a restaurant.

"What's wrong?" Nelson asked him immediately.

"You might want to take a look at this, boss," the man answered, his overclothes dabbed with brown stains, some still moist.

Hardegen remained still until Lamoureux motioned for him to come along. Feeling like a college student beginning an apprenticeship, the deputy felt uncertain of his boundaries. Apparently the investigator wanted him along for every part of the search, though he didn't know why.

Simply complying, the deputy walked a careful trail behind Nelson, Lamoureux, and the technician. They avoided the white Grand Prix because one of the county technicians was busy processing the vehicle and the surrounding area.

A third member of the forensic team stood near the pile, camera in hand, when the four men approached the makeshift burial plot. Two of the bodies had been unearthed, with the third remaining partially buried in the pile. Hardegen noticed the manure pile hadn't been affected by the cool overnight temperatures, separating easily when the technicians dug with their gloved hands and shovels.

He wondered how someone murdered three people in cold blood, then buried their bodies beside the barn with no one noticing. Perhaps the Wilsons kept to themselves, because it took two days for anyone to grow seriously worried.

A glance toward the ground revealed two bodies wrapped hastily in some sort of plastic drop cloths. One appeared to be an adult male, the other an adult female. Crouching down, he looked at the male body, still clothed, his eyes partially shut as though caught between a waking dream and the real world.

A dulled matte film overtook whatever life the brown eyes once displayed. Hardegen had seen his share of bodies, but never murder victims. Car wrecks and suicides provided most of the death scenes during his career, and though many of them were gory, he found it especially unnerving to know someone brutally killed the people laid out before him.

He would have studied them further, but Nelson's colleague spoke to the group.

"Take a whiff," he told Lamoureux, pointing to the body halfway recovered from the manure pile.

Instead of immediately complying, the Senior Investigator gave him a strange look, refusing to fall for any kind of prank.

"I'm not kidding," the man said. "Have a look down here, and let me know what you think that is."

Lamoureux finally leaned over, studying where the man pointed, then cautiously smelled whatever he found. To Hardegen, it simply looked like a tiny pool of stale water caught in one of the plastic's numerous folds, but he wasn't as close to the bodies.

"Goddamn," Lamoureux muttered. "That's piss."

Receiving the answer he wanted, the man nodded.

"It's all over their clothing, and pooled in the creases of each tarp. I accidentally touched it on the second victim's shirt."

Lamoureux thought a moment. Expired victims often release any stored waste in their bladders and bowels, but the mess typically stops within their own clothing. And, if the bodies had been moved after death, their own waste would not have followed.

He reached an obvious conclusion.

"The killer pissed on all of their bodies?"

The technician nodded.

"We haven't found fingerprints anywhere, but he left us plenty of DNA. Why the hell would he go through all the trouble of eluding detection, then leave us such damning evidence?"

Exhaling heavily through his nose, Lamoureux thought a moment, unable to readily answer the question. Though no detective, Hardegen decided the crime seemed exceptionally personal, though until they found a motive, they wouldn't know why.

Already two days behind in their investigation, the team had lost its golden forty-eight hour window. Crimes not solved within that time frame have a far lower chance of ever being resolved because trails quickly grow cold.

Lamoureux sought the sheriff, asking him for advice or permission when he found him. Though he couldn't hear the conversation, Hardegen noticed Gaffney readily agreeing with whatever Lamoureux proposed.

When Lamoureux returned, he plucked his cellular phone from its clip along his belt.

"I can't get inside this guy's head, and we're not making much headway with the evidence, so I'm going to call an old friend," the investigator informed Hardegen before walking toward the driveway to place the call.

CHAPTER 3

▼

"This absolutely sucks," Terry Levine said as he stood over the broken tombstone of his great-grandfather. "What kind of punks would do this?"

"It's a week from Halloween, Terry," Dan Schmidt, the local police chief, reminded him. "Kids will be kids."

Terry shot him a sour look.

Five other stones had received similar damage, which tended to unnerve a small New York town like Norfolk. The other grave markers didn't mean nearly as much to Terry, but at least Schmidt had done a kindness by calling him personally.

Standing near the back of the cemetery, both men looked down at the stone, which had broken in two pieces after falling off its base. Someone had evidently taken a lead pipe, or something heavier, to the stone.

A local state trooper, Terry had returned to his hometown area a year prior as a road officer, giving up a prominent position as an investigator. He and Schmidt had worked several cases together, putting their initial differences behind them as time passed.

Terry operated by the book, while the Norfolk chief tended to rough up suspects and investigate cases through unconventional methods. In their area, where small towns dotted the map across the county, Schmidt had to keep his methods under wraps, or risk losing his job.

"Are you saying you're not going to look into this?" Terry asked the chief, who continued to hold a flashlight over the grave site.

With dusk upon them, the flashlight provided the only means of visibility within the cemetery. Only a few overhead lamps shed additional light, but they were closer to the entrance, helping Terry and Schmidt very little.

Though the graveyard technically had a closing time, no gates actually closed to keep intruders out.

"I'll look into it," Schmidt answered, "but unless witnesses come forward, I'm not going to get far."

Terry bobbed his head solemnly.

He certainly didn't expect the chief to work any miracles. With a force of three other men, all of whom volunteered their time, Schmidt had more pressing worries than tombstone vandalism.

"I'd appreciate anything you can do," Terry said, allowing Schmidt to lead the way toward their vehicles.

He decided to change the subject, simply to let the chief know he wasn't upset, or holding any grudge from their previous work together.

"How's Amy doing?" he inquired, speaking of Schmidt's newlywed wife who worked as a state police investigator at a separate station.

"She's at an interrogation school in Syracuse this week, so I'm batching it."

"Any plans?"

Schmidt let a grin slip beneath his thick mustache, though Terry barely caught it in the low lighting.

"I'm going hunting with the guys this weekend. She gets to have her fun, so I'm not going to sit around the house."

Terry didn't regard any police certification classes as *fun*, though most of them proved fruitful at various points in his career. He wondered how Amy, an intelligent, beautiful, gifted investigator ended up marrying someone as gruff as Schmidt.

He had attended the wedding, wondering throughout the ceremony how long their relationship was meant to last. Before meeting his wife, Schmidt carried a reputation as somewhat of a ladies' man, which didn't exactly leave overnight.

"So what's been new with you?" the chief inquired.

"Same old thing. Raising three kids and working the road."

"No plans to go back to investigations?"

Terry shrugged lightly.

"There haven't been any openings at my station, and I don't feel like moving. Besides, it's a headache to investigate around here."

"How so?"

"All the action is near the cities. We don't get a whole lot of anything up here."

Schmidt chuckled in response.

"Yeah, like this past spring?"

He referred to a case that remained very personal to the state trooper. Terry had been asked by his former major, now part of his department's upper management, to investigate a case that followed him home. He solved it, but the courts kept it from reaching a definitive conclusion with delays from both the prosecution and defense attorneys.

Terry had a feeling the man who killed people in three different states would plead insanity when the case went to trial. He also suspected any reasonably intelligent jury would see through the defense and convict him to a life sentence.

While Terry would have preferred the death penalty, the state had abolished it years prior.

The delays proved helpful to the prosecution, helping them gather even more evidence and substantial witnesses to bolster their case.

"That prick needs to burn," Schmidt said with his usual lack of sugarcoating.

Terry agreed.

"I'd better get home before the wife calls," he said, extending his hand.

Schmidt shook it before opening his car door. He turned for some parting words.

"I promise I'll shake up the high school and see what I can find."

"Thanks. I'll talk to you later."

Terry slid into the driver's seat of his old S-10 pickup truck. Without the benefit of a take-home car from the state police, and a daughter about to obtain her driver's license, he found himself making sacrifices. The truck didn't burn much fuel, and cost him very little when he bought it from an individual two months prior.

He drove half an hour every morning to pick up a marked patrol car in Canton. The state cut costs by giving out few take-home cars, often making troopers double up in one car during certain evening patrols. The latter reason was as much for safety as helping the state economy.

The recent acquisition of the truck helped him temporarily, because he knew another family vehicle would be necessary once his oldest child received her license. Britney had already been informed that her first vehicle wouldn't be sporty, or expensive, which prompted her to think about getting a part-time job.

Schmidt pulled away as Terry's cell phone rang at his side. He picked it up, finding an old friend calling him. He hadn't spoken with Grant Lamoureux for months, and the two often had interesting stories to tell when they talked.

During his time as a fledgling investigator in the Buffalo area, Terry often teamed with Lamoureux. He solved the bizarre and the tough crimes while his friend conducted the interviews that got them answers and the hard proof prosecutors required. Lamoureux acted as a "closer" for Troop A, which encompassed Erie County, nearly reaching the top rung of importance on the NYSP ladder.

"What's up, Grant?" Terry asked when he answered the call, glad to hear from his friend.

"Well, a murder for starters," Lamoureux said, bluntly answering his question.

Terry said nothing for a few seconds.

"You okay?" Lamoureux asked over the line.

"I guess I was expecting an update on the kids, or something a little more personable. Got something tough on your hands?"

Lamoureux sometimes called when he needed help on especially unusual cases, or when he had no leads. Terry possessed the uncanny ability to think like serial killers and other predators, while his friend relied upon conventional techniques and science to solve his cases.

Since heading up A Troop's violent crimes unit, Lamoureux had complete access to forensic science. The New York State Police worked in districts known as troops throughout the state. Each troop encompassed several counties, covering a large span.

"I had to call and let you know something before someone else did," Lamoureux said, worrying Terry somewhat.

His mind raced with possibilities that perhaps a common friend had passed away, or someone they put away had been released from prison.

"What's wrong?" Terry asked.

"That murder I told you about is something of a strange one."

Terry heard strange noises coming through the phone.

"Where are you?"

"We had a triple homicide down here. I'm still on the property with the team."

"How can I help?"

Silence crossed the line over the next few seconds. Terry began wondering if their call had been severed until Lamoureux spoke again.

"Well, that's the thing. I've already arranged for you to come down here and give me a hand. I wanted you to hear it from me before your supervisor called you."

Absolutely stunned, Terry gripped the steering wheel with his left hand, infuriated that his friend had summoned him to the western part of the state without so much as a warning. He would have acted as a consultant on the case with a simple request from Lamoureux, but hated the sudden interruption of his personal life.

"You okay?" Lamoureux asked after a period of stunned silence.

"How could you do that, Grant? What if I had something going on with Sherri or the kids?"

"I'm *sorry*, Terry. I really am. This case can't wait. I'm already chasing a murder that's two days old, and this has all the markings of a fucked up scenario."

Terry fumed a moment. He knew Lamoureux wouldn't request him on a whim or a hunch unless he felt certain Terry's talents might prove useful. The Senior Investigator knew enough about murders to detect something truly deranged from the barrage of straightforward cases.

Most murders came with motives as obvious as tags on Christmas gifts. Terry specialized in finding the hidden clues and motives that other investigators overlooked. Lamoureux knew about his talents from firsthand experience.

"You couldn't just send me your files?" he asked his longtime friend.

"No. I'm already two days behind, and every second that passes I get further away from the guy who did this."

Terry looked skyward, only seeing the top of his truck instead of twinkling stars as he sighed to himself.

"It's a five-hour trip, Grant. I can be down there by late morning."

"Sorry ol' buddy. I need you down here tonight. The boys have already set up floodlights, and we're working through the night."

"Now you're just being plain unreasonable. I'm not going to be any good to you if I make the trip tonight."

"Then we start fresh in the morning," Lamoureux countered. "Believe me, you're going to want to see this."

Doubting his friend's words, Terry heard his phone internally beep, indicating he had an incoming call.

"I've got another call, Grant."

"It's probably your major telling you he wants you down here ASAP."

"It'll be hard for me to work effectively when I'm pissed at you. You should at least call Sherri and tell her you're the prick taking me away and leaving her alone with the kids."

"Ah, she probably needs a break from you anyway," Lamoureux said, trying to lighten his mood.

"Yeah, right."

Terry clicked a button to switch over to the incoming call, though he desperately wanted to avoid it.

CHAPTER 4

▼

Hardegen figured incorrectly his partnership with the state police was a short-lived experience. Gaffney informed the deputy he needed to work closely with Lamoureux until the investigator turned him loose. He wanted to argue that their own people were right there for him to shadow, but the sheriff had a reason for everything he did.

Around eight o'clock, the Senior Investigator did set him free, but only for the night. He said he wanted the deputy back at the crime scene by seven in the morning unless someone called to tell him otherwise.

Somewhat accustomed to being called out during all hours of the night, Hardegen didn't have an issue with getting up early, but he disliked feeling like Lamoureux's personal property.

So far he hadn't done anything except follow the investigator's lead around the crime scene, but Lamoureux had called an old partner for a fresh perspective on the killer's motivation.

Since he was now detailed to the state police, the deputy planned to trim his beard and get a more conventional haircut. He needed to look respectable to help with interviews, knowing his hair grew back quickly when he needed it to.

Now pulling into his driveway, Hardegen suspected his children were already in bed. It had taken almost an hour to navigate his way home through county roads and small towns. He resided several miles south of Buffalo in the country. Though he didn't own a farm, his water came from a well, and his yard took several hours to mow during the summer.

During his first few years working as a police officer, Hardegen tried living in Buffalo, but found city life expensive and foreign to him. He never grew accustomed to the way people dressed or acted, considering he grew up miles away from anything he considered a city. Anything urban felt dirty to him, unlike the green fields and clear ponds he knew as a child.

Finding Jamie had left the porch light on, he pulled up beside the house, shutting down the unmarked car before stepping out. She didn't greet him at the front or back door, so he suspected she might be upset with him.

He trudged up the steps to the back porch, finding the door locked. Letting an irritated sigh escape, he fished his keys from his jeans pocket, stepping inside seconds later. The odor of roasted pumpkin seeds, one of his favorite seasonal foods, entered his nostrils. Perhaps she wasn't entirely mad at him.

He found his wife doing dishes in the kitchen, confirming she was definitely unhappy with him. The kitchen window allowed her a view of everything he had done since pulling into the driveway, meaning she could have unlocked the door for him.

"I'm sorry," he said softly when he drew close to her from behind, putting several fingers into the back pocket of her jeans.

She continued washing dishes, saying nothing. At least she hadn't pulled away from him, meaning this was destined to be a moderate spat, not one that woke the kids.

"Sorry doesn't quite cut it," she said, noisily placing the last dish in the strainer before turning around.

To Hardegen, she looked as pretty as the day they were married seven years earlier. Her wavy dark locks flowed past her shoulders, but her green eyes had adopted a fiery glow that Hardegen suspected might turn him to stone any moment.

"When we got married, I knew what the life was like," she stated. "Everyone warned me about the long hours, the worry, and even how cops like to run around on their wives."

"Babe, you know I'd *never-*"

She pushed her index finger against his lips.

"I know, but I can't keep raising two kids by myself. This new position of yours is absolute torture."

There.

She had said it at long last.

For the better part of a month, Jamie had dropped subtle hints that she didn't like the hours Hardegen kept. Truth be told, he didn't particularly love the hours, but he felt more satisfaction busting drug dealers than writing tickets or fighting drunkards.

"You want me to go back on the road?" he asked, remaining more calm than he envisioned himself when he ran this inevitable conversation through his mind.

Of course Jamie had conditioned him for this moment during their fleeting conversations the past few weeks.

Rubbing his head, Hardegen walked to the refrigerator, grabbing a beer bottle before sauntering toward the living room. Jamie still hadn't answered him, so he turned to see a perplexed look on her face. Perhaps she hadn't expected him to be so compromising. She tended to plan her rebuttals in excess when she wanted to pick a fight with her husband. It came from living with two overbearing parents during her childhood, striving for the independence she never quite received.

Marrying a cop was one of the few defying acts she carried out against them, though they took to Hardegen shortly after the marriage. They still called daily, and Jamie's mother tended to stick her nose in their affairs more than the deputy wanted.

"I want you to be happy," Jamie said, drawing closer to him. "But I want help raising Brock and Emma Lynn, too."

Hardegen set down his beer, drawing his wife into a hug, saying nothing for a moment. He knew she wanted happiness for both of them, but he also knew raising two young children wasn't easy. When *both* of them were home to watch the kids, it sometimes proved to be a handful.

"Gaffney lent me to the state police since they're assisting with our investigation," he told her softly. "I'll be working some strange hours with them until we find the guy who killed those people, then I'll see what I can do about being here at night."

Enough people comprised the drug task force that Hardegen could slip out for the important things in his life, but he didn't want his peers thinking of him as a slacker. No longer the new guy in his unit, he could work fewer hours, as long as he logged enough to satisfy his department.

"What happened out there?" Jamie inquired as he walked with her to the couch.

He took a few minutes to explain the triple homicide without going into detail. She hated details, especially the graphic stuff. Even the crime shows on television creeped her out if they showed anything deeper than a small slit on a corpse.

"Do they have any idea who did it?" she asked when he concluded his recap of the events.

"No, but they're checking into the family's background. They'll find a red flag somewhere, and nail the son-of-a-bitch."

"Why would he take pictures?" Jamie asked, glancing toward their own family photos lining the mantle of the fireplace.

"Hard saying."

Hardegen drew close to his wife on the couch, reaching behind her as they kissed. Their work schedules had kept them from making love for nearly a week now, and the deputy quickly rose to the occasion as he undid a button, then a second, on Jamie's blouse.

He ran his hand up her thigh, drawing a subdued moan from her, ready to take their pent up passion into the bedroom when a voice killed the moment worse than inappropriate dinner conversation.

"Mommy, I'm scared," their three-year-old son stated from across the room, dressed in pajamas, holding his teddy bear.

Hardegen quickly assumed a normal seated position, dreading the day when his son caught them in the act of something more intense. Jamie corrected her blouse, trying to act normal, but Brock hadn't noticed, still rubbing his eyes.

"Did he take a nap?" Hardegen asked loud enough that only she heard.

"He did, but he was fussy."

Grunting to himself, the deputy knew this wasn't going to be an easy fix, so he patted the couch beside him.

"Come here, big man," he told his son, who lit up like a star upon hearing the words.

He ran over, jumping on the couch beside his father as Jamie headed for the kitchen.

"What's the matter?" he asked Brock, suspecting the boy simply wanted to see him.

Even at his age, his son knew how to push the right buttons to get away with murder, figuratively speaking. Luckily he and Jamie were on the same page when it came to discipline, so the kids could never bounce from one of them to the other hoping to get something. Their charms only worked on their grandparents, but he and Jamie expected their parents to spoil the kids by nature.

"There was a monster in my closet," Brock said sleepily.

"You don't seem real scared, kiddo," Hardegen noted with a chuckle. "Want me to tuck you in?"

Brock's blue eyes lit up again.

"Can you read me a story?"

"Sure," Hardegen said, reaching down to tickle his son along his ribs.

The boy laughed, swaying more defensively than a kick-boxer to avoid his father's strong hands. Hardegen finally picked him up, carrying him toward the second bedroom. He gave a quick look, along with a wink, to his wife when she looked up from the oven.

Jamie shook her head, as though to say he'd blown his one opportunity for the night, but the deputy suspected he could change her mind.

They had waited four years to have kids, but he still didn't have all of the newlywed fringe benefits out of his system yet. Carrying his son to bed, he found his daughter, not yet two, sleeping peacefully on the far side of the room.

As he tucked Brock into bed, Hardegen thought about how much time he lost with the kids when he worked. In a few years he would lose them to the school system, marking his last opportunity to act as a full-time influence on their lives.

He pulled his son's blanket up to his shoulders, gave him a gentle kiss on the forehead, then grinned as he simply studied the boy a moment.

"What story do you want to hear?" he finally asked, reaching toward the bookcase.

CHAPTER 5

―――――――――― ▼ ――――――――――

Terry reached the Batavia station around one in the morning, feeling more ready to call it a night than examine a triple homicide. His mind felt like a tire stuck in mud, unable to move, and barely able to spin.

State troopers refer to their buildings as stations or barracks interchangeably in New York.

Opened in 1976 just north of Batavia on West Saile Drive, the current Troop A headquarters possessed all of the amenities of other barracks, looking similar to several of them in design. Shaped like an "H" with offices, a communications center, a classroom, storage, a garage, and other necessary areas, the building brought back memories for Terry.

His career, in essence his life as he knew it, started in Batavia shortly after graduating the academy.

Sherri had taken the news better than he expected, but not without a few parting words.

For over a year Terry had worked the morning shift, allowing them the ability to plan every facet of their lives. She had no qualms with him leaving to assist on a murder case, but disliked the sudden nature of his departure. Terry explained the choice was not his, because Lamoureux had gone through proper channels to request him as a consultant.

While he didn't leave his wife on rocky terms, he drove away feeling guilty for something completely beyond his control.

Lamoureux met him at the station, driving him out to the old farm in person so they could catch up on old times.

His old friend wasted little time in whisking him away after an initial hand-shake and a hug. Terry felt far less enthusiastic than Lamoureux about seeing the farm, thinking a fresh morning start might give him the pep he truly needed to analyze the scene.

"It's been way too long," Lamoureux said, navigating the county roads rather easily in the dark.

"I just wish it could have been under better circumstances."

"You still raw over me calling you down here?"

Terry answered with unnerving silence.

He supposed the state paid him whether he patrolled the roads in his area, or solved a homicide near the state line, so he simply blamed the rules and regulations of his department.

He only blamed his buddy for drafting him without so much as a phone call until the deed was done.

"It couldn't be helped, Terry. There's something funny about this case, and I don't have any concrete leads yet."

Dried corn stalks barely showed in the headlights, creating a barrier between Lamoureux's car and the darkened fields beside them. Terry saw no lights in the distance except for a few stars in the sky. Though no stranger to miles of desolate fields, he found the current setting a distinct difference from the hundreds of lights and orange construction signs that guided him to Batavia.

"Have you found anything useful?" he asked Lamoureux.

"Our guy took some photos from two family albums, and pissed on the corpses. We also think the dad survived long enough to try and dig himself out of the pile. A deputy found his hand sticking out of a manure pile, or we might never have found the bodies."

"That's it? A guy urinates on a couple bodies and swipes a few photos and you think you have the next Ted Bundy on your hands?"

Lamoureux shook his head vehemently, then focused on the road ahead.

"It's not just that. The forensic guys can't find any footprints, and it's been muddy around here lately. There's no way the guy could have moved around the property without leaving something behind."

"Hair samples? Fingerprints?"

His friend gave him a scolding look.

"You *know* it takes time for the lab to get us results, even with a rush request."

Terry remembered periods of sheer frustration while he waited for lab results, but he wanted nothing more than to resolve this case and go home. He hoped exhausting every avenue might help him attain his goal a bit faster.

"How did Sherri take you leaving?" Lamoureux inquired.

"You should be asking how pissed off she is at you. And the answer to such a question is that you won't be invited to dinner anytime soon."

Lamoureux chuckled.

"For a five hour trip, it'd have to be a damn good meal. Don't worry, I'll send a card or something."

"It'll take a little more than that, I'm afraid. I'd tell you to send flowers, but that might throw fuel on the fire."

Both troopers remained quiet the next several minutes until enough lighting to illuminate a football field came into Terry's view. He couldn't recall seeing a scene more brightly lit, short of a major fire or rescue scene. Spotting a crime scene van, Terry wondered if A Troop splurged for specialty equipment. In his day, he never recalled having any vehicle with multiple lighting fixtures.

There were times he felt privileged to have flashlights with working batteries when he worked from the Batavia station. Now everyone had mobile task force centers, federal grants bought departments equipment they seldom used, and officers knew better than to step all over a crime scene.

Terry wondered why all of the great advances happened after he gave up his investigative position.

He noticed a handful of reporters and cameras at the end of the driveway. Several county officers held them in check while forensic technicians wandered purposefully within the yellow crime tape.

Everyone was herded to one side, allowing Lamoureux to drive past the media circus. He drove less than twenty yards into the driveway before putting the vehicle in park. Terry suspected his friend wanted to avoid contaminating evidence, though most everything should have been collected after six hours.

Taking a closer look at all of the positioned lights, he realized the scene had multiple points of interest, meaning their search might not yet be out of its infant stage.

"This must be a field day for reporters," Terry muttered.

"Damn right. This will probably make national headlines, which is another reason I wanted you down here."

When they stepped from the car, Terry heard several camera flashes pop behind him, proven by the orbs bouncing off every nearby object. A man Lamoureux introduced as Steve Nelson approached them at a brisk pace, shaking hands with both of them on the fly. No one missed a step as all three proceeded toward the modular home.

"Steve is one of the best in the state at what he does," Lamoureux noted, though it sounded sugarcoated, like he felt a need to stroke the technician.

"What do we have?" Terry asked, knowing Lamoureux had already told tales that made him sound like the Sherlock Holmes of his day.

A sound investigator in his own right, Lamoureux tended to exaggerate the abilities of his colleagues within his circle. Unfortunately, doing so hurt his credibility with some of the people he intended to impress.

And those he tried to hype in his stories.

"A lot of stuff is off to the lab, but we have blood spatter inside, concentrated in one area."

Nelson handed Terry and Lamoureux foot covers and latex gloves, since the processing wasn't completely finished. He led them inside, pointing out the spatter area immediately ahead of them. Terry made a motion with his hand, asking to step forward, receiving a nod from the technician.

What he found helped him little, considering his expertise came from mental angles, not forensic science. He looked for signs of normal life, or why someone might shoot a person in the middle of his or her own house.

Knowing one of the victims died from a gunshot wound, he filed the information into his memory, ready to move along. His mind felt like a boggy moat, unwilling to let information sink in. Terry hated simply going through the motions, fearful he might miss or forget something important.

"What else do we have?" he asked anyway.

"Here," Nelson answered, leading him down the hallway. "Upon Grant's request, we left everything we could in place for you."

"How kind of you," Terry said with a cynical tone directed toward his friend.

Terry followed Nelson down the hallway, stopping momentarily to peer into an undisturbed bedroom. Posters, plastic ponies, and a few stuffed animals created the visual center. No blood stains or signs of struggle marred the bedroom. Even the bedspread looked perfectly placed, without a crease in sight.

"That was the girl's room," Lamoureux said. "They didn't find any forensic evidence inside."

"I'd imagine not," Terry thought aloud, ready to move along.

Nelson led the way down the hallway, then stopped short of the door, allowing Terry to enter first. The former investigator did so, mentally describing the scene as slightly ruffled, but otherwise clean. Nelson's team had done a good job of leaving the scene intact for him, despite a desperate search for DNA and other evidence.

He felt like a kid searching for Easter eggs, but he wanted it that way. His colleagues waited patiently outside the doorway, giving him time and room to maneuver. Nelson started to say something, but Lamoureux shushed him as Terry took a peek under the bed, then thumbed through a few dresser drawers.

Sensing what he wanted all along awaited him in the closet, Terry slid open all of the doors, finding male and female adult clothing, several large cardboard boxes, and a few small shoe boxes atop the shelves. Along the floor, however, he discovered several photo albums, pulling them to his chest, then dropping them on the bed.

He had located the candy stash.

Nelson stepped forward, finally allowed to speak.

"We found photos missing in two of the books. The others appeared completely intact."

"Negatives?"

"We found several packs of photos, but they're all pretty recent. From the looks of the sticky patterns in the books, a lot of the pictures he stole came from an old 126 camera."

Terry recalled photos from his old Kodak 126 camera came back as perfect squares when he sent them away for development as a kid. He hadn't owned such a device in years, but distinctly recalled the unique prints. He wondered if the killer had stolen the negatives, or the family discarded them because few places still created prints from them.

He flipped through some of the pages, seeing a variety of people in the photos, including all three family members. An event, or more than likely, a person was captured inside the stolen prints. Perhaps the killer himself was the subject in question, stealing the photos to further protect his secret.

Feeling his thoughts clouded by fatigue, Terry stepped away from the albums momentarily. He wanted to see the rest of the crime scene, simply because the team was present to give him a guided tour. Retaining the information seemed impossible, simply because his mind felt like a field covered with fog.

"What's the matter?" Lamoureux asked him after a moment, causing Terry to realize his numb posture was openly apparent.

"Can I talk to you a minute?" he replied, which prompted Nelson to step back uncomfortably.

Lamoureux seemed concerned, but very patient as he took Terry's side.

"What's up, ol' buddy?"

"My brain is barely functioning after that five-hour drive," Terry admitted. "I just can't do this. Not tonight."

His friend appeared upset, but at himself for putting so much pressure on Terry.

"I shouldn't have pushed you. It can wait til morning."

"I'm sorry, Grant. Get me here in the morning, once your forensic team is done, and I'll have a much clearer picture for you."

Looking at his watch, Terry found two in the morning almost upon him. He hadn't slept since five the previous morning when he woke up early to jog before work.

He rubbed his head, realizing the chances of him falling asleep within the hour rested somewhere between slim and none.

"I don't even have a hotel yet," he told Lamoureux.

"Don't worry. You're staying at my place tonight."

"You sure?"

Lamoureux nodded affirmatively. He stepped outside the bedroom a moment to speak with Nelson, then returned.

"The team is going to comb the property through the night. They'll have most of it done by morning."

"And the press?"

"Sheriff Gaffney has that angle covered. They'll probably thin out once he offers an official press conference."

Both of them stared at the photo albums atop the bed a moment. Terry desperately wanted to begin hunting down the man who murdered three people, but knew his own limitations.

"Let's get you out of here," Lamoureux said, patting Terry on the shoulder, leading him toward the front door.

And to a much needed bed.

CHAPTER 6

▼

When Terry awoke the next morning, it took a few hazy seconds to remember where he was, and how he had gotten there. The smells of sausage and eggs crossed his nostrils from the guest bedroom at his friend's apartment at the outskirts of Buffalo.

Lamoureux had recently gone through a divorce, forcing him to sell a nice lakeside cabin to pay his bills in the settlement. Visitation with his two kids had been reduced to occasional weekends and holidays because of his work schedule.

During their recent conversations, Terry felt his friend sounded somewhat despondent, though nowhere near a suicidal low. Basically, the man lost everything during the divorce except his job. He never explained the reason for the breakup, causing Terry to wonder if Lamoureux was unfaithful. Something painful or embarrassing kept the man from revealing the details of his divorce.

Slowly sitting up, Terry rubbed his neck, finding it stiff from his deep slumber. Glancing at a nearby clock, he found a time earlier than he expected, though daylight framed the window shades.

7:14 a.m.

Attributing the fact he was awake to everyday routine, Terry stood and stretched. Lamoureux had presented him with the option of the race car bed, or the foldout sofa, and the sofa bed's springs weren't very forgiving. Terry spied his friend crossing the kitchen floor when he opened the bedroom door.

"Good morning," Lamoureux called, seeing him awake. "Coffee?"

Though he seldom drank anything caffeinated, Terry nodded. Today he needed a pick-me-up to jumpstart his morning.

Shirtless, Lamoureux wore tight bicycle shorts of a pastel lime green color. Like Terry, he kept himself fit, riding a professional-grade bike every morning up and down whatever street or trail he could find. Fast food dinners had taken some toll on Lamoureux's formerly slender waistline, but he still appeared fit due to his new weightlifting routine.

Seeing his friend in daylight for the first time, he noticed Lamoureux had grown a mustache since his last visit. Terry recalled his friend never being one to settle on one particular look or lifestyle. Perhaps his sporadic nature also doomed his marriage.

Somewhat surprised at the neatness of the apartment, Terry figured his friend kept the place clean for the visitation days. Though Lamoureux had never been a slob, any man going through a rough divorce might be tempted to let household chores slip for a few days.

"Feeling better?" he asked when Terry stepped into the kitchen, wearing only sweat pants and an old T-shirt.

"Still tired, but I'll survive."

Terry had packed enough essentials for a few days, expecting to stay in a hotel room. Considering he was acting as a consultant to Lamoureux, he brought slacks, sport coats, a few dress shirts, a necktie, and some casual clothes. To him, consulting and working as an investigator both required formal attire, and he suspected his superiors felt the same.

Terry doubted he would be required to speak in front of any cameras, but he wasn't about to have random snapshots taken of him if he didn't look the part.

"I need a shower," he told his friend.

"Towels are in the bathroom, and the water's usually hot."

"Usually?"

"The neighbors tend to take long showers."

Grunting to himself, Terry ventured into the bathroom to test the waters.

He emerged ten minutes later feeling more refreshed and rejuvenated than before. A full plate and a glass of orange juice awaited him on the table. His old partner remembered everything he liked for breakfast. Over the course of five years, they had shared many a meal together.

Terry often cooked full meals for his kids on weekends.

"You shouldn't have," he said.

Lamoureux shrugged off the compliment, sitting down.

"Probably not as good as your wife's cooking, but it's the least I could do after dragging you down here."

"So you're openly confessing your sins this morning?"

"I wouldn't call it a sin to want to catch the prick who killed three people in cold blood."

Instead of arguing, Terry took a bite of his toast, then washed it down. He felt a little surprised that Lamoureux hadn't helped him get dressed, then rushed him to the crime scene.

He didn't want to wait long either, but needed to clear his head first.

"How's apartment life?" he asked his friend.

"It sucks. I won't get back on my feet until the kids graduate high school."

"Then there's college," Terry added, knowing he wanted all three of his kids to attend, even though college was the furthest thing from any of their minds.

Both ate their breakfast a moment while Terry worked up enough courage to approach Lamoureux about a sensitive subject.

"You never said much about the divorce, Grant. Why is that?"

"I suspect you have an idea what happened."

Feeling a bit more uncomfortable, Terry shifted in his chair as he cleared his throat.

"Look, if you don't want to talk-"

"Let's just say I fucked up," Lamoureux answered, cutting off his friend. "It was my fault, and I got what I deserved out of it."

Terry started to apologize, then thought better of it. Silence during the remainder of their breakfast might ease the tension he created between them.

When Lamoureux's phone rang, he felt a wave of relief come over him. It broke up the awkwardness smothering them when his friend rose to pluck the cordless phone from its receiver.

He said very little, listening mostly, then hung up the phone a minute later.

"Change of plans," he informed Terry. "We're taking a trip to the morgue first."

∗   ∗   ∗   ∗

Terry dressed the part, donning a full suit. If he and Lamoureux had chosen to wear sunglasses, people might have figured them to be the covert government types.

As tall buildings blurred past either side of the vehicle, Terry questioned why Lamoureux wanted to visit the morgue first. They already had a sense of how the people were killed, and the forensic team probably knew where and when.

The drive along Route 33, through the outskirts of downtown Buffalo, brought back all kinds of memories for him. When he worked out of the Batavia station just into the next county, Terry made numerous trips to the morgue. He assisted Buffalo PD on several homicides, though pride typically kept them from calling him.

Smells of pizza and hot wings lingered in the air, even though the places that made them weren't yet open. City life could make him pudgy in no time if he fell victim to its charms. Though his rural home only offered smells of manure and swampy water in the summer, it felt safer raising three kids.

"You ever miss it?" Lamoureux asked, breaking the silence.

"Working here? Yeah, a little."

"I guess everyone has to go home sometime, don't they?"

Terry looked toward his friend.

"It was my time. I couldn't wait any longer for an investigative position up there. Hell, I wasn't sure I even wanted to investigate anymore."

"You *could* have waited. You had a lot of good years left in you, my friend. Being back on the road is no fun."

Shrugging, Terry disagreed. For him, it kept his mind from wandering to its dark recesses. The same thoughts that made him a good investigator were the reasons he remained a haunted man. He made strange leaps in his investigations by thinking exactly like the deranged people he tracked. It scared him, more than a little.

Such things made terrible dinner conversation, so he seldom found any release for his frustrations when he investigated crimes. As a patrol officer, he could tell his wife and kids he pulled a few people over, or stopped a drunk driver, without going into detail.

Or feeling a nagging guilt.

Lamoureux displayed uncanny talent as a closer. He could interview people and dissect them like master poker players studied their opponents at tournaments. He read body movement, changes in facial expressions, and even vocal patterns perfectly, tripping up many a criminal who might otherwise walk.

His specialty fit in perfectly once the legwork was done. Lamoureux also managed people well, monitoring every facet of an investigation himself, or through delegated authority. Putting him in charge of the violent crimes unit was someone's good idea, though Lamoureux lacked the ability to find the missing links in the investigative chain this time.

Which brought them to the Erie County Medical Center, where Terry officially began looking for the missing pieces.

Instead of wasting time searching for a good parking spot, Lamoureux parked along the street in a restricted spot, putting them closer to the entrance. A few minutes later, the pair found themselves in the basement, knocking on the morgue's door until a very attractive young woman answered.

Her blue eyes lit up when she found Lamoureux standing there, but she stopped short of giving him a hug upon seeing Terry beside him. Guessing her to be about ten years younger than his friend, Terry had a suspicion they weren't there just to view bodies and autopsy reports.

"Terry, this is Deanna Evans. Deanna, I think you've heard me talk about my old partner before."

"Pleasure," Deanna said, giving a formal handshake.

All three entered the morgue, no one saying anything momentarily.

Terry wondered if Deanna had expected Lamoureux for a different reason altogether. Assuming she was the one who called, perhaps she wanted to meet him before his workday started. Terry had a strong hunch Deanna was the reason Lamoureux no longer wore a wedding band.

"We, uh, came to see what you had on our triple homicide," Lamoureux finally stated.

Deanna led them toward a nearby desk, taking up three folders, opening the first for the investigators to examine. Multiple photos from different angles depicted her finds during the full autopsy.

"Did you do all of the exams?" he asked her.

"Yes."

"Yourself?"

"Yes. I worked through the night once I got the call."

Terry said nothing more, looking at photos of the young lady he assumed was Lacy Wilson, the seventeen-year-old daughter of Taryn and Francis Wilson. He noticed very few marks on her as he flipped through the stack, though the hair on the right side of her head had a circular bald spot. The area was a mix of fleshy chunks and matted blood, looking like Halloween makeup used to create a fake wound with a gory appearance.

"Gunshot wound to the side of the head from a .38 caliber weapon. The bruising around the wrist appears to be postmortem, likely formed when he dragged her body to the barn. We found blood spatter on her hands, so she probably saw it coming and put up her hands."

Terry couldn't argue anything he saw in the photos or the report. He noticed the blood droplets on the back side of her hands, which fit Deanna's theory. From what he saw of her face, Lacy appeared to be a fairly pretty young girl. What kind of monster walked up to a girl like that and shot her in the side of the head?

Deanna handed him the next file, making certain she kept it in a certain order. Terry had the feeling she wanted him to view this file last for a reason.

He opened the folder, finding a very straightforward image of Taryn Wilson lying on the autopsy table, a single red hole centered in her forehead. Her death seemed like a carbon copy of her daughter's, right down to the purplish marks around her left wrist.

"Why drag them like that?" Terry asked aloud, drawing stares from Lamoureux and Deanna. "Even an average-size guy like me would probably toss them over my shoulder and carry them, rather than risk leaving evidence all over."

"Maybe he's small in stature," Lamoureux suggested.

"Could be, but it doesn't feel right. Small guys don't knife someone through the ribs cleanly in one shot."

Terry ran ideas through his mind, but none seemed overwhelmingly accurate.

Perhaps he didn't want more direct contact with the corpses than necessary.

No.

Maybe he feared getting bodily excrements on him.

No. A bag or an old coat provided an easy enough barrier if he wanted to carry them.

Most people willing to kill so brutally in a repeated fashion didn't mind getting a little dirty in Terry's experience.

Perhaps dragging was convenient because the leaves covering the yard left no trace evidence behind when they blew away.

"Single gunshot wound to the head," Deanna said, gaining his attention. "Same caliber used on the daughter. The bullet exited through the back of the skull, which Grant's team recovered inside the house."

Terry began formulating a scenario inside his mind. He saw a shadowy figure enter the house, surprising Taryn Wilson as she emerged from the kitchen, callously firing a bullet into her forehead.

He tried to suppress the film playing inside his mind, not wanting to taint the evidence with an incomplete story. Seeing the modular home had already distorted some of his objective nature, so he pointed to the third file before his imagination ran further away from him.

"Francis 'Frank' Wilson," Deanna said. "Single knife wound to the abdomen, which we believe came from a survival camping knife. The type that has the little jagged teeth along the back side of the blade."

Terry held up his hand for her to stop talking a moment as politely as he could.

"What's wrong?" Lamoureux asked.

"Why kill your two easiest victims with a gun, then stab the man of the house?"

Instead of answering, Lamoureux referred to a file his team had comprised about the family, finding information about Francis Wilson rather quickly.

"Says he was a trucker for a local processing plant. Six-foot-three, about two-fifty-five. Not exactly a defenseless little fella."

Terry flipped through the photographs, finding no drag marks on his wrists. In fact, the only other injuries, aside from the puncture wound, were bruises found along his face.

He suddenly wanted to see the crime scene again, because the movie wanted to play inside his mind, but he fought it.

Not until I see everything.

"He probably remained alive at least fifteen minutes after the initial stab wound," Deanna explained. "Traces of animal feces were found inside his mouth and airway, meaning he was buried alive in the manure pile."

"A deputy discovered the bodies because a hand was sticking out of the manure pile," Lamoureux explained. "His."

"So he tried to claw his way out, but died from his wounds first," Terry theorized.

Lamoureux nodded in agreement.

"The killer knew a little something about anatomy as well," Deanna noted. "He stabbed Wilson just above the floating ribs so he wouldn't die immediately, but pulled the knife out so he certainly *would* die. The wound cut open several soft organs, which could only be achieved at the angle he used."

Terry looked at the photographs, finding evidence of a very deliberate stab. Considering Frank Wilson had been wearing at least a shirt when he died, the aim needed to be virtually perfect. No evidence of retries showed along his rib cage.

"What about the bruising on the face?" Terry asked Deanna.

"We think he struck Wilson several times, but most of the bruising barely penetrates the surface tissue."

"Maybe they were taunting blows," Terry said more to himself than anyone else in the room.

"Taunting blows?" Lamoureux questioned.

"Yeah. Meant to let you know I killed you, but I want you to die slowly and suffer a little more."

A look crossed his friend's face that indicated he understood, though not completely.

"I need to go back there," Terry told his friend, then turned to Deanna. "Do you have copies of your report, and the photos?"

Not wanting to waste time, he planned to study the information on the trip.

She nodded affirmatively.

"Those are yours to take."

"Thanks."

He looked to Lamoureux.

"Crime scene photos, Grant. I need to see everything as your team found it."

"You got it. Is the trail getting warmer, ol' buddy?"

"I can't make any promises, but I think I'm beginning to see what happened."

Lamoureux pulled out his cell phone, then put it back almost immediately.

"Damn basement," he muttered. "I'm going to have the team meet us over there in twenty minutes once I get a signal."

Terry nodded, indicating he was ready.

"Good to meet you," he told Deanna, shaking her hand once again.

"Likewise."

A few minutes later, the investigators emerged from the hospital.

"How long have you two been serious?" he asked Lamoureux before his friend could make any calls.

Before he answered, Lamoureux shot him a sly grin, because Terry's perception had caught the details he attempted to hide.

"Let's just say she's the reason I'm in the predicament I'm in, Terry."

"Maybe she'll let you move into her place, city slicker."

"That's *not* funny," Lamoureux said, opening his cell phone. "She's ready to take things to the next level, but guess who isn't?"

"Some things never change," Terry said to himself with a sigh, ready to see if he could outwit the man who killed three innocent people.

CHAPTER 7

▼

When they arrived at the crime scene, Terry felt like a groom late to his own wedding. Everyone stood in the driveway awaiting the arrival of the two troopers.

Thankfully the press had left, the only two holdouts being photographers from local newspapers virtually camping out at the driveway's edge. Apparently Gaffney's press conference satiated their hunger for information.

Based on the five people awaiting their arrival, Terry suspected most or all of the forensic sweep was complete.

"The four hoodlums on the left are part of my team," Lamoureux explained as he parked the car. "The other fellow is a deputy on loan from the sheriff's office. I think you'll find him handy for several reasons."

"Oh?"

"I'll explain later."

Everyone in the group held files in their hands, attentively awaiting their leader's orders. The deputy didn't appear as comfortable as the others, though Terry suspected he felt like a fish out of water. Terry remembered the first time he investigated a major case, knowing he had the ability to catch madmen, still intimidated by the comfort level of everyone else around him.

Now he and Lamoureux were seasoned pros, despite the mental baggage their numerous cases brought them.

Steve Nelson handed both of them a current dossier full of photos and compiled information. Terry thumbed through it, but Lamoureux preferred hearing news directly from his team.

"What have we got?" he asked without bothering to make introductions.

Nelson went first.

"We've been able to compare all of the prints to known friends and family, and we're down to three sets of fingerprints we can't identify. He didn't leave any tread patterns, but we estimated his shoe size to be an 11 normal."

"No treads?" Terry questioned.

"We think he wore plastic over his feet. There are indentations, but no tread marks."

"Tire tracks?"

"None that we could find."

Terry knew the gravel driveway would hold no clues, but he hoped for an outside chance they might find roadside tracks. Of course the media had quickly trampled any clues before the forensic team had time to set up their perimeter around the property outskirts.

"You'll see photographs of the bodies and the manure pile inside," Nelson revealed. "We have three distinct murder sites, but he buried them all in the same place."

"Any chance he bled, or left us other DNA?" Terry asked.

"Well, he *pissed* on the bodies," Nelson offered. "Other than that, we didn't find anything. No unaccounted blood stains, and the lab is still deciphering the hair samples from inside. I know we want a match for the urine sample he left, but he seemed to know how to avoid leaving us any gifts."

Terry wanted to see the three murder areas, but knew he had to hear any other details first.

"What else do we have?" Lamoureux prompted.

One of the other group members spoke up.

"The neighbors didn't know anything. Turns out none of them knew the Wilsons very well."

He appeared older than anyone present, but Terry didn't recognize him. In fact, he didn't know any of the task force members. Terry figured Lamoureux had moved quickly to assemble his personal dream team of investigators after attaining his current position. Years had passed since Terry worked at the Batavia station, and state police personnel tended to change assignments or troops regularly.

"Phone records?" Lamoureux asked, receiving an answer from the only woman on his team.

"Didn't take long to comb through them. Mostly calls to and from relatives, and some from the male victim's workplace."

The way she said "male victim" seemed a bit cold to Terry, but perhaps she felt a need to distance herself from the victims. He scolded himself, thinking he read too much into her logic. Analyzing serial killers and the people he worked with required altogether different levels of tact.

Like Deanna, she looked significantly younger than Lamoureux, her blonde hair reaching past her shoulders. Her firearm rested atop her hip, nestled within a clip-on holster. She wore dark slacks and an eggshell-colored top that displayed her form without giving away the details some men might drool over.

"We looked through the computer, but the hard drive had mostly games and business records. Nothing to indicate they visited any interactive sights, or any chat rooms. Of course that was a surface scan. The lab is going to perform a deeper scan for hidden files."

"What about e-mail?" Terry asked.

"Each family member had their own account, and none of them had threatening e-mails," the young lady answered. "Most of the sites they viewed were online merchants, but we saw very little buying activity."

"Thank you, Megan," Lamoureux said. "Anyone else? What about tax records and personal documents?"

The older investigator spoke up again.

"Nothing significantly strange. The family moved four times within the last nine years, but we didn't find a real good reason why. No bankruptcy or anything they might be running from."

Terry thought that explained the lack of photo negatives. After moving several times himself, he knew certain things became expendable when packing. Sometimes people ran out of boxes, or simply grew more tired and irritated about packing every little thing.

"How long had they lived in the area?" he inquired.

"Close to six months," the investigator answered.

"Hardly enough time to make mortal enemies," the deputy commented almost silently, entering the conversation for the first time.

Terry shook his head, though not in complete agreement.

"It doesn't take long for some people. But you're right in a way. It takes something drastic for someone to slaughter an entire family. Or someone not in his right mind."

He saw the deputy swallow hard, hoping he didn't scare the man away from active participation. Unlike the others, he didn't dress very formally. Wearing blue jeans, a green button-up shirt, and black steel-toed boots, he looked more like a neighboring farmer than a criminal investigator. Considering he kept a full beard, Terry guessed he worked some kind of special assignment for the sheriff's office.

"We know the two women died from the same firearm," Nelson added quickly, since the rendevous seemed to be winding down. "The lab made the announcement this morning."

"What about financial records?" Lamoureux asked. "Any bizarre political ties that might get them into trouble?"

Everyone shook their heads negatively.

"Their bills were caught up," the previously silent team member answered. "Credit cards were in order, and their loans looked current. Nothing to indicate they owed money to any other, uh, *outside* sources."

"I don't think Frank Wilson belonged to too many charitable organizations, but he wasn't a Klan member, either," the older investigator said.

Terry thought a moment on the subject. Even if one person maintained questionable beliefs, or belonged to a hate group, revenge typically wouldn't be taken out on an entire family. And if someone wanted to seek revenge involving the family, that person often murdered the family to teach the perpetrator a lesson.

This was a completely different animal.

Clearing his throat toward Lamoureux, Terry indicated he wanted to speak with him privately a moment.

"Yeah?" Lamoureux asked once they had stepped away from the group, turning their backs for some privacy.

"I need a look around, but I don't want everyone tramping around behind me."

"We have the files, and I can call them over if we need anything. Anyone you want to keep?"

"Nelson. I want him to show me the three murder origin points before he takes off."

"We're keeping Hardegen, too."

Terry took a half glance behind him.

"The deputy? You got a stiff one for him or what?"

Giving an innocent shrug and grin, Lamoureux turned toward the group.

"It's technically Erie County's investigation, so Gaffney put him with me. And I'm a big fan of his."

Terry looked from the deputy to his friend, his confusion evident. Lamoureux still refused to elaborate, though Terry suspected it had something to do with his alma mater. The Senior Investigator acted worse than a kid when it came to Syracuse University.

"You're going to thank me later," he told Terry before addressing the group. "Okay everyone. Great work, but I need you to keep beating feet to see what you can find. Steve, I need you and Deputy Hardegen to stick around, but the rest of you are dismissed. I expect all of you to call me immediately with any new developments."

The group members walked away, already knowing their boss's standard protocol. Terry considered all three very professional by their appearance and actions. He had faith that they would indeed continue to exhaust every lead until the killer was caught.

He felt reasonably certain only one killer had carried out the crime. Hatred seemed to resonate from the gruesome manner in which Francis Wilson died. Stabbing someone was certainly a violent crime in itself, but burying a person alive in manure after slapping him around took it to the next level.

"Just me and Nelson," Terry informed Lamoureux barely above a whisper. "You and your deputy can do your thing in the trailer once we're out."

"Funny. I tell you, you're going to thank me."

"Sure."

Terry motioned for the forensic team's leader to accompany him, which Nelson readily did.

"I need a tour of the murder areas, starting with the house."

"Sure."

CHAPTER 8

Terry walked inside the house, fighting to keep his mind on the facts before it ran wild with unfounded notions.

Nelson pointed to the wall where the blood spatters stood out against the otherwise white surface, in case Terry might have forgotten during his exhausted state. He stepped carefully toward the area, even though the team had photographed and tagged every piece of evidence they found.

"This is where the mother died," Nelson stated. "By all indications we believe she was taken by surprise, because the shot was centered in her forehead, and she would have been walking out of the kitchen, probably to greet someone at the door."

"How did you know it was the mother?"

"The bullet went clean through her skull. We retrieved it from the wall. In the daughter's case, the bullet remained lodged inside her skull. Our guy knew how to clean up after himself, or he was an excellent shot. Also, we found crumb particles on her fingers that matched a bowl of cheese puffs spilled on the floor."

"If he had the time and presence of mind to bury the bodies and avoid leaving trace evidence, aside from urine, why not dig out the casing from the wall?"

Nelson shrugged.

"Maybe he wanted us to know he killed all three of them. You know how some of these guys hate someone stealing their thunder."

"Or maybe it wasn't his gun."

"You know as well as anyone it's highly unlikely we're going to trace the weapon back to anyone on slugs and casings alone."

Terry indeed knew how few organizations and businesses kept ballistics records of firearms. If it had been used in other recorded crimes, their labs, or the FBI, might find a match in their files.

"How many cops do you know who use a .38 service weapon?" Terry asked the man, already knowing the answer.

"I'm not sure I know any. Hell, my father didn't even use one. I'm not even sure they'd be used as throw down weapons."

Terry looked around, finding an open novel planted face down atop the sofa. In the kitchen, beneath the table, he found an overturned bowl surrounded by little orange cheese puffs. An open bag of the snack food rested atop the table as though waiting for someone to return for a refill.

"I'm guessing she got up to get herself a snack, and that's when the killer made his way inside. He surprised her when she returned to the living room, probably making quite a noise when he did so."

"There was no evidence a silencer was used, so he probably did make some noise, which leads us to the next area."

Nelson led the way outside to the white Grand Prix, where blood spatters had dried like a sloppy spray paint job.

"We think the daughter heard the gunshot, came running from the barn, and got a warm reception from a bullet for her trouble."

"The medical examiner said she thought the girl put her hands up when she saw the gun."

"Probably did, which further proves my hypothesis that our perp was a good shot. I dare say he's been practicing."

Terry agreed, but he also suspected the man had been inhumanly patient, targeting this particular family for a reason.

"How far did your people check around the property?"

Nelson indicated with his finger, sweeping an area that went partly into two fields surrounding the farm. Terry looked around, seeing a tree line at the opposite edge of the field. He suspected a good pair of binoculars, or a camera with a good zoom, might provide someone with a fantastic surveillance base.

Raising both arms, he waved for Lamoureux and Hardegen to join him. They exchanged confused looks, then walked his way.

"What's up?" the Senior Investigator asked.

"I think our bad guy might have monitored his victims before killing them, perhaps as recently as the day he carried out the murders."

Lamoureux gave a strange look to Nelson, as though he expected better from the head of his forensic unit. Nelson simply raised an eyebrow, indicating he didn't know where Terry was coming from.

"I'm suggesting you two check across the field for a vantage point where he might have seen the entire farm."

Lamoureux had nothing better to do, so he signaled for Hardegen to follow him across the closest field. Long since dead, the tanned straw looked about knee-high, allowing an ample view while providing decent cover.

Terry watched them walk away a moment, then returned his attention to Nelson. The forensic technician suddenly looked a bit more uncomfortable, as though Terry had openly doubted his techniques.

"Your job was to search the place for evidence from head to toe," he told Nelson. "You *did* your job. I'm not trying to step on your toes. I just want to work every angle before this guy gets further away from us."

Despite not being completely convinced, Nelson led the way toward the barn.

"Best guess is the dad was doing some chores out back. If he was in the field, he might not have known where the shots originated. It looks like he was taken by surprise when he came around the corner of the barn."

"Our killer might have considered this personal, but he was no fool," Terry thought aloud. "How did you know he was the last victim?"

Nelson let a smug look escape.

"We found traces of blood on the grass leading toward the barn, but no blood or tissue leading toward the house. Based on bits of dried mud we found inside, we think the killer entered the house, killed the older woman, then stepped outside to kill the daughter, and finally the father at the barn. Only then did he return inside to pick out the photographs he wanted, then commence with burying the bodies."

Terry said nothing, stepping toward the barn. He saw Lamoureux and Hardegen trudging toward the woods, but something more pressing occupied his mind. He wanted to know why all three family members were completely separate.

Obviously the killer wanted them in one-on-one situations so he could pick them off, which reinforced Terry's belief he was monitoring them beforehand. This was no random killing, and the way in which he stabbed the father and buried the family in manure spoke volumes. He termed it a crime of passion, but in a different sort of way.

In his experience, when a jilted person murdered someone, the crime typically had a rushed feel to it. This anger had been a slow burn, smoldering over a period of months, perhaps even years. Standard vendetta crimes happen soon after a triggering event, lacking the planning and foresight he found here.

"What's the matter?" Nelson asked after a moment.

"If the father had been in the barn when the daughter was shot, he would have rushed straight out. You said he was killed when he came around the corner."

Nelson nodded affirmatively.

"If he had been inside the barn, chances are against it he would have come around the side," Terry deduced, knowing the barn had a few access doors along its front.

Having no doubt the forensic expert knew his job, Terry stepped into the barn, seeing everything from reins to feed. When Nelson followed him inside, a thought crossed Terry's mind.

"Did anyone feed these poor animals?"

"The deputy did. He came back this morning once we cleared the barn."

Perhaps Lamoureux had a good reason for keeping Hardegen around. If the deputy knew the local roads and haunts, the team might require his knowledge. State troopers also knew the roads, but Hardegen worked with the drug task force, meaning he'd seen a variety of hiding places and abandoned rural buildings.

Still, he wondered why Lamoureux didn't simply request a task force member from their department if that was his motivation. Perhaps he owed the sheriff a favor, or saw something in the deputy he liked.

Terry couldn't confirm that the killer was a recluse, or led anything other than a normal life, but a hunch told him the man preferred being alone.

If he felt this comfortable around a farm, he probably didn't reside within a city. Small town perhaps, but a rural setting seemed more likely. This killer was a serial killer in the making. If he wanted revenge on Francis Wilson, he could have waited for an opportunity to kill the man without murdering the family. After all, the man drove a big rig for a living.

Driving a truck required lots of time *alone*.

Terry's mind wandered to other possibilities. Maybe the killer also drove a truck, or perhaps he was a jealous husband of a woman Wilson slept with. Again, that didn't seem logical, simply because the killer murdered the entire family.

"Penny for your thoughts?" Nelson asked.

"Red herrings. Too many of them."

Allowing the complete vision to run through his mind, Terry saw the wife murdered as Nelson described. The killer likely killed the woman inside the house first to prevent any kind of 911 call.

He believed the daughter heard the shots from somewhere outside, possibly from the barn. Had she already been standing near the white car, she wouldn't have stood still until the killer took aim at her head. Terry envisioned her running from the barn, with the killer calmly stepping outside, making the timing of her death feel reasonably accurate.

Terry didn't believe the last part of Nelson's analysis sounded correct. Gunshots probably weren't uncommon in the rural parts of the county. He remembered his father sometimes sighting in a rifle, or simply taking target practice in their backyard during his childhood.

"I think Frank Wilson probably heard the shots, but didn't think much of them."

Nelson looked perplexed.

"Because he was probably riding a horse in the field," Terry explained.

Finding saddles and other horse riding equipment nearby, Terry pictured the man casually returning to the barn, putting up his gear, then exiting around the back to see if the girl had fed the animals. Farmers often have their children do chores, regardless of age or sex.

"He exited through here to check things over before closing up the barn," Terry explained, leading Nelson to the exit.

They walked around the side of the barn, spying the now disturbed manure pile.

"It makes sense that he rounded the corner to close the front door, and that's when the killer took careful aim and plunged the knife into Wilson's rib cage. You don't stab someone that cleanly the first time unless you know him fairly well."

"How do you mean?"

"Our perp had met Wilson before. He knew how tall the man was, and he knew better than to engage him in a physical confrontation, though he probably wanted to."

Nelson's face twisted in confusion.

"How do you know any of this?"

"It's my best guess. This guy wanted to savor the kill, so he murdered the women first to get his obstacles out of the way. Stabbing Frank Wilson, and making him suffer, was what the killer really wanted."

Saying nothing, the forensic expert seemed satisfied with the theory, though still confused about how Terry reached his conclusions.

Even Terry wondered how he thought like a killer, but his theories usually proved to be extremely accurate.

Though he didn't state them, Terry had a few other possible theories. Perhaps the killer viewed women as insignificant beings, which might stem from the lack of a maternal figure during his childhood. Or perhaps the maternal figure *was* the problem.

Often times, the lack of a father figure, coupled with grossly inconsistent affection from the mother turns a child against his mother. If such a boy matures from the act of mutilating small animals without restraint, women can become substitutes for the animals, also doubling as his mother during the act of murder.

Terry saw no such pattern here, based on the way the mother and daughter were killed. Frank Wilson was definitely the intended, primary target.

From his childhood, Terry recalled some farmers shooting their livestock as an efficient, cheap way of putting them down for the slaughterhouse. He wondered if the killer had witnessed similar acts, twisting what he remembered for his own purposes.

A call from across the field brought him, followed by Nelson, to the back of the barn. Lamoureux waved them over, indicating he had found something of interest.

Terry led Nelson with a brisk walk to a slightly cleared area surrounded by several tall trees. Lamoureux signaled for them to stop short of the area for the sake of evidence preservation. Hardegen remained in the field outside the perimeter, his expression relatively neutral. He may have been new to murder investigation, but he was seasoned enough not to get excited at every little find.

"What did you guys find?" Terry inquired.

From the corner of his eye he noticed Nelson already surveying the area, as though trying to make up for earlier oversights. He looked up a moment later to Lamoureux, whose eyes didn't indicate any negativity toward the forensic team leader.

"He was here," Lamoureux said bluntly. "Call your team back."

Nelson nodded, using his cell phone to place a call as he walked away from the group.

"Find anything concrete back here?" Terry asked his friend.

"He didn't leave any soda cans, or obvious trace evidence, but I found three indentations spaced about right for a tripod. You were right. He set up camp and watched them for a while."

Terry peered into the woods, trying to see if there might be a clearing on the other side.

"I wonder if he drove," he pondered aloud.

"I'm betting he did," Hardegen said. "There are some fields back there where farmers and hunters drive."

Everyone, including Nelson, stared curiously at the deputy as though he possessed inside information, or exchanged e-mails with the killer.

"What?" Hardegen asked defensively. "I just know the area."

Nelson returned to his phone call as Lamoureux smiled at Terry.

"I like this guy," the Senior Investigator confessed. "Did you know he played fullback at Syracuse?"

Hardegen suddenly looked both surprised and irritated as his eyebrows formed a "V" in the center of his forehead.

"That's not why I'm here, is it?" he virtually demanded of Lamoureux. "Am I some kind of sideshow for you?"

"Hardly," Lamoureux answered, showing slight irritation himself.

Terry had seen his friend pissed off, and this wasn't anywhere near that intensity.

"Gaffney says you know the area better than anyone, and he also wants you to get some investigative experience, so I'm doing him a favor. I want you here, but if you have better things to do-"

"No, no," Hardegen said quickly. "I'm ready for this. Sorry I jumped down your throat."

Terry detected something more to Hardegen's past than either of them revealed. Lamoureux seemed like a fan, but perhaps the deputy's athletic career went sour before he peaked.

Terry decided he wanted a look at the fields the deputy had mentioned.

"Can I borrow him for a few minutes to check those fields?" he asked Lamoureux, since the forensic team would require a few hours to set up and check the small clearing.

The Senior Investigator reached into his pocket for keys, but Hardegen held up his hand.

"I can drive him over there."

"Good luck you two."

Deciding some time away from the front line might do him some good, Terry welcomed some peace and quiet as he and the deputy walked toward the driveway.

"Did I strike a nerve?" Hardegen asked, unlocking the car doors with a keyless entry remote.

"I think you called him out and caught him in a lie."

"A lie?"

Terry slid into the passenger's seat, giving Hardegen a sly grin.

"He went to Syracuse, so he's probably a big fan of yours."

Without another word, the deputy looked forward, started the car, and began backing out of the driveway. When Terry looked over, he found the deputy silently content, perhaps because Lamoureux was a closet fan.

CHAPTER 9

▼

"The next time you miss a gear, this goes where the sun don't shine!"

Eric Toomey sat up from his bed as the words echoed through his mind, haunting him through his dreams.

What he called his bed, some people might refer to as shelter. He lived in an area long since devoid of human habitation, choosing a life of solitude after years of bouncing around from one home to another.

His last name had been "Foster" for so long, he nearly forgot his real identity. Not all of his homes were bad, but in the end, he simply meant one thing to the families that housed him.

Income.

Getting up from the floor, Toomey looked down upon the two tattered blankets he used to keep warm, along with the old wool coat he used as a pillow. Around him sat old school desks in various degrees of disrepair. Some were missing their writing surfaces, while others looked as though an ax had been taken to their wooden back supports.

Unable to choose between the first and second stories of the old schoolhouse he occupied, Toomey utilized both.

He tried to shake loose the dream that had embedded itself in his mind almost nine years prior as he looked in a small, cracked mirror in the old classroom's rear. Frank Wilson's voice had scared the shit out of him for almost the entire year he knew the man, but Wilson was no threat to him now.

In fact, that abusive son-of-a-bitch wouldn't be giving anyone trouble ever again.

The face of a man in his very early twenties stared back at him, his dark eyes staring beyond the reflection at the job yet to be completed. Another man knew the secrets that went on between the Wilson family and Toomey, but he never admitted one word of truth.

Years passed, even after the bizarre circumstances that removed Toomey from the Wilsons and the Buffalo area, and the man said nothing. Sheer murder had occurred at Frank Wilson's hands, yet the family friend let it go for years as the Wilson family moved several times to escape their sordid past.

Toomey looked to the knife lying beside his bedding. The very same knife that plunged into Frank Wilson's ribs, ending his existence. Wilson had been surprised by the attack in two ways, the second coming when he finally realized the identity of his attacker.

While Toomey's current location hadn't been utilized for years, he took no chances. Occasionally vandals or kids ventured past the no trespassing signs along the surrounding chainlink fence, but he simply hid out.

Practice hiding in closets as a child made him excellent at disappearing, but he now had what he called a home. Behind the gates, he was a single man with his first home, his first taste of true life.

Outside the gates, however, he cleansed the world of impure people who preyed on others, or kept dark secrets to protect heathens.

It required painstaking efforts to locate the Wilsons, forcing Toomey to keep up with modern advances. He used his computer skills at local libraries to search the internet for the Wilsons, and for their family friend. Amazingly, fifteen dollars bought a person virtually everything he wanted to know about an individual, short of a social security number.

At one time, Toomey failed in school, committing himself to the life of a prisoner the way he was treated by some foster parents. Not until the awakening he received when he was thirteen did he begin to apply himself. He obtained a high school diploma, attending no less than sixteen different schools during his young life, but considered himself self-educated.

Everything pertinent to his new mission he had learned through hard work and personal research. He held jobs long enough to save money, buying the essentials he needed to carry out his task. Murdering the Wilson family simply satisfied a thirst for revenge, but he had yet another mission to carry out. If more innocent people stood in his way, he knew what had to be done.

None of them would understand his motivation. None of them had endured the hardships of his childhood. The court system would consider him insane, not a fallen angel rightfully seeking revenge for the sins others carried out on him.

Turning around, he stared at the green chalkboard on the opposite side of the room. A math problem of **6+13=19** remained forever scrawled in yellowed chalk across its center. Several graffiti messages now surrounded it, but the equation itself could never be erased. Over the course of several decades, it had infused itself with the green surface.

He walked over, picked up the knife, and studied it closely. Though it had been wiped clean with a cloth, the coppery smell of blood lingered.

Frank Wilson had tasted its power, and known his assailant while he begged for mercy as manure covered his body. Moments later, he was reduced to mere whimpering and whining as the last of the appropriate burial material covered his face.

Grunting to himself, Toomey picked up his bedding, shoving it under the teacher's desk at the front. He never much wondered why the school looked as though it had suddenly been abandoned, and didn't much care. To him, it was sent by the Lord Himself, because Toomey carried out His work.

"Have faith," he told himself, knowing he had a few errands to do this morning.

He kept an old work vehicle hidden within the grounds, somewhat old and rusted, ensuring no one checked for a trespasser if they found it, because it easily looked abandoned. An expendable vehicle, it cost five-hundred cash, but ran like a top. Toomey had learned basic mechanic work from one of his nicer foster dads, knowing by then what his future held.

Stuffing the knife into a sheath along his right side, Toomey gave the room one last look, seeing his footprints along the otherwise dusty floor. They gave the room character, and anyone who saw them would simply think a one-time trespasser left them.

A dark film covered what remained of the windows, allowing some of the overcast daylight to filter through. Rocks from trembling hands had pierced corners of a few windows, because most kids believed the grounds were haunted. After all, who left buildings standing for decades after they ceased functioning unless ghosts inhabited them?

He walked with a purpose toward the door, planning to tie some loose ends before taking a weekend trip.

Most people would consider his trip a dangerous venture so soon after slaying the Wilson family, but he left the police no real clues. He planned to do exactly the same once again, while eliminating the last person responsible for ruining the one good part of his life.

Taking in a breath of fresh air, Toomey looked forward to the deed, feeling God had protected him thus far, rewarding him for his patience and planning. After all, God had not always been merciful to corrupt and disobedient human beings, so Toomey felt justified in his work.

He pulled the truck's keys from his pocket, ready for anything that came his way.

✳   ✳   ✳   ✳

"So how did you end up going from football to working for the county?" Terry inquired from the passenger's seat as Hardegen navigated his way toward the fields behind the Wilson property.

"Hurt my knee at the tail end of my junior year," Hardegen answered after a brief pause. "I came back strong for my senior year, but the scouts said I had lost some of my mobility and power. It was never a sure bet in the first place."

Terry looked directly at the deputy.

"You were being scouted for the NFL?"

"*Was.* My times dropped enough to scare them off, so I was left with a business degree and very few job prospects I liked. There were offers, mostly because of my football accomplishments, but I ended up testing for the state police a few times, then got a job with Erie County. Getting a job as the has-been hero didn't sit well with me."

"Why didn't we scoop you up?"

Hardegen shrugged.

"Not sure. I didn't get past the interview process either time, but I thought I interviewed pretty well."

"But you never tested again?"

"Nah. I was pretty content with my job, and I didn't want to get reassigned somewhere else, especially after I got married."

Terry looked forward as Hardegen pulled into the field. Because the worn tractor trail wasn't muddy, Hardegen avoided it, thinking like Terry that tire tracks might be preserved. He stayed clear of the trail until they reached the area parallel to the small clearing Lamoureux found.

"How are we going to do this without disturbing anything?" the deputy asked.

"Very carefully."

Hardegen chuckled nearly to the point of snorting.

"I figured that much."

Both men trained their eyes on the ground the second they stepped from Hardegen's vehicle. Terry looked for any flattened straw, seeing nothing until they drew near the edge of the tree line.

"Here," he pointed to an indentation in the ground, making certain the deputy didn't step near it. "He might have parked here."

If the killer parked there, and even *if* Nelson's team made a plaster cast of the tire tread, they were no closer to capturing him. Thus far, they had simply compiled evidence to put him away if the case ever made it to trial.

"This is Nelson's territory now," Terry said, thumbing toward the car. "At least we can assume he was here, and maybe he left us a clue in those woods."

He doubted it, but Terry held out hope that the killer got sloppy. In the meantime, he had other avenues to check, including a thorough background check of the Wilson family.

"What next?" Hardegen asked as the two men stared at one another across the car's top.

"There's a lot of paperwork left to cover. I want to know who this family was, and where they came from. If they just moved here, I want to know why. Our killer stole photographs for a reason, and I want to know what significance they have."

Hardegen nodded.

"Are we waiting to see what Nelson finds?"

"No. That would be counterproductive. We can't waste a second, in case this guy isn't done yet."

Both men climbed inside to escape the chilly breeze.

"I took the liberty of checking over state databases, and no similar murders turned up," Terry said. "That means our guy is new to the murder business, or he's covered up his previous crimes."

"He had two days to make these bodies disappear forever, and he didn't."

"Exactly. Which is why I think he's never done this before."

"But he's not stupid, either."

"Definitely not. Everything we've found indicates this is an isolated crime, but I'm not taking any chances. Anyone who commits murder, especially like this, gets a taste for it. It only gets worse with every kill."

Hardegen looked to him momentarily, his currently caramel-colored hazel eyes blinking with uncertainty. Terry had already learned his eye color changed more often than a mood ring.

"What now?"

"We're going to meet up with some of Grant's staff to sift through the family papers. If we don't find something soon, the trail is going to be colder than a witch's tit."

Hardegen smirked.

"Just point me in the direction, and I'll get you there."

CHAPTER 10

▼

Half an hour later, Terry stepped into a room with Hardegen in tow, finding Megan Reilly seated at a table with two boxes of paperwork spread out before her. She had put her hair up, possibly wanting to look more professional for the interviews she anticipated conducting.

"Like some help?" he asked, receiving a relieved nod and a smile in return.

"Would I," she said emphatically.

A phone call to Lamoureux revealed the VCIT members had split up to cover some different angles, leaving Megan by herself to analyze the family's files and documents. Terry thought it odd that the others found more important things to check upon, but seated himself beside her.

"Where do you want us to start?" he asked for himself and Hardegen.

Megan pointed to a small stack of papers on her left.

"Those are the things I've been through," she said. "It's been painstaking, and you know how guys are about doing the boring stuff. No offense."

"None taken. Just give us each a stack, and we'll start looking."

"What are we looking for?" Hardegen inquired as Megan gave him a short stack of documents to peruse.

"Anything unusual," Megan answered. "These people were brutally murdered for a reason. I've been focusing on their finances, and even though they moved several times, I haven't seen any patterns of mounted debt. The only thing I've questioned is why Francis Wilson quit a good factory job about eight years ago."

"Factories aren't all they're cracked up to be," Hardegen noted. "My dad worked in one for years, and he came home tired and miserable a lot, despite the money. Plus you're always in danger of getting laid off."

Terry thought a moment about what he knew of Frank Wilson.

"He became a truck driver, didn't he? That's not a bad job, except that he'd be away from home a lot more."

Megan studied the sheet in her hands a moment.

"At least they kept meticulous records."

While she appeared young for an investigator she had brains and good looks. Her blonde hair and blue eyes disguised her abilities according to Lamoureux. He had faith that she was going to take his place one day, because she showed incredible promise so early in her career.

All three settled in, examining records for nearly twenty minutes before Hardegen broke the silence.

"This is interesting," he said, pointing to a bank statement. "Nine years ago the Wilsons deposited nearly fifty-thousand dollars into their savings account."

Terry peered at the paper, finding the amount that stuck out like a sore thumb.

"Lottery win?" he questioned aloud.

"Awfully even number," Megan noted. "I'd guess an insurance settlement, or maybe a lawsuit win unless we see a pattern. Lottery wins are paid in annual increments."

He agreed, but knew no bank kept canceled checks a decade after the fact. He planned to call the bank just to cover himself, but suspected a field trip might be necessary to find the answer.

Atop the bank statement, plain to see, was the previous address of the Wilson family.

"Can you call this bank?" he asked Megan, receiving an enthusiastic nod. "I need any information they can pull about the Wilsons' account."

Without another word, she took the statement from Hardegen, then left to look up the bank's information. Terry didn't recognize the bank's name, so he hoped it hadn't closed. The state was speckled with local banks, many of which provided its small towns with a single banking option.

"Nice find, John."

"Wasn't hard. I just hope it gets us somewhere."

It took nearly fifteen minutes, but Megan returned flashing a smile as she waved the statement.

"Jackpot. The Naples First Mutual Bank is faxing over the documents as we speak. Not sure we'll find anything new, but it can't hurt."

Terry held out little hope that the documents would shed more light on the large deposit as he thought of other ways to trace the transaction. The most obvious and direct route led him to people who knew the Wilsons, which meant traveling to Naples and talking to neighbors.

Naples was about the same size as the town Terry resided in. Small enough that everyone knew one another, which he hoped might create the break they needed. If the Wilsons had done anything out of the ordinary, everyone living there would have gossiped about it.

"The bank is under new management, but they retained every file from previous clients," Megan revealed. "They were bought out a few years back."

Terry barely heard the words.

A nagging feeling that he had missed something at the farm bothered him. Between the forensic team delaying his personal search, and the hurried tour by Nelson, he felt as though his mind hadn't detected a major find.

"What's wrong?" Hardegen inquired, obviously expecting a more jovial disposition from him.

"I just feel like I've missed something."

Both looked at him helplessly. After all, *they* weren't the ones who jumped from nothing to a conclusion as easily as loggers hopping from log to log in the Adirondacks, back in the day.

He wanted to see the Naples lead carried through properly, but Lamoureux's faith in Megan prompted his next question.

"Do you want to make the trip to Naples and conduct the interviews?"

"You sure?"

"Yeah. We can finish this stuff."

"And Grant won't mind?"

"I'll deal with Grant. I would do it myself, but there's something I want to check after we get done sifting through these papers."

Megan looked pleased that Terry showed confidence in her. He knew Lamoureux tended to surround himself with good investigators, the types whose strengths complimented his weaknesses.

Everyone had already exchanged phone numbers, so Megan had little reason to linger.

"If we find anything helpful, we'll call," Terry told her as she stood.

The drive to Naples was just over an hour if traffic wasn't backed up, leaving her most of the day to prod the locals for information.

"I'll call as soon as I find something," Megan said.

"Good luck," Terry added with a nod before she left.

Hardegen picked up some more papers, but stared blankly at them a moment. He appeared lost in thought.

"Stunning revelation?" Terry asked.

"No. What did you want to see?"

"I want you to take me out to the Wilson place when we finish here. There's something I just didn't catch the first time through."

"Okay."

Terry began leafing through the stack of papers before him. He wondered what Lamoureux's other investigators found so pressing that they left Megan alone with the files. Of course he suspected they had other cases to work on, but a triple homicide took precedence over any cold case.

Perhaps they were looking for links in other recent violent cases. Sometimes arson fires and rapes were directly related to murders, but Terry suspected a different animal altogether. This murderer walked to a different beat, perhaps a sociopath, or maybe someone who simply wanted cold revenge.

After all, what fun was revenge if no one knew it *was* revenge?

Wrapping the bodies and urinating on them were part of the same act. The wrap was meant to keep the urine around for someone to find.

Hardegen had taken notice of Terry looking at the same page for almost a minute.

"You're gonna catch the thing on fire if you keep staring at it."

Terry returned a grin.

"I guess we're not doing a very good job at this, are we? Maybe Megan was right, and men just stink because our attention spans are so short."

"She didn't exactly say that."

"But she implied it. But let's say we prove her wrong, then we'll get back to the farm."

CHAPTER 11

▼

Megan stuck around long enough to look at the faxed documents before heading out to Naples. She made copies of them, simply for the address and contact information, then left them for Terry and the deputy.

She spoke with Lamoureux, because he needed to place a call to Troop E, where Naples was located, as part of their department's protocol. Basically the call provided a heads-up that they were investigating out of their troop area, and that they would contact Troop E supervisors if anything strange turned up.

Megan stopped at the bank first, only to discover all of the bank employees from nine years prior had retired or moved on to other jobs. Considering the bank only employed three tellers, a loan officer, and one manager, the idea didn't seem inconceivable. Megan realized she saw the same faces every time she walked into her own bank, so she took it for granted that bank employees hardly ever quit.

While she passed through town, Megan realized she had seen numerous little towns during her two years as an investigator. They all looked alike, yet different. While each had a unique flavor and look, they all seemed to have the same key components, and a lack of the spoils that cities provided.

Naples claimed to be the "Grape Pie Capitol of the World" just as many small towns attempted to make their mark. No less than seven motels and inns provided shelter for visitors seeking to visit the winery or marketplaces. Though one of the smallest communities in the Finger Lakes Region, it didn't lack for attractions.

Receiving several stares from residents, Megan tried to ignore them. Driving a state vehicle gave her unwanted attention, but it couldn't be helped. Trouble, and the police that followed, weren't welcome sights in such communities. Constables typically handled what small problems came about, and anything remotely newsworthy spread through the community like wildfire.

She wanted to phone her boyfriend, just to check in. Though she seldom called him during the day, she just wanted to hear a friendly voice.

Most men thought they were ready to date a female officer, but very few proved it. David was mature beyond his years, and secure enough that he didn't mind her carrying a gun, or being tough. In fact, he seemed to enjoy it sometimes.

He didn't tease her about work or judge her.

Working for a firm in Buffalo, David had put his engineering degree to work, allowing them to share an apartment in the city. They had been dating only eight months, but Megan felt comfortable enough around him to share her life completely.

Following the directions the bank teller provided, Megan made her way out of town toward the old Wilson property. She simply wanted to look at the property, then interview the neighbors. Hoping the neighbors, any of them, might give her some solid information, she considered the possibility of other avenues.

Everyone had an insurance agent, Frank Wilson had been employed while living in the Naples area, and most people in small communities attend church at least some of the time. Though any of those circumstances might have changed over the past decade, she imagined at least one would put her closer to the Wilsons.

Megan found the residence along a county road, appearing quite fit for an old farmhouse. Someone had taken the time and money to put up new beige siding, along with new windows. Where a barn had once stood, a large patch of dirt refused to yield to grass seed. In its place, a new prefab garage the same color as the house took up part of the lot.

One car was parked outside, so Megan pulled in for a look at the property. If the owner came out, she decided she could question him or her, but no one did.

She took several minutes to glance around the property, seeing nothing of interest. Perhaps she simply wanted to know the murdered family a little better, but the informal search failed to help.

Seeing an old doghouse to the side of the garage, she wondered if the family owned a dog. The doghouse looked as though it had been propped atop several bricks, indicating it wasn't being used.

Taking out her notepad, she questioned whether or not the Wilson family owned a dog at their last residence. If so, where was it?

Most families on a farm own dogs as a form of protection, and for practical reasons. They entertained the kids, but they also helped move other animals around, protected them, and kept them from escaping.

Dogs also sense danger from knife-wielding maniacs.

She supposed Terry had also thought of such a possibility. The way Lamoureux spoke of the man, Megan believed her boss worshiped him as a crime-solving god.

A few minutes later, she found herself driving up the road, trying to guess which neighbor might be the one to interview first. Considering the time of day, she wondered if anyone was home. Perhaps some of the neighbors were retired, meaning they had likely lived in the same place for a period of years, and might currently be home.

Of the four houses near the Wilson property, it turned out the closest one, a quarter mile away, had two cars in the driveway. She pulled in, hoping someone would answer the door, though every door and window appeared closed.

After a few knocks, a woman in her seventies answered with a perplexed look. She opened the door only a few inches, as though afraid Megan might be part of some home invasion ring.

"Can I help you?"

"Hello. I'm Megan Reilly with the New York State Police. I'd like to ask you a few questions if I could."

"Is something wrong?"

"Not around here, no. May I come in a moment?"

Megan provided her credentials.

In under a minute she trusted Betty and Tom Crouch as though they were her own grandparents. Holding a cup of hot tea, she sat on a country blue plush chair, across from the love seat where the older couple made themselves comfortable.

A diluted smell of mothballs hovered in the room, probably from the crawl-space beneath to keep critters away. Not a speck of dust covered any of the furnishings, which appeared brand new, though Megan felt certain they were not.

Paintings of farms and sailboats lined the wood-panel walls, while photos of their children and grandchildren stood proudly atop the coffee table and a nearby secretary.

"So, you knew the Wilsons?" she asked, receiving a nod from both.

"To say we 'knew' them isn't really how to put it," Tom said. "They kept to themselves, mostly."

"Can you tell me a little bit about them?"

Tom shrugged with a strange look, as though she had asked him to describe any typical American family.

"Frank worked in the factory, but he and the misses also grew vegetables. He had all kinds of deals with farmers and the Amish, selling his hay and some of his livestock."

Megan jotted down a few notes.

"Did they do something wrong?" Betty questioned, since Megan hadn't really explained why she was visiting.

She assumed incorrectly that the news had covered the story so extensively that only someone living under a rock hadn't heard.

"The Wilsons were all murdered three days ago at their new residence."

"Oh dear."

Megan gave the couple a moment to absorb the terrible news.

"Do you have any suspects?" Tom inquired after almost half a minute.

"Not yet," Megan admitted openly. "But we think it's an isolated incident. There's no need for either of you to worry."

Though shaken, the couple seemed to trust her words.

"Did they own a dog?"

Now the couple appeared confused.

"They owned a couple over the years. Why?"

"Just a thought I had. What about a lottery win, or some kind of court settlement? We discovered they deposited a large sum of money in the local bank before they moved away from Naples."

Both sat silently in thought a moment.

"The boy," Tom finally said. "Probably the life insurance policy."

An alarm went off in Megan's head. What boy?

"Their boy died in the field over there," he said, thumbing the direction. "Some kind of accident. The cops were here all day roping off the area and questioning everyone."

Megan sat stupefied a moment, until she realized the couple looked at her strangely, as though losing faith in her. She sipped her tea, trying to cover up her initial shock.

"I'd like to see the area," she said, standing up.

*   *   *   *

Tom led her across the field behind his house toward the only area where trees didn't appear abundant around the rear of his property.

He walked with a limp, which gave them plenty of time to converse during the walk, since Betty had remained behind. Megan could picture her picking up the phone to tell all of her neighbors the latest gossip.

"Can I ask how it happened? I didn't want to ask in front of the wife."

"The women were shot, and Frank was stabbed. I'm surprised you haven't seen it on the news."

"Television reception is terrible out here, and Betty doesn't want to spend the money for a satellite dish. She thinks the rays are going to fry her brain or some shit. Pardon my French."

Megan was amused at Tom's behavior. He was old-school, but his mind hadn't deteriorated one bit.

"Tell me about this boy," she said when they reached the halfway point in the field.

"He was Frank's son from a previous marriage, but you'd have thought he was a red-headed stepchild the way Frank treated that poor kid."

That explained why no one had rushed forward to inquire about the girl. She belonged to Frank and Taryn, and close relatives were either scarce or nonexistent.

"What was his name?"

Tom took a moment to recall.

"Kyle, I think. Poor kid never spoke, or he got smacked."

"How old was he when he died?"

"Maybe twelve or thirteen. The girl was a lot younger than him."

Megan found it difficult to jot notes while strolling through the uneven footing of the field, but managed to keep her writing legible.

"You mentioned possible abuse?"

"I didn't really say that. Frank just kept a tight leash on the boy was all."

"Smacking him for talking isn't abusive?"

Tom shrugged.

"Life on a farm isn't like you city folks have it. You gotta toughen up. If you can't take a few nicks, bumps, and bruises, you ain't gonna make it on a farm. I think Frank was trying to toughen the boy up was all."

Megan found his words sincere and truthful, but Tom hadn't made mention of the slaps for no reason.

"Can you give me a few examples of what Frank did to him?"

"He'd slap him a few times, especially when the kid didn't do his chores, or he didn't do well in school. He was, well, *forceful* in some of his teachings, too."

"How do you mean?"

"He'd threaten the boy if he didn't learn how to do something right. Like one time the boy turned their tractor too sharp and one of the tires snapped off part of the hay wagon's front end. Frank put a hay hook to his crotch and told him if he did it again the sharp end would end up in his pecker."

Megan wrote this down, but her mind raced with questions.

"And you don't consider that abuse?"

"That's tough love, missy. The boy was always running off, up to no good. Frank needed to keep him in line."

"Running off? Like running away from home?"

"Nah. Nothing like that. He had a friend across the street from us he always came to visit. Some foster kid who wasn't nothin' but trouble. Thank God those people moved out, because I couldn't stand half those foster rugrats they let run around the place. They were always getting on our property and-"

"Please, Mr. Crouch," Megan said, stopping him short. "Do you remember the kid's name? The friend?"

Tom looked at her as though she had suddenly gone mad.

"Didn't know any of their names. Didn't care to."

"What about the family?"

He thought a moment, then a spiteful look crossed his face as he said the last name with disdain.

"Ramsey. Lois and Bret. God were they a pain in the ass."

Megan stole a glance at the old house across the road, its wood siding faded to a puke green color as one half of the abandoned residence collapsed upon itself. She recalled a few belongings visible from the road, like an open concept museum displaying itself for all passers by.

She wrote down the names as they neared the accident site.

"When did they move out?" she inquired.

"About four years ago."

"How many kids did they have while they lived there?"

"None of their own, but they always had about four or five of those little bastards running around. Government fucking paycheck. 'Scuse my French again."

When they reached what Megan had initially thought was a clearing in the field, Megan found Tom putting his arm across her waistline like a crossing gate to keep her from falling into what looked like a small crater.

"Wow," she said, looking into the large pit, partially filled with junked automobiles, farm machinery, and some tires.

The vehicles had somehow been shoved or driven hastily into the pit, their metal exteriors split like slit skin, allowing rust to spread like a virus. None of the windows remained intact, and most of the tires had completely flattened.

Megan thought it looked like an incomplete junkyard, needing an industrial truckload of dirt to finish the job.

"It wasn't this full when the Wilsons owned the place," Tom admitted. "They found the boy down there with his skull cracked open by the rocks."

Megan noticed a number of large rocks nestled beneath the decaying machinery. Some might have been classified as small boulders.

"Who found him?"

"Not sure. A family member I think."

"Did the police investigate?"

"You'd think they called the National Guard in here with all the red lights we saw, but they said it was an accident in the end."

Megan made a note to check with local authorities about the death, knowing her department, or the Ontario County Sheriff's Department, likely had some of the original investigators on their payroll. Lamoureux had contacts everywhere if she needed expedited information, or she hit a roadblock.

"What did you think happened?" Megan asked him point-blank.

Tom raised a suspicious eyebrow.

"I think it was an accident, young lady. Frank Wilson was a lot of things, but he wasn't a man who'd kill his own flesh and blood."

Unsure of what to think, Megan took one final look into the large pit, then walked with Tom toward his house. She had any number of new avenues to check, and the Crouch family wasn't going anywhere in case she needed to check back.

CHAPTER 12

▼

Terry felt disappointed, though not surprised, that he and Hardegen found nothing else in the family paperwork. They decided to double-check one another by switching documents and looking again, but still found nothing.

They made notes of the companies the Wilson family dealt with over the years, which proved helpful when Megan called. Terry gave her the name of their insurance agent to aid in her search, giving her a few contact names in the Ontario County area. He doubted she needed any assistance, but having inside connections never hurt.

Her report about the neighbors intrigued him, particularly the development about the dead son and the neighbor boy. Terry wasn't going to fret about her discoveries until she found more, because his own leads were keeping him plenty busy.

"Are we meeting with your buddy?" Hardegen said in such a way that Terry believed the deputy preferred working with him a lot more than Lamoureux.

Perhaps the pressure of having a devoted fan worried the deputy a little.

"No. We're going to let Grant and his team do their thing in the field. I want you to go with me to the barn. If I say I need a moment alone, it's not that I'm being rude, but I'll need you to give me some space."

Hardegen bobbed his head in understanding as he pulled into the driveway.

A few minutes later, Terry found himself entering the barn as he examined his surroundings. He smelled the scents of farm animals as their banter filled his eardrums.

Without another word he stepped outside, walking to the nearby fence where a horse walked up to greet him. Hardegen stepped beside him, feeding the horse a sugar cube he'd found inside the barn.

"He'll be a friend for life now," the deputy commented.

Terry watched the horse savor the treat a moment as a thought crossed his mind. He knew the answer from his personal experience, but wanted a second opinion.

"When someone buys farm animals, is there a record of it?"

Hardegen chuckled.

"Maybe if it's an expensive animal, like a horse or a stud bull. Most transactions are done with cash and a handshake."

"Shit."

Terry suspected as much.

"Give me a minute, would you?" he asked, drawing a slightly hurt expression from the deputy, as though Hardegen's answer had irritated him.

"Sure."

While the deputy walked along the fence with the horse, Terry returned inside the barn, taking in the view. He tried opening up all five senses, finding the smells somewhat familiar from his childhood, the touch of wood all too common, and no sights that revealed anything new to him. The sounds, however, caught his attention.

A few hogs, goats, and sheep remained in their pens. They remained quiet until Terry drew closer, then they each spouted their individual cackles and calls his way. He approached the pens, finding most of the animals running up to him, their sounds growing louder as they requested food.

All of the animals crowded the pen's wooden boards near Terry as he examined them one by one. Every single animal beckoned for his attention with the exception of one large sheep that remained in the corner, staring at him momentarily before ducking its head toward the wall.

"What's wrong with you, little guy?" Terry asked, swinging one leg over the fence to climb over.

Because of their intense hunger, the other animals were slow to move aside for him, some virtually clinging to him as they begged.

He tried to approach the fluffy sheep, but it used evasive maneuvers, succeeding only in wedging itself into the corner face first. Terry blocked its path by placing one stiff arm against the wall where it tried to run, then cornering it by putting his opposite leg against the wall behind the sheep.

It made a few extended "bah" noises, continuing to move forward, then back, running into Terry or the wall with every movement. Taking a quick glance at the genitalia, Terry discovered testicles, realizing this healthy male sheep had little reason to be so shy.

Still, it wanted away from him in the worst way.

A thought occurred to him that the killer had plenty of time after the murders to search the house and the farm. He required time to erase certain aspects of his involvement, but that didn't mean he didn't take time to pleasure himself in other ways.

"John!" he called out. "I need a vet out here ASAP!"

✳   ✳   ✳   ✳

"Hey, babe," Terry said outside the barn when his wife answered her cell phone.

"You're calling me at work?" she said in response. "This is new."

"Well, I've got a few minutes, and it occurred to me I hadn't heard your sweet voice since last night."

Sherri gave a skeptical laugh. The one she always gave when she suspected he was up to no good, or about to apologize.

Glancing inside the barn, Terry found the local veterinarian examining the sheep's rectum after sedating the animal. He held a small flashlight, using Hardegen as an assistant for his every need, despite the deputy's initial protests.

"Have you caught the bastard?" Sherri asked, probably more for her own sake, since she had to watch three kids with him gone.

"No. But I'm getting some ideas."

"Was it worth Grant dragging you down there, or did he just want you for poker night with the boys?"

Terry chuckled.

"You always suspect the worst in people."

"And Grant usually proved me right."

"This seems like a legitimate whacko to me. I could give you the grizzly details if you want."

"I'll pass. Just let me know when you're coming home, so I can put the kids to bed early and get the bed warmed up."

Terry noticed the vet putting his face closer to the sheep's rectum than he would ever care to.

"You *are* a she-devil. I'll call you later with an update."

"Tease. You call me, then run."

"Can't be helped, dear. Love you."

"Love you, too."

Terry folded his phone shut, then walked inside the barn. Upon hearing about the new development, Lamoureux seemed torn between Nelson's work and Terry's bizarre hypothesis that the killer had somehow violated a sheep.

"Well?" he asked the vet when the older man stood up from the sedated animal.

"I dare say there was penetration," the vet answered.

A far cry from a James Harriot veterinarian, Bob Stillwell wore a tattered flannel shirt over the top of his coveralls. A pair of work boots covered his feet, a thin layer of dirt covering the gouges and scuffs they had endured during his many calls. His hair looked as though a comb had made one pass through it before the man considered his efforts complete.

By no means a handsome man, Stillwell had grown a beard that compared to those of mountain men and lumberjacks. Thick and untrimmed, it gave Terry the impression the man did his job well enough that he didn't care what people thought of him.

"I found blood in some of the stool," he reported, walking toward Terry. "His anus had tearing along the sides, so your theory may have some merit. I'd have to do more tests if you wanted to know for sure. How the hell did you think of such a thing?"

Terry shrugged. Thinking like creepy killers and rapists wasn't good conversation, so he usually refused to answer.

"Can you stick around while I call the forensic guys?"

"Hey, it's your time and money."

Actually the state police agency handled such bills.

"How does one corner a sheep and rape it?" he asked the vet.

Stillwell cleared his throat uncomfortably before answering.

"Sheep have a tendency to run. So you either have to be strong enough to manhandle one, which would still be tough, or you have to make them face a fear worse than being violated."

Terry pondered that a moment, trying to imagine what frightened farm animals.

Fire, drowning, strangulation perhaps.

All of those options seemed too complicated. Besides, subduing an animal took time. Perhaps even more than a patient killer wished to spend on the farm.

Taking a step into a nearby room, Terry found a wagon stored in the barn's center room. Above it, he spied a loft where hay was stored for winter. The only access points were a wooden ladder and a hay bale elevator.

He stepped over to the wagon, noticing part of it touched the bale elevator. Examining the surface of the wagon, he couldn't see any distinct footprints because of the scattered hay left over from summertime.

Peering into the elevator, he noticed bland footprints along some of the metal stops connected to the chain-driven lift. Compared to the layer of dust and grain particles accumulated on the machine, they seem extremely fresh, but lacking definition.

"He was here," Terry said aloud, drawing the deputy toward him.

"The killer?"

"Yeah. Do you remember that big sheep acting weird when you fed the animals?"

"He wouldn't come over to me," Hardegen answered. "Even after I put down the feed, he waited until I left the area before he ate. I thought he was sick or dying."

Terry thought a moment, looking from the loft above to the extension cord plugged into the elevator. Bale elevators typically escalate bales from outside a barn through an opening, not from inside. Any respectable farmer wouldn't leave the elevator plugged in so long after summer had passed, even if the opposite end wasn't plugged into a socket.

He remembered Nelson stating the loft had recently hosted some form of activity because of undefined footprints. He had distinguished between Hardegen's footsteps and those left to one side of the elevator above. A number of smaller tracks had also been found, which they attributed to a dog, because no other animal would be nimble enough to climb up a bale elevator.

Unless it had help.

"What exactly are you thinking?" Hardegen asked from below.

"A fear of falling over the ledge," Terry said in a whisper.

"What was that?"

"If you threaten to push a sheep over the edge of a heightened ledge, it'll push back against you to avoid falling over. Even if it's being probed from behind."

Looking somewhat suspiciously at him, the deputy was about to comment, likely with a joke of some kind, when Terry stopped him short.

"Don't even say it, or I'll tell Grant you want to tell him all about your college days over lunch."

Hardegen smirked, saying nothing as he held up his hands defensively and walked away.

Left alone with the bizarre thoughts running through his mind, Terry realized he had a killer who pissed on corpses and partook in sexual activity with animals. If he was correct, the theory that the assailant simply killed the Wilsons for revenge went out the window. It also meant this scene was destined to be the first of many.

He originally considered the idea of urinating on the corpses a form of revenge, almost the opposite of someone paying respects. While Terry held little doubt the Wilsons had somehow wronged the killer, at least in his mind, the urination might have been done for another reason.

Stillwell remained in the other room, awaiting further instruction.

"I have a question for you, Doc," Terry shouted as he stepped down from the wagon.

"Shoot."

"What kinds of animals mark their territory?"

Stillwell entered the room, his look indicating he was a bit baffled, but he answered quickly enough.

"A lot of animals, but typically those that hunt, or have to guard their area. I'm not sure any of the animals here would necessarily do so."

"Give me some ideas."

"Cats, dogs, deer, wolves, feral pigs, elk. Pretty much any animal in the wild. Even mice and reptiles to some extent."

Terry didn't regard the answer as much help.

"Thanks for everything, Doc. I'm going to get someone out here within the half hour. They'll want your help doing some further tests on the sheep."

"I can wait. Say, who do I bill for this?"

Terry pulled out one of his own business cards, deciding he would have Lamoureux take care of the invoice. He knew if his friend forgot, he could simply badger him until he sent the paperwork through.

"Send your bill to the local state police barracks, care of Grant Lamoureux."

He wrote his friend's name on the back of the card for Stillwell.

"If you don't receive a check within a few weeks, give me a call and I'll get it taken care of."

Terry had already decided to have the Erie County evidence technicians swab the animal's anus for DNA evidence. He suspected they wanted an animal expert around, and the veterinarian seemed cooperative despite his gruff nature.

"I'm going to grab a sandwich while I wait," Stillwell said.

As the vet walked toward his van, Hardegen returned.

"No jokes, I promise. I just want to learn something. How the hell did you make that kind of connection?"

Terry still wasn't certain he made a connection, and he was less certain his guess was accurate. They hadn't found any condom wrappers or additional linking evidence anywhere on the property.

"I think our killer is very much a loner. Nothing unusual there. But I think he has a fascination with animals that came from him seeking relationships with them to replace what you and I would consider normal courtship."

Hardegen stared at the wedding band on his left hand a few seconds before looking Terry in the eye.

"How? *Why?*"

"You've got to understand that these people don't have normal childhoods. They aren't born like this. Predisposed maybe, but they aren't born killing machines. Usually there's a lack of something basic that you and I had growing up, that these people didn't. Maybe they were abused or neglected beyond the norm, or there was an absence of a parental figure. Maybe both."

Terry held up both hands.

"That part is still a mystery to me," he admitted, "but I suspect our killer has no sense of belonging, little or no self-esteem, and what he knows he taught himself. There was little or no love in this man's life, and he's going to be adapted to living off the land and providing for himself."

"Holy shit," Hardegen muttered. "You major in psychology or something?"

"No. Based on what Megan uncovered, this *might* be revenge. You've got to look at all the angles, John. It's possibly linked with the death of the Wilson boy nine years ago. A typical serial killer is a white male, age twenty-five to thirty-five, if that's what we're dealing with."

"Glad I'm about to graduate from that category."

"I said *typical,* not *all.* That's a very generic but relatively accurate profile. What gets me is most serial killers, which I believe this guy is destined to be, torture and kill animals from a young age. Not always, but it's a progression, sort of like serial arsonists escalate their pleasure through violence when setting fires gets old. But this guy is different, and if I'm right, God help us all, because he'll be near impossible to track."

Looking more than a little concerned, the deputy glanced across the field before asking his next question.

"Then what's next for him? And for us?"

"We go where the evidence leads us," Terry answered. "I'm anxious to hear what Megan finds out before we go on a witch-hunt. As for our killer, he isn't done yet. He was successful here in more ways than one, which will only build his confidence. The unfortunate part is we can't put together a pattern because he's only killed once."

"Bummer."

"That pretty much sums it up."

CHAPTER 13

▼

Hardegen felt as though he wasn't learning a thing from Terry Levine. Not that Terry wasn't taking any time for him, but the investigator was an enigma all his own.

He drew conclusions from the air the way metal detectors spotted coins inches below the surface. Most police officers looked at the same evidence and saw nothing unusual. Terry found answers in everything, and Hardegen couldn't argue with the man's analysis of the killer.

Simply trying to do his part, the deputy took off for the day just before suppertime. Lamoureux and Terry asked him to look over his local maps to plot some areas where the killer might be hiding.

No one lived entirely off the land. Horror movies made it sound like killers could live off bugs and small animals for years, but they neglected to mention how even the meanest of killers survived harsh winters. Man needed food to survive, but he also required shelter.

Terry and the deputy had discussed marriage and work, which was another reason Hardegen didn't stay into the evening. The state trooper revealed his marital secrets, which included making time for his wife and kids, no matter how much work beckoned. He also explained that him coming to Buffalo was Lamoureux's doing, and couldn't be helped because his friend had used proper channels.

"My wife understands the work I do saves lives, and she knows I'll be motivated to find this guy because it means I'll be home that much sooner," the investigator revealed that afternoon as they stood inside the barn. "You're new to your division, but you've been around. You don't need to earn respect from the guys, and they could give two shits how many hours you put in. Just work your day and go home. Simple as that."

With a county map spread across the kitchen table, Hardegen heard Jamie in the other room with the kids, giving him some time to think. He tried to picture abandoned houses, hunting camps, or seldom used community buildings. The thought occurred to him that the killer might kill someone to use their home if he knew no one would call or come looking.

Such a bold move required absolute certainty the murdered party wouldn't be missed, and he couldn't account for such people, so he focused on his original idea.

He looked at the map, circling several key areas, but his mind kept wandering to the results, or lack thereof, from the workday.

Megan had reported several snags from her trip, deciding to stay the night in one of the Naples inns. Reviewing the case file from Kyle Wilson's death provided several more leads for her to check.

Steve Nelson found evidence that the killer had indeed spied on the Wilsons before killing them. It proved he intended to murder them in advance, but he left no physical evidence in the small clearing. Nelson admitted he was dying for a fingerprint, a footprint, anything that might be traced through archives.

A possible tire track was still being analyzed when he called, so Nelson reported he would contact everyone when he knew something more.

Hardegen knew Lamoureux had connections with the FBI, so if they needed evidence rushed, or compared through a national database, the Senior Investigator could get the job done.

The deputy had just circled another area on the map when his daughter tapped his right arm for attention. She was holding her favorite doll in one hand, and a picture book in the other.

"Got your hands full?" he asked her a rhetorical question, receiving a toothy grin in response.

Emma Lynn said very little, but Jamie had faith their daughter was going to be a better scholar than either of them could ever have been. Brock showed signs of advanced intelligence, but he also liked sports, computer learning games, reading, and collecting bugs. At this point, Hardegen figured his son might be anything from a biologist to a computer programmer when he grew up.

He just hoped his children didn't follow his path, not because he feared for their safety, but he wanted so much more for them.

"I'm sorry," Jamie said, coming into the kitchen to retrieve Emma Lynn.

"It's okay. I need a break anyway."

She bent over to give him a kiss before he scooped up his daughter, carrying her to the living room. Jamie looked at him with concern, but he said nothing as he sat down, placing Emma Lynn in his lap. His wife worried about the mental toll the case might take on him, because he dwelled on the welfare of others so often in his job.

He found a Halloween cartoon for the kids to watch while he and Jamie talked. Despite their best efforts to keep the house clean, several toys were strewn across the living room floor. Brock played with a Tonka truck and several wooden blocks, while Emma Lynn danced gleefully before the television as the cartoon came to life.

Hardegen doubted he was so well-behaved as an infant, and his mother swore he was nearly the death of her. She said they needed to have one more child so he could endure the same trials she went through raising four children.

"How was your day?" he asked, deciding to keep her mind off his problems.

"The usual. Little Billy Tyson is going to put me in a padded room by year's end. Why they don't put that kid in a special needs class, I'll never know."

Saying nothing, he simply grinned to himself. Every year, Jamie had one demon child who gave her problems on a daily basis. She felt positive the staff programmed the computer to give her the worst possible student when selecting classroom placement for the kids.

"I picked up some pumpkins on the way home from work," he told her quietly enough that the kids didn't hear.

He had left them on the porch without saying anything to them on his way inside. By not telling them, Hardegen maintained the secret a little longer, because he didn't feel like getting his hands gooey from pumpkin innards just yet. Neither child was old enough to carve a jack-o-lantern yet, meaning he or Jamie needed to get messy when the time came.

"You going to clean up the mess?" she asked.

"I figure if I'm here while we carve them, I can provide damage control."

"Like last year when Brock threw pumpkin guts at the dog and I had to give them both a bath?"

"I don't seem to recall that."

Jamie's look soured a bit, warning him that they were about to tread on the one subject he hated more than anything.

"That's because you were on assignment somewhere in Buffalo. Seems you missed taking your son out for trick-or-treat, you missed most of Thanksgiving, and the family barely got you for a cameo on Christmas."

"We just had this conversation. If I go back on the road, it's going to be the same thing. I'll still be missing a lot of things, and if I get stuck on midnights, I'll be miserable because I'll be sleeping like a vampire half the day."

"I'm not asking you to give up your position, but after this assignment, maybe you can start making time to be here when you're not studying a map, or finishing arrest reports."

Hardegen looked at his kids in the living room, occupying themselves with the television and computer. He didn't want couch potato kids, and to avoid such a fate, he needed to be around them more often. Gaffney liked his work, and impressing everyone else did very little to advance his career.

The desire to win at any cost followed him after college graduation. He put in countless hours of training to compete in football, and now he did the same putting away drug dealers. For every one he put away though, another two rivals took his place on the streets.

It never ended. The vicious circle continued, no matter how much he figuratively broke his back to curb the drug syndicate.

He realized what Terry told him wasn't just the physical act of being home. Hardegen needed to be a family man, and leave the police work at the front door when he walked inside. Still, admitting to Jamie that she was right never came easy. Like a wild animal, he hated being leashed and kept home without the freedoms his job brought.

"I've told you I'm going to try and be here more," he said, putting forth an understanding tone. "And I will. I'm here tonight when I could be out looking at places where this creep might be staying."

"You already know all of these roads, John."

"But I don't know this guy, or how he thinks. It's going to take someone else dying before we figure out more about him."

Jamie knew he didn't want more people hurt, so she didn't probe any further.

"I may know these roads, but we're taking stabs in the dark. He could live in New Mexico for all we know. It could be a professional hit made to look like something else."

"But you don't think so, do you?"

Hardegen shook his head negatively.

"Levine thinks the guy is a nut-job, and I can't disagree. Terry has a sixth sense that gets him inside the mind of the bad guys. The more evidence we find, the more detailed his profile of the killer becomes."

"Is that so unusual?"

"Based on the evidence we've found, I would never come to the conclusions he's telling me. But the funny thing, the really strange thing, is I think he's right on almost every count. It's hard to describe, but it's like he knows what makes the killer tick even more than the killer himself."

He looked to the map on the table, then folded it shut. Glancing at his children, he decided it was beyond time for them to start doing things as a family, even if it meant the dog getting pelted with pumpkin guts.

"I'm going to grab those pumpkins," he informed Jamie, who appeared both relieved and apprehensive at the same time.

Finally getting her way, Jamie would never gloat, because her husband's pride wasn't something to toy with.

She called the kids into the kitchen as her husband stepped onto the porch to fetch the orange vegetables.

CHAPTER 14

▼

Terry settled into his motel room just outside of Batavia. Though he appreciated Lamoureux putting him up for a night, he needed to keep everything about his investigation official.

Including where he stayed.

Lawyers sometimes pick apart the strangest things in court, so he didn't want his efforts to be wasted when a defense attorney grilled him about why he stayed with a fellow investigator as he tracked the Wilson family's killer.

Jurors typically rose above cheap tactics used by defense lawyers, but it only took one to prevent a rightful conviction.

Psychologists would argue that such bizarre killers needed to be studied, but Terry already knew this serial killer in the making was a one-of-a-kind monster.

He paced the floor inside his room, occasionally looking out to the darkness through his window. In the distance, city lights broke up the moonless night, reminding him that he was truly far away from home.

Instead of calling Sherri, he ran the events of the case through his mind once more. His head ached from thinking about it so much, but the pieces they found weren't fitting together for him. Terry felt positive another important clue somehow eluded him, but it hadn't come out of hiding.

"It's your first murder, and you're so damn smart," he said to himself. "You knew not to leave fingerprints. You knew not to leave *footprints* for that matter. And you didn't molest the bodies, did you? So you're not very touchy-feely, are you? And the only souvenirs you took were family photos."

Terry thought a moment until an idea hit him like a hammer.

"Family photos."

Why had there been no family photos with the boy in the residence?

Why was there no record of Kyle Wilson in their documentation? Several investigators, including himself, Megan, and Hardegen had painstakingly checked records, but it was as though Kyle Wilson never existed.

At least in the eyes of the Wilson family.

It took knowledgeable neighbors to bring Kyle Wilson to light, or he might have forever remained lost.

"Was it too painful?" he pondered aloud. "Who erases *everything* about their deceased child?"

No one he knew of.

Terry knew several people who had lost children, from infants to young adults. None of them ever truly stopped grieving. All of them kept photographs, videos, and keepsakes of their children around to ensure they never forgot. Most people assume their child is in a better place, wanting their loved one to know they will never forget them.

Guilt, he thought. Many parents feel guilty when a child dies, believing they could have done more.

Unless they're responsible for the child's death, Terry deduced.

Megan had mentioned checking records of the boy's death with local authorities, but Terry initially believed it was a formality on her part. When he last spoke with her, she was about to review some case files with an investigator at the local state police station, then talk to the man who investigated the death in person.

He decided to check on her progress as he pulled out his cell phone.

She picked up after two rings.

"What have you got?" Terry asked before she could say anything.

"Just got done reviewing the file with Ralph Conrad, the original investigator," she answered.

Terry heard her walking outside, opening a car door momentarily.

"Seems Frank Wilson wasn't up for Father of the Year when it came to Kyle."

"Oh?"

"The investigators talked to some neighbors after the kid's death, and they said he used some tough love on the boy, but they didn't think he was capable of killing him."

"What did our people think?"

"Conrad seemed to think the father knew more than he told investigators, but he couldn't prove anything."

Terry stared outside, a blinking airport light in the distance seemingly waving directly to him caught his attention.

"So we're no further than we were."

"Not necessarily," Megan answered. "I found some new people to talk to, and it seems Kyle Wilson had a very close friend down the road. If I can find this guy, maybe I can shed some light on what happened."

"Don't waste all of your time on that," Terry warned. "What else have you got?"

"I have more neighbors to talk to. Hopefully none of them have weekend plans."

"*We* certainly don't, do we?"

"Not anymore."

Terry wanted to tell her his theory about possible revenge for Kyle Wilson, if he was abused or murdered, but didn't want to taint Megan's search. For all he knew, the son might be a red herring his mind created, meaning he didn't want to put it on the table just yet.

Work the facts, not theories, he kept reminding himself.

"Anything new on your end?" Megan inquired.

"Nothing phenomenal. We discovered the killer stalked the Wilson family for some time before acting. He wore out a little area across the field from the barn."

"Any new evidence?"

"Not really. This guy was careful. He's dangerously smart."

A moment of silence passed before Terry's mind traveled a different avenue.

"Did it occur to you that the Wilsons had no reminders of their son around the house?"

"Maybe the stolen photos were of him."

"Could be, but still, doesn't it seem odd?"

Terry looked out the window, down at the parking lot. A woman carried her baby in a carrier while her husband struggled with two suitcases from the open hatch of their SUV.

"Well, you're right," Megan said. "We didn't even find paperwork about the boy, did we?"

"I thought maybe they left it with someone when they moved, but they didn't have local relatives. Grant called the families, but it didn't seem right to burden them with subjective questions right after telling them their family had been massacred. We're hoping to catch some of them at the calling hours or funeral."

Lamoureux had asked them some basic questions, but nothing pressing.

"If it's that important, why not call them back?"

"It won't bring back the Wilsons, and Kyle certainly isn't a suspect, so it's not a priority."

"I'm hoping to talk to some family friends tomorrow. Maybe we can learn something that way. It's been hard tracking them down, because the Wilsons didn't keep many friends."

"And they never stayed in one place very long."

"You know, they never really moved until their son died. Well, Frank's son."

Megan made a good point. Taryn Wilson was Kyle's stepmother, leading him to wonder what Kyle's natural mother made of the boy's death. Surely if he suffered abuses, the boy would have told his mother when he stayed with her.

"Does the natural mother live around there?"

"I think she left the state, but I can find out tomorrow for sure."

"Please do. I'd like to do a phone interview, if nothing else, to see what she thought. And maybe she knows the friend's name."

"It would save me from drowning in foster care records. I talked to the county today, and only records from the last five years are in their database. Until I get a court order, I can't look at the files, or order them to hurry up. They have an intern entering the old cases at a rate of about fifteen a day, so I'll be lucky to be home by next week."

Terry chuckled.

"Grant's too tight to let you get overtime, so you'd better hurry."

Now Megan let a brief laugh escape.

"I'll do my best. And I'll call you tomorrow when I know more."

"Take care."

"You too. And good luck."

"Thanks," Terry said as he severed the phone call from his end.

He took one last look out his window, drew the large blinds, then stared at the open file atop his made bed. After a long shower, he planned on calling Sherri, then brainstorming through the evidence one more time. His mind was stuck on the evidence, unable to think creatively, because his head ached whenever he stewed over the case.

In desperate need of sleep, he hoped the shower might revive him enough to concentrate. Lamoureux had a full day planned for him, despite it being a weekend. Terry had a to-do list for his friend, which included checking out Frank Wilson's past employers, the man's associates and friends, and why the man kept his own son a secret.

Fifty-thousand dollars went a long way toward happiness, but everything seemed to change for Wilson after Kyle died. Had the man killed his son? Had someone else killed Kyle, and the father was forced to keep a secret?

Or was the boy's death a genuine accident?

Terry knew most people didn't keep life insurance on children unless their job allowed for free or cheap family life insurance. He could never put a price tag on any of his three kids, much less imagine taking one of their lives.

Frank Wilson had been the killer's intended target, but the killer also took his wife and stepdaughter.

"He didn't *have* to," Terry said to himself, taking off his shirt as he turned on the shower.

A glance in the mirror revealed a washboard stomach, which he maintained by religiously riding a mountain bike and jogging daily. He noticed the bags under his eyes, but looked away to remove his pants as the hot water's excess steam snuck around the shower curtain like a thief.

Stepping into the shower, he held both of his hands outward, letting the water caress him from head to toe. It felt excessively hot, but he didn't care. The discomfort only served to make him more alert.

"He didn't have to kill them," he said again. "Were they a guilty party? Were they witnesses to something?"

Terry's envisioned scenario had Frank Wilson dying last, never knowing his wife and stepdaughter had already been murdered when he was attacked.

If the killer knew their habits, he likely knew when Frank Wilson would be alone at the farm. Therefore, he had ample opportunity to kill the man without excess bloodshed.

No, Terry reasoned, the killer wanted Taryn and Lacy dead as well. They didn't deserve the slow, painful death the male figure received, but they deserved death in the killer's eyes. And they apparently deserved to be buried in manure.

He doubted the killer had time to bury the first two bodies, much less move them, before Frank Wilson returned. The killer likely stabbed him, left him to bleed a bit while he collected the wife and daughter, then buried them first so Wilson could see the error of his ways.

Terry washed his hair while thoughts from the murder scene plagued him.

When had he taken the time to piss on them? In front of Frank Wilson? Obviously Wilson was alive when urine trickled down his face, and atop his clothes, but the fatal wound kept him from retaliating.

The killer had to know the wound was fatal, because he didn't bury the man very deep. Wilson managed a partial escape before expiring, meaning he might have sat back and let the killer have his way to conserve strength.

Terry stepped from the shower, chastising himself for over thinking trivial details. He needed a connection between two events, people, or actions before making a definite analysis about the killer and his motives.

Good profiles typically happened after several murders. This case was different, because there was no particular day of the month, no moon cycle, a particular area, or even a type of victim to trace. Terry felt confident such things were forthcoming, because the killer was just getting started.

He looked into the mirror, wanting to say something macho about how the killer's days were numbered, but he lacked both the confidence and energy to do any such thing.

Glancing from the case file to his phone, he decided to call his wife, then see if sleep or reviewing case files sounded better.

CHAPTER 15

▼

Thomas Crotteau walked the property line of the hunting lodge he and several friends owned almost seven miles southwest of the Adirondack Mountains. A wooded property sprinkled with occasional fields, the area was one of the few remaining hunting retreats not bought up by the state for park use.

He stared at the tree line ahead, noticing the sun beginning to rise beyond the horizon. Based on the orange glow, Crotteau guessed he had about half an hour before daylight overtook the woods.

On this Saturday morning several friends were coming to the camp early, prepared to hunt in the morning, then play poker, drink some beer, and awaken early enough to do more serious hunting. In their region, archery season was in for deer, and this was the first weekend the entire group could get together.

A former petty officer with the United States Navy, Crotteau had received an honorable discharge, moved home to New York, and began a family. Now, nearly twenty years later, he had two teenage children and a job as a foreman for a reputable construction company.

His children hunted with him occasionally, but they were busy this particular weekend. Instead, his brother's son had come along to join the group for the first time.

After checking in at the camp, he grabbed one of the portable radios the group used to communicate when they weren't hunting. Sometimes a few of the camp co-owners met to check the property boundaries and make certain their cabin hadn't been disturbed.

While the land remained in a friend's name, Crotteau and several others split the fees involved with purchasing and maintaining the camp. Everyone had a key, and they all looked out for the place whenever possible.

Remote enough that most people couldn't find it, the cabin received extensive damage one spring when a bear tore through one wall to eat peanut butter and other stored goods. None of the hunters were present, and it could have occurred any number of days during a month when no one visited the camp.

Hardly a place to rough it, the cabin had a fireplace, stove, generator, four-wheelers, radio units, and even a stereo to give it a sense of home when the hunters joined together.

Crotteau walked along the property edge to check some tree stands before the group set out to hunt. While the group planned on bucking tradition and hunting later in the morning, he wanted to enjoy nature as he surveyed the area.

Armed only with a Smith & Wesson .22 revolver, he wore a camouflage jacket and pants, along with an orange cap. While he doubted anyone would hunt on their property without permission, it never hurt to put safety first.

Old, but reliable, the pistol had been passed down from his grandfather and his father to him. While using firearms to finish off wounded deer was illegal during bow season, he kept it as protection from the unexpected.

He looked around as he neared a bordering fence, fighting the urge to free his bladder from its full state. The cold weather, combined with the fact he last used the bathroom prior to leaving his house that morning, left him in agony. With no one around, he unzipped his pants and conducted his business behind a tree.

As he spotted someone in the distance, Crotteau nearly thrust his zipper into his private parts as he yanked it up. Standing like an English Setter on point, he stared over the fence at a man dressed partially in camouflage with a rifle slung over his shoulder. Crotteau carried his pistol, which was the largest firearm allowed to be carried by a civilian during archery season.

Either this man had little regard for the law, or didn't know better. Plus he walked directly toward their camp, which meant he would be trespassing once he crossed the fence.

He considered confronting the man directly, but decided to use his radio to call for some backup from the camp. With their four-wheelers, they could meet him within minutes, and might scare away the rogue hunter before he got too far into their property line.

Stepping aside, he called over the radio while he maintained eye contact with the trespasser, who now stepped over the fence. The young man appeared to be on a mission, and Crotteau wasn't certain he was after a deer. Perhaps he had wounded one, and had to track it down, but no gunshots had echoed through the woods, and he wasn't moving very quietly for someone hunting game.

Scotty Helton called him back on the radio, stating that all of them were bringing the four-wheelers to his location.

Crotteau told them which edge of the property he stood upon as he slowly stalked the trespasser through the open area, then the trees. Following him proved relatively easy, since the noise of dried leaves being crunched continually preceded Crotteau. He occasionally lost visual contact with the young man, but managed to keep track of him without being seen by listening intently.

When the sound of three four-wheelers drew near, Crotteau stepped into a fairly open area to flag down his fellow hunters. He pointed out the direction where the hunter had been walking, never saying a word. All three vehicles took off toward the trespasser, Crotteau pursuing them in a lazy jog.

He wanted to get his two cents in when they started berating the trespasser. His wife said he had a quick temper, which Crotteau couldn't deny. His years in the military, followed by life on construction sites, certainly developed his sailor mouth and a short fuse. As a team leader on most jobs, he dealt with the impatient, the rude, and the oblivious.

Both his workers and the people who hired his company proved to be problematic at times.

When he caught up to the others, which only took a few seconds, he found them dismounting from the four-wheelers as the trespasser merely stopped to look at them. He pointed his rifle toward the ground, prepared to talk, as Bob Hagen addressed him first.

"Care to tell us why you're on our property?"

"I didn't know I was."

"The 'No Trespassing' signs weren't hint enough?" Crotteau asked, his voice laced with sarcasm.

A brief glare came his way, but the hunter seemed more interested in addressing Bob Hagen, as though he had business with the man. Despite five other people surrounding him with somewhat menacing stances, he studied Hagen.

"What are you doing back here?" Scotty Helton asked, prompting the hunter to finally look around at the other people.

As he looked, he didn't make much eye contact. At first Crotteau thought he might be shy, or scared, but the young man looked them up and down with cool eyes. He obviously contemplated something, and Crotteau wondered if he *wanted* to be held up by the group.

"I was tracking a deer I shot about fifteen minutes ago," the young man answered without skipping a beat. "He headed this way."

Members of the group looked suspiciously at one another. Crotteau didn't buy it, because he had been outside nearly an hour, hearing no shots of any kind. Besides, gun season wasn't in within their region, meaning this young man didn't know the law, or deliberately broke it.

"This is bow season," Hagen stated. "You can't legally shoot a deer. We're going to have to ask you to leave."

Now the man looked very distrustful of the six property owners, as though they might be out to steal his prize. Crotteau sensed something very disturbing about the entire situation, and especially about this young man with the rifle.

When the young man hesitated, for some unknown reason, Crotteau stepped forward to display his support for Hagen's decision.

"He asked you nicely once, kid. Now get the fuck off our property."

Without another word, the young man turned and left, crunching orange and red leaves as he headed toward the fence. Crotteau watched without blinking until the stranger straddled the fence, then turned to confer with Hagen.

"What the hell was that?"

"I don't know, but it was weird."

"He had his eye on you almost the whole time," Carrie Helton, Scotty's wife, noted aloud.

She sometimes came to hunt with her husband. They owned a stand that allowed them to work back to back if they chose, scouting for deer in either direction.

"You know him from somewhere?" Crotteau asked his friend.

Hagen appeared perplexed as he struggled to recollect any previous encounters with the young man.

"I don't think so."

Everyone shook their heads, muttered separate complaints, then turned to retreat to the warmth of their camp. Only Crotteau bothered to turn and look, just to make certain the young man left their property. As he did so, however, a shot rang out through the air.

Drew Greene, the hunter closest to him, made a brief sound as his body stiffened. If Crotteau hadn't heard the noise, he might have thought Greene took a punch to the gut. A red mist exploded from the front side of Greene's chest as a bullet ripped through his heart, then he slumped to the ground like a tower collapsing to one side.

Everyone stood in complete shock for a moment, knowing one of their own lie dead beside them. It took a second shot, which threw Scotty Helton's head back, to make the survivors scramble for cover.

Stuck in an open area, the four remaining hunters had only the four-wheelers or strewn leaf piles to duck behind. Crotteau began running, but ducked down to a combination of crawling and slithering until he rounded one of the four-wheelers. With no one left at camp, help might be miles away.

Or nonexistent.

He stared at the open eyes of Scotty Helton as his wife ran to his side, too late to save him from the round lodged in the center of his forehead. She had initially run for cover when the shot rang out, but after shrieking her husband's name, she dove to his side.

If he had been watching a horror movie, Crotteau might have shouted for her not to make such a stupid move, but in real life emotions took hold of people. His survival instincts had kicked into high gear already, while the events around him passed like a strange dream.

For her trouble, a shot pierced Carrie Helton's chest, allowing her only a few precious seconds of life before she expired.

Crotteau felt a strange combination of shock and his mind racing, as though he had no control over his own body, or his destiny for that matter. Over the course of less than a minute, three people he cared for were reduced to corpses just feet from him. It seemed as though random chance, if anything, kept him from being the next victim.

"We have to get out of here!" Crotteau's nephew, Brian, shouted at him from behind one of the other vehicles.

"Don't do it," he said calmly enough to surprise himself. "He'll pick us off if you try and ride out of here."

A look at Bob Hagen revealed the man shaking like a leaf. Aside from Crotteau, only Drew Greene had carried a firearm, but retrieving it from his corpse would bring certain death that much sooner. Crotteau reached for his sidearm, but without an idea of where the gunman was hiding, his revolver was useless. His hand touched the leather holster, leaving the gun in place.

"If we each take off on one of these, he can't get us all," Brian reasoned aloud, obviously panicked.

Barely two weeks removed from his twenty-first birthday, the young man had the best years of his life ahead of him. He had good reason to live, but his plan meant someone had to die, and Crotteau didn't particularly like playing Russian roulette under any circumstances.

"Don't do it," he ordered his nephew.

"Why? So he can get a better view of us through his sights?"

Brian tried making an escape attempt by keeping a low stance as he mounted the four-wheeler, but a shot rang out, returning him to the ground in a heap. Like a fatally wounded cowboy from the old westerns, he slammed to the ground, his arms falling out to his sides.

Crotteau wanted to run to his nephew, trying to rationalize how he would tell his brother the kid was dead.

What the fuck am I thinking? he asked himself with a mental slap to the face.

I've got to survive this thing.

He tried to remember how many rounds a hunting rifle held. Five, he thought, remembering how many his held. Even so, the man probably had time to reload, so the number proved irrelevant. Trapped behind skeletal metal, Crotteau tried to contemplate his next move when the answer came with the sound of another gunshot.

A bullet tore through his abdomen, leaving him in complete agony as he rolled on the ground, trying to reposition himself behind the four-wheeler for better cover. The killer had found an opening and shot him, despite Crotteau ducking behind the vehicle.

Now he looked up, finding the young man returning from his hiding spot, walking with a purpose. His eyes locked on Hagen, who appeared absolutely traumatized, but awakened with a terrible realization. Crotteau realized Hagen now knew the identity of this young man, but he was more helpless than an upended turtle. Stuck behind the four-wheeler, with the killer coming directly at him, Hagen had two choices.

Stay and die, or run and die.

"No! Please!" the man shouted when the killer drew within earshot of him.

Crotteau clutched his wound, trying to roll out of the way. He didn't want the young man noticing he had two live victims. As he wriggled his way around the four-wheeler, Crotteau quietly undid the snap on his holster, pulling his pistol up to his stomach. There, it provided ready access, allowing him to use both hands to apply pressure to the hole at his side.

If the killer turned his back, Crotteau would attempt to fire, but his hands felt far from steady. Missing completely, which seemed quite possible at the moment, would leave him at the killer's mercy.

And right now, the killer seemed to have no mercy to give.

Maneuvering for cover left Crotteau with a poor view of the action unfolding before him. He saw Hagen, hands clasped near his chest as though in prayer, continuing to shiver. His eyes welled with tears, the thought he was about to die obviously paralyzing his mind. The insulated beige pants he wore looked wet around the crotch.

Crotteau could relate, knowing his composure hung by a thread. Nothing they said should have sent this man into a killing frenzy, and it seemed as though Hagen somehow knew this cold-hearted individual.

His hazel eyes looked through his thick spectacles at the unarmed Hagen, pleading for mercy, perhaps forgiveness, in any form.

A swift kick sent Hagen to the ground, because the man dared not defend himself. As though rubbing in his cleverness, the gunman reloaded the rifle with a full five shots, indicating he had used five already.

Crotteau had missed an opportunity to shoot him while he had no ammunition in his gun. His forefinger inched toward the trigger, but he remained silent, allowing it to rest on the gun's cold steel.

"Did you think I forgot you?" the killer asked Hagen before shooting him just above the knee at close range.

Crotteau cringed as Hagen screamed in pain after tissue and blood spurted from his leg. He tried to say something, but only stuttered as the injury affected him in every way.

"P-Please," Hagen finally stammered.

"No. You could have done something. What you did was unthinkable, and now you've gotten five of your friends killed because you retreated to your precious camp. What I did to the Wilsons won't be the half of what you get."

Another shot rang out as Hagen's other knee became a useless appendage. His pained groans didn't cease this time, even as the young man grabbed him by the cuff of his jacket to drag him away. He turned his back on Crotteau, pulling a crippled Hagen in the direction from which he came, allowing the injured hunter one opportunity to avenge his four dead comrades.

In seconds the killer was almost two dozen paces away, tugging Hagen along. Any chance for Hagen's survival rested with his aim, which grew less accurate with each foot put between Crotteau and this ruthless murderer.

Crotteau sat up, steadied his pistol with both hands, then squeezed off a round.

He froze in horror as his shot missed completely, because without so much as flinching, the young killer turned around, took aim with his rifle at Crotteau's head, and fired a round.

CHAPTER 16

▼

A combination of mental fatigue and the necessity to be around his family kept Hardegen from studying the county map as much as he planned to. Though fully able to visualize the landscape and buildings by tracing the roads and highways, he wanted to see the areas in person.

Occupancy could change suddenly in any building, so the deputy wanted a firsthand look at every stretch of highway, and every country road. He already knew the haunts where meth dealers had set up shop. While they likely wouldn't return, other people might move in.

Understanding the danger involved with searching some of the buildings, he didn't argue when Terry Levine asked to tag along.

The task force had already checked buildings within a two-mile radius of the crime scene. Few houses dotted the surrounding roads, and Hardegen knew things never fell into place easily on major crime investigations. The killer had played it smart if he stayed in the county.

Gaffney authorized limited overtime, despite the county tightening its pocket-book. While he didn't sneak out like a thief in the night, Hardegen took advantage of the opportunity to start early, not bothering to wake Jamie or the kids.

Hardegen pulled up to the hotel where Terry had spent the night, trying to imagine the best place to begin their search. He hadn't slept well because ideas and images ran through his mind, making him restless. Never before had his knowledge of hiding places and rural roads been so important.

"You ready for this?" Terry asked when he climbed into the car.

"As I'll ever be."

Hardegen started toward the highway, only to turn on the first of many county roads a few minutes later. A virtual cobweb of interconnecting roads, like most of New York State, Erie County harbored few secrets from the deputy.

"Is this really the most effective way to be tracking our killer?" Hardegen asked.

"No. Megan is our best shot at getting answers right now, but even if he doesn't currently reside in this county, the killer stayed someplace while he spied on the Wilsons. Your uniformed officers are checking out every hotel, motel, and inn, so we're going another route. If we can verify where he stayed, we might get some more information about him, or dust for fingerprints."

Hardegen looked out his window at the sparse selection of old houses. Half a mile down the road, an old green house had missing windows and an overgrown lawn during the summer. Checking every single abandoned house would take days.

Time they simply did not have.

"We can't begin to search Buffalo, can we?" he asked the trooper.

"Your sheriff is working with Buffalo PD to arrange sweeps of all the good hiding spots."

"I feel like I'm being spun around and asked to hit a pinata without any hints. This guy could be hiding anywhere."

"No. Not anywhere. I don't think he's able to function in society, so he wouldn't stay in an apartment, or somewhere that other people frequent."

Hardegen threw up his hands for only a second.

"See? Right there. How do you know that?"

"Basic psychology."

"There's nothing basic about that. I had psychology in college, and *I'd* never reach that conclusion."

Terry gave no further reply, only adding to the mystery behind his sleuthing technique.

A moment later, Hardegen spotted the house in the distance, looking somewhat creepy with its faded paint and disintegrating roof. The early morning sun resembled an intense dusk, causing Hardegen to wonder how many more sunsets the house would survive.

"When was the last time anyone lived here?" Terry inquired as the deputy pulled into the overgrown remains of a driveway.

"Years. I don't remember it ever being occupied when I patrolled."

Both men stepped from the car. Hardegen left it running, because he knew their examinations were going to be quick by nature. Considering the driveway showed no disturbances from tire tracks, he doubted the killer had resided here.

Terry now knew the killer had driven some kind of vehicle, which helped quickly eliminate several residences.

He watched Terry draw close to one of the completely smashed windows, then picked another partially broken window to peer through. Weather had stained the living room carpet, creating a foul, rotten smell that virtually stung the deputy's nostrils. They found no evidence of habitation, and a stroll to the back revealed that both doors remained intact and locked, despite the damaged windows.

"Good enough for me," Terry said after little more than a glance.

He never once indicated he wanted to step inside.

They returned to the car as Hardegen began wondering how many empty houses they needed to visit before they found something, or grew disheartened from the lack of answers.

What seemed like incidental information the previous day now came in quite handy as their search began. Nelson had phoned Lamoureux and Terry to reveal his team couldn't identify the tire tracks left at the field across from the Wilson residence. Precipitation had washed away tread details, but the lab had analyzed the width of the tracks as those from a fairly large truck, or perhaps a van.

Every hint aided their search, but Hardegen wondered if they were putting together a 500-piece puzzle with half of the pieces missing.

"Where to next?" Terry asked him.

"Wherever the road leads, my friend."

✳   ✳   ✳   ✳

Megan wondered if her luck could get any worse.

After spending the night in Naples, she discovered some of the key neighbors had gone away for the weekend, including Bob Hagen. She especially wanted to speak with Hagen, because he had spent a great deal of time around the Wilson family.

Taking time to subpoena the county child protective services kept her from making contact with important witnesses. Even the subpoena provided limited access, because Megan was searching for a possible witness to Kyle Wilson's death and a remotely possible tie to the deaths of the remaining family members.

How a subpoena reads makes all the difference when investigating a crime, depending on the jurisdiction and nature of the search. If Megan had proof that she knew the man she searched for had anything to do with either crime, full access would be a snap. While she suspected the neighbor boy might have some information about Kyle Wilson, she worked from simple hunches at this point.

She needed information, but the state protected individuals and records until guilt was proven or highly suspected. Megan both respected and hated the system at the same time. While some investigators might abuse privileges, she did not consider herself among them.

Gaffney had provided a great service by speeding up the subpoena process, then putting her in touch with the director of child protective services. Considering Laura Carlson was willing to meet her on a Saturday was a testament to the sheriff's effectiveness, even several counties away.

As she pulled into the empty county building parking lot, Megan thought about an earlier call from Lamoureux, catching her up on the team's progress. He had dispatched two of her team members to other areas where the Wilsons lived after exhausting the family's belongings and paperwork. No evidence of financial gain existed from their deaths, virtually eliminating distant family or friends as suspects.

Of course that had never been a focus of the group in the first place, but every angle they dismissed created more dedicated focus on the remaining avenues.

Megan stepped from her vehicle, finding a woman with shoulder-length brown hair in her mid-forties outside the main entrance. She wore business casual attire that looked as though it had been pulled from a hamper, or at least put on in a hurry.

"So glad you could meet me," Megan said, assuming the lady was Laura Carlson as they shook hands.

"No trouble at all," Laura replied. "Paul Gaffney and I worked together when I was the county assessor in Erie, so when he called, I put everything else aside to dig up the file."

Megan felt a bit insulted, since her call and credentials weren't enough to elicit any assistance.

Laura turned to unlock the door as Megan sifted through her notes. A few minutes later they stepped into the Department of Social Services office as fluorescent lights buzzed to life overhead.

An odor of stale coffee lingered inside the room.

Megan suspected Laura wasn't thrilled about giving up her weekend. After all, it took a subpoena to gain access to the records, and the office had shown little initiative to assist her until Gaffney made some calls.

Apparently helping the authorities in the name of justice only applied Monday through Friday.

"Everything around here is a mess," Laura confessed. "Our intern is putting archive files into the computer, but after you called yesterday, I searched for the Ramsey files. It seems they left our program about five years ago after an incident with one of their foster kids."

"What kind of incident?"

"It never went to court, but one of their children came up missing. He was found days later in the woods, alive, but quite, well … disturbed."

"Was he molested?" Megan asked, trying to cut to the chase.

"Yes. The Ramseys were accused of negligence, but nothing ever came of it."

"Why not?"

"Apparently the prosecutor couldn't make a case against them. They had a spotless record, and our internal investigation found nothing wrong."

Megan discovered some local bleeding hearts for the couple during her search. Tom Crouch didn't seem to think his former neighbors were angels. She made a mental note to pursue their past later, and perhaps interview them if they could be located. At the moment, she wanted to find the boy who befriended Kyle Wilson in the months before his death.

Most murder investigations center around immediate evidence, often pointing to obvious suspects. Everything in this triple homicide pointed toward revenge, which meant unconventional investigation methods, including the family background. Megan disliked spending time on leads that produced nothing, but process of elimination was necessary.

If everyone on the team worked their leads to a conclusion, eventually one of them would produce the clue that led them to the killer. Megan felt positive Kyle Wilson had something to tell her from beyond the grave about his family, if not the identity of the man who killed them.

"What do you have on the kids the Ramseys fostered about nine or ten years ago?" Megan inquired.

"I dug out their file yesterday, and it looks complete from beginning to end."

"Does it include their last known whereabouts?"

"Yes, but I think they've since moved."

Laura flopped a thick file atop the conference table where Megan had seated herself.

"Luckily the intern hadn't been given this particular file, or we might still be searching for it."

Megan looked through the list of children they housed over the years. In chronological order, the roster included stays as short as a few days, and as long as a few years. Her eyes quickly scanned the few years prior to Kyle Wilson's death, finding five boys who seemed reasonably close to his age in the correct time frame.

"I need information about these five boys," Megan informed Laura. "Is it possible to get photos of them?"

Her reply came in the form of a quizzical look.

"I'm hoping the old neighbors can recognize the boy."

"Their individual files should have photographs," Laura said. "I'll make you a copy of each boy's photograph, but for the sake of their privacy, I can only give you one complete file at a time. I suggest you make your best guess, or be specific in what you're looking for."

Damn subpoena, Megan thought.

"I'll think about it a minute. Thank you."

Laura jotted down the names, then left to search out the five files.

Quickly glancing over the sketchy information the Ramsey file provided, Megan tried determining which boy might be the most likely to befriend Kyle Wilson. She had to assume they were roughly the same age, which would have made him around twelve at the time.

"Shit," she muttered to herself, wishing she could have found a more sympathetic judge in Ontario County.

As she looked over the list, Megan couldn't imagine how foster kids dealt with their situations. She knew some of them were placed in homes or centers because of behavioral problems, but many simply came from bad situations. Bad parents, or a complete lack of parents, sent already troubled kids into unfamiliar surroundings.

Some turned out okay and normal, but others remained troubled for life.

She wondered how Kyle Wilson's friend had turned out.

CHAPTER 17

▼

Bob Hagen had never experienced the taste of urine before.

He once heard it possessed healing or cleansing powers, but never partook. The taste was indescribable, and he had no regrets about not sampling it earlier.

Drawing in agonized breaths, Hagen couldn't help but experience the terrible taste. Sour milk tasted better than the bitter liquid raining down upon his face and chest. The sound of pants unzipping provided hint enough that a piss shower was coming his way, but Hagen couldn't defend himself against it.

Pain now shot through the remains of his knees as blood oozed from the two gunshot wounds. Nearly two-hundred yards removed from his five dead hunting buddies, Hagen doubted anyone had heard the gunfire. He had no cell phone, and his radio only called people at his hunting camp.

Besides, he doubted his life expectancy exceeded another two minutes.

Crippled, and lying in two small pools of his own blood, Hagen looked up to see his young assailant zipping up his pants after marking his territory with a hardened, unwavering expression.

Angry at life was how Hagen termed it between fearful thoughts of how his own life was about to end.

"Don't do this," he pleaded, unable to maneuver himself to any kind of defensive position.

"You saw what happened on that farm, and you didn't do a thing," the young man stated. "Even at the end you didn't tell the truth."

"I did," Hagen insisted, his voice breaking up. "You've got it all wrong."

He felt tears welling in his eyes because of intensifying fear and pain, but tried to stay strong, keeping his mind focused long enough to talk his way out of this mess. Short of finding a weapon and subduing his attacker, Hagen had no means of escape.

To simply move meant using his elbows to crawl over almost a mile of landscape before reaching the camp.

Able to only watch helplessly as the young man drew a knife from the sheath at his side, Hagen saw the blade emerge with a slow, methodical motion. Not only did the knife look sharp, but its one side displayed jagged teeth.

The kind that catch on ribs when plunged and withdrawn.

Wearing dark green gloves, the killer had covered his bases, making certain he didn't leave fingerprints, or allow blood to spatter upon his skin. Hagen tried noticing details, because he hoped to overpower the younger man and wrestle the knife away, because he now knew the knife was coming for him.

Considering the blade was far too big to throw at someone, Hagen knew the young man had to draw close to use it.

When he saw the news about his former neighbor's entire family being murdered, he never believed it might be someone he actually knew committing the crime. Of course he didn't really *know* the young man except by sight. In fact, he couldn't recall the kid's name, but Hagen knew exactly what this disturbed human being wanted.

Vengeance.

"Stay away from me," Hagen stammered as the knife loomed overhead, gripped in a hateful hand.

The blade turned from an upright position toward Hagen's stomach. He tried to back away by using his arms until the knife plunged toward him, causing him to reach out in order to block the attack.

Hagen quickly discovered he had been duped.

Instead of aiming for the chest, the young man slashed the blade across Hagen's right leg, causing far greater blood loss from several ruptured veins. He moaned in pain momentarily, then returned his attention to his assailant.

The loss of blood began to take a toll, however, as the world around him began spinning.

"How does it feel as your life slips away?"

Hagen had just enough sense left to realize the man was toying with him. His body betrayed him, weakening by the second as his hands lay uselessly atop his stomach. He fought to raise his head, wondering if his assailant might be content to just let him drift off to sleep.

Over the next few minutes, the killer assaulted him by ramming the butt end of the rifle into his face repeatedly. Bones broke, while new and different forms of pain kept Hagen aware of the beating's new twists. He glanced at the sneering face of the angry young man just before the rifle smashed into his jaw, dislodging several teeth.

Hagen spit them out as a survival technique to keep them from blocking his windpipe.

When the pummeling finally ceased, he breathed in heaves, trying to recover enough to see beyond the welts now forming around his eyes. His head slumped against the ground, as Hagen wanted nothing more than to let an unconscious state overtake him.

A sharp, incredible pain brought him back to reality, if only for a moment, when the knife lodged itself between two of his upper ribs. He felt his life slipping away, wondering what had spawned such incredible hatred in the young man. Hate or dislike was one thing, but slaughtering an entire hunting camp of strangers seemed extreme.

Insane, perhaps.

Hagen felt his consciousness wavering once more as the knife was ripped from his gut, expediting the death process. He looked up at the blurred figure wiping off the blade, feeling his heart rate quicken as his body grew cold from blood loss.

Too weak and tired to fight for his life, Hagen laid his head down for the last time.

*   *   *   *

"How sure *are* you about this?" Hardegen asked again after a check of nearly twenty abandoned buildings.

"About what exactly?"

"That our guy stayed in Erie County while he spied on the Wilsons."

Terry watched a farmhouse pass by, jack-o-lanterns set across the front porch steps. Most years, he found a way to trade shifts, or get the day off so he could take his kids out for candy on Halloween. Unless he worked a miracle within the week, Sherri might take their two youngest into town, or designate their teenage daughter to do so.

Terry finally turned toward the deputy to answer the question.

"Because when you're in the mind set to stalk someone, you don't want to be too far away from them. You want to see their every move, know their habits, and learn their schedule."

"You're saying he stalked them? Like a jealous boyfriend might stalk his ex?"

"Sort of, but this is much more serious. Serial killer types have to do things a certain way, almost like an obsessive compulsive disorder. They have to know the details, and when they carry out the murders there's a ritual. Nothing is more important to them than the kill. It has to be perfect, because they relive it to satisfy themselves."

Hardegen made a left turn.

"Call me stupid, but I just can't get my mind around all this."

Neither said a word for a few minutes as another decrepit house came into view.

"We get stuck in our ways, don't we?" Hardegen asked a rhetorical question that Terry didn't try to answer. "My day usually consists of knocking down doors, busting drug dealers, and doing a little undercover work. I like to think we're doing our part to keep the world a little safer."

"And you are," Terry said reassuringly.

"You ever worked on a drug task force?"

Terry shook his head negatively. It was one of the few things he hadn't done in his fifteen years with the state police.

"It's like a brotherhood, because it's so dangerous. We have to watch each other's backs, and we do some things we don't always like to talk about to get the job done. What happens in the task force stays in the task force, we always say. Some of the people I have to deal with, pushers and users alike, make me cringe sometimes, but I just think of how much safer the streets will be when my kids get older.

"What we're doing here is a completely different animal to me. Everyone has their own part to carry out, but there's no real unity. It's a lot of phone calls and short meetings. I mean we're virtually grasping at straws for a lead. *Any* kind of lead. I guess I'm just used to immediate gratification for my work."

Completely understanding what the deputy meant, Terry knew how methodically homicide investigations worked, but he also recalled the natural high that came with busting a murderer. Hardegen hadn't experienced such a revelation yet.

"People out there don't want to see what we see," he told Hardegen. "They don't want us there until they need us, and most of them wear blinders through life, trying to believe the dealers, hookers, and gangs aren't in plain sight. And they certainly don't want to worry about some psychotic stranger gutting them like a deer. Most of the guys I work with don't want to see what I've seen."

"How do you describe what you've seen?" Hardegen asked as he pulled into the driveway of an old house that looked dingy, but mostly intact.

"When I get called out, I'm the witness to the creative pallet someone else has left for me. They don't always leave it for my viewing pleasure as much as their own, but it is the byproduct of a warped childhood."

Hardegen put the car in park, giving him a strange stare.

"Why can't someone have a shitty childhood and overcome it?"

"Some can," Terry replied. "When someone turns killer, their mind no longer functions normally. Most times they can blend into society, but it's a wolf amongst sheep disguise. They walk around and analyze who makes the best choice for their next victim. It usually takes a very traumatic childhood, completely devoid of love and compassion for someone to snap. Not always, but much of the time.

"Only by killing can these people satiate their hunger for a need they've gone without. Love is easily substituted with some part of the killing act that satisfies a basic need for them. While you and I might go home and put it to the missus, they have a certain part of the killing ritual that really turns them on."

Hardegen smirked at the last statement, but he still didn't appear entirely comfortable with his role on a homicide investigation. Terry suspected he missed his comfort zone and some of the freedoms it provided.

"I think Gaffney has big things planned for you," he told the deputy. "He wouldn't have taken you from your work if he didn't think you could help us, and maybe learn a little something. I don't know you that well, John, but I appreciate everything you've done for me."

Hardegen scoffed, making a strange noise out of his nose as though the compliment was insincere.

"Really," Terry stated. "You've given me insight on things that have helped me piece together a profile, and you're saving me countless hours by chauffeuring me around the county. I don't remember a lot of these county roads."

"Your buddy said you worked here for five years. How could you not know them?"

"I worked as an investigator, so I didn't get to scour the back roads like our road officers. Hell, I doubt most of them know all these haunts like you do."

Opening his door, Hardegen stepped outside before speaking, once Terry joined him.

"I grew up in this area. Going to Syracuse was one of the most difficult things I ever did, especially after the knee injury."

Both men sauntered toward the house, taking a halfhearted break from the dull grind of driving county roads.

"I felt like I let everyone around here down when I finished college with a business degree. Everyone thought I had what it took to go pro."

"Did you ever walk onto a team, or join a practice squad?"

"Nope," Hardegen said with an air of finality, lacking any hint of regret. "The NFL has enough washed up running backs who don't want to call it quits, so I came home. Funny thing is though, I found out who my real friends were. Calls and e-mails stopped coming from certain people after they found out I wasn't going to be worth millions."

As though on cue, both men turned their attention to the old house set back nearly fifty yards from the road. Without a neighboring house for almost a mile in either direction, the place seemed ideal for farmland, if nothing else.

"How do places like this just sit vacant for so long?" Hardegen pondered aloud. "I should deal in foreclosure properties on the side and set up my retirement fund."

Terry peered into one of the windows, seeing a fairly clean house inside. Pieces of dusty furniture remained present, as though left for ghosts to use at their leisure. Drapes hung in some of the windows, yellowed and dirty from years of neglect and direct sunlight.

Hardegen disappeared momentarily, then returned with a satisfied look.

"The door's secure in back," he said, thumbing behind him.

The only other building on the property was a storage shed at the end of the driveway. Because the door and two windows appeared intact, Terry didn't ask the deputy to check it. A gaping hole in the roof made the tiny building nearly inhabitable for a stowaway, no matter how badly the person might want to rough it.

When his cellular phone rang at his side, Terry nearly jumped out of his skin because it broke the otherwise dead silence.

"Holy," he muttered to Hardegen before answering it, receiving a chuckle from the younger man. "Levine."

"Terry, I've got some news," Lamoureux's voice said from the other end. "Megan has narrowed it down to five boys who might have been friends with Kyle Wilson. And Nelson managed to figure out what the murder weapon used on Francis Wilson was."

"Something tells me it won't be a rare collectible knife sold only at auction only twice a year."

Lamoureux shared his sense of humor.

"We couldn't be that lucky, could we? As a matter of fact, it's the exact opposite. We're dealing with one of those cheap survival knives sold at flea markets across the country."

"The ones with the compass on the handle?"

"*The* one. Nelson compared the teeth mark wounds to the knife itself and got a match."

"I got one of those things for Christmas once."

"That makes you and about two-million other people our prime suspects, then. I'm checking every flea market within a hundred mile radius. Maybe someone had a weirdo customer they remember."

"You might look into the state fair vendors, too. I think some of them sell that junk."

"Good idea. You sure as hell can't take something like that on a flight anymore."

"True. You know, I was hoping you were calling with good news for a change."

"I have to deliver good news in pieces, so you guys keep your morale at a steady level."

"Oh?" Terry asked, suppressing the urge to chuckle at his friend's expense.

"I learned that at one of those leadership seminars last spring."

Terry once poked fun at his friend for seeking a higher position, but it fit Lamoureux. He felt certain the man would command a troop one day.

"Steve is having the medical examiners check for any metal shavings along Wilson's rib cage. He thinks the lab might be able to figure out what the knife was sharpened with."

Terry recalled the knife he received being very dull. Perhaps the manufacturer intended it that way, since kids ran around with knives more frequently back then. If Nelson got lucky, the lab might figure out exactly which company produced the knife, because several imitators had come along. The task force desperately needed solid leads to put them on the right track.

"How are things on your end?" Lamoureux inquired.

"Slow. But I don't think I'm wrong about this."

"Not that I doubt you, ol' buddy, but I'm having the uniform guys check out hotels and apartments just in case."

"Ye of little faith."

Lamoureux laughed momentarily.

"I'll have John pull the knife out of my back after I get off the phone," Terry teased his friend.

"You're awfully testy. I'm just covering every angle."

"As well you should. I just have a really strange feeling about this guy, Grant. He's dangerously bold, yet clever enough to get away with it. It's like he has a natural talent for perfectly concealed murders."

"He's only done this once that we know of, Terry," Lamoureux was quick to point out.

"That's what scares me even more. He has room to improve, but not by much."

Terry looked over to Hardegen, who now stared across the field at something in the distance.

"I'll call you if we find anything new, Grant."

"Good enough."

Terry hung up the phone, joining the deputy at the edge of the field.

"What's the matter?" he asked.

"Nothing. I was remembering all the crazy things I did as a kid, many of which took place in fields just like this one."

"Me too, but I got over the shock of urbanization when I took the job near New York City."

Hardegen nodded.

"Yeah. I've seen my share of the big city, too. Changes your perspective, doesn't it?"

"I suppose."

The deputy swung his arms out, then brought his hands together in a clapping noise, indicating he was ready to drive again.

"Ready when you are," he said, turning toward the car.

Terry followed, realizing they were burning daylight. He hoped Nelson or Megan might dig up some tangible leads for him to follow, but then again, he realized their jobs were to follow real leads. His job was to think in the abstract, and stop the killer before he grew into something more potent.

What he wanted was to be home with his wife and kids, simply patrolling roads in the north country, but his reputation sometimes acted like a dog collar, dragging him where he was needed most.

He opened the car door, hoping for a sign, a thought, even a premonition about the killer's identity, or where he remained hidden.

Any good news would help him make it through the day.

CHAPTER 18

▼

When Paul Gaffney took office as sheriff, he planned on avoiding a dull retirement, making a little extra income until he collected social security, and sticking with the career he loved a bit longer.

He retired as a captain from the New York State Police with over twenty-five years of service. During that time he investigated crimes, patrolled in nearly two dozen counties, worked with task forces covering everything from drug deals to homicides, and headed up a division that covered juvenile crimes.

Since taking office, he had attended various classes put on by the state police, secret service, and even the FBI. He doubted his constituency much cared about his furthering education, but dealing with new threats and terrorism required new information. The world had become a network run on communications and computers.

Whether they knew it or not, the people he protected needed him to educate himself for their safety.

In the back of his mind, Gaffney always knew a highly publicized crime might come his way. The state of New York historically drew bizarre crimes, so a triple homicide didn't surprise him, but the media attention felt like someone breathing down his neck.

Sitting behind his desk, Gaffney stared at the file from the Wilson farm. His secretary had screened his calls all week, giving him some temporary peace from the media and concerned area residents. Panic typically ensued after brutal rapes or murders, more so if they occurred continually without solid leads.

On this Saturday morning he had the entire county building to himself, with the exception of a few custodians.

Surrounded by plaques of his successes and accomplishments along three walls, Gaffney put his feet atop the desk, scooping up the photos and documents for closer examination. Not much of an "open door" sheriff, he preferred privacy and time to himself during the day. His evenings were often filled with charity events, political fund-raisers, retirement dinners, and other miscellaneous functions.

While not a recluse, Gaffney enjoyed time to himself. He owned a duplex in Orchard Park, just outside of Buffalo, with a small garden he tended with his wife. Their anniversary was fast approaching, so he needed to ponder what gifts seemed appropriate, while appeasing the general public.

He studied the crime scene and autopsy photos with great interest, wishing he could join the investigative team. One of the most difficult transitions proved to be removing himself from the action as an administrator. Gaffney had yet to completely remove himself from standard policing, occasionally helping out with sobriety checkpoints, or drug raids.

A few of his young bucks like Hardegen provided him with hope that his department would remain in good hands for many years after he left. With the public deciding his fate every four years, Gaffney never took his job for granted, particularly since he neared the end of his first term.

Like a dark cloud, the election a mere two weeks away loomed over his head.

He worried about it occasionally, and he fretted over the triple homicide, but for different reasons. Gaffney didn't want to use the case as political leverage.

He simply wanted it solved.

Technically, the state police were steering the investigation, but his was the face plastered across every news station. He and Lamoureux revealed very few details about the murders, because they needed to weed out the crazies from legitimate suspects. When it came time to interview the true suspect, if one emerged, the authorities needed to make certain they held exclusive details about the murders.

When someone could reveal the hidden details of the murder scene, it would prove without a doubt that person committed the murders.

Today Gaffney wore his regular uniform, but a fully pressed gray suit hung inside a nearby closet. His favorite black suit received some spaghetti sauce stains at a lunch, prompting his secretary to send it out for cleaning before he could object.

She knew him far too well, but she also kept him in line, and organized.

He kept several changes of clothing on-hand at all times, including casual wear for golfing and his full dress uniform.

Ordinarily, Gaffney wore blue jeans and flannel shirts on fall weekends, but today he had promised the news crews an informal update outside the county building. This wasn't meant to be a leisurely weekend, touring the countryside with his wife, or staying at a cabin with a large fireplace. They often traveled the state, and when his vacation time permitted, the country.

With his shined, gleaming black shoes atop the desk, he stared at the photograph of Francis Wilson, who had received special attention from the killer. Gaffney agreed with many of Terry Levine's assessments, not just because the man had a winning track record, but because they sounded plausible.

Based on the single crime scene, Gaffney felt the two women had been shot quickly. On farms, disposable animals were shot once in the head, mainly for efficiency of bullets, though also to keep them from suffering. The sheriff felt reasonably certain Francis Wilson had pissed someone off during his travels, and the women were simply objects in the way of the real quarry.

His theory stemmed from the idea that this was the only set of murders the killer might commit. If that held true, and the man never said a word to anyone about them, he would likely elude custody forever, because the task force had discovered no concrete evidence. What disturbed Gaffney even more, however, was that Levine felt these murders were not the last.

Gaffney agreed, because there was no reason to kill Taryn or Lacy. Murder for revenge might have spilled over to thrill killing.

Evidence trickled from the scene and autopsy results, but most of the new facts were insignificant. They knew the killer was right-handed, and probably around six-feet in height. Nelson theorized his strength as above average based on how he dragged three bodies with ease, and the depth of the blade into Frank Wilson's torso.

Even a hair sample would help the task force begin to piece together a composite of the killer's appearance through length and color. No footprints, no tire tracks, no fingerprints, and no witnesses. A complete strikeout so far as leads went.

He set the files down as his phone rang, swinging his feet to the ground before answering it. Few people had direct access to his office phone, because the number on his business cards led to county dispatchers or his secretary.

"Gaffney," he answered somewhat gruffly, thinking some reporter had purchased the number from an unreliable member of his staff.

"Paul, this is Greg Higgins from Oneida."

Major Higgins commanded all of Troop D, which included Herkimer County, the Utica area, Syracuse, and part of the Adirondack Mountains. He and

Gaffney had worked several cases together over the years. They occasionally spoke at public functions, but Higgins wouldn't call him just to chat.

"Something the matter, Greg?"

"I think your triple homicide just poured over to our area."

Gaffney stiffened.

"What do you have?"

"Word just came in from a conservation officer that we have five dead hunters about thirty miles northeast of us, one of which had traces of urine on his skin and clothes."

"Five? What the hell happened?"

"We're not really sure yet. Four of them were shot, and the one he pissed on had a knife wound in his rib cage."

A strange tingle ran through the sheriff's arms when the words reached his ears. It sounded like a carbon copy of Frank Wilson's murder.

"We have one survivor," Higgins reported. "Shot once in the gut, and once more in his skull. They rushed him into surgery, but his condition is up in the air."

"If he makes it, we probably have an ID on our killer."

"Probably. Our VCIT is scouring the scene right now, but I figured you or your people might want a look."

"You bet your ass I do. Can I ask you a huge favor?"

"Shoot."

"If you can, please have your people leave the scene as intact as possible. I have kind of a special investigator working down here who can piece things together just by looking at them."

Higgins remained silent a moment.

"He's one of yours from Troop B. Terry Levine."

"Sure," Higgins finally answered. "I'll try and keep everyone from tromping up the scene once they're done."

"I appreciate it. If that guy doesn't survive the surgery, Terry might be our only hope of finding our guy."

Higgins sighed uneasily.

"We can always hope for the best, can't we?"

"I suppose. Thanks for the heads up, Greg."

Gaffney hung up the phone, slightly overwhelmed by the news for a moment. He took in a deep breath, debating where to start, and how to alter what he planned to say at his impending news conference.

He plucked the phone from its cradle, deciding to call Lamoureux. Hopefully the Senior Investigator established a good working relationship with Troop D immediately, so the exchange of information went smoothly.

Gaffney had opened the door for Terry Levine to do his thing, so he hoped Lamoureux's faith in the man's abilities wasn't misguided.

CHAPTER 19

▼

Terry and Hardegen had been standing in the center of an abandoned house when the call came from Gaffney that five hunters were murdered near the Adirondacks.

Since Troop D's commander had offered full cooperation, Gaffney made certain Terry could see the scene firsthand. He informed Terry to take the deputy along, since he had approved Hardegen's assistance in any way possible.

"I just can't believe this guy would strike a second time so soon," Hardegen noted as they drew near the scene.

According to the directions given by the VCIT investigator they spoke with, they were less than a mile away after about three hours of high speed drive time. Gaffney wanted to offer his departmental helicopter, but a medical emergency had taken it out of the county. The backup chopper, an old military surplus model, was out-of-service for repairs.

"It has me thinking," Terry said, letting the thought openly drop.

He had remained silent most of the trip because his mind raced with all kinds of ideas. The investigator provided some details over the phone, so he knew what to expect when he walked into the woods.

For the most part, Hardegen said little, but the few words he spoke didn't hide the fact that he wished he hadn't been ordered to accompany Terry. He seemed understanding of the situation, but obviously hated missing time with his family. Terry questioned how he worked on a task force if he was always so torn between work and family.

Investigators don't always get to choose their own assignments or hours. Weekends are occasionally mandatory because crime doesn't take vacations.

Terry recalled many a weekend of being on-call for the state police. Having a normal schedule on patrol helped console him when he gave up his investigative position to come home.

Moments later, Hardegen pulled up to a county police officer blocking the road. He and Terry produced identification and explained their purpose. The officer let them pass with minimal conversation, obviously expecting them, as multiple red strobe lights came into view.

"Want me to make small talk with the locals while you poke around?" the deputy asked.

"Sure. Unfortunately they only gave us one invitation, so I hate to leave you, my friend, but I have to. Just don't get yourself into trouble."

Hardegen laughed sarcastically.

"Yeah, there's *so* much to do around here."

The last part of their journey took place over a dirt trail filled with potholes and bumps the unmarked car didn't handle particularly well. If not for specific instructions, the two officers might have spent an hour or more searching for the crime scene. While the land was privately owned, the acreage covered miles of woods. Countless trails went deep into the dark woods, providing turns and dead ends that would baffle the layman traveler.

Perhaps that was the idea.

Hunting camps weren't much of an escape if they were within earshot of the highway. Unfortunately the location made it much easier for the person Terry now felt certain was a serial killer to target a group of six.

No longer was the man a potential serial killer. Within days he had lived up to the prophecy Terry uttered.

"Wow," Hardegen muttered as they neared a perimeter that looked better lit than most football stadiums.

Over a dozen police cars, an ambulance, and two fire trucks sat in a semicircle around the main portion of the crime scene. The two fire trucks were local rescue trucks, there simply to provide lighting with their extendable towers. While blinding to gaze upon, their halogen bulbs dispersed light over great distances.

Despite being early afternoon, the combination of overcast skies and tall, full trees created a dark atmosphere. Terry assumed the lighting was to aid in the search for smaller evidence, rather than create artificial daylight.

"Make some friends," Terry suggested. "I'm going to get the grand tour, then decide for myself what really happened."

"Sounds good," Hardegen said as they stepped out of the car.

The deputy hadn't seemed enthused about driving halfway across the state, but Terry had little choice. Picking up Lamoureux, or even driving alone, would have delayed him another precious hour or more.

Seconds counted when dealing with a serial killer who left so few clues. Terry stepped forward as a man dressed in a dark suit approached him. Sporting buzzed blond hair, the man appeared as though he had dressed in a hurry to investigate the scene.

"Duane Peterson," the man said, shaking hands with Terry as Hardegen leaned against the hood of the car. "You must be Terry Levine."

"Guilty," Terry said, following Peterson through the obstacle course of parked vehicles.

Many officers stood back from the scene, several conducting perimeter security. Terry thought the presence of so many lights and vehicles might attract the media more than a subdued setup. Helicopters sounded in the distance, indicating word had already spread to the television stations.

"It's a circus," Peterson commented. "Our forensic people are still working inside, but the boss man said I could take you in."

Not that it mattered to him, but Terry figured Peterson was the boss.

"Who's in charge?" he asked.

"Bill Chambers is the Senior Investigator, but he's off giving a quick update to the news people to keep them off our backs. He promised a statement if they kept the helicopters away until we were done."

"Your forensic people won't care if we walk through the scene?"

"Well, we can't walk through, per se, but we can walk, skip, or jump across anything they've been over. We're not calling the coroner's office until we're finished, but I think they'll have an idea what's coming their way."

Terry certainly didn't want to endanger any forensic evidence. The lack of physical evidence at the first scene made him desperate for any links to the killer.

"So you had a homicide like this in your area?" Peterson inquired.

"I'm going to reserve judgement until I see the bodies, but it sounds eerily similar."

Peterson lifted some crime scene tape as he led Terry into the actual area. A glance back toward Hardegen showed the deputy on the phone, likely trying to explain the situation to his wife.

"He one of your new guys?" Peterson asked.

"Not exactly. He's been helping us on the triple homicide."

A thick man with a full head of red hair intercepted them as the two investigators drew near the heart of the crime scene.

"Terry, this is Bill Chambers, the man in charge," Peterson said, making introductions.

"Former man in charge," Chambers said with a slightly perturbed tone, though he shook hands with Terry. "Aren't you the one who stopped that Kimmerling guy last spring?"

Terry nodded reluctantly, sensing the conversation was about to change direction.

"ADS Duggan just called me personally and said we were to do whatever you asked of us," Chambers stated. "I translate that as he wants you in charge of this operation."

Assistant Deputy Superintendent David Duggan once served as the major in Terry's old troop. Serving as an influence in several ways, Duggan put Terry on the fast track to investigations, and sometimes lured him back, as Lamoureux had, on bizarre cases.

While Terry sought the comforts of home in the Canton area, Duggan put himself in a position to become part of the New York State Police upper brass. Now he occasionally, and unnecessarily, stuck his nose in when it came to high profile cases.

"You're in charge," Terry told Chambers. "I'm just here to help however I can."

Chambers didn't appear very comfortable brushing an order from an ADS off his shoulder like a gnat. Taking the lead on a major homicide meant leading a team, dealing with the media, and often dealing with distraught families that didn't rest until justice was served.

Terry had just met the Troop D Senior Investigator, and already felt certain the man was fully able to handle it. He wondered if Chambers might even enjoy the responsibility in some twisted sort of way.

"I need to see the bodies as soon as possible," Terry said. "If this is the same guy, God help us because he's just getting started."

"The team is combing the ground for trace evidence," Chambers revealed as Peterson broke away from them. "All five bodies are exactly as we found them. We've identified all five, but we're not releasing any information."

He started walking toward the central area where the crime occurred. Terry followed, surveying the area carefully for any details outside the realm of physical evidence.

Despite the dense woods surrounding them, the area looked more open, with only a few trees and shrubs dotting the otherwise tall grass and dirt trails.

"Who found the bodies?"

"A hunter from a nearby camp heard multiple gunshots," Chambers said as they approached four face down bodies, lined up like beds in an army bunkhouse. "Since its bow season, he decided to check it out."

Terry examined the bodies, seeing very little distinguishing about any of them. They all wore camouflage gear, which hid the bloodstains. One of them had a strawberry blonde ponytail, causing him to think it was a male with long hair until he saw the pink and white striped band holding it in place.

It occurred to him that some of his own friends brought their wives or girlfriends on hunting trips with them. He exhaled a sigh through his nose, wondering why five people had to die on a weekend getaway.

Since their faces were against the ground, he couldn't see their features. He pulled a pair of latex gloves from his back pocket, snapping them into place over his hands.

"Has your team been over the bodies?" he inquired.

"They photographed the bodies and identified them from wallets and hunting licenses, but nothing else."

Terry would have to be careful if he moved them at all. He wanted to see their front sides, but didn't want to disturb evidence. Typically morgue attendants removed clothing, then sent it to the state police lab for analysis. Terry couldn't risk knocking off the least little shred of DNA evidence if any remained attached to their clothing.

"It took him some time to find the bodies," Chambers continued. "These four were here, along with the fifth guy they took to the hospital. The other body is just over the hill."

"Was he originally lined up with the others?"

"No. Up here is where we found him. I don't think he was in any condition to crawl anywhere."

Terry followed the direction of the Senior Investigator's pointed finger to another area encompassed by yellow tape.

"Did the killer leave the one guy alive on purpose?" Terry asked.

"I don't think so. He was face down like the others. The man who found them was an EMT, and he barely found a pulse on the guy."

"Where's he?"

"My people are interviewing him. He was up here with two friends, so it doesn't seem likely he had anything to do with it."

The fact that he reported a survivor immediately informed Terry that he had no part in harming any hunters.

"Any good leads so far?"

"We think we have the tire tracks from whatever the guy drove back here," Chambers replied. "There will be slugs retrieved from the bodies, if not the ground. If we're damn lucky, he left fingerprints on the body up there."

Terry looked up at him.

"Why's that?"

"He manhandled the guy like a professional wrestler before he finally killed him with the knife. If he wasn't wearing gloves, we'll definitely pull something from the body or one of the shell casings."

Chambers walked with Terry toward the last body, carefully tracing the edge of the perimeter where his forensic team had already checked for evidence.

Despite investigating multiple homicides several times over, Terry's mind felt like mush as he tried to reason what steps to take. Chambers had likely followed the same procedures perfectly, but Terry wanted no rock left unturned.

"How would anyone know these people were up here except for friends and family?" he wondered aloud.

"We're on it," Chambers replied. "I don't have much spare manpower, so we're going to work it in when we inform the families about their loved ones. Two of the people down there were married, so it's hard telling what we'll be getting into with their family."

Hoping they didn't leave young children behind, Terry ascended the hill until Chambers stopped at the top.

"We found indications he was dragged up here, away from the others," the Senior Investigator said as Terry dared look at the harrowing sight before him.

Much of the man's face appeared swollen and bruised, and not by human hands, either. Purple and red puffy spots covered whatever areas weren't readily bloody across the face. The eyes appeared swollen shut, leaving Terry a guess that several facial bones were broken. Based on the nature of the wounds, he assumed the injuries occurred before death.

No, he *knew* they occurred prior to death. Quit second guessing yourself, he thought. You've been away from the game, but it never once left your mind.

Someone had used a blunt object to punish the man before ultimately stabbing him in the ribs with a large knife. Terry doubted the killer used his fists in any way, and even if he did, he likely wore gloves. He wasn't stupid about leaving blatant evidence behind.

Unlike the other bodies, this one remained upright for all to see.

A strong odor of urine crossed Terry's nose, making him cringe as he turned his head. Strangely, none of the other bodies were defaced like this one. Nor did they smell of urine. Like Francis Wilson, this man had received special treatment from the killer.

"What was his name?" Terry inquired, kneeling down to examine the unsightly corpse.

"Bob Hagen. We found a government ID on him, so we did a quick background check with the Post Office." Chambers conferred with his clipboard for more information. "He worked as a postman around Ingleside and Naples."

Terry's head turned so fast he felt a slight pain in his neck.

"Naples?"

"Yeah. Why?"

Standing up quickly, Terry plucked his cellular phone from his side.

"I need the name of every victim, including the guy in surgery, right away."

"Okay," Chambers said, his face registering that he understood the urgency of the situation.

He turned around, snapped his fingers several times at someone waiting downhill, and returned his attention to Terry, who had already placed a call to Megan's cell phone.

"A good break?" Chambers dared asked.

"Quite possibly."

Chambers stared at him intently, as though waiting for an elaboration, but Terry desperately needed to speak with Megan. Though she did not know it, she might be staying in the town with all of the answers, and worse, she might be in danger if she spoke with the wrong people.

CHAPTER 20

▼

Megan returned to the Crouch residence, armed with five photographs.

Her enthusiasm quickly faded when the older couple couldn't recognize any of the faces.

"There were so many of them," Betty said. "And it's been years since they moved."

Her husband appeared more gruff about the Ramseys, but he didn't recognize the kids either, citing his lack of concern over any of the "rugrats" he saw across the road.

Instead of picking one file, Megan convinced Laura Carlson to meet her later, once she had more neighbors look at the photographs. If she could just find one neighbor who recognized the best friend of Kyle Wilson, she wouldn't waste more time with subpoenas or vague file searches.

A wrong guess meant returning to the court and asking for another subpoena. Asking and receiving were two different monsters when it concerned juvenile records.

Tom Crouch informed her that the Hagens were the only other former Wilson neighbors still living in the area. Everyone else had moved away, and in one case, passed away.

Megan had already visited Eileen Hagen once. Another visit would likely make her a nuisance in the woman's eyes, but she just needed one question answered.

The purpose of her first visit had been to see if Bob Hagen was available for a few questions, but he wasn't due back until Sunday afternoon at the earliest.

Megan decided she needed to know if Eileen knew the identity of the foster child before she made the trek to the Adirondacks.

With no answers forthcoming, she felt a need to travel to the hunting camp was the only way to attain solid answers before moving forward. Terry and Lamoureux had nothing new, or they certainly would have called.

Pulling into the driveway of the Hagen household, Megan noticed a beautiful arrangement of shrubs, bushes, and flowers lined in front of the house. Though the flowers had long since wilted, she produced a mental image of how they probably looked during the summer. The lawn appeared nicely kept, while a small vegetable garden sat to one side of the house.

Tomato vines and their support cages lined an otherwise plain dirt patch dotted with browning foliage. Megan felt a stiff breeze as she stepped from the car, which heralded a predicted storm front sweeping across the state of New York.

Taking a deep breath, Megan stepped toward the house when the phone clipped to the left side of her slacks rang.

"Damn," she said, taking it up to see Terry Levine was calling.

Putting off the inevitable task of speaking to Eileen Hagen seemed inviting, so she answered.

"Good news for me?" she asked lightly.

"No. Terrible news."

He sounded genuinely distressed.

"Megan, we have five people dead in the southern part of the Adirondacks, and I think you might be in the Mecca of information for breaking this wide open."

"Five people dead?" she asked, his words still stunning her. "Same guy?"

"Looks like it. And his primary target was someone from the area you're in."

Megan knew it before he even stated the name. Everything had already fallen into place for her.

"Bob Hagen?"

Terry's moment of silence provided all the confirmation she needed.

"Damn it, Terry. I'm in his wife's driveway. How bad was it?"

"The guy shot four dead. One survived, but they don't know if he'll make it through surgery. He tortured Hagen and knifed him just like Frank Wilson. I can't see how this couldn't be our guy. Gaffney never revealed the details of the first crime, so this *can't* be a copycat."

Megan took a moment to absorb the information, noticing the blinds from a living room window moving slightly.

"I'm about to ask Hagen's wife for some information. I can't barge in there and ask her any questions knowing her husband is dead."

"She doesn't need to know yet. They aren't releasing the names of the victims until later. Someone will call when the time is right."

Megan remained silent a moment.

"I'm not trying to sound cold," Terry added, "but notification isn't your responsibility."

"I know, but she'll think I'm a complete bitch, because she'll know I knew."

Megan doubted she would need Eileen for any further information after this line of questioning, but guilt already consumed her.

"Do what you think is right," Terry said. "Just keep in mind that more lives may be at stake."

Megan rolled her eyes skyward. Eileen already knew she was back, so turning around and leaving might look even worse when the woman heard of her husband's murder. Consoling herself with the notion other lives might be spared, Megan still didn't feel right about pumping Eileen for information while hiding certain facts.

"I'll call you when I know something more," she told Terry before clicking the phone's end button.

Composing herself before she approached the front door, Megan tried to put the new information out of her mind.

An impossible task.

While she hoped to be invited inside during her first visit for an extensive talk with Bob Hagen, Megan wanted the opposite now. She envisioned herself showing the photographs to Eileen, then the woman gasping with apprehension as she immediately recognized one of the young men.

Things never went that smoothly, so when the door opened before Megan even knocked, she found herself a bit startled.

"Back so soon?" Eileen asked, far more friendly than Megan anticipated.

"So sorry to bother you again, but I had a quick question."

"Certainly. Would you like to come in? I was just making some fresh tea."

Megan weighed the consequences of being rude against what Eileen might come to think of her later. A terrible storm blew toward Eileen, one that might leave irreparable damage with its unexpected swiftness.

"I've got a few minutes," the investigator said as she stepped inside, praying no one called Eileen with the terrible news until she left.

Pleasant odors of scented candles floated throughout the living room as Megan stepped inside. Eileen walked briskly toward the kitchen, almost openly thankful for the company. She and her husband were about ten years short of retirement age, and Eileen worked out of the home.

Fighting back the urge to rush out the front door, Megan stood in the living room until Eileen returned with a server set complete with teapot and saucers. Megan had never informed anyone of a loved one's passing in a criminal case. Such tasks were typically done by the coroner's office, or an investigator in charge.

As a trooper she had told people of a loved one's passing several times, but most of those were from expected natural causes. Once she informed a family of their teenage son's demise along a county road after his motorcycle was struck by an oncoming tractor trailer. Firefighters spent hours collecting every piece of him from the pavement and nearby ditches, and the family provided mixed reactions, none of them pleasant, when Megan gave them the news.

"Very nice place," Megan commented, hoping she didn't blurt out anything about the woman's dead husband.

She felt like a heel for trying to extract information, harboring such a dark secret.

"So how can I help you this time?" Eileen asked as she poured them each a cup of hot tea.

"Did you and your husband spend much time with the Wilsons when they lived down the road?"

Eileen shrugged easily.

"Bob spent time during the summers helping them put up hay and doing odd jobs for extra money. I sometimes helped Taryn cook for the men just to keep her company. Shame what happened to that poor family."

If only you knew, Megan thought.

"Did you see much of Kyle Wilson before his death?"

"Sometimes. I got the impression his father didn't always want him around."

"How's that?"

"He sent Kyle to his room quite often. The boy was usually doing chores or playing with his friend."

Bingo.

"What friend?"

"A boy from the foster home he spent a lot of time with. His father didn't really approve, which I never understood. All kids that age have friends, and I never saw any other playmates for the poor child."

Pulling out the five photographs, Megan laid them in front of the housewife once she sat on her couch.

"Can you recognize any of these children as the friend?"

Megan took her first sip of tea as Eileen studied the photographs. Once she received her answer, she couldn't simply jump up and leave. Yet she didn't want to be present when the doomsday phone call came.

"It's been so long," Eileen uttered just above a whisper, leading Megan to think another crushing blow was coming.

Her blue eyes studied one particular photograph nearly half a minute until a look of complete recognition showed in her expression.

"I'm almost positive, no, I *am* positive that's the boy."

"Do you remember his name?" Megan dared ask for the sake of an airtight identification.

Eileen started to say a name, then stopped, as though it remained stuck on the tip of her tongue.

"Aaron maybe?"

"Eric?" Megan asked, thinking of her best guess from the five foster kids.

Eileen pointed directly at her with a broad smile as the name connected the dots for her.

"That's it. I remember Frank always calling to them both, as though they were both his mischievous kids. He acted a bit differently when the friend was around, but not much."

"What can you tell me about the way Frank treated the boys, especially Kyle?"

Eileen's expression soured exponentially. She crossed her legs, took a sip of tea, and prepared to tell a tale of woe.

"I didn't see much firsthand, but Bob told me some of the stuff he did. When company came around, Frank tended to put on a front, but he abused that boy."

"Abused? How?"

"Mentally, physically, you name it. He treated that boy like dirt and said he was no good, but at that age no kid is going to be perfect. I'm not sure how anyone could hate their own child, but Frank Wilson never said one good word about his son."

Megan found her words interesting, because it confirmed more of what Tom Crouch stated, only more factually.

For a moment she found herself removed from the harrowing truth that the woman she sat beside no longer had a husband. Her life was about to turn upside down, but Eileen might have saved any number of lives with the information she just provided.

Megan scooped up the photos, replacing them into their original folder. Terry never spoke truer words than when he said the connection might center in the

Naples area. Megan realized a killer had stalked and killed the Wilson family, and now Bob Hagen. Within the next hour she would start down a path to discover if Eric Toomey was that particular individual.

If he was, she planned to find the connection between him and the victims, though the answer already seemed to be Kyle Wilson.

Now Megan needed to find an excuse to leave before someone called or stopped by with the bad news. While she felt bad for the housewife, Megan didn't want to be someone's shoulder to lean on because she found herself hot on the trail of the killer.

She took a sip of tea as her mind raced for an excuse to leave. Wishing she had told Terry to call her back, she began sorting her materials, hoping Eileen Hagen could cope when the bad news found her.

CHAPTER 21

▼

By suppertime, Terry had exchanged the deputy for his old friend.

Lamoureux drove to the state police station in the town of Herkimer, named the same as the county, where the two friends exchanged handshakes and talked over hot coffee.

Patiently waiting for answers from Troop D's Forensic Investigations Unit, they had little else to do except talk and compare notes. Though Chambers said they were more than welcome to stay at the scene, the offer was only half sincere, because he wouldn't show them around until his forensic team finished.

While Terry knew his function was important, forensic evidence could only be collected once, and quickly, before it vanished, evaporated, or weather diminished its value. With rain moving into the area, the team worked doubly fast to finish, while trying to maintain their high standards.

While thunder rolled in the distance, Terry heard raindrops pelting the roof above. Meteorologists said the rains were coming hard and fast, but the storm was a small front. When it came to collecting evidence, it didn't matter if the rain lasted five minutes or an hour. Wet DNA evidence wasn't usually admissible in court, and damp grounds made a search much tougher.

After visiting a nearby vending machine, Lamoureux returned to the interview room they had commandeered, plopping several wrapped pastries on the table. Considering he barely ate breakfast before joining Hardegen that morning, Terry didn't much care what he put in his body.

"Sorry the selection wasn't better," Lamoureux said as he sat down.

"It'll do."

"So this guy, Tom Crotteau, was flown to Syracuse for surgery, right? He might be the best lead we have if he survives."

Terry nodded, though not in complete agreement.

"Megan might have our best lead. If our killer is somehow tied to the Naples area, she's standing on the answers as we speak."

Lamoureux clasped his hands together with a boyish grin.

"I hope he screwed up, Terry. I really do."

After seeing the crime scene, Terry saw no outward physical evidence to indicate the killer left them any early Christmas presents. Trace evidence and tracks were something the FIU people might discover that he couldn't with the naked eye.

"Things look a lot more promising," Terry admitted, "but even if we find out who he is, I'm not sure we can find him."

"We'll track him," Lamoureux vowed. "If he had an apartment, or a cardboard box, we'll find him."

Terry knew his friend wanted nothing more than to grill the man in the interrogation room once they arrested him, but they remained two steps behind. The fact that the latest murders went undiscovered for several hours gave the man ample time to clean up his mess and leave undetected.

"Who do we have at the hospital watching over our victim?" Terry asked his friend, since Lamoureux had spoken with the higher authorities once he arrived.

"Syracuse PD has an officer stationed nearby during every second of the surgery, and will continue to monitor Crotteau around the clock if he makes it. I was going to send one of my guys out there to do the interview, unless you want to handle it personally."

While he hoped the hunter survived the surgery, he didn't create false hopes. Gunshot wounds to the abdomen and cranium complicated matters terribly, but the second bullet basically cracked the man's skull as it glanced off the bone matter.

He should have died instantly by all rights.

Since Crotteau was found beside the four dead hunters, face down, Terry figured the killer thought he was dead. Fate kept him alive, because his head was found angled at a position that allowed him to breathe, rather than suck in dirt and grass.

His breaths must have been too shallow for the killer to notice in his hurried pace.

"Something bothers me about my original analysis," Terry confided aloud.

"What's that?"

"If these events are tied to a location, he might not be a serial killer so much as a man targeting specific individuals."

"But he's killed eight people we know of."

"True, but the way he's going about it makes me wonder if he's more of a sociopath than a serial killer. He has little regard for human life, that much we know, but what's motivating him isn't a need for a trophy, or a fix like I originally thought. I mean, he doesn't touch the bodies after he's done, Grant."

Terry realized he had animated his speech by using his hands more than usual.

Lamoureux smirked at him, then his cellular phone rang. The Senior Investigator stood up to find a quieter area to talk as he answered it. Because of the multiple homicide, the station looked and sounded much like a beehive.

With time to wait, Terry ate one of the wrapped pastries, almost feeling worse because he wasn't accustomed to so much sugar at once. He wanted something to wash it down, but soda pop didn't sound good, and the coffee grew staler by the cup.

He walked to the restroom to relieve himself, then cupped his hands to drink water from the sink after washing them. Looking at himself in the mirror, Terry decided he wanted to interview Crotteau if the man survived and awakened. No local officer could possibly ask all the right questions or ask for elaboration on what might sound like complete answers.

Details.

Terry wanted the man to be his personal video of exactly what occurred in those woods.

What struck the investigator as somewhat amazing was how the killer took down six hunters without one of them injuring him, or escaping the situation. They knew Crotteau had fired once, but a recovered shell proved he missed. Because of how the bodies were placed, Terry might never know the entire truth.

Waiting around to hear of more deaths didn't suit Terry, but he couldn't interview Crotteau, assist Megan, and help Hardegen search for clues all at once.

Megan seemed to have a grasp of the situation, Hardegen required no assistance to search, and Crotteau might never wake up. Still, sitting around felt perpetually useless.

"Some good news," Lamoureux announced when Terry returned to the room. "We have a very good plaster cast of the tire tread, and they recovered a few of the slugs."

"What about casings?" Terry asked, knowing they were much easier to find at a crime scene.

"None. He must have picked them up."

Efficient, Terry thought. Able to backtrack to every single casing and pick it up so police couldn't possibly trace his weapon.

Comparing slugs hadn't helped the team one bit in the Wilson triple homicide. What comparison meant was simply testing against bullets used in other crimes. Very few handguns or rifles, sold new or used, had useful records on file with the government, or the dealer who sold them.

"Forgive me if I don't applaud, Grant."

"I'm not done, ol' buddy. The forensic guys are wrapping it up because the weather rushed them. They said you could come back down and trample all over the scene with them."

"Like a bull in a China shop," Terry said, already starting for the door with his friend in tow.

*   *   *   *

Megan didn't leave Eileen Hagen's house as soon as she'd hoped.

She stayed in case the notification came from the coroner or local authorities to comfort the woman, but the call never came. To pass the time, she continued to ask questions about the Wilson family, gathering a few more firsthand accounts from Eileen, and a few stories told to her by her husband.

Frank Wilson treated his son worse than most people treat stray dogs according to Eileen. He fed the boy and provided a bed, but standard parenting drew a line after that concerning Kyle. Worked to the point of exhaustion on their various farms, the child was expected to make straight A's in school. Anything less than that came with severe consequences, which Megan found odd.

Anyone who mistreats children doesn't typically care how well they turn out, much less what grades they bring home.

With the conversation still floating through her mind, Megan pulled into the county building parking lot, finding Laura waiting for her once more.

"I think I have exactly what I need," Megan said, unable to hide her excitement as Laura unlocked the door. "Thank you very much for meeting me here again, and for giving me the time to dig up some answers."

"You're welcome, but I did it for my benefit as much as yours. The fewer times I have to come here on weekends, the better."

Megan understood.

Giving up her weekend wasn't her idea of fun, either.

If not for the satisfaction of finding some answers, she might have returned to Erie County already. Coping with the news of another five deaths felt surreal, but knowing Eileen's husband wasn't coming home again made her want to go home and throw her arms around David.

Following Laura inside, Megan soon found herself seated at the table while Laura searched for a file on Eric Toomey and the young man's life.

Too little too late, a faxed death investigation report came from division headquarters in Albany, revealing the state police had interviewed a subject named Eric Toomey. Because the case was older than seven years, it was no longer kept at the original barracks, meaning it took time to track it down.

Though he claimed to be Kyle Wilson's best friend, Toomey provided no useful information to the investigating officer.

Megan wondered how the young man turned out, mainly for her own sake when it came to tracking him down and interviewing him. Until she learned differently, Megan considered the man a material witness to Kyle Wilson's life, and perhaps his death.

"Here we are," Laura said when she returned a moment later, flopping a rather thick file down in front of the investigator.

"Thank you."

Opening the dingy, tattered manilla folder, Megan found a different photograph of a young boy with a flat affect. In terms of psychology, a flat affect represents a complete lack of expression upon one's face.

No smile.

No frown.

Wanting to cut to the chase, Megan decided to ask for Laura's help to save them both valuable time.

"Do you have his last known address, or any idea where I might find him?"

"Once these kids become adults, we lose touch with most of them. Unfortunately, it's not a situation where we exchange Christmas cards every year and keep up."

Megan laughed, then cut herself off until a smirk emerged from Laura.

"Sorry."

"It's okay," Laura said. "I don't mean to sound cold, but our job isn't easy. We have regulations to follow, kids with all kinds of problems, and more headaches than I ever anticipated when I took this job."

"What about job search assistance?" Megan asked, flipping through the papers. "Could your agency have helped him find a job?"

"Possibly. What *kind* of job would depend on his skills and education."

Leaning over Megan, Laura flipped through the pages, scanning them quickly with experience that came from dealing with the various forms.

"No," she finally said with a defeated tone. "No job, no contact information."

"What about family?"

Laura found a few pages bound by a paperclip that gave Toomey's family history. Yellowed and dry, the pages looked as though they might crumble into pieces without a delicate touch. They offered records almost two decades old that told a tragic story of Eric Toomey, the sole survivor of a car accident that claimed his parents and younger sister.

Too young to truly remember his family, yet too old for most families to consider adopting him, Toomey bounced between foster homes from age six until he legally became an adult. Megan found it incredible that no one adopted him, but knew most couples wanted infants or toddlers to raise as their own. Perhaps Toomey was lost in the shuffle of foster care, preventing enough exposure for him to be adopted.

"Can you think of any other avenues that might help me find him?" Megan inquired.

"I can check with some other county agencies. Surely if he's worked or resided somewhere, you can track him down."

"It's not always so easy," Megan replied with a sigh. "If he has a criminal record, that could shorten my search time, but might make things uneasy in an interview."

Megan realized she hadn't completely gone through the file, but she was certainly ready to head home.

"Can I get a full copy of this file?"

"Your subpoena doesn't call for that," Laura noted. "I would love to help you out, but I can't let you take it, or any part of it, with you."

Megan figured she could attain a new subpoena, but she simply needed to find Eric Toomey. A need for further information wasn't necessary unless she discovered reason to investigate him as more than a witness.

"I understand," Megan said, knowing Laura risked jeopardizing her job if she helped in any way not stated by the court order. "I'll need some time to go through these papers, then I'll probably head home."

Laura nodded.

"Coffee?"

"Yes, please."

Megan suspected she had at least another hour of note taking before she felt secure enough to head home. Anxious to see David and compare notes with the task force, she hoped to discover where Eric Toomey currently resided.

Yawning to herself, she flipped through the pages, pen in hand.

Ten minutes later, she made a discovery that Toomey had spent time, off and on, living with an uncle. He apparently resided with the uncle, youngest brother of his father, until the man went to prison.

While the paperwork made no mention of why Michael Toomey went to prison, Megan found a remark that the charges were unrelated to his nephew.

She jotted down the little available information, deciding to check with Michael Toomey concerning his nephew's whereabouts.

A simple phone call would give her the name and location of whatever jail or prison the man currently resided in. She hoped for better luck than the string of nothings coming her way thus far.

CHAPTER 22

▼

Terry followed Chambers and his forensic team leader around the crime scene as raindrops smacked his face and body. Cold and wind made the rain irritating, and though Terry wasn't drenched, he shivered against the elements while Chambers gave a guided tour.

By now the bodies had been removed to free up the ambulance service and because the lab needed to further examine the corpses, and their clothes, for fiber evidence.

"We're not sure if the hunters were taken by surprise, or they knew the killer," the Senior Investigator explained. "We found several sets of footprints going back and forth, probably from when he moved the bodies and murdered Bob Hagen up close."

"Did you get any preserved footprints?" Terry asked.

"Plenty. Two sets of tracks come from further out, which led me to think he might have engaged the hunters once, then come back after firing from a distance."

Had the killer covered his feet this time, the hunters might have looked at him very suspiciously, so he took the gamble and left tracks behind.

Terry stared at the area, now saturated with rain. It sounded as though the team had finished up their search with moments to spare.

"We're still trying to match up all the footprints with the treads on the hunters' boots, but we think one of the hunters might have come this way to hunt, or check traps. There's a foot trail that comes this far from the camp, circles around this area, and ends up behind one of the four-wheelers."

Terry followed, but the scenario sounded complicated. He couldn't envision the five deaths inside his mind, because the evidence trail snaked in so many directions.

"What else?" he asked Chambers, his good friend remaining unusually quiet.

"There are indentations behind the four-wheelers, indicating the hunters might have sought cover behind them when the killer started shooting."

Chambers led them to the vehicles, unmoved from their last known positions. He pointed out some indentations in the ground where the hunters had knelt and crawled, attempting to preserve their lives.

"Any chance of fingerprints?"

"Not that we found," the forensic team leader answered. "There's a good chance the assailant wore gloves."

Terry nodded. He suspected as much, but the opportunity for true linking evidence continued to elude both investigative teams.

"Killing the entire group is senseless," Terry noted aloud. "If he wanted Bob Hagen, he took an awfully big risk confronting six experienced hunters."

"What are you thinking?" Lamoureux inquired, turning his attention from the local investigators to his friend.

"I'm thinking one of the hunters found him and forced a confrontation. Someone said something about portable radios, right?"

Chambers nodded.

"They kept radios at their camp."

"So one of them could have called for backup, so to speak."

Again, the Senior Investigator bobbed his head.

"How could none of these people defended themselves?" Lamoureux asked.

Everyone stood silently a moment, indicating no one had a clear answer.

"Only two of them even *had* guns," Chambers stated. "One of them was our guy in surgery, so maybe he'll know."

"If we're lucky enough for him to make it," Lamoureux muttered, clenching a fist in frustration.

"We might be missing an obvious point here," Terry said.

"What's that?"

"If someone is plinking your people off from a distance, a handgun doesn't do you a whole lot of good."

Chambers cleared his throat, breaking up the negativity that loomed over them like the rain clouds.

"We've been through the camp as well, and our perpetrator did not pay a visit. We swabbed this area and we'll have positive links of where the hunters were shot by tomorrow."

"That won't really give us what we need," Terry thought aloud, almost to himself. "We need to start looking at the possibility he monitored Bob Hagen at the man's home. If he saw Hagen pack up his hunting gear, and knew the man owned part of this property, he probably took the same route."

"He might have followed Hagen," Lamoureux suggested.

"We need to see if any gas station attendants saw any unusual customers, or if Hagen stopped anywhere on his way through. Maybe a security camera picked something up."

Chambers didn't disagree. His attention had been focused entirely on the scene before them all morning.

"Have you made notifications to the families yet?" Terry asked the Senior Investigator.

"No. The victims lived in different counties, so we're setting things up with local coroners and police agencies. We wanted to let the families know something before we held any press conferences. Everything should be taken care of by tonight."

"We need to get on this immediately," Terry said with resolve. "If you can get the word out to our road officers, we might catch some of the gas station attendants before their shift changes."

Chambers took up his phone.

"Any other ideas before I make the call?"

"We need to talk to his wife and neighbors to see if anyone was seen hanging around the neighborhood yesterday or today. A personal notification might be in order."

"You wanting us to do it?" Chambers asked, openly unenthusiastic about being stuck with such a task.

"No. It's on our way home."

Now Lamoureux gave him a questioning look.

"Are we doing the notification?"

"I owe it to Megan for putting her in a pinch."

Lamoureux appeared uncomfortable, but said nothing more.

"Does that mean we're done here?" Chambers inquired, ready to make his phone call.

"I think so," Terry answered. "Can you call me or Grant personally once you get more results?"

Chambers nodded, handing him a business card with his information on it.

"Have Mrs. Hagen give me a call to make arrangements at the morgue."

"Okay."

Terry gave his friend a nudge to gain his attention before they walked toward the edge of the crime scene.

"You're insane if you want to personally do a notification," Lamoureux complained.

"I'm not doing it, *you* are. I'll be the rebound guy who follows up with a few questions."

"You know these things never go well."

"I've done notifications before, Grant. Stop treating me like this is my first dance. You're the one who called me down here, remember?"

Lamoureux walked away from the scene, openly pissed off about having to speak with a victim's spouse. Terry didn't feel sorry for him, because he had already given up several days away from his family at his friend's request. Consoling a grieving widow was just the beginning of what Terry expected from his friend to return the favor.

Now the closest he had been to his home in days, Terry wasn't able to make a two-hour trip home because he had no vehicle. The thrill of the hunt kept him devoted to the scene, because he felt closer to the killer than before. Soon enough the killer would slip up, leaving him an essential clue to close the case.

Then his arms could wrap around his wife and three children again.

Rain continued to pelt Terry as he followed his friend, stopping to take one last look back at the scene. Still artificially lit by two fire rescue trucks, it looked completely natural, as though five deaths never marred its soil.

*　　　*　　　*　　　*

By all rights Hardegen should have been home already, but fate dealt him a strange hand when he spotted two members of his regular task force just west of Batavia.

Now sitting in a corner café where the members typically met up, the three men occupied a table covered by a stained, plastic tablecloth. Not upscale, but not trashy, the café catered to mainly middle-class laborers, cops, and folks who enjoyed a meal made from scratch. The atmosphere, nothing fancy, consisted of several faded framed prints, an air-conditioner sticking awkwardly out of one wall, and two ceiling fans with dingy lights and coverings.

Hardegen found himself being probed by a state trooper and a fellow county officer about his involvement in the homicide investigation.

"Did Gaffney put you up to it, or did you do him some favors to get that gig?" Sean Blair, his fellow county officer, asked of him as they sat in a booth toward the rear.

Hardegen snickered at his buddy's tone.

"I got volunteered, Sean. The sheriff said he thought it'd be good for me to do some investigative work."

Blair had grown his dirty blond hair out long enough to create dreadlocks that appeared dirty in a different sort of way. He intentionally put on a little weight because his usual buff appearance didn't make for good undercover work.

Meetings such as this were often kept from the wives. Hardegen didn't hide much from Jamie, but some occurrences were best kept under wraps. He knew dirty little secrets about everyone he worked with that could ruin their marriages or get them killed if the wrong people discovered such information.

They literally depended upon one another with their lives, so indiscretions that didn't directly affect work remained buried.

"You're not going to up and leave us after this, are you?" Ian Warner, the state trooper, asked.

Hardegen shot them both a disparaging look.

"Why are you guys so freaked out about me getting reassigned for the week?"

"A week?" Blair asked skeptically. "I heard a month, maybe two."

Another thing Hardegen hated was how rumors spread like wildfire amongst the ignorant masses. Some people had nothing better to do than gossip.

"The sheriff didn't tell me much, but I'm hoping we nail this guy quick," he said instead of bellyaching about the rumors.

"What do they have you doing?" Warner asked.

Taking a sip of the hot chocolate he ordered, Hardegen burned his lip slightly. He tended to it with a napkin before answering.

"Well, I'm looking for anywhere the killer might have stayed while he stalked the family members."

Both gave him quizzical stares.

"That's it?"

"We've been sifting through paperwork and doing interviews. Guys, there isn't a whole lot to go on. And now he's struck again."

"The hunting camp?" Blair asked. "It's all over the fuckin' news."

Hardegen nodded.

A couple passed their table, the young woman drawing Blair's attention to her backside, despite the gold wedding band usually found on his left hand. Hardegen wasn't comfortable with everything his team members did, being a devout Christian, but he said little. He didn't waste time trying to save their souls, because they already knew his stand on life issues.

He didn't pretend to fit in when they celebrated after big busts. Though he took some ribbing, Hardegen didn't have to bother turning them down on certain outings because they knew not to ask.

While he would sometimes drink beer with the guys, he didn't partake when they visited strip clubs or went to parties to find a one night stand. His partying days took place during his college years, and those were well behind him. Even then he moderated his questionable activities, acting more mature than most of his football teammates.

Some things never changed, though not all of his colleagues had thrown their morals to the wayside.

"Where have you been checking?" Warner inquired.

"Abandoned houses mostly. We figured he wouldn't stay too far from the crime scene because he wanted to know their every move."

Blair drew a cagy smile, nudging the trooper.

"He even thinks like a detective. We're gonna lose him yet."

Warner grinned, but he seemed more concerned about the case.

"Why would he stay in a house?"

"Renting a place doesn't fit his profile, and we've checked apartments and motels in the area."

"No, I meant we have a number of abandoned factories and businesses around here. Wouldn't it make more sense to stay somewhere where a realtor or the owners wouldn't stop by?"

Hardegen saw his point.

"Do we really have that many vacant industrial spots?"

Warner nodded.

"Especially in Buffalo. You seen the south side lately?"

"Yeah, but this guy isn't going to stay in the city. It's too far, and he's antisocial."

"Where do you come up with this shit?" Blair asked.

"It's not me. We've got a profiler helping us out, from upstate."

He wanted to drop the conversation right there. His mind raced, picturing several rural businesses and factories he had neglected. They were probably easier than houses to access, because no one really cared. Graffiti and vandalism were expected in and around abandoned businesses, so no one checked on them.

How could he have been so negligent, simply following Terry's request to search houses?

"Guys, I've got to split," he said, pulling out his wallet to leave payment for the hot chocolate and a tip. "I'll catch you later."

Warner and Blair exchanged strange looks, as though they had said something wrong, but didn't get a word out before Hardegen exited through the front door.

"The wife must need him," Blair commented, receiving only a tired sigh from Warner in return.

CHAPTER 23

▼

With everyone on the task force moving in different directions, Terry decided to call for a meeting Sunday evening. While Saturday provided them with more answers, the wheels of the investigative vehicle came to a screeching halt soon after.

Thomas Crotteau survived his surgery, but had yet to awaken. Doctors assured Lamoureux over the phone they would call when the man was well enough to speak. Terry had two problems with their promise. One, he might never wake up, and two, family members and medical staff might not call the authorities immediately for fear of Crotteau's recuperation being jeopardized.

Megan continued to track the whereabouts of Eric Toomey, with little success. She found two businesses where he had worked, but both spanned brief periods of time.

Her lead concerning the uncle turned out to be a waste of time. While in prison, the uncle ended up in a scuffle with two other inmates that cost him his life. Prison officials informed her that Michael Toomey was never a model inmate, and quite an eccentric human being.

Though he received medication for depression and a form of schizophrenia, they said he still behaved quite erratically at times. One of the guards Megan spoke with commented that he didn't know how Michael ever received custody of his nephew, much less a dog from the local SPCA.

Megan wanted more than ever to speak with Eric Toomey, but he proved far more elusive than she originally figured.

What Terry considered the only useful new lead came from the latest murder scene. The lab picked up bullet casings from the ground, retrieved slugs from the victims, and matched the knife used on Bob Hagen as the exact weapon used to kill Francis Wilson. None of this mattered to Terry until they caught a suspect.

They had yet to find one single fingerprint, and so far they had no witness testimony.

The only useful information came from footprints they determined to be the killer's based on process of elimination. He wore a size 11 boot, and the forensic team obtained several excellent samples for comparison if and when the time came.

While most investigators found such evidence compelling, Terry knew the boot print was of limited value because the prints came from a common brand. If they found the host boot, the print's usefulness jumped exponentially. The tire tracks the team found, however, gave him more hope.

A wide tire tread used on only a handful of trucks was found almost half a mile from the crime scene. Very fresh, and easily photographed and cast, the tread matched the width of the track Nelson found at the triple homicide. Chambers' team had already begun researching where the tire was manufactured, and which companies sold them.

The team determined the track was somewhat worn, meaning it might have been purchased months, maybe years ago, depending on how much use the truck received.

Now he found himself waiting in Gaffney's conference room for the sheriff and the rest of the team to file in. To provide neutrality for task force meetings, Gaffney had negotiated use of a community center recently put on the market.

When various agencies met, they disliked any one branch having a home field advantage during an ongoing investigation.

Megan did excellent work in digging up information in Naples. He left her a message telling her so on her home phone, but suspected she and her fiancé made good use of what little time they had together.

Hardegen went to church that morning, which seemed to be the only break the man took. He informed Terry that he planned on checking any business or warehouse not in use at the moment, explaining some of them might still have live electricity to run basic elements such as lighting. While frigid weather hadn't come to stay in the Northeast, anyone living off the land might want an environment with light and heat whenever possible.

When Lamoureux came in ahead of his team, he gave Terry a deep stare before breaking off to speak with the sheriff.

Informing Eileen Hagen of her husband's untimely death hadn't gone particularly well, and worse yet, she provided no useful information. Though she seemed rather distraught, she had her wits about her enough to answer a few basic questions.

Any hope of drawing closer to the killer rested with Tom Crotteau's recovery. Or a lucky break.

"We may have some company tomorrow," Gaffney revealed to Terry and Lamoureux, far enough toward the front that no one heard them. "I got a call from the Special Agent in Charge of our Buffalo division today."

Terry and Lamoureux exchanged questioning glances.

"I'm not going to refuse the help," Gaffney insisted sternly. "They have better resources, and I'm not going to look like a horse's ass if we don't get a break in this case soon."

In the past, Terry had maintained good partnerships with the Bureau, but a few times they had strong-armed their way into taking over. He felt relatively certain Gaffney and the SAC knew one another fairly well, which hopefully meant a beautiful partnership in the making.

"I welcome the resources, but I'm not about to get bullied if they send some hotshot in here," Terry said. "We need manpower more than ideas right now."

"Agreed," Lamoureux said, though he virtually turned away from Terry.

Gaffney nodded that he understood their position, but said nothing more.

A few minutes later, everyone from the initial task force took a seat around the conference table except for Terry and Gaffney.

"The media wants another press conference tomorrow," Gaffney said to everyone, though he shifted his eyes toward Terry. "What, if anything, do we want to reveal this time around?"

Gaffney was implying that giving the press more to work with might generate more leads. At this point, Terry wanted to invite the general public to assist in the investigation without stating the task force had failed.

Failure and a lack of leads were two different things.

Terry hadn't experienced much failure during his career, because he remained tenacious until his cases were solved. In time someone always blabbed about a crime, or other investigative avenues presented themselves.

"We want to enlist the public's help," he finally told Gaffney. "We can't sound desperate, but anyone who knows anything helpful about the Wilson family needs to come forward."

"Maybe we *are* desperate," Lamoureux pointed out, directing his stare toward Gaffney in response to the sheriff calling in the Bureau.

Lamoureux took a seat with the others, apparently expecting Terry or the sheriff to run the show, possibly inviting them to a roundtable discussion to avoid formality.

Considering Gaffney had already asked his advice once, Terry decided to take the lead without sitting down.

"We have some solid avenues, people," he began. "I'm going to admit my original analysis of this guy may be slightly askew. He may simply be a sociopath carrying out revenge on certain individuals. That makes him highly dangerous, perhaps more so than a serial killer. My guess is our perp may have some sort of social deficiency, or at least *thinks* he does. He may be scarred, he might stutter, or could have a physical deformity of some sort."

Everyone looked at him with keen interest, including Hardegen, who seemed more in tune with his place on the task force.

"Paul, I think we should call for a press conference tonight. What I want you to say should be in every morning paper, and on every television across the state. We can't afford to have him strike again without making him at least a bit nervous."

"If he's living off the land, how will he even know?" Hardegen asked, though not pointedly.

"My suspicion is he's probably proud of his accomplishments, based on the way he leaves his victims. He'll want to see his work in the newspapers, and he'll want to know that we're helpless to stop him. I'm hoping we can unnerve him a little bit."

Lamoureux drew a concerned expression.

"You're not going to put yourself in the open, are you, Terry?"

A simple, slow nod came in response.

"I called you down here to help us find him, not stick your neck out," Lamoureux argued, obviously worried.

"It's my call, Grant. We can't wait around for more innocent people to get gutted and pissed on."

Everyone shifted uneasily in their seats. Terry hadn't planned on any outbursts from Lamoureux, particularly since he gave no details. Lamoureux indeed had some good detective skills to accompany his interrogation techniques.

Gaffney cleared his throat rather loudly to break up their conversation before it grew more heated.

"Okay," Lamoureux said, surrendering as he threw up his hands. "You win. But if you do this, you'll have someone with you at all times."

While Terry felt fully capable of defending himself in most any situation, he had no further desire to argue with his friend. They both knew he planned to publically take responsibility for the investigation, and possibly say things about the killer that might infuriate him.

Gaffney had refused to give details about the investigation team thus far to the media. He simply stated the county and state police created a joint task force to handle the matter.

Taking from a stack of papers at his end of the table, Terry handed out dossiers to each team member with updates and potential leads.

"These stay with you, and aren't to be shared with anyone else," he warned. "Does anyone else have any news to contribute?"

Everyone took a moment to skim the material listed on the papers, then looked to one another, waiting for someone to speak.

No one had news, so Terry decided to wrap up the meeting so he could speak with Gaffney to plan their press conference.

"We're waiting for the Herkimer folks to get back with us, but it looks like what we have is what we've got."

"Who's handling the interview if the shooting victim wakes up?" Megan asked.

"I will. They have strict orders to call me the minute he's conscious and alert. I don't trust the family and staff, so I have the local police monitoring him around the clock."

Lamoureux smirked. He often teased Terry about being untrusting, and overly cautious, when they worked as partners.

"Any other questions?"

No one spoke or raised a hand.

"Fine. I won't torture you any further. Tomorrow we start tracking this son-of-a-bitch again. See Grant if you have any questions about your assignments."

Some filed out of the room, while a few others milled around, talking amongst themselves.

Lamoureux approached Terry, which the investigator expected from his friend.

"There are other ways to do this," Lamoureux argued. "I know you get some kind of charge out of challenging these guys, but this one's dangerous, Terry."

"We're running drier than a well in the Sahara on leads, Grant. I'm going to do whatever it takes to trip this guy up. Even if he wanted to come after me, which I *doubt* mind you, he can't find me."

Lamoureux shook his head.

"Let me do it, Terry. I got no family waiting for me at home. If you want to lure him out of hiding, let me be the bait."

"No offense, ol' buddy, but I need this to seem completely natural. You tend to freeze up on camera."

"This is still my investigation, Terry. I can call you off if necessary."

Terry couldn't help but grin, especially after seeing Gaffney's sour expression when Lamoureux implied the investigation *belonged* to the state police.

"You're bluffing. And that's why I don't want you doing this press conference, Grant. It's a risk, and I'm not going to saddle you with it."

"Goddamn it, Terry, let me do this for you."

"No. Protect me all you want, but I'm doing this my way."

Gaffney stepped in, seeing no end to their argument otherwise. He addressed Lamoureux immediately.

"If you want what's best, maybe you should help us shape what we're gonna tell the public."

Terry nodded.

"I could use some constructive criticism, buddy."

"That's what I just gave you, but if you want more, I'm game."

Gaffney reached for a nearby phone, looking to Terry first.

"You sure this is what you want?"

Terry didn't like the idea of putting his own family at risk, but he planned on catching the killer before ever needing to worry about it. Locally, he couldn't be traced, so he felt reasonably certain about his own safety.

"I want to do this," he told Gaffney.

"An hour be enough time?"

"Make it eight o'clock," Terry answered. "That should still give us good coverage, and with what I plan to say, they'll hold the presses."

CHAPTER 24

▼

An hour after the press conference ended, Terry looked out the large window from his hotel room at the Buffalo view. For the night, he changed venues, beginning to cover his trail in case the killer did seek revenge against him for the words spoken at the press conference.

Intentionally putting off calling home, Terry wondered what he would tell his wife. Sherri tended to know when he was hiding something. He knew better than to lie to her, but delaying the call put up red flags as quickly as dodging subjects during the conversation.

He looked to the bed when his cellular phone rang, bringing the inevitable conversation to him. Terry walked over, scooped it up, and looked at the number in the box.

Not his home number, but from the same area.

"Levine," he answered.

"How's the vacation Trooper Levine?" Dan Schmidt asked from the other end.

"It's not exactly luxurious, Chief Schmidt," Terry answered, using the equally formal tone to mock his colleague.

"I might have some leads on who knocked over your granddad's tombstone. Some concerned parents called me this afternoon, and I'm having a talk with a few kids in school tomorrow."

Terry walked with the phone toward the window, watching several people pass along the streets of downtown Buffalo below. He suddenly missed jogging on his own property in open fields, feeling confined in a prison of steel and asphalt.

"In the school? Is that wise?"

"It'll get the other kids scared, and I can put some real pressure on them."

Schmidt liked intimidation tactics, apparently giving no free passes to teenagers.

"If you prefer, I can take them to my office and rough 'em up a little bit."

"Dan!"

"Kidding. I'll have something for you tomorrow afternoon. You coming home anytime soon to celebrate?"

"Celebrate?"

"These punks'll be busted within a day or two."

"I think you're blowing this out of proportion just a bit."

"Hey, you're the one who wanted vigilante justice in the first place."

Terry wondered if he needed to separate himself from the hometown investigation entirely. Schmidt liked to push his buttons, but he occasionally roughed up suspects to the brink of getting himself into trouble. Luckily for him, no hospital personnel had ever pushed the issue when he brought in injured criminals.

"Cat got your tongue?" Schmidt asked when Terry said nothing for a moment.

"I recall saying I wanted the individuals responsible for smashing my grandfather's grave site brought in, but that's it."

"You sound like you're on a wiretap, Terry. I was just messin' with ya."

Terry sighed, saying nothing momentarily. He seldom worked around the police chief, easily forgetting the man's sense of humor was almost as brash as his methods.

"Sorry. I'm a little distracted by my case, Dan. I know you wouldn't harm a hair on any adorable teens for my sake."

"I never said that. What happens in the Norfolk Police Chief's office stays in the Norfolk Police Chief's office, if you get my drift."

"Quit jacking with me and get back to work, Chief."

"Catch that bastard and get your ass back here, would you?"

"Yeah. I'll see if I can convince him to turn himself in right away."

Schmidt laughed.

"Now who's messing around?"

"Let me know when you hear something, Dan. And do me a favor?"

"Name it."

"Keep an eye on my house, would you?"

"Any particular reason?"

Terry hesitated, not wanting to raise hairs with the chief, and in turn, his wife.

"Just as a precaution."

"Will do."

"Thanks."

Terry looked out the window after a goodbye, then used the remote to turn on the television, catching a recap of the press conference on the local NBC station.

Faces of all eight confirmed victims flashed across the screen, haunting him because he never turned over the four hunters lying face down at the second scene. The screen switched to him standing beside Gaffney, taking credit for heading up the investigation, though the job truly belonged to Lamoureux and the sheriff.

He recalled the dangerous quotes clearly, having rehearsed them several times before meeting the press.

"The man we're looking for likely resided in Ontario County at one time," Terry heard himself say on television, always amazed that he never sounded like he thought he did. "He probably had ties to the Wilson family, as well as Bob Hagen. I believe this individual dislikes society as a whole, and carries out sexual fantasies with animals."

He debated revealing his find from the first scene with Lamoureux and Gaffney, but ultimately decided the fact carried more weight as an informational tool than damning testimony later. Whether or not it held true, it needed to be cast as bait.

"Fantasies with animals?" one reporter probed, nibbling like a bass at the worm.

"We have reason to believe he had intercourse with an animal at the first scene. Disturbing, yes, but we believe he expresses dominance over animals because they're the only things he can overpower. When he kills, he must surprise his victims because he's too weak to confront them."

A blatant lie, and the only part Terry made up to draw the killer out. Slandering the killer was a job better suited for the tabloids. He handled the questions his statement brought about from reporters, Gaffney deflecting several for him.

He spent much of the press conference skirting sensitive information, revealing only what they dared about the victims and circumstances. Without conferring with the group in Herkimer, he focused mainly on the local investigation, refusing to give away their techniques.

Whether the general public knew it or not, he had challenged the killer. He awaited an answer, praying no more innocent people took the brunt of the man's anger for his words.

When his phone rang, Terry suspected his time was now up concerning the impending conversation with his wife.

"Hello?" he answered, seeing his home phone number first.

"You sporting a bull's-eye these days?" his wife asked from more than half a state away.

"Been watching some television?"

"Yes. The kids were thrilled to see their dad on TV, since it's the only way they see him these days."

Terry felt the verbal dig.

"You did look kind of sexy in a suit," Sherri added, letting up a bit.

"It seems I traded those for a gray and purple uniform because my beautiful wife asked me to."

Sherri laughed in an almost maniacal tone.

"Now that's not fair. Look where you are right now."

Clearing his throat, Terry decided he wanted a more constructive conversation.

"Can we start this over? So, honey, how was your day?"

"It was wonderful. You'll never guess what was on the evening news."

"Wow. I was hoping you might say the dog fathered bastard puppies, or the kids all came home with straight A's on their report cards."

"To be truthful, your dog has been a pain, but your teenage daughter has been worse."

"And all this time you led me to think she belonged to both of us," Terry said, playing along, since Britney was indeed their firstborn. "I feel deceived."

"As I was saying, your daughter wants to go to a party this weekend that is completely unsupervised, though she swears there won't be alcohol present."

"Right. Do I need to have a talk with her?"

"I've got it handled, though I received 'I hate you' and 'You never let me do anything fun' for my efforts."

"So it ended well then?"

Sherri didn't share his sense of humor this particular evening.

"She's in her room doing God knows what. Please tell me you're close to finding the guy, and that you're vague pleas for help during the press conference were just a ploy."

"Did I come off as sounding desperate?"

"A little, but the layman probably won't catch it."

"That's good, because truth be told, we're struggling. This guy isn't helping me one bit by leaving anything except his piss behind."

"If he did both sets of murders, they're related, right?"

"Yeah. The two primary targets were former neighbors."

Silence crossed the lines for a moment. Sherri didn't usually ask much about his cases, unless he was away from home.

"So he tracked one of them down, or what?"

Terry pondered a question he hadn't really asked himself. The Wilsons moved, several times over, meaning the killer did indeed track them, and didn't begin with them. He probably began searching for them in the area he was familiar with, which meant Ontario County.

"Can I call you back?" Terry asked his wife in a tone she probably knew all too well.

"Have a revelation?"

"All thanks to you, dear."

"Just call me tomorrow, hunk."

"Love you. Bye."

Terry shut his phone, prepared to call Megan. He wanted her opinion, but if his hunch proved correct, he might travel with her to Naples in the morning to conduct more research.

CHAPTER 25

▼

Danny Russell started his Monday morning like any other, not quite certain he wanted his weekend to end so soon.

Sitting in a local café, he took a sip of coffee, having just placed his breakfast order, while he looked at the sports section of *The Buffalo News* morning edition. Sold primarily in Buffalo and its suburbs, the newspaper sparsely made its way as far as the Naples area. This particular café had two copies waiting every morning, which helped them maintain Russell as a regular customer.

Regrettably, the newspaper had abandoned its evening paper some years earlier, closing the chapter of his life where he relaxed at home, reading the day's events after work.

"More coffee, hon?" the red-headed waitress asked when she breezed his way, carrying a fresh pot with her.

"Sure," Russell said, seeing her eyes dance across the left side of his chest.

New waitresses often read the company logo on his neatly-pressed beige work shirt. His personal truck had similar vinyl emblems applied along the sides and back, because advertising simply added to his clientele.

He wanted to believe they were studying his handsome features, but those years had long since passed.

Most people his age planned for inevitable retirement while Russell continued selling products for the same company after twenty-five years. He worked his own fields, which gave him a decisive edge over competitors and the other sales people within his own company.

Working on commission, Russell sold bulk seeds for a living to local farmers and growers. Everything from soybeans to alfalfa sold in his region, and he found himself in the harvest season, prepared to meet with clients in the field all day long.

His clients came from every walk of life, working in fields from 60 to 6,000 acres. Some worked full-time, while others leased their fields to other farmers.

Over the course of a year his job description changed slightly. After the harvest season, Russell became a hardcore salesman, receiving orders and cold calling, which meant touching base with perspective customers to attain new sales.

Today was one of the days he felt lucky, because his four contacts were all in his home region, which meant he wouldn't be on the road much. He spent much of the fall riding in combines with his clients, listening to what they liked and disliked that particular season. Often, simply listening to them let them know he cared, but they also gave him informal research data.

Scanning the newspaper for football scores, then local news, Russell soon found an article about the triple homicide and five hunters killed on the south end of the Adirondacks. The story revealed police believed the two sets of murders were connected, and State Police Investigator Terry Levine asked for anyone who had contact with the Wilson family to come forward.

Even seemingly irrelevant information might prove useful, he said in the article. Russell felt his body stiffen at the sight of the words. Several images marched through his mind like kids crossing the street to school.

He read the rest of the article, finding a generic contact number for the state police. Looking down to his cell phone, Russell figured his information would warrant a quick forwarding of information to Trooper Levine.

Before he called the state police, he wanted to check with his first client, to see if arriving late was an acceptable option. More often than not, relationships with his customers drove his business, but occasionally they skated atop thin ice. Russell spoke for his product and service, but if either of those facets failed to meet expectations, he often received a customer's wrath.

He planned on spending anywhere from an hour-and-a-half to almost three hours with each client, leaving himself travel time and breathing room between meetings.

With another two hours before his first meeting, Russell took up his cell phone. He decided to see what the state police told him before altering his schedule. Perhaps they didn't care what he had to say, and their plea served a completely different purpose.

*   *   *   *

Lamoureux had no objections to Terry borrowing Megan for a trip to Naples. While Terry's theory held merit, it still felt like a longshot, though not as tedious as checking houses with Hardegen.

Considering the Wilsons had an unlisted phone number, he knew their address wasn't public record. In order for the killer to locate their house, he needed to know the county or region. Realistically, he wouldn't go from county to county checking property records, and doing so might draw unwanted attention.

"Run this by me again how the guy might have gone about finding the Wilsons," Terry asked Megan when they drew within minutes of the town.

"Short of some kind of inside source, like the post office, he would have to use the internet."

"Post office?"

Megan looked to him, thinking the same exact thing.

"Surely Hagen wasn't an accomplice," she stated in awe.

"I don't think so," Terry replied, quickly changing his mind. "The Wilsons moved a few times before settling at their last residence. Using Hagen as a resource doesn't seem likely, especially if the man might have known him."

"What if Hagen could be bribed?" Megan suggested. "Then kill him before he puts two and two together and spills the beans."

"Hagen probably didn't even know where the Wilsons moved to. They seem almost like a family on the run to me, so I doubt they left much to chance."

Terry crossed the town limits, seeing the business district.

"Where could our guy readily get internet access around here?"

"The library has a few computers," Megan said. "I used them to check my e-mail and do a little research."

"If he did a search for the Wilsons, it would still be in the memory, right?"

Being no expert on computers, Terry often relied on younger officers, or his kids, to guide him.

"Possibly. It depends on several things. If the hard drives were cleared, the information might be gone, or if it's too old, it'll get overwritten by other files."

"Realistically, I don't see another way to quickly locate a family. My only concern is he didn't use a public venue, or he located them a long time ago."

"Can't be that long ago," Megan noted. "They hadn't lived there very long."

Terry gave it some thought, but they had already discussed a rough plan. While Megan checked the local public internet connections, he would speak with the seed distributor.

While Danny Russell wasn't a former neighbor or friend, it sounded like he possessed some good information about occurrences at the Wilson farm. Terry decided he warranted a personal interview based on the sketchy information he provided the deputy over the phone.

"If you can't find any signs of a search, try finding the top ten people search engines," he suggested. "We can have the FBI guys put some pressure on the companies to reveal who went looking for Frank Wilson."

"Can they do that?"

"They can do pretty much whatever they want to when they choose to involve themselves in a case."

An appreciative expression crossed Megan's face.

"And if they can figure that out, we know who killed the Wilsons."

"In theory. It's still a long way from finding the guy and convicting him."

Terry pulled up to the library, Megan's starting place, to drop her off.

"I'm sure the townsfolk will be thrilled to see me again," she said before opening the door.

"Good luck. I'll call you when I'm done with the interview."

"Sounds good."

Megan shut the door before walking up the library stairs.

Instead of immediately driving away, Terry looked at the small town around him, already growing homesick. The time he spent in New York City, Buffalo, and Albany provided him with a reputation that never left, but at heart he was a small town boy who missed the serenity of the north country during those fifteen years.

His phone rang beside him, bringing him back from the scenery of snowy fields and orange autumn leaves at his property.

"Yeah," he answered, suspecting Lamoureux had news, after a look at the caller ID box.

"Terry, we got some work records back on Megan's character witness. I'm going to interview his bosses and see if we can track him down."

"He'd have to put references on the application," Terry surmised. "Where did he work?"

Sounds of leafing papers reached his ears.

"At a Burger King, and a high school as a custodian."

"Custodian?"

"Yeah. He worked afternoons there until a few months ago."

"And no job records since?"

"Not that we've found."

Terry mulled over the news momentarily.

"You're thinking, which scares me," Lamoureux confessed.

"I'm thinking there's something odd about this kid, whether he's hiding from someone, or *something*."

"How do you want me to proceed?"

"It's your show, Grant. I say do what you were going to do, and see where the pieces fall. I'll let you know what we find out here. And one more thing."

"Name it."

"Ask them if he had any physical deformities, was shy, or maybe had a speech problem. Anything that made him stand out."

Momentary silence before Lamoureux spoke again.

"You think there's a chance it was him?"

"I'm just covering the bases, buddy. I'll see you in a few hours."

"Okay. Bye."

Putting down the phone, Terry began wondering if the noose was about to tighten around the killer's neck, or their efforts were hurling toward brick walls.

He put the car into drive, prepared to hear what the seed distributor had to say.

CHAPTER 26

▼

Terry drove to Danny Russell's house, wondering exactly what he offered to the investigative mix. Over the phone he told Lamoureux he had seen some strange events during his visits to the old Wilson farm. Knowing Terry and Megan had business in Naples, he decided to let Terry handle the interview in person.

Russell lived outside of town, working in a regional center with other seed sales representatives. Terry once lived a mile down the road from a farmer who worked his own fields. One time, when his neighbor needed to take a tractor to town for repairs, he asked Terry to sign for his seed delivery.

Terry spoke at length with the distributor, learning a few things about the unusual occupation.

He recalled the salesman having a very liberal schedule, so he suspected Russell probably rescheduled some meetings, or told the office he would be in late. Terry doubted the man had many people to answer to if he worked on commission.

After three knocks, the man answered his door, wearing a long-sleeve shirt with his company's emblem on the left side. He wore blue jeans and work boots, indicating his job required visiting work areas, and might have an informal sense about it.

Light brown and gray hair combined for a peppery mix, parted atop the man's head.

"Danny?" Terry asked to be certain, producing his identification.

"Come on in," Russell said, quickly waving him inside as though he didn't want anyone seeing a cop visit his premises.

"I appreciate you seeing me on such short notice," Terry said, stepping through the door.

"After hearing about what happened to Frank and his family, it left me uneasy, but when you said anything might help, some things came to mind."

A few minutes later, the two sat down in the living room. Terry noticed two mounted deer heads, and one of a black bear. The house had the feel and smell of a hunting lodge, lacking feminine touches everywhere he looked.

He suspected Russell was a widower, because photos of children and various adults with the man, including a wifely figure in a few, adorned the fireplace mantle.

Terry took down basic information about the salesman first, then formally began the interview.

"What was your relationship to the Wilson family?"

"Frank leased his land to one of his neighbors, but he often had the seed delivered to his property."

"Did you deal with Wilson or the neighbor?"

"Both, but mainly Frank. He had more storage than the neighbor, who I believe passed away a few years back if you were thinking of looking him up."

"Thanks for the tip," Terry said, already knowing the information held true from Megan's report. "So, what kinds of things did you see at the Wilson farm?"

"A couple times, I saw him give that kid of his a thrashing," Russell stated, admitting what no one else had courage enough to tell police. "These weren't simple scoldings, mind you. Farm kids have it a little rougher than most, but there's no call to hit your kid when he's not doing anything wrong."

Terry knew from personal experience that life on a farm wasn't easy.

"Can you elaborate?"

"One time Frank told the kid to help me put up a seed delivery, which he did, but afterwards he hauled off and smacked the kid upside the head from the blind side."

"Why?"

"Said the kid forgot to do some of his chores that morning, but Kyle argued that he had done all of his chores. He got another slap upside his head, but the kid didn't cry. He just hung his head and walked away, kind of defeated if you know what I mean."

"Yeah. I think I do."

Terry jotted down some more notes, beginning to understand that Frank Wilson wasn't a nice man. If he treated his own child that way, Terry wondered how he handled other relationships.

While he didn't work with abused kids very often, Terry knew the signs.

Both mental and physical.

"I wasn't at the farm a whole lot, but there was another time I saw Frank strike his boy. Pretty much the same circumstances. Don't know why he beat the kid like that, almost like it was second nature to him."

Terry now knew Frank Wilson had been a victim of child abuse himself, reaching a culmination when the man's mother killed his father, then turned the gun on herself. Unfortunately the cycle of abuse didn't end that day, leaving a bloody trail that didn't stop when it reached the investigator's doorstep.

"Anything else you can tell me about Kyle?" he prompted Russell. "Do you remember him having any friends around the farm?"

Russell suddenly appeared uncomfortable.

"There was a boy from down the road. The few times I saw them together, he and Kyle were inseparable. I'm not sure how much Frank knew about them being around each other, because I doubt he would have approved."

"They were kids, Mr. Russell. What are you implying, exactly?"

Clearing his throat, Russell continued.

"I mean the other kid wasn't well-kept. He lived down the road in a foster home. I guess he didn't seem all there, either."

Terry suspected the salesman continued to hold back information, mainly out of discomfort with the information itself, and not the interview process.

"How exactly did the kid strike you as odd?" he pressed.

Though he hesitated, Russell finally conjured up the words.

"The year Kyle was killed, I had to bring out some bags of soybean seed to round out Frank's order. On small loads like that, I bring the stuff to customers myself. Anyway, I got there and no one was home, so I decided to just unload the bags myself, then find someone for a signature.

"I walked into the barn, and made my way toward the center, where they stored the seeds and feed when I heard some strange noises from the pen area."

"What kind of noises?" Terry asked, his pen poised above the notepad.

"I couldn't exactly place it, so I threw down the bag and walked into the pen area to find the boys, uh, nestled with a sheep."

"*Nestled?*"

Russell fidgeted his fingers uncomfortably atop his lap.

"When I got in the room, I saw both boys lying down with a sheep," he explained. "At first I thought maybe they were just fooling around, but his friend jumped to his feet and zipped up his pants in a hurry as he turned away from me."

"What were they doing ... exactly?"

"I'm not sure, and I didn't want to stick around for answers. I turned around, finished my job, and left after Taryn signed the paperwork."

Terry wasn't about to let Russell turn around and run a second time. Even if it was circumstantial, he wanted the man's opinion.

"Okay, Mr. Russell. Tell me what you *think* happened in that barn."

"They were boys, Trooper Levine. They're experimental at that age."

"With animals?"

Russell hung his head.

"I don't know. I really don't. There was nothing openly pornographic going on, if that's what you're looking for."

"I'm looking for the truth, sir. Did you ever tell Frank Wilson, or anyone, about this incident?"

"No way. He didn't need much of an excuse to beat the kid, so I kept quiet. But I think he knew something was up from the way his neighbor talked. Kyle died that summer, and I couldn't help but wonder if his father had something to do with it."

"Why is that?"

"Call it a hunch, but he didn't seem real broken up about Kyle's death. You know, I guess the only people who probably know the whole truth about all that died last week."

Terry agreed, though he said nothing.

"Did Frank Wilson ever speak with you about his son's death?"

"No. That soybean drop was one of the last times I stepped foot on the property."

"Kyle's friend," Terry said, tapping his notepad with the pen. "Anything else about him seem odd to you?"

Russell searched for the words.

"Creepy. Dirty. He just didn't say much. Just one of those kids you somehow knew wasn't going to turn out well."

He may not have, Terry thought.

Turning his line of questioning toward Bob Hagen, Terry discovered Russell knew virtually nothing about the murdered postal worker. He remembered seeing friends on the Wilson property sometimes, but couldn't recall if Hagen was among them.

The links between Hagen and Wilson seemed weak at best. Interviews of the neighbors and Hagen's wife revealed little to no connection between the two men, aside from neighborly friendship. Terry found no business dealings between the two, which narrowed the list of possible motives and suspects considerably.

If anything, the talk with Russell simply reaffirmed his growing suspicion that Eric Toomey might be his prime suspect. He wished he could find the young man to confirm or eliminate him as a suspect.

After a few more questions, he thanked Russell, handed him a card, then left to pick up Megan.

CHAPTER 27

▼

While Gaffney and Lamoureux awaited their first meeting with the FBI, the other task force members continued to track down leads. Investigators and road officers checked everything from convenience stores to Wal-Marts and gun stores for hits on ammunition purchases and possible firsthand witness accounts of anyone driving an older style pickup truck.

The lab determined the tires were an obsolete make known as H78-15. While some tire companies made modern versions under a different model number, these tires were very scarce. As a bonus, very few vehicles still on the road used such tires, new or old. Gaffney hoped the FBI might help the task force create a list of potential suspect vehicles, and discover further information about the tread.

Because they were no longer manufactured, the tires had to be located through junkyards or dealers of vintage equipment. A group of officers were dispatched to speak with the appropriate sellers.

At this point they wanted to pick up a new lead because most every avenue they had already checked led to a dead end.

With a local map riding shotgun, Hardegen continued to check abandoned houses and buildings, crossing them off his list. While it wasn't a wise idea to check properties alone, he didn't want to burden anyone else. Lamoureux didn't object to him traveling alone, though he seemed a bit concerned. He stated his desire to tag along, but the FBI meeting superseded all else.

He now knew recalling vacant buildings from memory wasn't a foolproof plan. Several residences and businesses had been renovated, while other new abandonments caught his attention as he drove along county roads.

Drinking coffee to artificially keep him alert, Hardegen noticed a thin line of smoke rising in the distance. If the rainy weather hadn't stopped, or any wind stronger than a breeze passed through the area, he might never have noticed.

His interest in the smoke stemmed from the fact that it appeared to originate from a property he believed had been abandoned.

Hardegen dismissed it as a work in progress, purchased since the last time he laid eyes upon it, until he drew closer.

An old farmhouse sat half a football field's length from the road, but the smoke came from behind the deteriorated structure. The structure had begun to collapse upon itself, beyond repair in the deputy's estimation.

He pulled into the driveway, wondering exactly where the smoke came from, and what caused it. A number of trees and bushes continued to obscure his view.

Cautiously, he shut the car down, then stepped out, quietly closing the door behind him. A moment later he stepped around the shrubbery to discover a detached work building or garage of some sort. The lingering smoke came from a heaping pile of charred debris stacked near the building, but puffs of smoke emitted from the building's few windows, along with a strange odor not common to fire.

Reaching behind him for his firearm, Hardegen approached the building, finding a partially loaded van parked on the opposite side. He wondered if someone got wind of the police checking vacant county buildings. This had the earmarks of a meth lab operation, but one that might have met with foul circumstances.

Carefully pushing in the front door for fear of backdraft conditions, Hardegen stepped back as a strange yellow smoke rushed out to greet him like a friendly dog. Luckily no fire accompanied the toxic substance, so the deputy waited a moment for the hazardous materials inside to clear.

He knew his priority was to call for backup immediately, but Hardegen wanted to check for any loss of life.

Or any chance someone might be saved from inside the building.

Sucking in as deep a breath as he could, Hardegen stepped inside, feeling his eyes tear up and burn from the lingering chemicals. He dropped to his knees to avoid the heavier smoke, and almost immediately found two fairly young males face up, victims of their own concoction.

Both wore patchwork jeans and T-shirts, sporting unconventional haircuts. Their bodies showed signs of light charring, one on the side, and the other along his front.

He wondered if they had tried to mix one final batch of whatever drug they were creating, while preparing to move their operation. He figured they weren't too far removed from high school, assuming they attended. Seeing young people throw their lives away so recklessly bothered him, despite the hardened shell his job provided.

Based on the amount of smoke, and localized fire damage, he knew they had blown themselves up trying to mix a batch of chemicals. Trying to run a meth lab while moving out, and burning their junk behind the building, had probably provided enough distraction for one of them to do something careless.

They were too far gone for him to revive, even if he could work on two patients at once with his basic CPR skills.

"Damn it," he muttered, crawling toward the door to escape the fumes. "This isn't my week."

On the way out, he spied both neo-Nazi and anti-war materials strewn about. The latter didn't protest war so much as it protested soldiers in general, which bothered the deputy. He felt kids had less respect for authority, even police, with each passing day.

Once outside, he had half a mind to simply call the local dispatchers anonymously to report a fire, but thought better of it. He had already entered the crime scene, and suspected if he falsified the information it would catch up to him.

Hardegen wanted to keep searching the vacant houses, and avoid the stack of paperwork that was likely coming his way, but he walked to his car, scooping up his portable radio instead of the phone.

Not only was his day going to be wasted, stuck at this crime scene, but Jamie would question why his clothes were stinky.

He sighed audibly, then pushed the transmit button on the radio, hearing a miserable coughing sound as he did so.

Clipping the portable radio to his belt, Hardegen drew his firearm once more. Walking toward the back of the building, he ignored the dispatcher calling him back to see if he had intended to transmit.

Realizing he had barely examined the area around and behind the building, Hardegen chastised himself when he spied a third victim, older than the other two near the pile of burning debris.

He too appeared burned, though not as extensively. A strewn pile of containers and trash had settled near him, giving the deputy the impression he had been adding to the intentional fire outside when the explosion rocked the building.

"Help me," the man muttered upon seeing the deputy.

"Hang in there, buddy," Hardegen said, reporting the situation to dispatch, requesting an ambulance, along with county and state police units.

He knelt beside the man, seeing the back window of the house had blown out from the explosion, but a thick curtain imprisoned the smoke inside. The surviving victim had burns along his face and arms. Glass shards had acted as missiles when the explosion rocked the small building, piercing the survivor's flesh in countless areas.

While the man seemed able enough to speak, he said nothing as they waited for additional help to arrive. Really, what was there to say? Both of them knew exactly what the garage had been used for, and the man knew the deputy wasn't stupid enough to fall for any excuses.

Hardegen had nothing inside the unmarked car to treat burns, so he simply kept silent company with the man, dreading the impending paperwork and media blitz.

Gaffney would be proud, but he doubted Jamie was going to plan a hero's welcome for him. Then again, maybe she would.

*   *   *   *

When Terry and Megan arrived at Gaffney's office, they were unceremoniously introduced to the two FBI agents assisting them on the case. While they weren't the *only* agents available, they were sent to be liaisons between the task force and their agency.

He filled the group in about his talk with Russell. Megan had found nothing useful on the computers, which meant the information was old enough to be flushed from the memory, or the killer never accessed them.

Megan soon left to check for any messages or new information with the desk officers.

Terry approached the older of the two agents, Greg Murphy, once everyone in the room had received an update.

A tall, slender man in his mid-forties with thinning brown hair, Murphy firmly shook hands when Terry offered.

"What can I do for you?" the agent asked.

"I was wondering if you might be able to check on a hunch for me. I'd have to cut through a lot of red tape to get it done on my own."

"Sure."

Terry explained his idea that the killer might have located the Wilson family through an online search.

"Can you pinpoint the top ten search companies and see if they had any hits for Frank or Francis Wilson within the state of New York? The family had an unlisted number, and I doubt our guy went county to county checking property records."

"Shouldn't take too long," Murphy shrugged with a thin smile. "I hear they dragged you down here from up north?"

"Kicking and screaming."

"Grant can't say enough about you."

Now Terry gave a reluctant grin.

"He's trying to suck up, because he's the one who ordered me down here."

"Anything else I can do for you?" Murphy asked.

"Did the sheriff ask you to dig deeper on the tire tread lead? He thinks you might be able to narrow down the field of play."

"Possibly. We're only allowed one miracle per day, so we'll see what happens."

Terry took the agent's humor well, but wondered how many miracles might be required to find the killer before he struck again.

"I like that particular lead," Murphy admitted. "There were only so many vehicles that used that kind of tire back then, so there are *extremely* few now."

Used for certain recreational vehicles, as well as some trailers, the task force already knew they weren't from a trailer. Terry personally doubted the killer would risk bringing a vehicle into the slushy field, or the hunting lodge, without four-wheel-drive capability.

"I hope it gives us the break we need," Terry simply replied.

Lamoureux had informed him of Hardegen's discovery while checking the houses. While he might have saved a man's life, he was a loss to the team for part of the day while he assisted at the crime scene and filled out paperwork.

Terry blamed himself for the deputy's misfortune, but still considered checking the houses important until the team came up with a concrete lead.

Megan returned with a far cheerier look than Terry could ever recall, carrying some paperwork with her. She sought him out, placing the papers atop the table with a deliberate thud to ensure she had his complete attention.

"What have we here?" Terry asked.

"Information about Michael Toomey."

"Thought he was dead."

"He is, but he's speaking volumes from the grave. Turns out he was arrested twice for possible abuse on Eric. While he was never put away for *that*, Eric was taken away from him several times and placed back into the foster care system."

Terry scratched his head, trying to decipher the information before him. Murphy, too, had taken an interest since he was present when Megan returned. He also stole some glances toward Megan's shapely features, which Terry stopped with a disapproving stare.

Blushing a bit because he was caught, the agent returned his full attention to the paperwork.

"According to the reports, he did some strange things with Eric. He didn't beat the kid, per se, but locked him in closets, starved him for petty things, and didn't let him play with friends. Sounds a little bit like the boy was a caged animal most of the time."

"The fact that he's fallen off the radar completely worries me," Terry stated his worst fear. "He's definitely a person of interest, and not in the interview sense, either."

"There's more," Megan said. "Seems Michael was incarcerated for drugs, both trafficking and using. Eric probably had some bad influences in his life whenever he lived with his uncle. In prison, his uncle was treated for depression and a mild form of schizophrenia, so who knows what that kid saw growing up in that house?"

"What exactly happened to the uncle?" Murphy inquired.

"Seems he got off his medication and picked the wrong fight with some dangerous gang members," Megan replied. "I've got written accounts from the boy's school about possible abuse through stories he told teachers and guidance counselors. No one stuck up for this kid, and he may have kept a lot of demons inside."

"Psychological abuse isn't always easy to prove," Terry said. "Especially when the kids deny everything they said to the people that matter."

"There could be a history of psychosis in the family," Megan prodded. "I'm going to see about his parents, and possibly the grandparents, since they're all dead."

"All of this is dandy," Terry said, "but we need to focus on finding the nephew. I'm beginning to worry that he might have disappeared for other reasons."

Megan didn't appear convinced.

"I think you had it right a minute ago when you said he was a person of interest for all the right reasons. Some of the things his uncle did to him made me cringe. And that's just from reading the third-party accounts."

Gaffney's secretary walked into the room, heading straight for Terry. She talked in a tone that sounded like a made-up voice for a cartoon or sitcom, though it was very effective and easily understood over the phone.

"Dr. Juracek from University Hospital just called to say Tom Crotteau is awake and talking. He said you wanted to know immediately."

"He wasn't lying," Terry said, fighting the urge to plant a kiss on the older woman's forehead. "Thank you."

He looked over, noticing his friend's eyes meeting his.

"Want some company?" Lamoureux asked.

"You've got a task force to run. I can handle it."

Lamoureux nodded neutrally, not hurt or surprised by Terry's answer.

Terry started for the door, fully prepared for the drive to Syracuse. Every possible lead or clue he and Megan compiled ended in a dead end, while the forensic evidence results were caught in the quagmire known as the state lab. Talking with Crotteau might give him the break he needed to change the course of the investigation.

While his prayers had been answered, he wondered where Eric Toomey might be found, because one way or another, the task force needed to speak with the young man.

"Terry," Gaffney called from across the room, barely catching him.

"What's up, Paul?"

"You heading to Syracuse?"

"Yeah. I want to talk to the survivor in person."

Gaffney beamed like a candle.

"You wanting to go?" Terry asked.

"Nah. But I think it's in our best interest you get there ASAP."

"What are you suggesting then?"

"Follow me."

Terry trailed the sheriff, wondering if he was about to get a ride in the highly touted helicopter. Though he had never experienced such travel, he decided it sounded better than six hours of total drive time for a simple interview.

CHAPTER 28

▼

16 Years Earlier

Living with his Uncle Mike turned out to be anything but a smooth transition for Eric Toomey. After two months in a foster home, he felt great relief when a relative came to claim him from the facade of family life that came from living with six strangers.

None of the other kids took to him, because he didn't speak correctly all the time, stuttering when he grew nervous, or hurried his thoughts.

All of them saw a stupid kid who couldn't pronounce his eloquent thoughts, but he knew better. One day he would become their better.

When Toomey's foster parents informed him that his Uncle Mike was coming to pick him up from the foster home, Eric felt a wave of excitement and confusion at the same time. For one, he had never met his uncle before, which seemed strange. Not that he thought too much of it at six years of age, but later in life it occurred to him that maybe Uncle Mike wasn't welcome when his parents were alive.

His expectations were falsely high, because when he dashed to the window to spy his foster parents speaking with his uncle, Eric saw a man with stringy hair down to his shoulders, a mustache that reached the bottom of his jawbone, and a few days of unshaved stubble.

He wore tattered jeans and an old flannel shirt that seemed a few buttons shy of being properly donned. The little Volkswagen Bug behind him looked like a lemon, figuratively and literally. It resembled the yellow crayon Eric sometimes used to color the sun in his drawings.

Uncle Mike wasn't exactly the shining knight Eric had envisioned in his dreams for the past week.

When he was finally brought outside, Eric looked up at his uncle, who gave a strange smile to him, then a look of disdain to the foster parents, when just a moment prior he had been chummy with them.

"Aren't you a little darlin'?" he asked his nephew.

Eric said nothing, afraid he might immediately say something wrong in front of his new guardian.

"Let's go," he said, waving an arm toward the car, taking up the boy's two small bags of belongings.

During the ride to his uncle's house, neither said anything for a few miles. Eric watched the trees and landscape pass by, very uncertain of what his future held.

"You know what a black sheep is?" Michael asked his nephew.

The boy's confused look provided the answer.

"A black sheep is what I am, kid. My whole family didn't like me because of how I live my life."

How could a family not love one of its own? Eric wondered.

He remained quiet the rest of the trip, until they pulled up to a small yellow house with large flakes of paint missing, or clinging for dear life. The roof looked worn, though nowhere near collapse, or even leaking. Chunks of the topmost dark gray shingles were missing, revealing another set of red shingles beneath them in several places.

The backyard looked like a junkyard with old rusting cars sitting neatly in a row. A broken down bus and an old tow truck helped give the row a stair step effect. Eric had grown accustomed to having his own bedroom, and a fantastic play area in one corner of the living room.

What he discovered inside his uncle's house dashed his hopes of ever playing again.

Not only did useless junk lie in heaps, there was lots of it. Items that looked worse than some trash his parents threw away stood atop desks and tables, as though any day now they might find a use.

His new residence contained a living room, kitchen, two bedrooms, and a common bathroom with no running water in the tub. Tattered posters lined the walls of his uncle's bedroom, and even the living room, whereas beautiful paintings adorned his former residence.

Somehow leaving the foster home now felt like a regrettable decision that was never his to make.

But the worst had yet to come.

*   *   *   *

It didn't take long for Eric to realize living with his uncle was an undertaking like no other. School provided the only escape from the routine madness shielded within the small yellow house.

Torn between what seemed like a normal, safe world at school, and the behavior of his uncle, Eric felt confused. He had no one to turn to, because kids at school picked on him, and telling the teachers might get him in worse trouble at home.

In his former life, Eric's parents adored him. They knew beyond the occasional slips in his speech that he possessed more intelligence and ability than his peers. His uncle went from treating him similarly to the opposite extreme, sometimes within an hour's time.

Michael seemed to have good days and bad days, and Eric never knew which environment to expect when he returned home from school.

On Halloween, Michael went digging around in the attic for nearly an hour before he returned, carrying a costume with him.

"Let's go out and have some fun," he told his nephew. "Maybe we both need to feel good for a change."

Eric thought of his uncle's gesture as a healing process, perhaps a fresh chapter in their relationship, but Michael kept him out well past dark, venturing from house to house in town.

The costume, as it turned out, smelled musty from years of storage. Michael revealed that it was one of his childhood costumes, though Eric wasn't impressed with the hand-sewn heirloom. With floppy ears dangling from either side of his head, and a round pink nose that looked somewhat like a clown's, he preferred the imitation plastic store costumes.

At least they had themes, and really a nice fragrance for a few days.

Even the tail on his uncle's old doggy costume weighted him down as though he had fallen into the deep end of a pool. Brown, with a few distinctive white spots, the costume was mistaken several times for a dairy cow, despite the details created for the facial area, including the floppy ears.

Michael took such comments in good humor when the people said something, but called the people derogatory names after he and Eric were on their way to the next residence.

Three hours of door to door travel and brisk weather took a toll on young Eric.

"I need to go to the bathroom," Eric said at one point, his faded orange jack-o-lantern container almost filled to the brim with sweets.

Until this moment, his uncle had been unusually kind to him, treating him more like a son than a house guest. Now Michael gave an exaggerated sigh, looking down at the boy.

"Use that bush over there, doggy," he said, nodding toward the community center and a row of shrubs lining the front and sides of the building.

Hesitantly looking at the public building, then to his uncle, Eric questioned the seriousness of the statement. People continued to walk past, not done celebrating the holiday as a bank clock informed him it was already past nine.

Michael's look didn't waver, meaning dead seriousness on his part. While Eric didn't want to relieve himself in public, he knew his uncle wouldn't let them move on until he did so. He waited until no one on the street looked in their direction, then tried to look natural as he headed toward the building, ducking behind a shrub to conduct his business.

"That's a good little doggy!" Michael called, bringing embarrassment to himself because Eric had ducked out of sight behind the bush.

People on the street thought his uncle was drunk or insane, yelling at the vacant community center.

Eric peeked around the bushes, seeing people from the sidewalk staring at his uncle in disbelief, Michael oblivious to them.

During the ride home, Michael continued to berate his nephew.

"You need to toughen up, boy," he said. "If you can't hold it longer than that, I'm not going to let you sleep in your bed."

Some nights Eric slept on the floor anyway because his mattress smelled like rotten eggs. It also felt uncomfortable unless he found just the right spot on which to sprawl beneath the covers.

Complaining about anything to his uncle simply brought on a verbal tirade that might go on for hours, and do little or nothing to improve conditions. Over time, Eric began to question if life with his parents had been as typical as he figured, or if he lived more of a normal life now.

When they arrived home, Michael ordered him into the closet with no light, and barely space enough to sit down and move his legs.

Surrounded by newspapers he couldn't read, and the musty smells of clothes hanging overhead, Eric watched the door close behind him, the beam of light entering the closet narrowing into nothing. He heard the latch slide outside the door, leaving him isolated in the darkness.

"And you stay in there, filthy dog," Michael said angrily. "You stay in there until tomorrow morning."

Footsteps echoed down the hallway.

"And don't you mess, either!"

Feeling tears well in his eyes, Eric fought the urge to cry. He wasn't going to give in to his uncle's bizarre will. He pulled an unused neon light stick from inside his costume, shaking it and snapping it. As it glowed to life, he began staring at the newspapers around him, finding interest in the crime section writings.

He spent some of the night reading material far above the skill level for his age, interested in the crime and murder stories. He learned one important factor that got every one of the criminals caught in the end. They all blabbed about their crimes to someone, even if it was someone they trusted.

Eric pondered on ways to get his uncle in trouble at work, knowing direct talks to authority figures would only result in worse treatment at home. He plotted at some length as the light stick drew dimmer by the hour. Eventually Eric drifted off to sleep, the smell of the costume enveloping him as he dreamed up more schemes.

CHAPTER 29

▼

Before Eric ever hatched a plan against his uncle, fate sent his life in a different direction when Michael lost his job.

Returned to foster care, he ended up in a house with two other children, cared for by an ordained minister. Though strict rules and more chores than he was accustomed to took up much of his time, he slept in a normal bed, excelled in school, and began to learn about the Bible.

He learned biblical passages and attended church, but he didn't feel very Christian. The foster situation left him without a true sense of family, and friends never came easily. Eric wanted a sense of belonging, but found none.

During the time with his uncle, Eric found himself treated more like a household pet on a daily basis. Michael forced him to sit on the floor to eat food, despite a kitchen table being present, and sometimes forced him to relieve himself outside. After reading several books, and watching several movies that focused on animals, he began realizing all mammals shared similarities.

Not all animals were intelligent, nor could they all fend for themselves, so Eric eventually took up for them on the playground, or after school. The kids already hated him, so befriending animals gave him a purpose.

One Sunday, his new foster father gave a sermon about how God had placed animals across the world for mankind to do with as he pleased. While the speech interested Eric, he didn't agree with all of the views. He began reading more into the Bible about how animals were sacrificed to the Lord, and how men should never lie with the beasts.

Taking in the information, Eric reevaluated his stand toward animals, beginning to see himself as their only true protector. Veterinarians and animal rights groups did only so much. They worked regionally, not in the field on a case by case basis as Eric did.

After a year or so with his new family, Eric found himself with Michael once again. In the beginning, things seemed much better. His uncle had found a new job with benefits, so he took medication, transforming him into a completely different person.

He wore decent clothes, behaved like most people Eric had encountered during his youth, and traded the lemon for a newer car. Most of the time, he held civil conversations with his nephew, concerned about his schoolwork and social activities.

In time Michael was laid off, meaning things went back to normal. He treated Eric much like he had before, sometimes even worse. The living conditions, which had been reasonable, deteriorated quickly when Michael stopped doing any housework. The clean environment soon looked like a recycling center as stacks of junk appeared throughout the house.

Eric endured his punishments well, believing they taught him valuable lessons about how animals must live under human care. He suspected his time with Michael would be short-lived after the loss of income. Even at a young age, Eric knew much about the world through his uncle's rambles.

The government indeed caught up with Michael when the financial well ran dry, and Eric found himself off to a new destination at a time when things couldn't get much worse.

✳   ✳   ✳   ✳

Because of his inability to conform to normal standards, Eric lived with three different families before becoming a neighbor to Kyle Wilson, the best friend he ever had.

The two boys shared much in common, including the unusual nature in which each was raised. Though Kyle had lived with his father most of his life, he took equal amounts of physical and mental abuse. When his father wasn't striking him with something, he informed Kyle of how worthless he was around their farm.

Eric disliked Francis Wilson, and the feeling seemed mutual, so the boys kept their friendship low-key around the families. Regardless of what the boy's father said, Eric felt his best friend had a complete grasp of life on the farm.

Kyle used the tools, picked up hay bales with ease, and treated the animals with respect, even if forced to handle them roughly sometimes. Francis Wilson never respected animals, sometimes beating them unnecessarily, because it was his way.

One day he found the boys together, playing in the barn. With a cross look, he stood there momentarily before addressing Kyle.

"You're going to learn how to drive, son," he said sternly.

Usually on the weekends he left them alone, too occupied with his own leisure to be bothered with anything else.

"Bring your little buddy."

Eric wondered momentarily if the man might be warming up to him, but quickly dismissed the thought when he found himself virtually crushed against the passenger side door of the old work truck.

A manual-drive truck seldom used around the farm, covered equally in rust and light blue paint, felt like a deathtrap to Eric. Few of the handles and gauges worked, but since it never left the property, it didn't much matter.

Kyle brought the truck to life with ease, but shifting proved burdensome for him. What Eric didn't know, and later learned, was about manual clutches, and their tendency to wear out over time. The one thing Kyle had little or no control over provided his father with the means to punish him.

When the truck turbulently reached second gear, Frank pulled a hay hook from the floor, putting the pointed end into his son's crotch, his hand gripping the handle to keep tension on the tool.

"Do that again, and this goes where it'll hurt the most," Frank threatened.

Openly nervous, Kyle did his best to keep the truck running smoothly during shifting, which he only had to do two more times before Frank let them return to the barn.

Eric learned about most of Kyle's troubles through his friend. The father carefully orchestrated the times and places Kyle received his wrath. His sickness wasn't like Uncle Michael's, because he knew exactly what he was doing to Kyle. He didn't know any other way to raise the boy, Eric decided.

What seemed more unfortunate was that two of the neighbors, Frank's buddies, knew about the abuse. Kyle said his father was never quite as blatant when they were around, but they knew. Eric wondered why the world was against them, because there seemed to be no way out of the adult world and the consequences it brought.

"People expect farm kids to take a licking," Kyle sometimes said. "When I get bumps and bruises, everyone thinks it's from working here."

Bob Hagen witnessed several smacks upon Kyle's head from his father, but he simply turned the other cheek, quite literally. The look on his face told Eric he knew better than to watch like a lackey, but the man never said one word to Frank, or the authorities.

The other neighbor, a truck driver older than Hagen, condoned the actions far more easily than the postman. He often talked about life on the open road, which Frank appeared to like hearing. Eric later deduced that Wilson took driving jobs because of the stories the truck driver told him.

Eric witnessed his friend being smacked along the back with a coarse, coiled rope. The truck driver smirked at the action, though Kyle had done nothing to deserve any kind of punishment, much less a thrashing. When Kyle lifted his shirt, Eric saw the deep red bruises along his back, thinking back to how the man laughed, simply encouraging the inappropriate actions on Wilson's part.

On a late spring weekend, Eric went to find Kyle in the barn. They often met inside the barn to keep the family from knowing. Frank's wife and stepdaughter reported everything to him, which alienated Kyle from everyone.

What Eric found inside the barn that warm spring morning wasn't his friend, but something dark and disturbing.

Following the sounds of grunts and groans, Eric cautiously rounded corners, passed through doors, and peered through hatchways until he found Kyle's father violating a rather large hog at the end of a narrow pen.

Horrified, he stood and watched momentarily until a door creaked beside him, drawing the man's attention his way.

Reasonably certain he wasn't spotted from his vantage point, Eric quietly navigated the familiar barn until he reached the safety of the outdoors. He ran to the nearby woods, taking a very long way home to ensure no one knew he had visited the farm that morning.

He didn't visit the farm for a few weeks, though Kyle called him several times. Finally, when Frank took his stepdaughter to town one morning, Eric visited his friend. He explained himself, then proceeded to go through the motions of what acts Frank performed on the hog using a nearby sheep.

Eric didn't reenact the unspeakable act, but unzipped his pants for visual effect while explaining the situation to Kyle. Bad luck followed the boys as usual when the seed distributor walked into the barn, finding them near the sheep. His shocked expression didn't require an explanation, and the boys failed to provide one before he turned and left.

Over the next few months, the relationship between Kyle and his father grew more tense. Eric wasn't allowed over to the farm at all, which led him to believe Kyle said something about the unspeakable incident.

In early fall, Eric walked to the old makeshift junkyard where he and Kyle sometimes met, despite the families insisting they not play together. There, he found Frank Wilson pacing around the deep crater where several old cars and appliances had met their ultimate demise. Hiding behind a tree, Eric heard the man make guilty utterances just above a whisper.

He stayed for a few minutes, fearing Frank might see him, then left for the equally terrible sanctuary of the foster home.

Later, he saw the swarm of emergency vehicles in the same area, knowing before the media confirmed his suspicions that his friend was dead. In his mind, he suspected Frank followed his son to the meeting place, confronted him, and inevitably killed him. Whether he meant to or not, Wilson killed the boy he had a legal obligation to protect and raise to adulthood.

Eric grew distraught over the loss of his friend, even into late fall. By the holiday season he was moved to another home, though the agency and his foster parents never said why. Deep down, he always suspected Frank Wilson had something to do with it.

The remainder of his life after that day never matched the ten months of intermittent happiness with his best friend. One man was responsible for deflowering various farm animals, and ultimately killing Kyle. Eric decided, gradually over a period of years, that Frank Wilson needed to pay for his sins.

Even though the pastor talked of forgiveness of one's fellow man, Eric's life had taught him that a boy could only depend on one person.

Himself.

CHAPTER 30

▼

Terry made good time to the hospital because Gaffney let him borrow the Erie County Sheriff's Department's helicopter and Captain Jim Covington. He appreciated the gesture, because none of the six state police helicopters were immediately accessible, and only one of them was remotely nearby. Gaffney made a call to the medical center in Syracuse for landing clearance at a nearby soccer field, while Terry arranged a ride from a trooper in that area.

During the abbreviated trip to Syracuse, Terry received a brief history lesson about how the department received their first helicopters after the Vietnam War from military surplus sales. When one of the choppers broke down and crashed, with no casualties to speak of, the county purchased a state-of-the-art helicopter used for police and medical emergencies.

A father of two, Covington was about to send his daughter to college, while his son neared graduation with a degree in accounting. Still happily married, the captain mentioned entertaining thoughts of retirement within the next few years. He liked working for Gaffney, but three decades of military, then police life had worn his mind and body.

One of the other deputies had taken lessons on flying the bird, so Covington wouldn't leave his department in a pinch. Terry suspected the captain had definite retirement plans, whether they be touring the country in an RV, or hunting for a new house with both of his children leaving the nest.

While he didn't use words any more than necessary, Covington had a smooth voice Terry likened to Sam Elliott. He wondered if the man had ever considered a career in radio, or television show narration.

Covington landed the machine with practiced expertise in the fading grass. Terry cautiously exited the chopper, meeting with a fairly young road trooper who drove him to the best entrance at University Hospital.

Terry spoke with a young woman at the reception desk, then made his way to the intensive care unit where Thomas Crotteau had spent the better part of the past two days.

After a few words from the doctor, and assurances from Terry himself that he wouldn't push the man too hard, the family left the room. A few gave him protective glares as they brushed past him.

Crotteau looked a bit pale, but doing fairly well considering he had survived two separate surgeries. Most of the danger stemmed from the abdominal surgery, because the bullet fired at his head damaged the skull, but ricocheted without penetrating the brain.

The white bandage wrapped around his head looked somewhat like a biker's skullcap. His rugged face, accented with a thick brown mustache, displayed the hardness that Terry recognized in survivors. Luck and sheer will brought the man out of the woods both literally and figuratively, but Terry had only one survival tale he wanted to hear.

Sitting up in bed with his hands folded atop his lap, Crotteau looked relatively comfortable as his eyes studied the visitor. A gold wedding band adorned his left hand, informing Terry the man would have all the support he needed.

For a man who brushed against death the day before, he looked remarkably healthy.

Keeping his expressions minimal to avoid additional pain, Crotteau extended his hand as Terry introduced himself, producing his identification.

"I'm sorry for your loss, Mr. Crotteau," Terry said. "How are you feeling?"

"Not bad, considering I had two holes in me yesterday."

Terry knew more about the victims than he cared to, after perusing their files for hours in search of answers. Losing his nephew had to be hard, but the medical staff warned him not to mention too much about the deaths if possible. Thus far, they had tiptoed around the subject of the slaughter near the hunting lodge.

Terry saw no way around the subject, though he decided to be sensitive. Anyone suffering the loss of four friends and a family member deserved respect and courtesy more than a typical witness.

"I need to ask you some questions about what happened yesterday morning."

"Can you promise me you'll catch the son-of-a-bitch?" Crotteau asked in such a deliberate manner that Terry worried about his mental well-being.

"I can promise you I won't rest until I do," Terry answered properly.

He knew to never give victims false assurances.

"What do you want to know?"

"Start from the beginning if you would. Tell me everything about the incident."

Terry pulled out a tape recorder to catch every detail.

"Mind if I tape this?"

"No," the injured man said after painfully attempting to shake his head.

Crotteau told him about spotting who he thought was a hunter, calling the group, and the shootout transpiring after the group figured they were safe.

"Hagen was the last one?" Terry questioned, because Crotteau skimmed over the details fairly quickly.

"He knew Bob. I think Bob was the reason he was there."

"What makes you say that?"

"He just stared at Bob whenever he talked, and when he had Bob at his mercy," Crotteau paused as the painful memory entered his mind, "he, he talked about something Bob could have prevented. Or something like that."

For about half a minute the room went silent, except for Crotteau's forceful exhalations through his nostrils. Terry gave him this time to collect himself, knowing it couldn't be easy to relive such an ordeal.

"Did he say anything else?"

"Not really. He blamed Bob for something, but it sounded like he meant something a long time ago."

"Did the guy talk with any kind of lisp, or did he stutter?"

"No. He spoke very, uh, deliberately. It was like he measured his words carefully before he said them."

Terry knew of instances where people didn't stutter when they were nervous. He also knew the opposite sometimes held true, when they were dead serious.

"How old was the guy? And what did he look like?"

"Late teens, early twenties, I guess. He was pretty much covered up, except for his face, so I didn't get to see much. Uh, no facial hair or anything like that, but he didn't look very well kept, either."

"What exactly do you mean by that?"

"It's hard to explain. His teeth were fine, but what little bit of hair stuck out seemed stringy, almost needing a simple cut. His face seemed kind of pale, too, like he hadn't eaten well for some time. *Gaunt* is the word I think I'm looking for."

Unkept and malnourished hardly sounded like a combination for a cold and confident killer to the investigator, but he listened intently. Of course he knew people with psychotic tendencies often neglected themselves in every way.

He strongly suspected Eric Toomey was the man he sought. If that proved true, a family history of mental illness might have provoked his wrath toward his former neighbors.

"If I could get someone to show you a photo lineup, do you think you could pick him out?" Terry asked.

"Yeah. I won't forget those eyes for anything."

"Is there anything else you can remember?" Terry prompted. "Did you see what he drove, or any distinctive clothing on him?"

Crotteau thought a moment.

"He wore gloves and a camouflage jacket. I don't remember nothin' else."

He seemed to sense Terry knew more than he let on.

"Do you have a suspect?"

Normally he hated to reveal any specifics of a case, but Crotteau had earned the right to know a little something.

"I had someone in mind before I came here, sir. What you've told me pretty much verifies who I believe is the killer."

"Then I hope you'll put a bullet in him for me."

Terry shut off the tape recorder, standing up to leave.

"I'll do what I can, Mr. Crotteau. Rest easy, and I'll check on you in a few days."

Crotteau forced a grin.

"I won't be going anywhere. I've been dying for a smoke, but they say in my condition I can't."

"They're paid to look out for your best interests, sir."

"I'd even settle for a chew at this point."

"Can't help you there," Terry said, putting forth a sympathetic smile. "Take care of yourself, and I'll be in touch."

*   *   *   *

While riding back to the helicopter, Terry placed a call to Lamoureux to have a photo lineup prepared for Crotteau.

"Is it Toomey?" Lamoureux asked the loaded question, because he implicitly trusted Terry's judgment.

"If it's not him, someone's doing a great job of framing him. Didn't you say he did custodial work at a school?"

"He worked at the local Boces School in Newark."

Boces schools dotted the entire state. Basically trade schools with specialized training for high school students, they provided necessary job skills as the state made the transition from industrial to tech jobs.

"I'm going to have a talk with the staff, Grant. Maybe they can shed some light on what kind of guy he was. And I can probably get a recent photo of him."

"I'll hold off on the lineup until you call me back. Want me to call the school for some landing clearance?"

"I appreciate it, and I'm sure they will too."

"I'll call you back when I get some information."

"Thanks."

Terry knew the way to the school, hoping Covington didn't have anywhere to be for the next hour or two. Gaffney had instructed Covington to do whatever Terry asked, considering it was part of their high-priority case. Terry also hoped the captain could find a place to land near the school, but Lamoureux would use his charms and have the school officials eating out of his hand before Covington even landed.

Terry stepped from the trooper's marked car, thanked him, and approached the helicopter. Inside, the captain thumbed through the pages of sports magazine as though he never heard a car door open or slam shut.

Opening the chopper's door, Terry gave Covington a wry smile before speaking.

"Feel like going to school?"

Covington looked a bit apprehensive, knowing there was no right answer to the loaded question.

"That depends."

Half an hour later, Terry found himself speaking with a gray-haired supervisor inside the custodial break room, centered within a hive of school's indispensable machinery. Closing the door behind him to drown out the roar of the heating units, the supervisor offered Terry a seat, then pulled out the wheeled chair from behind his desk. He sat down, taking up a familiar, comfortable position as he propped one leg atop the opposite knee.

"Eric wasn't with us very long," the man stated immediately. "Smart kid, but the staff kept their distance from him. They weren't quite sure what to make of him."

"How so?"

"He was kind of distant. Not shy, but distant. I guess he creeped people out the way he stared holes through 'em."

Terry looked to a desk under repair beside him. Carved graffiti covered part of the surface, taking him back to his own school days.

"How was his work ethic?"

"Good. He got stuff done in plenty of time."

Terry figured as much. He wondered if Toomey had other objectives to accomplish that work interfered with.

"Do you have a file on him, or any photographs?"

"The administration should have his records."

Terry doubted the school had its own yearbook, since it accepted kids from multiple local schools for part-time training. The very same employment records might have an address and contact information, hopefully accessible without a subpoena.

He decided to pursue a different avenue.

"Did he have any speech problems?"

"He stuttered sometimes. The kids always made fun of him, sometimes to his face. Punks these days have no respect for anyone at all, I tell ya."

After working as the School Resource Officer at the local consolidated school for a year, Terry knew all about how society and kids had changed.

He sometimes wondered if he was simply older and grumpier, but tragic news stories verified his initial thoughts more often than in years past.

"Why did he leave?"

The supervisor shrugged.

"Just told us not to expect him in here anymore one Friday. He never showed up again."

"Is there anything else you can remember about him that stands out? Did he ever talk about his childhood or life outside of work?"

"Not really. He just followed orders and went home."

Running a hand through his hair, the man seemed to remember something.

"He sometimes used the computers in the lab for personal reasons, Mr. Levine. We never said much, because he always got his work done in plenty of time, and he used them after school hours."

"What kind of stuff did he use the computers for?"

The custodial supervisor shrugged helplessly.

"Do you remember what he drove by chance?"

"Sure. It looked like one of those old Jeeps. The enclosed kind."

Terry nodded.

"Remember the color?"

"Uh, red. Kind of faded, too, with one of those tacky accent pieces that looked like wood paneling down each side."

Some older vehicles had molded pieces from the factory that run down their sides, rather than stripes, until the fad passed.

Terry thanked the man, then visited the administrative offices. Without hesitation, they allowed him to view Eric Toomey's employment records, giving him an address and the recent photo he wanted.

He felt better about their chances of locating the young man, though he suspected the trail might have gone cold months after Toomey quit his job.

Things that usually assisted police in tracking people, such as tax forms, property records, credit cards, and utility records didn't seem to apply in this case. Toomey's few links to society disappeared like dandelion seeds in the wind when investigators drew close to solid answers.

Armed with new information, Terry hoped Crotteau would identify Toomey as his attacker, allowing every cop in the state to know exactly whom they sought in the murders of eight people.

As he left the school, he pulled out his cell phone to update Lamoureux on his progress. If the task force's luck continued, by day's end they might confirm Eric Toomey as their prime suspect *and* discover his current residence.

Seldom did high profile cases end so easily, but Terry had experienced fortunate conclusions much sooner than expected in some of his toughest investigations.

Listening to the phone ring against his ear, he opened his door, hoping to be home by afternoon the next day.

CHAPTER 31

▼

Hardegen had barely walked through the door of the new task force command center when Lamoureux snared him for a ride to an undisclosed location.

Gaffney had worked out a temporary lease of the old community center, contacting everyone on the team that morning. The building contained a small gym, one sizeable meeting room, restrooms, and a small office. While several officers moved necessary equipment into the facility, Lamoureux had caught the deputy looking around.

After spending most of the day filling out reports and checking on the condition of the meth cook at the local hospital, the deputy wanted nothing more than a status report and some sleep.

Now late in the afternoon, the sun set in the distance as the two cops walked toward Hardegen's unmarked car. Because the air had cooled considerably, Hardegen zipped his leather jacket halfway, fishing in his pocket for his keys.

"Where are we headed?" he asked Lamoureux as he unlocked the doors using the keyless remote.

"Terry thinks we have a solid suspect, so we're going to check his last known residence."

Lamoureux handed him a piece of paper with a somewhat familiar address on it.

"Yeah. I know where that is."

If he remembered correctly, the address came from a small apartment complex on the eastern border of Erie County.

"Quite a little commute to Newark from there," Lamoureux commented thoughtfully, looking at the address.

"Not that bad, really."

Hardegen started the car, wasting little time finding the nearest highway to begin their journey. He wondered if Lamoureux had picked him for his professional expertise, or to pick his brain about his Syracuse football days.

Five minutes later, Lamoureux started a conversation.

"You okay after that mess this morning?"

Hardegen still felt a bit shook up about the incident, not so much because of the deaths, but rather the items found at the scene. Drug dealers with political stances were a far worse breed than the simple junkies and cooks Hardegen usually locked up.

"I'm doing okay," he answered.

His own guys would never pose such a question. They went about their business with the efficiency of worker ants, never stopping to evaluate emotions or assess their own condition. The only critiques came from their leadership, who evaluated their performance in drug raids to educate the group for their next assignment.

"You familiar with this place?" the Senior Investigator inquired, waving the paper with the address.

"It's a shoddy apartment complex, not too far from your Batavia station. We've had some busts there before."

"Not exactly a country club?" Lamoureux asked, openly struggling to remember the place.

"Hardly."

Apparently the Senior Investigator hadn't worked the meaner streets of the Batavia area lately.

Though not government housing, the complex was part of a low income neighborhood. Even college students knew to avoid living in such apartments for fear of their lives.

"So what have we learned about the suspect?" Hardegen asked.

Lamoureux told him about the photo lineup heading to Crotteau, the possibility of a Jeep as Toomey's vehicle, and why they heavily suspected Toomey as the killer.

"Do we have a search warrant for this?"

"We're just finding out if Toomey lives here, and if he does, we have to wait for the hunter to positively ID him before our next move."

"And if he doesn't live here?"

"Then we get creative and see what we can find out."

Hardegen's stomach growled, reminding him that his early lunch no longer contented it.

"Need to hit a drive-thru?" Lamoureux offered.

"I'm good, thanks. My wife is already going to kill me."

Giving a grunt at the statement, Lamoureux's displeasure showed.

"Is it marriage in general that's bothering you?" the deputy decided to ask.

"The lack thereof," Lamoureux answered, pausing momentarily. "I haven't told Terry the whole story, but I think he knows."

Hardegen said nothing, being patient. He expected to be interrogated by the investigator, but now the man was about to open up to him.

"Maybe I'm ashamed of what I've done, especially since Terry and I were so close, but this past year I lost just about everything I ever cared about. All because of one mistake."

"You know, you don't have to tell me anything you don't want-"

"No, John. I do want to talk about it. And maybe it's because I *don't* know you that well."

A few silent seconds passed. Hardegen kept his eyes on the road, already somewhat jittery about the impending confession.

"What should have been a one-night thing turned into a few weeks. It's hard to keep anything secret nowadays, so my wife eventually found out. She got the kids, the house, everything."

Hardegen found it difficult to summon sympathy for anyone who cheated on a spouse. The world had fewer good Christians in it these days, but he went to church and honored the commitments he made to his wife and children.

He questioned exactly why Lamoureux confided in him, or what he expected in return. Perhaps just telling the story was relief enough for the man.

"I understand why you wouldn't want Terry to know, but why do you feel obligated to tell me this?"

"It's not obligation. I know what I did was wrong and there's no forgiving that. You suppose God forgives mistakes like that?"

Hardegen pondered the question a moment.

"I suppose He forgives just about anything a person's sorry for. But is this … infidelity an ongoing thing?"

The lack of an immediate answer told Hardegen it was.

"I shouldn't have to lecture you about the chances of a relationship born out of impurities lasting, should I?"

"No."

"Then I won't."

Hardegen navigated his way through traffic, keeping an eye on his speed as he looked for the upcoming exit.

"I guess maybe I trust you, John," Lamoureux admitted. "It's why I wanted you on this case. Well, that, and you're Syracuse alumni."

Both men smiled at the comment, breaking the tension.

"I was Terry's best man at his wedding," Lamoureux said. "We've always kept in touch and trusted one another, even after he left for the big city. He probably thinks I called him down here to solve *all* my problems."

"You know, life is what you make of it. If you spend all your time worrying about what other people think of your situation, then you never make the situation better. I've been riding with the man for almost a week now, and he hasn't said one bad word about you."

"I guess that's what I really wanted to hear."

Hardegen left out the part about Terry cursing Lamoureux for dragging him down to Buffalo, deciding to give the investigator some peace of mind.

"You've got about five minutes to ask me whatever football questions you want to before we reach the apartments."

Lamoureux lit up like a kid on Christmas morning.

✳   ✳   ✳   ✳

It took closer to ten minutes for Hardegen to navigate the streets before finding the apartment complex. He parked outside the manager's office, stepping from the car the same time as Lamoureux.

"Did you call ahead and get us a reservation?" he asked.

"We couldn't get an answer over the phone, but Gaffney said he'd keep trying."

Hardegen let Lamoureux knock on the door, since the investigator was appropriately dressed. People tended to look at the deputy as though he were an untrustworthy intern when he wore plain clothes.

Both men were surprised when a man in his mid-fifties opened the door, apparently expecting them. He invited them inside immediately, acting far more friendly than most people finding police officers on their property.

"George Hackett," he said, quickly introducing himself as the property manager. "How can I be of service?"

Hardegen felt certain the man spoke with an accent that sounded very much like Brooklyn. He based his theory on movies and a person he worked with from Brooklyn earlier in his career.

Looking around, Hardegen noticed the manager lived in a carbon copy of every other apartment in the complex. He figured the man would have more deluxe accommodations.

"Did Sheriff Gaffney contact you?" Lamoureux asked.

"Yes. He asked about one of my former tenants, so I dug out all the information I could find."

"Former?" Hardegen asked, sensing a complete waste of time.

Time he might have spent at home, trying to catch up on much needed rest.

"He moved out about two months ago."

"The same time he quit the school," Lamoureux commented as the two officers locked eyes momentarily.

"I don't suppose his old apartment is vacant?" Hardegen inquired.

"It was for about a month."

"Did you find anything left behind when you cleaned it?" Lamoureux asked without missing a beat.

Hardegen saw the same tenacity and experience in him that Terry exhibited.

"Not even a used napkin. The boy cleaned everything up before he left."

Lamoureux grunted to himself, indicating he knew exactly why Eric Toomey left nothing behind. Hardegen too suspected the young man knew exactly where he was heading when he moved out.

Most likely to visit the Wilson family from the edge of their property.

"Did he leave a forwarding address, or anything behind that might help us find him now?" Lamoureux asked.

"Not really. He's had a few items arrive in the mail for him that didn't get forwarded."

"Please," Lamoureux said, holding out his hand toward the tenant file Hackett had laid upon the counter top.

After examining the postal contents, he handed them to Hardegen. The first item was a mercenary magazine with commentary about assassination, abduction, and close-quarters killing. While Hardegen never took such magazines too seriously, Eric Toomey apparently wanted some vital information from them.

"I threw away most of the junk mail, like the ads and missing kid fliers," Hackett said.

Hardegen found a few common pieces of mail like credit card applications and bank loan offers, but the last appeared to be a bank check of some sort with three perforated edges.

"May I?" he asked Lamoureux, who nodded affirmatively.

Opening it, the deputy discovered a check for over a hundred dollars from a bank that had closed his account.

While none of the mail appeared to be from individuals, some of the letters seemed worthy of postal forwarding, like the check. Hardegen believed Toomey gave no forwarding information to the post office, indicating he didn't want to be found.

"Can I get copies of his information?" Lamoureux asked, handing the file back to Hackett.

"Certainly. I'll be right back."

Hackett stepped outside, briskly walking to his office in the closest building to make copies.

"What do you make of it?" Lamoureux asked, eyeing the check.

"I think our boy wanted out of here in a hurry, and didn't care enough to pick up his mail."

Lamoureux looked displeased.

"He didn't leave anything for us to go on. His old phone number was on that file. You suppose he took it with him?"

"I doubt we're that lucky."

"Me too."

At least with the phone number, they might be able to track some of Toomey's calls and figure out his plans leading up to the Wilson murders. Of course, such an action required documents and permission from a judge, which he hoped might be a real possibility.

CHAPTER 32

▼

By the next morning, the task force felt rejuvenated with the news that Eric Toomey was positively identified by Crotteau as the killer of his five hunting buddies.

Gaffney expedited the subpoena process by contacting a state supreme court judge, saving the team valuable time. Toomey moved around more than some vagabonds, and with less provocation, covering multiple jurisdictions.

While his friend made arrangements to scrutinize Toomey's life in every detail, Terry joined Gaffney to conduct a morning meeting. He hoped for some positive results, particularly when the two FBI agents walked into the room carrying portfolios.

Terry revealed Lamoureux's current whereabouts to the group, citing several new leads the group members had discovered.

"Thanks to Sheriff Gaffney getting in touch with Judge Cooper so quickly, we should have Toomey's phone records by this afternoon."

Gaffney took an informal half bow toward Terry, acknowledging the compliment before the trooper continued.

"We're hoping to track down Toomey's whereabouts through some of his calls, because his driver's license has an old address, and he's moved since his last job. Megan, can you tell us about your newest finding?"

Megan nodded, looking around at the group, including the FBI agents who continued to stand at the back of the room.

"Toomey inherited his uncle's house, property, and what little money the man had set aside when he died in prison. He made short work of selling the house. He also received a trust fund left by his parents once he turned eighteen, meaning he has financial means without working. We have every indication that he left his last apartment with the intent to murder the Wilsons because he covered his tracks."

"At the moment, we have no clue where he's staying," Terry said to emphasize the urgency of the situation. "He left no forwarding address, and his old phone number is still an unused line with no forwarding number. At this point, we plan on providing news stations with his photograph in the hope that someone recognizes him."

He looked to Gaffney for confirmation, receiving a nod. The sheriff dealt more often with the media than Terry, and had experience in all sorts of abduction and murder cases, which sometimes required help from the public.

"We also have another new development," Terry said. "Our computer guys finished searching the hard drive from the Wilsons' computer, and they found some interesting things to say the least. Someone in that household regularly surfed the internet for photos, videos, and articles about incest and bestiality. What that means is Toomey may not be the one responsible for violating a sheep at the farm, and worse, my profile may be more than a little inaccurate."

"You've gotten us this far," Gaffney said close enough for only Terry to hear. "Don't be too hard on yourself."

"I'm not," Terry replied before addressing the group. "Greg, do you and Leo have anything new to share with the group?"

"Our people contacted some of the search engine companies from the internet as you requested," Greg Murphy replied. "One in particular had a search done for anyone named Frank Wilson within New York State about two months ago. The information was sent to a generic e-mail that had no trace value, and paid for with a prepaid credit card, which also had no traceable content."

"Anything on our tire tread yet?" Gaffney asked.

"We have one of our best technicians examining your evidence," Murphy replied. "If anyone can get you specific information, it's him. He's about to retire, and we're going to hate losing him. There's probably no one better at matching treads to makes and models."

Everyone remained silent a moment. Terry thought it peculiar how Eric Toomey had fallen off the radar by his own doing. He knew exactly what he wanted to accomplish months before he executed his plan.

Sitting right in front of him, Megan caught his thoughtful look.

"What's the matter?"

"I'm just wondering who our guy might target next," addressing only her, since several people had begun talking amongst themselves. "He's got to be running out of former neighbors."

A realization crossed her face the same time Terry's mind reached a dire conclusion.

"Maybe we should go talk to your retired couple again," he suggested.

"I suspect we can just give them a call," Megan said. "We're on good terms since they showed me their pottery collection."

Terry chuckled at the comment because Megan had informed him they weren't an easy interview, since they kept changing topics to keep her company longer.

"Did they mention other neighbors?" he asked.

"They did, but one has since moved, and the other died."

"There have to be others. I'm sure Frank Wilson was no social butterfly, but it sounds like he made friends with most of his neighbors wherever he went."

"We can check on the foster parents who had Toomey for a year, and I'll ask about anyone else the Crouches might have known."

"Sounds like a plan. I'll meet back with you in a few. I've got my own call to make."

He pulled Gaffney aside, asking him to conclude the meeting, then left the room.

*   *   *   *

"I can't believe you're going to miss trick-or-treat with your kids," Sherri chided him when he called her cell phone.

He stood outside the community building command center for maximum signal.

"Have your party daughter take them out and take the night off."

Sherri was not amused.

"If anything, Britney is staying here tonight to hand out candy while I take Jess and Corbin into town."

"You want me to make the five-hour commute home so I can take them out? I might have time enough for some role playing with handcuffs before I head back."

"The *only* place you'd better be putting those cuffs is around your suspect, and soon. You getting anywhere on that front?"

"I'm pretty sure we know the who, but the where isn't so easy."

"They always slip up, don't they?"

"Usually, but this guy has covered his tracks pretty well. He's either living off the land, or he's changed something that keeps him from getting noticed. We're going to plaster his mug all over the news tonight, so hopefully some good Samaritan will turn him in."

"Can you be so lucky?"

Terry watched tourists checking out the antique shops across the street from him. An older couple hunched over to see something close up, reminding him of Megan's interviewees.

"I doubt it. If this takes too much longer, I'll just transfer back here and make it easy on us."

"I'll start packing," Sherri said sarcastically. "And I'll go ahead and turn in my two weeks at work, since I'm about to get fired anyway for neglecting my duties by talking on the phone."

"Good. Tell them it's police business, and if they fire you, you can get an early start on that packing."

"I should hang up on you."

"But then you wouldn't hear me say how much I love you."

Sherri paused for effect.

"You said that too sincerely. You doing something down there that you shouldn't be?"

A laugh preceded his next statement.

"By the time my work day is done, I'm too tired to even *think* about doing anything I shouldn't be."

He watched the older couple scuffle along, wondering if he and Sherri would retire and survive long enough to escape the highs and lows of raising three children.

Megan peeked her head around the corner to signal she had finished her call.

"Hon, I've gotta run. Have fun tonight if I don't catch you later."

"Don't worry, dear. I'll find time to pack your bags after my night on the town."

"Love you," he said, trying to refrain from laughing in front of Megan.

"Love you too, handsome. Stay safe down there."

"Okay. Bye."

He turned to Megan.

"Well?"

"It seems there was another neighbor, about two miles past the old Wilson farm from the Crouches. He's a truck driver who visited the farm very regularly, and he's the reason Frank Wilson took up driving when his factory job was going under."

"Where do we find this guy?"

"That's the hard part. They can't remember his name, and he moved away about six or seven years ago."

Terry doubted Toomey ever forgot the name.

"Shit."

"My sentiments exactly," Megan revealed. "We can get the address and check property records."

A car passed, delaying Terry's next question because it's lack of a good muffler drowned out any conversations within earshot.

"Why didn't they mention it before?"

"Tom forgot, and Betty thought he had told me."

Terry rolled his eyes with a sigh.

"We've got to find this trucker guy at all costs, but we can't focus exclusively on him, either. Any of the neighbors might be potential targets, especially if they befriended Wilson."

Murphy stepped out to join them, bearing a look of good news.

"Leo had our people check several databases concerning your suspect," the agent began, "and it turns out he spent two years in the military."

"I'll be damned," Terry said. "That explains how he gunned down five people so easily."

"And why he fell off the map for so long," Megan added.

Motioning with his hand, Murphy prompted for them to be quiet so he could continue.

"He spent two years in the Marines, then received a discharge due to conduct unbecoming a soldier. The records don't say why, but it's a safe bet he did something to get himself out of there when the time was right."

"Meaning he's had all of this planned for a lot more than the months to a year I originally figured."

"He had money, so why work at the school?" Megan questioned.

"Access to their computers," Terry answered. "It was close proximity to his old home, plus he led what by all accounts seemed a normal life to those around him. He probably never expected anyone to link him to the murders after planning them so well."

All three exchanged worried looks, now knowing Eric Toomey was far more than a leisure killer with luck on his side. He had been trained for combat, which taught him how to better murder people from a distance and close up.

Terry had run a criminal background and firearms check on Toomey that morning. He had no criminal background, and no record of gun ownership, which worried the investigator. If Toomey inherited his uncle's guns, or received them through other means, they would be impossible to trace if and when Toomey discarded them.

"Okay," Terry said. "We know who he is, and who his next victim may very well be."

"We do?" Murphy asked skeptically.

"We just got new information about Frank Wilson's former neighbor, who might possibly be targeted."

"All's I need is a name and we'll find him."

"Steve Lancaster," Megan answered, waving a freshly-faxed property tax form.

"We'll get right on it."

Murphy retreated to the community center's warmer interior, opening his cell phone as he did so.

"Can it be this easy?" Megan dared ask Terry.

"Probably not. Now, more than ever, I'm worried that Toomey is one step ahead of us."

"I still don't understand why he kills innocent people, instead of just waiting for his intended victims."

"That's something I don't know. If he went into the military simply for training in extermination, it only fueled his confidence and resolve to carry out his plan."

"What's at the end for him? I mean, what kind of life does he lead when he's killed the last of the neighbors?"

Terry peered across the street at the antique stores and groups of shoppers milling about, any of which might be targets for Eric Toomey in the correct situation. Several Halloween decorations flapped in the wind, reminding him of the minor holiday he was about to miss with his family.

"Assuming we're right that he's going after the neighbors, he hides away. But if he has a taste for this sort of thing, and money saved back, we may be tracking his murders for a long time."

Wondering if Steve Lancaster might be their solution to finding Toomey, Terry looked inside at the task force members. He felt confident they were getting close, but not so much that more blood wouldn't be shed.

CHAPTER 33

▼

Hardegen followed his son around the town of Clarence, where his parents lived, occasionally carrying him. Dusk came around suppertime during the late New York fall, despite daylight savings.

The deputy's first real night home felt wasted. He wanted to spend time with Jamie and the kids instead of driving and walking around town.

Already exhausted from the past two days, he didn't plan on spending much time trick-or-treating with two young children.

Emma Lynn protested at the thought of being in costume until she saw herself in the mirror. Her ladybug disguise covered everything except her face, and she entertained herself by playing with the two pipe-cleaner antennas above her head.

"You okay?" Jamie asked him between houses as Brock ran ahead.

He had quickly learned how to knock on doors and spout something that sounded like "trick-or-treat" on his own.

"It's nothing," Hardegen answered. "We're just so close to finding the guy who committed those murders. I know we're missing something simple."

"Is that all you ever think about is work?"

"Sorry."

Rushing up to the next house so the residents didn't think Brock was abandoned, Hardegen arrived just in time to hear his son's attempt to ask for candy.

"Isn't he a darling?" a lady with permed gray hair asked.

Hardegen placed her about a decade past retirement age, then chastised himself for analyzing every stranger he encountered.

Because Terry had figured out the killer's identity and possible next move, the deputy wondered how much longer his services were going to be required on the task force. He found it surprising that Toomey stayed close to his original home, choosing his locations to fit the task at hand.

Jamie nudged him, bringing him back to the present as Brock received a few pieces of candy in his plastic bag.

"Can you carry her for a while?" she asked, handing him Emma Lynn, whom he readily accepted.

As they walked from house to house, Hardegen noticed kids too old to be asking for candy just ahead of them. He wished people raised their kids with more common sense, remembering he gave up trick-or-treating well before high school.

He spied broken eggs along the sidewalk, then looked up to see a vacant parking lot a few blocks away. A factory had closed there several years earlier, but a few single bulbs remained lit inside the place. Rumors of a potential buyer, or imminent destruction of the large building circulated throughout the town, but no one ever provided evidence either way.

Emma Lynn made a low moan beside his ear, but Hardegen drowned it out like conversations in a restaurant, his thoughts condemning him for not thinking of a particular hiding place earlier.

South of Alden was an old factory that had closed years prior, probably during Hardegen's college years. He recalled it running during his childhood, though it now sat much like the factory down the street with minimal power.

At night a few light bulbs illuminated the graveyard of unrealized dreams outside of Alden. A small village built up around the factory remained a fixture behind layers of mesh wire fence.

An hour later, after bedtime stories and lights out, Hardegen stepped onto his porch, calling Gaffney at home. Not that the sheriff was likely to be upset with him, but Hardegen felt he had a reasonable excuse for calling.

"Hello," he heard a familiar voice on the other end after two rings.

"Sheriff, it's John. I need some information, and I can't think of anyone better to ask."

"Happy Halloween, John."

"Happy Halloween, sir."

Gaffney chuckled, obviously not upset by the call. Hardegen envisioned it taking the sheriff away from candy-giving duties for a few minutes.

"What do you need?"

"That old factory just east of Alden. What can you tell me about it?"

"The one on Sawmill Road?"

"Yeah. That one."

"It's been everything from a lumberyard to a lid and top producer for canning companies. It closed about fifteen years ago when the owners relocated their operation to Indiana. I think they got bought out."

"It still has lights on the property, and a big ass fence all around it. Why wasn't it ever torn down?"

"Well, some people had grand plans to officially create a village called New Alden, but that fell through when the company moved. They had some stores and restaurants in there as I recall. All of it's probably still there. I'm not sure who owns it these days, or why they haven't done *something* with it."

"That's kind of what I was thinking. I haven't checked it out yet, and I can't believe I forgot about it."

"Don't kick yourself too hard. Take someone with you and check it out in the morning. Hell, I'll go if you want."

"That's okay, sir. Levine and Lamoureux have been keeping me company, but thanks."

Hardegen looked at the woods behind his house, missing the summer nights when fireflies blinked intermittently like green warning flashers. Crickets chirped while the smell of grilled meat lingered across the porch for hours.

"Anything else?" Gaffney asked.

"Yeah. Why hasn't someone tried to buy the property?"

"It was a big EPA stink. Someone tried to purchase it, but the EPA came in and said all of the buildings were contaminated with fuels and bacteria. Would probably cost more to tear it down or clean it up than to start fresh."

"Typical. Leave the mess behind for everyone else to deal with."

"Hey, they *did* fence it off," Gaffney said, showing his seldom seen lighter side.

"How kind of them. Thanks very much, sir. I'll see what's out there in the morning."

"Good luck, and be careful."

"Will do."

Closing his phone, Hardegen looked through the window, finding Jamie staring back at him with a look he couldn't quite read. He stepped inside, pulling her into an embrace before she found time to resist, letting his hands lock around her waistline.

"How can I make things up to you?" he asked.

"Dinner and a movie for starters."

"You're letting me off cheap. Any *services* I can do for you?"

"Well," she said, placing her forefinger along his lips, "there is one thing I can think of, but it's too cold outside, and we got caught in the living room the last time."

"Oh," Hardegen said with realization. "*That*. Well, I think there's a vacant room over yonder."

Jamie smiled, giving him a long kiss.

"Let's go find out."

CHAPTER 34

▼

Only one new development presented itself the next morning at the task force meeting. The FBI technician informed Murphy that the tire came from a 1985 Scout International Tracker II.

"How could he possibly know that?" Hardegen asked in awe, knowing the state labs had no way of matching a tire tread to a particular make or model, since numerous vehicles typically used the same tire sizes.

"He got lucky, and he knew where to look," Murphy answered. "He's a pack-rat, and a case he had about eighteen years ago dealt with the same exact tire tread. This pattern is from an *original* tire off a Scout."

"That's impossible."

"Improbable, but not impossible. That's what he told me."

"So we're now looking for a Tracker instead of a Jeep."

"They look very much alike," Lamoureux interjected, standing beside Megan. "The custodian told Terry he thought it was a Jeep, which is close, but the important thing is we now have a full description of the vehicle."

"Everything except the plate," Terry thought aloud. "Strange that he never registered it, but he probably thought of that, too."

Lamoureux drew close to him.

"I think my buddy, who's a very good profiler by the way, already deduced that this guy is very intelligent and plans ahead."

Terry smirked, though he wasn't going to let himself off the hook as easily as Lamoureux might.

"Your buddy has a lot of mistakes to atone for. He's going to start by trying to find Steve Lancaster."

Thanks to the Bureau's resources, they knew the man's address, phone number, hobbies, friends, and haunts, but not his current location. He had recently switched trucking jobs, and they had yet to determine his new employer because none of his friends knew the company.

"Well, if you see him, tell him to stop referring to himself in the third person," Lamoureux said. "John and I are going to check on some new hiding places."

"You two forming a bond? I'm jealous."

Lamoureux appeared amused, cautiously forming his next words.

"You're still my favorite."

"But I didn't play football at Syracuse," Terry said just above a whisper, "so I know that's a lie."

"Hey, who was your best man?"

"You were, Stephen," Terry answered, paraphrasing a quote from a particular movie they watched a few nights before the wedding.

"That's right, little brother," Lamoureux said, continuing the playful banter with the appropriate quote that followed the first.

Megan approached them after speaking with Gaffney a moment.

"Seems John has quite a location picked out for you," she informed Lamoureux.

"Oh?"

"All the kids think it's a spook town these days. They dare each other to climb over the fence and go inside the factory."

"Then I guess we'll answer some of their burning questions, won't we?"

Terry looked around at people seeking a purpose. Every newspaper across the state, and possibly the nation, had released the photograph of Eric Toomey. Soon, they would scramble to scoop one another when Gaffney released the vehicle description. If Toomey ventured into public, Terry felt confident some concerned citizen would take notice.

"We've got our own errands to run," he told his friend, nodding toward Megan. "Ready to roll?"

"As I'll ever be."

"I'll let you guys know how the haunted village turns out," Lamoureux said.

"We'll be waiting with baited breath," Megan said as she and Terry walked out the door.

"Yeah. Me too."

*   *   *   *

Luckily Hardegen kept his car stocked with essential tools at all times, or the search of the abandoned village might never have begun.

Lamoureux hadn't been very talkative since the meeting ended, or the least bit friendly. The deputy wondered if the man was upset with Terry, or the investigation in general. Evidence of their preexisting friendship hadn't been openly apparent during any portion of the task force meetings.

Perhaps Terry wasn't tolerant of his friend's actions.

Or maybe time had worn away the bonds formed during their partnership like weathered fenceposts ready to snap during the next big thunderstorm.

Pulling a bolt cutter from the trunk, Hardegen stared at his temporary colleague until Lamoureux returned his gaze.

"What?"

"I'm wondering if your head is in this or not."

"I'm in."

Hardegen said nothing, simply staring.

"Seriously. I'm in."

"Ready to do an illegal search?"

Lamoureux grinned for the first time in an hour.

"It's only illegal if someone finds out about it. Besides, we're the good guys, remember?"

Hardegen stared at the fledgling town left for dead behind the mesh wire fence. Potential trespassers might consider the barbed strand lining the top a mere nuisance, with little chance of them being discovered in the remote area.

"Something tells me no one's going to tell on us."

He walked with the bolt cutters toward the front gate as a thought occurred to him. Veering off to his left, Hardegen stared at the fence, though parts of it were covered or partially obscured by bushes and vines.

"What are you doing?" Lamoureux questioned.

"Following a hunch."

Fencing completely surrounded the factory and the remains of the small town. Hardegen guessed the enclosed area to be at least a square mile. It looked preserved, like an amusement park shut down for the off-season, ready to open up at a moment's notice.

From a distance, it simply teased Hardegen to come in for a closer look. He itched for an opportunity to see everything up close, but his instincts told him to think before acting.

Looking through the fence, he saw the factory looming in the distance. Several trees shaded its roof, partially blocking his view. He glanced in the other direction, seeing a small school, a church, and several general stores.

"What are you looking for, John?"

"They really had this place up and going, didn't they?"

"No. It wasn't even a thought in anyone's mind when they started it. Couldn't even get a gas station out here because it was too far from the highway."

"Someone had it in mind," Hardegen said, pointing toward a covered vehicle beside one of the vacant stores.

Lamoureux squinted, anxiously looking through the fence toward the old faded tarp. The several rips in the synthetic material failed to provide details about what the tarp covered.

"Looks like a compact car," he finally stated. "*Not* a Scout."

Unaffected by the words, Hardegen continued to walk until he found a separation between two sections of fence that looked accelerated by human intervention.

"Someone's been here before."

"Like Megan said, it's a dare thing with kids. Besides, if Toomey was staying here, he'd have to find somewhere to park the Scout."

"You sound like you're wanting to back out without checking."

"Hardly," Lamoureux said defensively. "This is an ideal place to hide out. Utilities, roominess, your own hardware store around the corner."

"Funny."

Hardegen slipped through the opening with Lamoureux in tow. His eyes immediately surveyed the area for anyone watching them. Even if Toomey hadn't chosen to hide in an abandoned town, that didn't mean others hadn't considered it for shelter.

Seeing no pairs of eyes staring back from any windows, or around any corners, he walked a straight line until he reached the back of a nearby building. He moved with the same anticipation he might when approaching a potentially dangerous scenario like drug busts.

"Want to split up and cover more ground?"

Lamoureux shrugged.

"Sure. I'll cover the factory and school if you want to check the ghost town."

Hardegen nodded.

"I'll meet you at the school when I'm done."

He moved to his right, finding a makeshift alley that led him to the old retail stores lining the main street. Strangely, Main Street was the only named through-way in the deserted town, aside from Sawmill Road, which became an afterthought when one reached the town limits.

Standing in the center of the street with shops on either side of him, as though living out some kind of western high noon showdown, Hardegen looked to his left, then to his right. To his right, a clothing shop with mannequins dressed incredibly out of style struck poses behind a dingy display window.

A "CLOSED" sign remained hanging on the other side of the door, but only a few empty racks remained as evidence that the store ever truly existed. Hardegen wondered if the residents thought they might be coming back, leaving certain expendable items behind.

To his left, the deputy found an old drug store. Faded candy wrappers, still clinging to their chocolate hosts, adorned the window beside the front door. Several other small items sat nearby, never having found the opportunity to live with a family, or find peace inside a landfill when their purpose reached an end.

Weaving between the buildings, Hardegen checked fronts and backs, along with every side. He found no broken windows or doors in the first four buildings, surprising him very much. Vandalism was common in abandoned buildings, though typically by drug addicts and the homeless. Rural proximity likely kept the area free of people who didn't have adequate transportation.

Hardegen found damage to the building nearest the school. A small white church's fairly common billboard reported that Pastor Tim Michaels offered Saturday evening and Sunday morning services. His eyes glanced over the magnetic white letters atop the faded black sign, which all rested beneath a cracked glass casing.

For some reason, the church sustained more visible damage than the other buildings. Not only had it begun deteriorating on the outside, but several windows were cracked or smashed. Wondering if someone might have sought shelter inside, Hardegen peered through a few of the windows.

Finding nothing, he returned to the street, staying on one side to avoid detection in case anyone else had trespassed.

Once he neared the school a moment later, he stared at the partially collapsed brick structure, wondering why one side had fallen in upon itself. A placard brick placed within the exterior walls revealed a 1913 construction date, meaning the building had likely served several purposes before becoming a school within the doomed community.

Birds flocked atop a steeple, which might have housed a bell at one time. The steeple's point, made of wood, appeared cracked and broken in some areas. Wooden boarding planks in the windows had long since fallen prey to severe weather, or been torn out. Trees and shrubs had grown outside the main entrance, as though to deny more meanspirited individuals ready access to the helpless building.

Hardegen studied the building as he walked around it, spying a different covered vehicle in the distance.

A vehicle large enough to be a Scout remained under a militaristic canvas covering, flapping as the wind caught its edges. Though momentarily stunned, Hardegen regained his composure enough to walk toward the vehicle, carefully placing his hand atop the firearm holstered at his side.

CHAPTER 35

▼

Toomey started his day by planning the final phase of his revenge against the people who aided and abetted in Kyle's murder.

Living in an abandoned town had certain advantages, but receiving news from the outside world was not one of them. When he went into public places, which happened every day or two, he bought a newspaper or watched the news at a coffee shop. He planned on making a trip by early afternoon, mainly to use a disposable cell phone to make a very important call.

As a child, Toomey passed the unofficial village of New Alden several times on trips to small towns or farmers markets with his uncle or foster families. He always wondered why the village looked like such a lonely place, barricaded like a military facility out of the movies.

He never understood why the grounds were left for dead until he researched it during his teenage years. Because it remained standing while he was away in the military, and he didn't fear the EPA's findings, he decided to make it a base of operations for his current mission.

Buying the Scout was a bargain for five-hundred dollars, and stealing current plates lessened the chance authorities would pull him over. Careful scraping and chemical solvents allowed him to steal valid registration and inspection stickers from the same vehicle, virtually ensuring his safety from eager young officers.

Years of planning had brought him this far, but he had no real plan beyond exacting revenge against the last man who knew of Kyle's abuse.

After waking early, as usual, he rolled his sleeping bag and tied it off before sliding it under the teacher's desk. He usually slept in the one room on the second story that remained intact for a full view of the grounds, and to hear anyone trying to sneak in downstairs.

All of his money remained with him upstairs, as well as his weaponry and paperwork. One box contained most everything he needed in case a quick escape became necessary.

Living alone provided him time to read and study, mostly from mercenary and military magazines. He knew little else aside from misery and death.

Bird calls and chirps filled the school all morning long until the noise suddenly ceased. Toomey opened the door to the adjoining room, looking across what little bit remained of the classroom's floor. Jaggedly broken in a diagonal pattern, the partial floor contained traces of bird shit everywhere, but no birds perched atop the remaining exterior bricks as usual.

His attention turned to the ground below, causing him to stiffen as he realized his sanctuary had been breeched.

At the front gate sat a dark sedan which looked to be standard police issue. Looking frantically around him to the ground below, Toomey saw a man dressed in plain clothes, but packing a firearm, scouring the grounds near the old stores.

Only seconds later, he heard the sound of the downstairs door closing as someone entered the one place he called home. Whether they knew it or not, they were trespassing, and Toomey knew all about how to punish trespassers.

Silently crossing the old floor, he grabbed his survival knife from his old canvas pack, mentally debating how he wanted to handle the situation. He considered collapsing the old floor atop the intruder, but decided it might take too long, or create too much noise. If it worked, it might pass as an accident, if not for the second officer lurking outside.

No, he decided, if they came looking he would deal with them individually.

The first kill had to be silent in order to provide him enough time to formulate the secondary plan.

As he heard the unseen officer ascending the stairs, drawing closer to him, Toomey disliked the idea of murdering a cop. They were only doing their job, but more importantly, he didn't want a statewide manhunt on his heels while he tried to carry out his plan.

Despite his lack of planning a life after the plan, Toomey didn't envision himself getting caught, and certainly not this soon. Had they accidentally stumbled onto the site? Had someone followed him, or tipped off the cops?

All kinds of possibilities passed through his mind as he held the knife close to him, posting himself against the wall adjacent to the door. Feeling the pressure of his sheathed smaller knife against his right side, Toomey changed his mind at the last minute.

Knowing that hiding was an impossibility, he waited for the door to open as he held his breath. His hiding place would be compromised the moment the cop stepped inside and looked around the corner, so he tossed the survival knife toward the corner closest to the door as it began opening.

Guessing correctly, the noise distracted the investigator long enough for Toomey to silently draw behind him. In a rehearsed motion, Toomey clasped the man's mouth to muffle his cries, wasting less than a second before thrusting the knife into the center of his back. A stifled moan escaped the man as the knife lodged partway into his back, then stuck on cartilage or bone.

As the investigator grasped for the firearm at his side, Toomey lifted a knee to prevent an easy grab, then snagged the nearby rifle he used on the hunters. In one swift motion, he raked the butt across the injured cop's skull, sending him to the ground in a heap.

Assured the man was at least unconscious, Toomey quickly removed the investigator's firearm from its holster.

He tossed it into the box of items essential to his plan. Taking up the box, he gave the room one last look around for any missed items. With his home compromised, he could never return, because other officers were sure to swarm the area by the day's end.

Toomey searched the fallen officer for car keys, finding none. He liked the idea of having an unmarked car, particularly for the next phase of his plan. The Scout had outlived its usefulness, destined to eventually die within the ruins of New Alden either way.

While he hated to leave any evidence behind, Toomey knew his own preservation overtook all other priorities at the moment.

"Grant?" he heard a voice from downstairs call as the door opened.

Setting the box down, Toomey quickly dragged the first cop out of the way, knowing the sound was sure to carry downstairs. As he expected, the plain clothes officer began climbing the stairs.

"You find dirty magazines up there?" he called as his footsteps clomped against the old wooden stairs.

Toomey growled to himself at the words, searching for a new weapon to use against the second visitor, since the small knife remained planted in the first officer's back. The survival knife sat uselessly in the corner. With the door open, Toomey would expose himself if he tried to retrieve it, and he knew the plain clothes officer had a gun.

Quickly finding a useful item under the desk, Toomey scooped up an old iron skillet, hiding beside the door once again. When the plain clothes officer stepped through the door, his eyes were immediately drawn to his fallen comrade.

"Grant?"

Without bothering to check the area, the man knelt beside the investigator, allowing Toomey to clock him in the back of the skull with the frying pan.

Landing with a thud beside his friend, he no longer presented a threat to Toomey, who struggled to decide his next move. Searching the second man for car keys, he found some, pocketing them immediately.

He debated what to do with the two prone officers, ultimately deciding neither had seen his face. That fact alone did not provide Toomey any kind of sanctuary from police scrutiny, or ultimately, his arrest, but might keep them from unleashing all of their figurative dogs upon him.

Within a few minutes, he packed his box with absolutely everything he needed and decided exactly what needed to be done in his best interest.

And the interest of his plan.

CHAPTER 36

▼

When Hardegen awoke he had no idea of the time, and not just because his head was throbbing from the unseen attack.

Pushing himself up to a crawling position, he found Lamoureux, knife still in his back, then scrambled over to him. He tried to avoid moving the investigator while he checked for a pulse, finding a weak heartbeat as he noticed the man's back moving up and down slowly from his shallow breaths.

Blood had begun to pool around the knife, but not as much as Hardegen might have figured. He knew better than to remove the blade, deciding he needed to call for assistance immediately.

Feeling for his cell phone at his side, he couldn't find it, so he frantically searched the area, finding it smashed against the large desk near the front of the classroom. His wallet's contents were strewn across the floor, his license missing from the stack, instantly sending warning alarms through his mind.

"Jamie."

Torn between the thought of a murderer stalking his wife, or worse, or saving Lamoureux, a valued colleague, Hardegen looked around to assess his situation. He had no gun, Lamoureux had no gun or cell phone, and Toomey was long gone.

Finding the covered Scout outside left the deputy no doubt Toomey had holed up there for an extended time. His words entering the house, and coming up the stairs, were a test to see if Lamoureux had beaten him there, or encountered foul play.

His answer came too late.

Knowing he needed to find a phone or a radio quickly, he found an old shirt in the opposite corner, carefully placed it around Lamoureux's knife wound, then darted down the stairs. Flinging open the door, he ran around a building blocking his view of the front gate, then felt complete dismay when he found his car gone.

"Damn it."

Clenching his fists, he scoured the grounds for anything useful. The Scout sat behind him, but without keys it did him little good. Without a phone, his radio gone with the car, and his family in potential danger, Hardegen needed means of communication immediately.

Like most state police investigators, Lamoureux carried a cell phone to contact fellow officers or his dispatchers because they didn't carry radios. Hardegen hadn't found the man's cell phone in the room, or clipped to his belt, causing him to believe Toomey took it or disposed of it elsewhere.

Returning upstairs to check on Lamoureux, and search one last time for the phone, Hardegen tossed the room hurriedly. Though he verified Lamoureux's phone was indeed gone, he found a set of keys inside one of the desk drawers. They looked as though they might possibly be a spare set, based on the generic key ring holding them.

He hoped Toomey had accidentally left his second set of keys for the Scout behind.

Checking one last time on Lamoureux, he heard the investigator groan painfully when touched near the wound.

"Hang in there, Grant. I'm getting help."

Hardegen ran so quickly from the building that he nearly stumbled several times. Within a minute he found himself inside the unlocked Scout, fumbling to get the key into the ignition.

If he remembered correctly, they had passed a convenience store about a mile away from the deserted town.

He turned the key, and after several seconds of struggle the Scout roared to life. Hardegen floored the gas pedal, smashing through the front gate without hesitation, irritated that Toomey had outsmarted two police officers and taken a head start across the county.

He feared for Lamoureux's life, but almost as much so for the safety of his own family. Finding the main road that led out of the compound, he stomped the gas even harder, almost hoping some county or state police officer might pull him over.

Luckily Toomey hadn't bothered to steal money or his credit cards, meaning he had sufficient funds to directly call his wife after dialing 911 for an ambulance.

Saying a silent prayer to himself, he hoped neither call proved too late to save lives.

*   *   *   *

Steve Lancaster, Jr. purchased a Pepsi, cigarettes, and a few snack cakes after fueling his semi on the way back to New York. Just north of Nashville, Tennessee, he stopped at one of the many fuel and shopping centers designed with truck drivers in mind.

Opting not to use their shower service, he wanted to make it home by the next morning at the latest. Traffic stops had been heavy through the Midwest lately, meaning he needed to keep his logbook accurate. Any discrepancies in his driving hours might result in stiff penalties for him and his employer.

Like his father, he decided to drive a truck on the open road instead of settling for a regular job.

Many of the good jobs had left the state, and Lancaster came from a blue collar background, unable or unwilling to learn any more about technology than necessary.

Only five years removed from high school, he had driven a truck the past two after passing the test for his CDL. His father coached him through the process and they talked frequently on the phone while on the road.

His father had divorced twice, moving to different counties both times. The senior Lancaster lived in a trailer park a few miles outside of Syracuse, while his son took up residence in a rural home a few miles away.

While he shared similarities with his father, such as occupation, choice in clothing, and some hobbies, Lancaster hadn't yet tried his hand at marriage. Because of his father's occupation, he spent more time with his mother growing up, though he found himself closer with his father. He understood the commitment and long hours his father's job demanded, but the man made time for him on weekends and days off.

Inheriting premature hair loss from one of his parents, Lancaster found his blond hair beginning to thin along the front. He had already grown his beard in anticipation of the cold winter months.

At the moment, Lancaster was on a return trip from Utah, carrying a load of power tools for a Home Depot warehouse. After the drop, he had two days before his next trip west. Sometimes he drove for weeks without a day off, so the break would be welcome. If his father was around, they might go hunting or fishing, and if not, he would treat himself to a nice dinner.

Home never felt like the right place to be for very long. Growing up, he seldom saw his father, but their time together meant a lot to him.

After paying for the fuel and sundries, Lancaster lit a cigarette while walking back to the truck, ready to hit the road. His cell phone rang at his side, but he waited until he was nearly to the truck before answering without looking at the number.

"Hello?"

"Mr. Lancaster?"

"Yeah," he replied gruffly, expecting some telemarketer to work him over for a sale.

"My name is Terry Levine. I'm an investigator with the New York State Police."

Lancaster had begun to reach up for his door handle, but stopped short, his arm falling limply to his side upon hearing the words.

What could possibly be wrong?

He wondered if something had happened to his father.

"I'm investigating a homicide. You might have information related to my case, if I could ask you a few questions."

"Sure," Lancaster said, curious to see what this investigator wanted.

"I understand your father used to live near the Wilsons?"

Suddenly Lancaster knew what homicide the investigator eluded to.

The man on the other end of the phone spoke very deliberately, almost as though he had to carefully craft his words before saying them. He spoke intelligently, but not with a natural flow that one might assume any police officer would craft after years of discussions.

"That's right," Lancaster said, taking a final drag from the cigarette before tossing it aside. "What does this have to do with me?"

"We're afraid you and your father might be in danger. I'd like to go over the details with you in person. Are you home at the moment?"

Lancaster looked around the area to see if anyone might be monitoring him. He suddenly felt worried that the person who murdered the Wilsons might think of him or his father as targets. The news had covered the story the past few days, but Lancaster ignored most of the segments after the first day.

"No. I'm in Tennessee, but I'll be home tonight or tomorrow morning."

"I'm going to give you my number. I'd appreciate a call as soon as you get in."

Fishing for a pen, the truck driver used his receipt to jot down the number and the trooper's name as it was read to him.

"What about my father?" he asked after writing down the information.

"We've been trying to reach him. If you get in touch with him, I'd gladly explain everything to both of you tomorrow."

"He's probably on the road. He just started with a new company."

"I understand."

Lancaster realized he wasn't being fed very much information. Whether that was for his own good, or the well-being of the investigation, remained unclear.

"Are we in serious danger, sir?" he decided to ask.

"Not necessarily, but we want to take every precaution. One of the other murder victims lived near the Wilsons around the same time as your father."

Lancaster also lived there, at least part of the time. He spent time with his mother as well, when his father went on the road, following their divorce.

"Who was it?" Lancaster asked, wishing he had paid more attention to the news.

"A postal worker named Bob Hagen."

"Oh, God."

The name certainly struck home. Hagen often visited his father, as well as the Wilsons. They sometimes went fishing and camping when the postal worker had weekends off. His father and Hagen spent summer nights drinking in the backyard, watching fireworks on the 4th of July, or staring at stars in the sky.

They talked for hours on end about the simplest things, but Lancaster learned at an early age he wanted to drive on the open road. As a child, he always thought the chrome rims of his father's truck looked as beautiful and exotic as the Ferris wheel at the state fair.

A moment passed without any exchange of words.

"Are you okay?" the trooper finally asked without much emotion attached.

"Sure. I'll, uh, call you tomorrow when I get back into town."

"I appreciate your time, Mr. Lancaster."

As he hung up the phone, Lancaster took one last look around before climbing into his truck and examining both the front seats and the sleeper. Finding nothing, he took a deep breath, setting his new purchases in the seat beside him before starting the truck.

He had a lot of road to cover, and lots of information and memories to keep his mind occupied until he reached New York.

Waiting until he had merged with traffic along Interstate 65, he opened his cell phone to call his father.

*   *   *   *

Hardegen discovered how terrible a loss of identity and authority truly affected people when he reached the convenience store. The combination of driving a ragtag vehicle, along with his missing driver's license and badge, caused the clerk to question him when he requested use of the store phone.

Deciding against an argument for the sake of time, Hardegen stepped outside to use the payphone, first calling 911 with a free call to report the incident at New Alden. Though he told the dispatcher who he was, the woman on the other end of the line didn't seem to believe any part of his story.

Since the area had no local police department with a dispatch system, the call had gone through to his own dispatch center, but this woman's voice was unfamiliar.

He knew dispatchers dealt with pranks all the time, and to outwardly question a caller was a major taboo, but she was indirectly testing him to see if he was pranking her. The dispatcher had given him no indication she truly believed his story, leaving him to feel she was going through the motions, possibly as a new hire.

"Hard again?" she asked.

"No. Hardegen. Like it sounds. This isn't a joke. I'm with Grant Lamoureux of the New York State Police. Officer down, *he's* down, at the old New Alden village with the gate around it. I need EMS started this way *now.*"

"I'm starting the medics right now. So you're not with the injured party?"

"No! He's a mile down the road. The suspect stole our phones, and our car, so I'm at a payphone outside Kreiger's Gas n' Go. I need county and state police started this way."

"Can you describe the suspect, or what he's driving?"

"Suspect is Eric Toomey. The task force in Buffalo has all the information about him. He's driving my unmarked brown Crown Vic, plate number CCB 5198 from Erie County."

He waited a few seconds, hearing typing on the other end. Hardegen didn't want to wait for his story to check out. After giving the plate number, he realized he should have provided his unit number immediately to avoid any delay. His mind functioned on a different plane when his colleagues and family were in peril.

Suddenly thinking how everyone, especially Terry, would blame him if Lamoureux died, Hardegen wished he had stopped Toomey, or at least been more cautious. After seeing the Scout, he should have called for backup, but wanted confirmation, and to remove Lamoureux from potential danger.

Confirmation seemed to have a way of biting him in the ass lately. Saving face wasn't as important as protecting lives, and regardless of how Lamoureux fared, he felt like a failure.

"The ambulance is about ten minutes out, but the county has a unit in the area," the dispatcher finally said.

"I'll meet them at the gates over there," he said before hanging up, not giving the dispatcher a chance to interrogate him further.

He picked up the receiver once more, prepared to call Jamie, but slammed it down on the hook. She was at work, with the kids safely at his mother's house for the day. Unlike Lamoureux, her life wasn't in immediate danger, so he climbed into the Scout, ready to salvage any part of his workday he could.

A few minutes later he pulled up to the front gate of the abandoned town, quickly searching the old utility vehicle for anything that might break the gate loose. When he drove through the gate, the Scout knocked it over instead of breaking it open, leaving it awkwardly leaned away from the property with a few hinges still attached. Now it forbid him reentry until he cut the center lock, or the remaining hinges.

One of his fellow county officers pulled up before he could locate anything better than a crescent wrench.

"I've got an officer down in there, Neil," he told the man who looked bewildered at the sight before him. "You got any bolt cutters?"

"I think so," Neil Cuthbert answered, popping his trunk with the keyless remote.

It took the two officers less than a minute to snap the old padlock and move the gates aside for the incoming ambulances and police officers.

"The ambulance is on the way," Hardegen told his fellow officer. "Can you get the cars out of the way so they have a clear shot?"

Cuthbert nodded, allowing Hardegen to dash toward the old school. He sprinted up the stairs, questioning how carefully the medics would need to transport Lamoureux. The jagged walls and floors were anything but accommodating for treatment of a patient, particularly if they needed to carry him down the stairs atop a bulky cot.

As he found Lamoureux lying face down in the same position a wave of guilt swept over the deputy. He hated leaving the trooper alone for any length of time, but Toomey had ensured the necessity of his actions.

"Hang in there, Grant," he said, feeling for a pulse along his neck.

It took a moment, gravely concerning Hardegen, but he found a weak, occasional thump through the artery.

The small pool of blood surrounding the wound hadn't grown much, meaning Lamoureux had internal bleeding. Hardegen heard the wailing of sirens in the distance, praying one of them was the ambulance. He heard someone clamber up the stairs behind him, then stop suddenly at the threshold.

"Holy shit," Cuthbert said, kneeling down beside Hardegen. "What happened?"

No words could explain what occurred, and Hardegen knew questions, accusations, and paperwork beyond his comprehension were coming his way.

Over Cuthbert's radio he heard his department's helicopter was already in the air, responding to the officer down call. An ambulance would likely run Lamoureux to the nearest accessible clearing, then the chopper could fly him to ECMC's trauma unit.

Hardegen remained silent, simply hanging his head as he waited for fate to reveal its hand.

CHAPTER 37

▼

Word of Lamoureux's condition soon reached members of the task force, bringing about mixed feelings of grief for the fallen investigator and a subdued joy that came with knowing Toomey would soon be caught.

Stealing a police officer's car was a bold move, and one that made the job of patrol officers much easier. Gaffney's office provided exact information about the vehicle, including the vehicle identification number, in case Toomey switched the plates.

Unfortunately, Hardegen's car was unmarked in every way. The only emergency flasher lights were built in with the headlights and taillights, meaning it didn't stand out as a police car.

Terry had just returned with Megan from a few minor interviews when the news reached the community building, where Gaffney received the call. Though flushed red from anger and frustration, the sheriff relayed the information to Terry who remained stunned at the news. He felt the color drain from his own face before bolting from the building faster than a kid facing punishment for being late to school.

When he bullied his way past the emergency room personnel at the ECMC, drawing the attention of security officers, Hardegen provided an intervention.

"How is he?" Terry asked first and foremost.

"He's in surgery," Hardegen replied. "He's been in there for twenty minutes. They haven't said anything yet."

Terry looked down the hallway as though he might be able to catch a glimpse of the surgery, but he had no idea where to look, or if he even stood on the correct floor. Often waiting rooms were spaced far enough from the surgical ward to keep friends and family from getting too curious.

"How could this happen?" Terry posed a question that he didn't really want answered.

His friend had to be equally responsible in whatever terrible thing happened on those grounds if he was stabbed in the back. He didn't want to think of Lamoureux as careless or negligent in any capacity, but truth be told, the man had changed.

Hardegen explained the situation to Terry with fair attention to the details.

"Why didn't you call for backup the second you found that Scout?" Terry inquired more skeptically than he might when interrogating a murder suspect.

"My radio was in the car. My main concern was for Grant, so I went into the school to meet with him as we'd arranged. I should have called him, but I didn't want him distracted, or Toomey getting any kind of warning signal."

Terry understood the situation, wishing he'd been there. Searching the grounds was as routine as the dozens of houses he and Hardegen had explored, but they had never split up to the point that either was out of eyeshot for more than a second or two.

"If the road officers don't find him, I will," Terry said, speaking of Toomey. "He'd better hope it doesn't come to that."

Stepping away from Hardegen a moment, he spotted Deanna Evans down the hall with tears readily flowing down her cheeks. Caught in a moment of weakness, she thought about turning away from him, but decided ultimately to approach him. His suspicions that Lamoureux and the medical examiner had more than business ties had just been confirmed.

Obviously a *lot* more than the business of death went on between them.

"Why him?" she asked hesitantly, keeping just a short distance between them, openly more vulnerable than she cared for her hospital colleagues to see.

Terry pulled her into a careful embrace for support, and to keep wandering eyes from fixing upon her.

"I don't know," he said. "But I'm hoping the man who did this winds up on one of your slabs."

Before long, members of the task force filed into the waiting room, anxious to hear any news about Lamoureux. Several people Terry didn't recognize joined them, and once Gaffney showed up, he ushered many of the people out of the area who worked under him. He eyed Deanna, then Terry, as though asking if she belonged there.

"They're pretty close," Terry said as he leaned over to Gaffney, who nodded in understanding.

He seemed to comprehend the entire story without being told. Gaffney had seen more in his years on the state police than most officers see in a lifetime. Working as a road officer, investigator, and now an elected official, he understood the intricacies of human relationships from every aspect.

Nearly three hours passed before anyone emerged from the operating room. One of the doctors who had been assisting on the operation stepped out to speak with them after washing her hands and removing the outer portion of her surgical gowns.

Everyone anxiously stood up to hear.

"Grant pulled through the operation just fine," she reported. "He had some internal bleeding, which we managed to stop rather quickly."

So far, everyone felt optimistic about the news, but the doctor's look changed like sunny skies to dark gray clouds threatening dire storms.

"However," she said slowly, "there is a possibility of nerve damage along his spine."

Terry turned away, immediately knowing the ramifications of such an injury. Though thankful Lamoureux had survived the surgery, a terrible image of his friend confined to a wheelchair entered his mind.

"Is there still any danger?" he heard Gaffney ask.

"He's stable," the doctor answered. "They're finishing up right now."

"When can we see him?" Terry turned around to inquire.

"Only family members will be allowed to see him. He may not awaken until late tonight or sometime tomorrow."

Gaffney didn't appear pleased about family members only seeing Lamoureux. Terry suspected the sheriff would have some pull if they wanted to check on the investigator in person. He assumed Lamoureux's parents were still alive, and he had a sister, though Terry couldn't place her name.

Frustration had blocked certain brain functions, irritating him to no end. He wanted closure for his friend, but the lack of news from patrol officers had him worried.

Toomey somehow remained ahead of the law, even after being flushed from his hiding place. Intelligent and trained for all kinds of combat, he had proven his willingness to attack police officers. The realization that Toomey now had a head start on the next phase of his plan weighed heavily in Terry's mind.

"Are you going to be okay?" he asked Deanna, taking her hand between both of his.

"I'm a lot better now."

He couldn't imagine the harrowing thought of her finding Lamoureux's body inside her morgue freezer until a funeral home came for his body.

Gaffney seemed determined to stay until further news came his way.

"The press is going to want some information, Paul."

"Fuck them," he said, leading Terry away from the slowly dispersing group. "I take it you have somewhere else you want to be."

"I might not know where he is, but I know where he's going."

"You want me to organize surveillance teams?"

"Not yet. I need to find Lancaster before we start protecting him."

"Let me know when you're ready. I'll authorize whatever manpower you need."

Terry nodded.

"I'm going to give Murphy a shout and see if he found more contact information for our newfound bait."

"I'd appreciate a call if you find anything new."

"Will do."

Terry left the hospital with a numb feeling that came with the loss of someone important. He hadn't lost his good friend, not yet anyway, but he feared for Lamoureux's future. Being wheelchair bound, on disability from the state, would cripple his friend in other ways. Lamoureux lived for his job, the one thing he had left to care about aside from his kids.

About to call Murphy, he spied Hardegen stepping out of the hospital looking rather distraught over the day's events.

While everyone waited for news about Lamoureux, Gaffney ordered his deputy to undergo precautionary X-rays and tests. After Hardegen was given a clean bill of health, he was taken to a room and interrogated for the better part of three hours by state police and Gaffney, likely adding to his headache. Losing one's firearm and badge was bad, but letting another officer get injured or killed sometimes ended careers.

Terry turned around, deciding to approach the deputy, partly out of guilt, but also because he didn't feel like taking on his next task alone. He planned on calling Murphy, checking Steve Lancaster's address through local authorities to see if the man was home, and going through Eric Toomey's last known address personally.

He planned to put out an ATL (attempt to locate) on Lancaster, even before heading out to the man's home. In essence, the alert would say Lancaster was a possible serial killer target, or might have information regarding a serial killer. Anyone locating the man was to call NYSP immediately.

"Feel like going for a ride?" he asked Hardegen.

"You driving? I seem to have lost my wheels, along with my pride."

Terry didn't feel like entertaining humor or self-pity, though he suspected Hardegen was going to feel the wrath of his colleagues, Lamoureux's family, and the media very soon.

"Come on, John."

✳   ✳   ✳   ✳

Following Gaffney's orders, Hardegen asked Terry to stop by the Erie County offices where he was issued a new firearm. He also took his old badge from his locker so he had some form of identification with him. Technically, the deputy needed to qualify with the new gun at a firing range, but Gaffney said it could wait until they returned.

While Terry drove toward the scene, Schmidt called to inform him two boys confessed to the tombstone desecration. Apparently it took intellectual persuasion from the chief to obtain their confessions, but the parents had already agreed to pay for the damages. While the parents saved themselves embarrassment, and worse consequences for their boys, Terry hoped they demanded restitutions from the students so the boys learned something.

When Terry pulled up to the New Alden gates, Hardegen stared at the grounds as though they somehow haunted and captivated him simultaneously.

"This is a lot different," he said, staring at the vehicles and lights invading the small village like fire ants finding a new host area to overthrow.

Steve Nelson and his forensics team continued to comb through the area, where they had spent the better part of the three hours.

"Any news?" Nelson asked as he approached the two men, paying Terry more attention than Hardegen.

"Grant made it through surgery. They said he's stable."

"Good," Nelson said with relief. "We're picking up all kinds of prints and trace evidence, but nothing that definitively links Toomey to the murders. The DNA will probably be enough, but I'd feel better if he would have left us some firearms or some paperwork."

"Kind of a tease, isn't he?"

Terry looked around the area for the first time, seeing the decay that over a decade of negligence left behind. With so many buildings, he imagined Toomey felt safe inside his own barricaded compound.

"Can I see where he lived?" Terry asked the forensics expert.

"Sure," Nelson said, leading them toward the old school. "We found a concentration of personal belongings on the school's second level, or what's left of it."

"Anything juicy?"

"We were saving the reading material for you, since we're uneducated folk who just like tweezers and plastic bags."

Terry chuckled, which he could now do with his friend alive and recovering. "Lead on."

A few minutes later he found himself squatting inside the room Toomey called home. He found more magazines about combat and mercenary training, and a few knickknacks. Nothing he considered damning remained inside the small, dangerous living area.

He couldn't fathom living on a floor supported by three out of four brick walls and randomly fallen debris beneath the floor. One wooden support beam fell in such a way that it accidentally helped stabilize the second floor, but only loose bricks kept it from kicking outside the building completely.

Terry hated having only circumstantial evidence. Unless Lamoureux had seen Toomey's face, they had no concrete proof he perpetrated the attacks on the two officers.

No firearms or identification had been left behind, so Toomey had at least some idea of how the law and court system worked. In theory he had left his urine at the two crime scenes, which Terry hoped the lab could confirm with collected DNA from Toomey's lair. Nelson and his crew had several utensils and objects to fingerprint, and despite the harsh environment, Terry figured hair and fiber samples had to be present.

Toomey had been hurried, putting forth less effort when it came to cleaning up his messes.

Terry now suspected Toomey didn't mind eventually getting caught, never planned to get caught, or worse, wanted to carry out his plan and end his own life.

Dealing with suicidal people, much less proven killers, ranked as high on his list as being shot, which he had experienced once already.

"Can you find anything he might have jotted notes on?" he asked Nelson.

"You mean like writing that bled through to another surface?"

"Yeah. Anything that might indicate his next address or target."

"When you're done looking, I'll forward the stuff to our lab. The white coats can usually lift any writing samples pretty quick."

Terry began stacking the magazines together, thinking they might be the only possible surfaces where stiff writing might have left indentations.

"I need these processed doubly quick, Steve."

"I understand that, but arm-twisting from me doesn't always do the trick."

"Maybe our FBI friends can get some faster results."

"It's possible. I'll call the lab and see if they can put a rush on these. If not, talk to your boys in the Bureau."

Terry wanted to find one of the stolen family photographs amongst the remains, but Toomey probably watched over such keepsakes like a mother hawk over her young. He believed Toomey stole any photograph with Kyle Wilson in it, simply to remind himself of something good in his life.

Perhaps the Wilsons hadn't erased every memory of Frank's dead son after all.

Noticing Hardegen hadn't said one word since they entered the compound, Terry turned his attention to the deputy.

"You okay?"

"I'm coping. If I'd thought of this place sooner, or been more careful, none-"

"Don't put this on your shoulders," Terry interrupted him. "The point is you *did* think of it, and now Toomey's on the run."

Hardegen frowned.

"Lot of good that's done."

Terry scooped up the magazines, handing them over to Nelson for processing.

"It's not over yet," Terry said, directing his focus on the deputy. "No one feels worse for Grant than I do, but I'm not resting until we find Toomey. He's getting predictable, so we're going to stop him. Soon."

Saying nothing, the deputy turned away, milling around the room. Terry knew the man felt very much outside of the investigation from day one, now feeling worse than ever. While Terry had never worked much with drug task forces, he knew their kind was never satisfied waiting for things to happen. Cops like Hardegen created their own action, taking down the bad guys at their leisure. He wasn't happy when control slipped through his fingers as it had in this case.

While searching for more comforting words, Terry heard his phone ring. Seeing it was Megan, he stepped toward the edge of the safety zone, then answered.

"Good news, Megan?"

"Not exactly. I've been reading the psychological profile of our prime suspect, and he is definitely a piece of work."

Following up on the subpoenas Lamoureux requested before his injury, the group had been granted access to Toomey's full records, including those sealed by the court system.

"It seems his uncle wasn't the only one in the family with psychological issues," Megan said, the sound of flipping papers coming over the line. "Eric was diagnosed with schizophrenia by no less than three court psychologists."

Terry cursed under his breath, wondering how the military accepted him.

"He tended to imagine things that weren't real," Megan continued. "No imaginary friends that they knew of, or any voices in his mind, but he reported people and events that just weren't there, or didn't happen."

"What else?"

"They put him on medication, which seemed to help, until he stayed with his uncle."

"What happened?"

"His uncle typically refused to buy, or sometimes give Eric his medication. Those were the times when the boy struggled in school and had problems making friends."

Terry suspected several bad habits were passed on by Michael Toomey, one of which might have been neglecting medication. Perhaps the nephew's military discharge had something to do with the discovery of his past medical issues.

Since the records were likely sealed because Toomey was a minor, the military might never have known about his issues when he enlisted.

"So, basically what you're telling me is Toomey may be going after people he blames for a tormented childhood that may never have happened?" Terry asked of Megan.

"The doctors who examined him came up with similar findings. They felt his illness might have been hereditary."

At this point Terry had to believe anything might have happened on the Wilson farm years prior. It wasn't entirely inconceivable that Toomey killed his own best friend, then conjured up an alternate story in his mind.

"We have to assume anyone he came in contact with during his stay near the Wilson family might be in danger, Megan. Can you interview your couple and the neighbors again to compile a list of potential victims?"

"Sure. Are you still going to sit on Lancaster?"

"Yeah. He's still the best bet."

Terry's hypothesis felt sound because Lancaster was the only significant person who visited the Wilsons regularly left alive. His son of the same first and last name also lived near the Wilsons for a period of time, during his teenage years.

"I've got to go console a deputy, Megan."

"He still blaming himself?"

"Yeah. Your boss may be one of my best buddies, but he should have been more careful."

Megan gave no reply to the comment, remaining silent a moment.

"I'll let you know if I dig up anything new in Naples," she finally said.

"Okay."

Terry hung up, noticing Hardegen had left the second floor. He wondered what Toomey thought after subduing two police officers with minimal effort. Was his confidence soaring, possibly making him susceptible to capture? Or did he remain continually cautious and plotting?

"This guy must be a cool customer," Nelson noted as he returned to Terry's side.

"How's that?"

"He didn't leave us anything useful. Either he took his sweet time boxing up his goodies, or he had everything packed up and ready to go."

Considering Toomey stole a police car that had yet to be recovered, much less spotted, Terry believed he had at least one contingency plan in place before his hiding place was discovered.

He hated having to wait for Lancaster to return home, leaving Toomey the opportunity to find the man elsewhere first. The neighbors provided him with very little information, saying the little time the truck driver spent at home he usually kept to himself.

None of Megan's contacts had current, or useful, information about the man, making Terry's job extremely difficult, despite the FBI agents tracking him down quickly.

Murphy had begun looking into Lancaster's employment, attempting to discover his current trucking company. If they located his employer, tracking and contacting him would be child's play.

He was about to leave when Nelson spotted something pinned by the legs of a student desk in the far corner. Bending over to pick it up, the evidence technician studied the white receipt a moment.

"What is it?" Terry asked.

"If I had to guess, our guy bought a cell phone."

He handed the paper to Terry, who immediately discovered Toomey paid cash for what looked like a disposable cell phone. He sighed, thinking they had reached another roadblock. Then figurative sunlight peered through dissipating storm clouds.

The phone had been sold at a cellular phone specialty shop, and not a typical retailer or drugstore.

"Think they might have a phone number in their records?"

Nelson winced.

"Depends on the type of phone, but it's possible. Some can be recharged, and some are a one-time deal. Most of them don't have contracts or paperwork."

"But if it gets recharged, doesn't the buyer have to tell them the phone number to add the minutes to?"

"Usually. I'll have one of the guys check it out."

"Thanks."

Terry walked downstairs to find Hardegen seated on the front steps of the old church. He seemed sullen, leaving Terry with the option of removing him from the task force, or involving him more so he could forget his costly mistake.

"Penny for your thoughts."

"I've been thinking Gaffney was wrong for assigning me to the task force, and maybe that's true, but I'm done feeling sorry for myself."

Hardegen seemed to have found himself again within a day's time.

"I want to help you catch this guy, no matter what it takes."

"Good, but I think your wife is going to be pissed."

"Why?"

"Because we're going on a stakeout unless our FBI friends come up with new information."

CHAPTER 38

▼

When the younger Steve Lancaster made his way home the next morning, he pulled his big rig into the driveway of his county home. Most of the gravel in his driveway had disappeared over the course of the year, leaving a bumpy dirt surface behind.

If he planned on keeping the house long-term, he needed to pave at least part of the driveway to maintain the weight of his truck. For now, he parked it in a dry spot beside the driveway in case he needed to take his Ford pickup to meet the investigator who called him.

A few attempts to call his father ended in futility, because the man was apparently going through one of his phases where he charged his cell phone, forgetting to turn it on again.

Stepping down from the rig, he surveyed his house and property carefully, as he always did when he returned home. He glanced to the two-bay garage, then the rear door to his house, finding nothing disturbed. Pulling out his house keys, Lancaster started to unlock the door when he realized it wasn't locked.

Hesitantly turning the knob, he let the door swing inside, stepping back as he debated calling the police, or specifically Trooper Levine. The sounds of his own breathing thumped within his eardrums as he reached for his cell phone.

A noise from within his house changed his mind as he started toward the rig to retrieve his gun. He opened the door, reached under the seat, and tucked the gun and phone into his pants as he tried to decide his next move.

Absolutely infuriated that someone invaded his house, he wanted to exercise some vigilante justice if the person was still inside before calling the police.

Returning to the same door, he looked behind him at the garage's side entrance, noticing the entrance door's frame had sustained damage.

Exhaling heavily through his nose, he walked over to the door, pushed it inside, and found a car parked beside his truck that didn't belong, since he only owned one vehicle.

"What the fuck?" he asked himself.

What looked like an unmarked police car caught his attention, giving off a gleam when he turned on the overhead lights. Fighting the urge to investigate the car further, he pulled the gun from behind him, heading toward the house to find some answers.

If someone was inside, that person had to know Lancaster returned home from the sound of the rig. Either the intruder had dashed out the front door and down the road, or remained inside, hiding from the impending confrontation.

He pushed the door open, carefully peering inside before stepping in, holding the gun in a ready position like he often saw during cop shows. With an overcast morning sky behind him, Lancaster found it difficult to see inside his residence without any lights turned on.

Once fully inside, he closed the door behind him, standing perfectly still while he listened for movement. After a few seconds with no indications, he stepped forward to begin searching for an intruder.

Not once had he ever felt so uncomfortable inside his own house.

He stepped slowly, but the cowboy boots he often wore while driving made enough noise to echo throughout the house. A few curse words ran through his mind as he bent over awkwardly to take them off. The second boot caught on his foot, causing him to hop around momentarily as the gun dropped to the floor.

Picking it up quickly, he continued into the living room, finding everything in order, despite the dark surroundings. Furnished with a couch, chairs, and two end tables bought at flea markets or handed down from his father, the basic room provided no places to hide, except behind the couch.

He checked the room within seconds, moving into the kitchen. Seeing his home phone beside the refrigerator, Lancaster thought momentarily about calling the police for a direct 911 feed. Deciding against it, partly because it would take at least ten minutes for police to arrive, he moved through the kitchen into the secondary living room.

The home advertiser had called it a family room, but Lancaster didn't usually share the room with anyone. Stocked with more used furniture, his large television stayed in the room, ensuring he could rent movies while home for a few days instead of visiting a theater. His computer sat atop a prefabricated desk, still powered down.

When his eyes finally reached the front door, Lancaster noticed a vertical crack of light because the door wasn't quite closed tightly. With no damage around it, he quickly deduced someone had made a hasty exit.

"Shit."

He briskly walked to the kitchen, picked up the phone, and reached his free arm toward the mounted part of the phone to dial the number after setting the gun on the counter before him. His finger had just hit the '9' button when he felt a strong arm reach around his waistline, trapping one arm, as a cloth pressed against his nose and mouth.

Struggling and flailing immediately to get free, Lancaster knocked his gun to the floor after grazing it with two fingers. He then attempted to touch the last two digits of his urgent call, but the attacker batted his arm away.

By the time he realized the dire consequences of his situation, he neared unconsciousness. He felt himself fading, slumping to the floor as his eyes saw more and more black, like a cut scene in an old movie, fading into the next important sequence.

✳   ✳   ✳   ✳

A few miles outside of Syracuse, the Shady Acres mobile home park provided housing for predominantly older residents. Quiet and off the beaten path, the court contained nearly two-hundred units, sitting off a quiet county road.

Close enough to several towns to provide easy shopping and entertainment, the park provided isolation, along with peace and quiet due to the wooden fence surrounding the property, and the numerous tree groves outside and amongst the mobile homes.

Sitting in the passenger seat of Hardegen's car, Terry stared at Steve Lancaster's trailer, used but in good condition. Its white exterior mirrored many of the rented or purchased trailers around it, though his yard contained no ornaments or intentional shrubbery. Several trees loomed over the narrow rear of the trailer in the small corner section that contained six units.

Both men watched the trailer until early morning for signs of Lancaster returning, or Toomey stalking his next victim. Instead of heading back, Terry charged two nearby motel rooms to the state. Though Hardegen mentioned very little about it, Terry knew the man's wife wasn't pleased about the suddenness of the news he wasn't coming home.

Terry had phoned Gaffney, discovering Lamoureux drifted in and out of consciousness throughout the night and into the morning. He never remained conscious long enough talk about his condition, particularly if he had any use of his legs.

Lamoureux's kids had visited the hospital the day before, once their school day ended, but Terry didn't speak with them. They wouldn't have remembered him, and he didn't feel comfortable giving them a history lesson since he was a stranger in their eyes.

While waiting the night before, an idea struck Terry to call Murphy, so the agent could triangulate any calls the trucker made from his cell phone. Murphy reported they had yet to locate his cell phone provider, something fairly typical when dealing with the business world. They didn't always rush to aid law enforcement, or their information got tangled up between offices.

Terry turned futility into another idea as daylight finally entered the grove of trees surrounding Lancaster's area of the trailer park.

"How long are we going to wait?" Hardegen asked, though not impatiently. "These guys are sometimes gone for a week or better."

"We're not going to wait," Terry answered. "All of the neighbors but one are gone for the day. I'm going over to chat with her while you find a way inside Lancaster's trailer."

Hardegen rolled his eyes when the idea was spoken.

"Hey, we don't have to worry about civil rights, John. He's not under suspicion for anything, and we're trying to save his life."

Nodding reluctantly, Hardegen understood the need to do a technical wrong to accomplish a greater good.

Typically one to go by the book, Terry felt disgusted that he couldn't accurately profile someone for the first time in his career. Now one of his best friends remained bedridden because of his shortcomings, meaning he needed to do whatever it took to catch Toomey.

When they stepped out of the car, he pulled his identification from inside his sport coat, nodding toward Hardegen before heading to the neighboring mobile home. He knocked on the door several times, receiving no answer. His only reason for believing someone might be home was because a car remained in the driveway, as it had the previous evening when the owner raked his small yard.

Terry wondered if he simply wasn't answering his door, or had alternate transportation. He peeked through a few of the windows, seeing no activity inside, while he listened for movement or conversation that never passed through the trailer's walls.

Fairly convinced the residence was empty, he walked toward Lancaster's trailer, his blue eyes panning the nearby grounds and roads, finding no one watching. He rounded the corner of the trailer, finding the deputy's activities concealed by the thick trees and good fortune that no one could see into the back of Lancaster's yard. Standing on a wood stump, Hardegen struggled with his objective.

Hardegen fought in vain to open a single, narrow window that worked from an inside turn crank. Terry approached, figuring the deputy heard his footsteps, so he tapped him on the shoulder, causing the man to jump.

"Holy!" Hardegen exclaimed as he stumbled, barely catching himself before giving Terry an irritated stare. "You should have said something!"

"Sorry. I thought you heard me."

"Well I didn't."

Terry looked from the deputy to the window.

"Can you get it?"

"Not without breaking something. Either the glass has to go, or if we force it, the hinge arms will probably bust apart."

"Something tells me Mr. Lancaster probably doesn't leave anything unlocked when he travels," Terry sighed.

Hardegen shrugged.

"We can try the other windows, but someone might see us."

The idea of local police questioning their interest in a trailer didn't appeal to Terry, and unless Murphy came up with some good contact information in the next few minutes, he needed to act.

"Stay here," Terry said, walking around the trailer, examining and trying each window as he went.

Finding no success, he returned to Hardegen, who continued to work at the original window.

"I might be able to jimmy it with one of the flag posts in the yard," he commented, examining it like a raccoon sniffing the air for food.

A few minutes later, Hardegen pried the window open with a metal rod barely thicker than a pencil, discovering the extending arm was on the verge of a breakdown before they ever thought of breaking in. Terry followed the deputy inside, conscious of the fact he was breaking laws he swore to protect, even if his actions were potentially life-saving.

To Terry, the place looked like someone lived there only a few days of the month. Two chairs and a small television set atop a stand comprised the living room's furniture. The kitchen had no table or chairs, though it appeared tidy.

Curtains hung in every window, ensuring snooping eyes didn't see much when the trucker wasn't home.

"Look for any phone numbers, contacts, work papers," he told Hardegen. "Anything that might help us find him."

Seconds later, Hardegen stopped at the refrigerator.

"How's this?"

Magnetized to the appliance were several people to contact in case of emergency.

"Write those down."

Terry continued to search until he found a phone bill stub, but the number wasn't anywhere on the paper. Since the bill was two months old, he suspected the carrier would be current, cutting Murphy's search time down considerably.

After about ten minutes of searching and jotting, Terry sensed a danger light going off in his mind. A look to Hardegen confirmed the deputy felt the same way, so they exited the trailer through the window, securing it as best they could.

They had been careful to leave everything undisturbed, though thorough in their search. While no overwhelmingly positive information came their way, Terry felt they had several solid avenues to search.

Hopefully they found Steve Lancaster before Toomey did.

CHAPTER 39

▼

When Lancaster awoke, he found himself inside his own garage, the dim overhead lights casting shadows everywhere his groggy eyes looked. He felt sluggish, almost sick, then he remembered being attacked from behind.

He suspected some kind of drug or agent was used on the cloth placed over his mouth, which explained the nauseous feeling in his stomach. A pungent smell of fresh paint remained trapped with him inside the sealed garage, adding to his queasy feeling.

Regaining his senses, he looked around, realizing his hands were bound behind him and his legs tied to the metal legs of the chair he was strapped to. Except for the extra vehicle, his garage appeared normal. Tools hung from various pegs, or rested upon any one of his work benches. Cans of oil and paint lined shelving units while his air compressor sat away from its usual corner, close enough to him that he felt as though it might have come to life and moved itself.

Fighting back the urge to close his eyes, Lancaster discovered the unmarked car now had primer paint on one front fender, one of the four doors, and barely visible on the opposite fender. A few selected areas had been dented intentionally, making the car look more like a beater.

His truck's license plates were removed, now placed on the car to keep it from being readily identified. Lancaster had some idea of who was holding him captive, which worried him even more, because this man had posed as a police officer over the phone to pinpoint his arrival time.

While he knew only a little bit about police business, particularly investigations, Lancaster imagined an investigator would have found him in person, or asked to meet him immediately. The line of questioning had been rather vague, but Lancaster hadn't noticed until this very moment.

Looking around for a way to escape his predicament, he found no tools or loose objects anywhere nearby. He tried scooting the chair in the direction of one of the work benches, but the chair didn't move more than an inch or two at a time because his feet remained bound to the legs. Short of a major impact, the chair wasn't going to shatter, but if he dumped himself to the ground and failed, he would be upended like a turtle.

A good opportunity never presented itself before the door opened and a man close to Lancaster's age stepped through. Saying nothing, the trucker simply craned his neck for a look at the individual, wondering if he knew him.

"Expecting someone else?" the stranger asked.

He didn't look like someone who abducted people for kicks. Dressed in blue jeans, a college sweatshirt, and new tennis shoes, he was no vagrant, nor did he appear suave and sophisticated. His black hair had been cut short, looking very contemporary. No scars or blemishes marred the smooth features of his face, causing Lancaster to believe he might actually be a college student.

"Who are you?" Lancaster demanded.

"Someone who wants to meet your father very much," the stranger answered, crafting his words very slowly and carefully as he had on the phone. "He owes someone an apology."

Lancaster's mind scrambled for the right thing to say or do. Since his father's cell phone number wasn't listed, and he had no property on public record, he was virtually unreachable by anyone outside of his friends and family.

If this man had killed Bob Hagen and Frank Wilson, there was little doubt he plotted the same fate for the elder Lancaster. Sensing his life was over, regardless of what he did, Lancaster decided to protect his father.

"My father died last year," he answered, putting forth the most straightforward face possible.

Smirking, the stranger walked toward the air compressor, taking up a framing nailer and a one-inch thick board just over a foot in length.

His actions were about to speak louder than words.

Placing the board over the thick portion of Lancaster's right leg, he let the trucker think nervously about the situation a moment before pulling the pneumatic nailer's trigger three times within a few seconds. Though the board stopped an inch of nail penetration, Lancaster's leg took the brunt of the nails in three different areas.

He screamed in agonized pain as the nails entered his flesh, muscles, and in one area, bone. It took several seconds, but he finally collected himself enough to look his captor in the eyes.

"This can be easy or hard, Steve. Your father's number is in your cell phone. Just call him, and we can reunite for a gathering, just like the old days."

Despite searing pain, Lancaster decided his next move.

"I haven't erased my father's number from the phone yet."

Toomey wasn't buying one word.

"Slipped your mind? Or does it have emotional attachment?"

"I guess both."

His expression turning grimly serious, Toomey ripped the board upward from Lancaster's leg, bringing bloody nails with it. Unable to suppress more tormented outbursts, Lancaster watched as red droplets fell to the floor after failing to cling to the cold steel of the nails.

Cursing himself for using the barbed framing nails to put up his garage over the summer, he saw bits of flesh clinging to the barbs. Each nail possessed four areas of twisted wire to help them cling to the material they were used to fasten. They clung to everything they touched upon entry, and exit.

"If I hit an artery, it's all over," Toomey warned. "You can call your father, or I can do it."

"Who *are* you, damn it?"

"You should remember me. I lived down the road from you."

Lancaster studied him, failing to place the stranger's face.

"I lived in a lot of places," Lancaster said, the stinging throbs in his leg reminding him of how he wanted to avoid further torture.

"You lived near Kyle Wilson. You could have done something."

Now Lancaster felt genuinely infuriated.

"I was something like twelve years old! How in the fuck could I have done anything?"

Incensed, Toomey placed the board over his leg once again, letting Lancaster squirm a moment before punching three more nails into the meat of his leg, threatening to turn it into hamburger with each entry and prying of nails.

Screaming in pain during the nailing, and after the board was yanked out, Lancaster refused to give his father to the maniac standing before him.

"We can do this all day long," Toomey said, holding the bloodied board near his chest. "Your father isn't dead, and we both know it. He's running from his sins."

"You can't have him, you sick fuck."

Toomey grinned, holding up Lancaster's cell phone.

"Your noble efforts will be for nothing. One call from me, and he'll come running to save his baby boy."

"There's no way."

Flipping open the phone, Toomey searched the contact list until he found the listing for "Dad" and hit the send button. It immediately went to voice mail, but he received confirmation that he had indeed reached the senior Lancaster's phone after listening to the message.

"When will he turn on his phone?"

"He forgets, sometimes for days."

Toomey held up the nailer as a threat.

"I swear," Lancaster said with defeat in his voice.

"Then we'll wait. We have nothing but time, do we?"

*   *   *   *

It took Terry very little time to get the information he needed.

Murphy's people contacted Lancaster's cell phone provider, but calls placed to the man's phone resulted in immediate forwarding to voice mail.

Megan returned home after speaking with all of the neighbors surrounding the former Wilson farm. Everyone had been accounted for, warned, and given contact numbers for the task force if they discovered or thought of anything new.

Terry received some help from Troop D, who temporarily took over surveillance on Lancaster's property while he attended to other business.

After a brief meeting, which resulted in very little new information, Terry decided to visit Lamoureux after hearing his friend had regained consciousness. Unfortunately the prognosis wasn't good, because the injured investigator wasn't feeling much, if anything, below his waistline.

He asked if Hardegen wanted to tag along, but the deputy declined, unable to hide his guilty feelings. Terry doubted Lamoureux would place any blame on Hardegen, and shame on him if he did. A lack of arrogance prevented Terry from assuming he might have captured Toomey without a hitch, but he once believed Lamoureux exercised at least as much caution as he did in the field.

Now he approached the hospital room with his friend lying helplessly inside. He stopped at the door, finding Lamoureux bathed in white, from the clean linen to the hospital gown. Tucked beneath sheets like a burrito, possibly because the window was open enough to allow the fall air inside, Lamoureux stared vacantly toward the sunlight as the curtains gently blew inward.

Terry recalled the times they ate breakfast together, jogged, and teamed up to break suspects once they had solid proof of guilt. Their lives paralleled in many ways when they worked together, but years and life choices had made them different men.

Instead of speaking when he stepped inside, Terry made enough noise that his friend turned to see him, forcing a smile as they clasped hands.

"I feel like I should say something cliche, like ask how you're doing."

"Don't. My sympathy meter is in overtime."

"We've always been straight with each other, Grant," Terry said, taking a seat beside the bed. "What the hell happened out there?"

Lamoureux groaned, turning his torso away from Terry as he answered.

"I got careless, thought Hardegen was on a wild goose chase. By the time I sensed danger, Toomey already had the jump on me."

"John didn't fare much better. I don't need to lecture you on proper procedure. You're the one who broke me in, remember?"

"Yeah," Lamoureux answered, his mind recalling better days when they were green investigators, absorbing information like sponges.

He turned serious before looking to Terry.

"Are you close? Can you find him?"

"It's a matter of time, buddy, but I'm worried he's going to get the trucker before we can find him."

Terry brought him up to speed on the recent finds.

"So what have they told you?" he asked afterward.

"They're running tests, but I can't feel much in my legs. They think there was nerve damage where he stabbed me."

Lamoureux seemed dejected, almost sensing that his days of active duty were behind him. While Terry agreed with people being realistic, he didn't want his friend starting out any kind of rehabilitation on a pessimistic note.

"Don't be giving up on yourself just yet," he warned. "I may need a closer someday, and I can't think of anyone I'd rather drag up to my neck of the woods."

Lamoureux flashed an unenthusiastic grin.

"I'm sorry I brought you into this, especially since I let you down."

"You didn't let me down, Grant. Just get yourself better so you can close Toomey for me."

"I want you to take him alive so he can suffer. Killing him would be too easy."

"I can't make any promises. He's proven himself a pretty dangerous adversary."

While he had worked with cops who shot first and asked questions later, Terry never followed the philosophy. His firearm had been drawn only a few times during his career, and only once while he served as an investigator.

"Promise me you're going to fight this," Terry said, trying to avoid being overly emotional.

Over the years, the two had maintained a very up-front friendship, never mincing words and actions around one another.

"I'll listen to the docs," Lamoureux replied. "I don't plan on being in this bed, or a chair, the rest of my life."

"Good."

Terry stood, briefly taking hold of his friend's forearm to show his support. Had Lamoureux not been blanketed so tightly, he might have given a rare hug. He stepped over, shutting the window.

"How's the food?"

"Better than my ex used to make, but not that great."

"How'd your kids react?" Terry asked, prolonging the inevitable goodbye.

He wanted to stay longer, but to do so kept him from searching for Toomey.

"They were okay," Lamoureux said. "They're old enough to understand, but they didn't like seeing me like this."

Terry remembered his days in the academy, how instructors stressed that cadets needed to maintain awareness every second on the job so they could go home to their families.

"Hey, I've gotta get back to work," Terry finally said, though uncomfortably.

"I know."

"I'll check on you tomorrow."

"Bring me a present, okay?"

Terry understood his friend meant for him to find Toomey.

"I'll do what I can."

Even as he left the hospital, determination and guilt pulsed through his veins. He wished he had accompanied either Hardegen or Lamoureux to the abandoned factory. He felt like a failure after being summoned to the area to put away a killer he couldn't quite figure out.

Knowing about Toomey's psychological history helped a little bit, but only to let him know the man was more unpredictable than he might ever have predicted.

He was halfway across the parking lot when his phone rang.

"Levine," he answered.

"Terry, this is Paul Gaffney. We checked on the contact numbers that you and John mysteriously came up with."

The sheriff's tone indicated he knew something more than he stated, but wasn't going to press the issue. Terry wondered if the deputy had somehow let information slip out, or Gaffney was simply that crafty that he knew such good information didn't simply materialize.

"Your person of interest has a son who also drives a rig. I'm arranging for someone in Onondaga to see if the guy is home."

"I'm available, Paul. Where is he?"

"No. You and John have done enough to uncover some new leads."

Terry wondered if the sheriff had just given him a double-edged compliment.

"Are you running the investigation?"

"I don't recall ever giving it up," Gaffney said. "I've got Randy Gosser, my senior investigator, taking the helm."

"Where is your protégé?" Terry asked.

"Home. I ordered him to rest up."

"Anything else I need to know?"

"Not really. You need to take it easy, too."

"Unlike John, I don't have a whole lot to do, Sheriff."

Gaffney chuckled.

"The day is still young if you want to come up here."

"I'd rather work dead end leads than sit around my hotel room."

A few seconds passed before Gaffney spoke again.

"How's Grant doing?"

"Understandably depressed, but I think he'll get on track."

"Any word on his nerve damage?"

"No. They're still running tests."

"I see. So I'll see you in a little bit?"

"Sure. Take care, Paul."

"You too."

Terry shut his phone, wondering if Gaffney wanted him and Hardegen out of the picture, or the task force had things handled without them. He imagined someone from the task force had been phoning Steve Lancaster all day without results. The only question about Lancaster's lack of phone etiquette was whether his phone was shut off, or dead with him in a ditch somewhere.

Getting into his car, Terry hoped to know one way or the other very soon.

CHAPTER 40

▼

As cold as the early November air felt outside, the inside of the garage had a hot, sticky feel to it by early afternoon as Lancaster remained bound to the chair. Toomey had left for the better part of an hour, leading him to believe his captor was planning, or packing.

His right leg throbbed continuously with pain from the six bloody holes created by the framing nailer. Some of the wounds began to clot, but without medical assistance fairly soon, Lancaster doubted the leg could heal correctly.

Somehow he doubted Toomey was going to call for an ambulance.

Thoughts of escape came and went like gusts of wind. Doubting his ability to walk, much less run, Lancaster decided to wait, since he wasn't able to move the chair more than an inch at a time. If Toomey caught him, nails through the upper leg would surely pale compared to the next level of punishment.

When Toomey finally stepped through the door, Lancaster sucked in an anticipating breath until he noticed the man appeared rather nervous. He shut the side door behind him, placing a nearby board under the doorknob to brace it. The sound of gravel crunching in the driveway meant someone was paying the property a visit.

"One peep from you and I kill the cop out there," Toomey said, holding out a revolver to prove his point before turning out the garage lights.

Lancaster tried to remember if any visible damage to the house or garage stood out. If so, any reasonably intelligent police officer might investigate further, or call for backup. Lancaster had no idea why someone might be sent to his property, unless they wanted to warn him about Toomey.

Too late, he thought with the last bit of humor in him.

Sitting in complete darkness, he listened to the sounds of the police officer climbing the two steps to the back door, knocking, then scuffing his feet on the top step. He tried knocking a few more times, then ambled down to level ground, possibly examining the garage.

"Mr. Lancaster?" he finally called out. "I'm Doug Everett from the Sheriff's Department."

Lancaster thought it sounded like he was yelling toward the garage door, or perhaps toward the house, but pressed his lips together. He knew Toomey was capable of carrying out his threat, and didn't want anyone's death on his conscience.

He heard the deputy take a few steps on the gravel, possibly examining the garage, or looking for a different access point. Seconds seemed like an eternity until the deputy gave up, returning to his car and pulling out of the driveway.

When the lights flickered overhead, Lancaster felt his eyes blink, hurting from the sudden brightness and the lingering effects of the drug used to render him unconscious earlier. Toomey did not appear the least bit pleased with the latest development. He stewed in his juices as he paced the garage floor, occasionally shooting a stare toward his captive.

After a few minutes he examined the downgraded car, exhaling loudly through his nostrils, before looking toward Lancaster.

"We're going on a road trip."

*   *   *   *

On a return trip from Nevada, Steve Lancaster, Sr. stopped for the first time after leaving the western border of Illinois shortly after dawn. Both trips contained hazardous chemicals, which paid substantially more than standard loads, providing more figurative headaches for drivers.

Pulling near a pump at a Pennsylvania gas depot, he let the pump automatically fill his truck while he searched inside the truck for his wallet and cellular phone. The notion of calling his son occurred to him when he grew bored with traffic jams and watching the same old signs pass by. He hardly ever phoned people while driving, but when stuck in traffic he sometimes updated his dispatchers and family.

Turning on his phone, Lancaster discovered a few new messages. One was from his mother, wanting to check in, and the other from a poker buddy inviting him to play cards that coming weekend.

He had a few days off before his next trip, but wasn't sure he wanted to spend it playing cards. Once his truck registered full, he replaced the diesel nozzle, then stepped inside to pay for the gas and buy an orange soda.

Over the years little changed about the truck driver, which explained his two divorces. He currently had no steady girlfriend, and rarely found time to socialize, except with his son when they made their way home at the same time. His hair receded a bit more each year, and his goatee sported more gray hairs than he cared to see, particularly at his relatively young age of forty-four.

He married his high school sweetheart soon after graduation. Their son arrived three years later, which marked the beginning of the end concerning their marriage. With him working long hours to buy them a house, his wife grew tired of watching the baby. She claimed to be a slave to their apartment when she informed him of the divorce.

In time Lancaster bought his own house, which he lost during the second divorce years later. He chose to live in a trailer because he owned very little, simply stowing his money in the bank as a personal retirement bonus.

When he stepped outside to overcast skies, Lancaster fished inside the pocket of his flannel shirt for a cigarette.

Lighting up without missing a step, he heard his cell phone ring at his side, making him wonder if someone had been trying to reach him.

Exhaling toward the sky as he neared his truck, a look at his phone informed him the call came from his son's mobile phone.

"Hello," he answered in his usual gravelly voice, a bit more chipper than usual.

"Is this Steve Lancaster?" an unfamiliar voice inquired, making him wonder if something had happened to his son, and a concerned bystander or hospital employee was trying to reach family members.

"This is," he answered after a few seconds. "Where is my son?"

"He's with me, sir. We've been catching up on a few things, like how you let Kyle Wilson die at the hands of his father."

Now Lancaster's mood changed, from one of concern to confusion and growing rage.

"Where is Steve? Let me talk to him."

"I'm afraid he's a bit, uh, tied up at the moment."

Having no patience for games, Lancaster took a squeaky drag from his cigarette, then tossed it aside, now standing beside his rig.

"You have about three seconds to tell me what you want before I-"

"If you want to see your son alive, you're going to do exactly what I say."

Completely stymied by the caller and his threats, the trucker took a moment to absorb such a bizarre revelation.

"This is bullshit. Is this some kind of sick joke?"

"No. No joke."

Lancaster heard the phone set down, then a few footsteps, before an agonizing scream reached his phone.

"Don't do it, Dad!" his son's voice called. "Don't give him what he wants!"

Feeling his heart race with fear, Lancaster realized he was definitely caught in something that placed his son's life in jeopardy.

"What do you want?"

"I want to meet with you, Steve. You, and you alone. Involve the authorities, and the next time you see your son will be in a casket, just like the one you helped put Kyle Wilson in."

"Please," Lancaster said, trying to maintain his composure. "I don't have a clue what you're talking about."

"I think you do."

He remembered Kyle Wilson, because he befriended the boy's father a number of years. Police ruled the boy's death an accident, which satisfied everyone concerned at the time.

Looking around him, Lancaster searched for anyone who might be watching him from the gas station or the dozens of rigs parked nearby. Truckers filled their gas tanks, strolled toward or from the store, or used one of the payphones outside the store.

"I won't call the cops. What do you want from me?"

"If I tell you that, you won't come. Where are you?"

"The middle of Pennsylvania," Lancaster answered nervously, not wanting to irritate the abductor of his son.

"I'll call back with instructions in a few hours, once you're close to Buffalo."

"What about my son?"

"He'll go free once I have you. Remember, don't tell anyone, or he dies."

An abrupt click reached Lancaster's ear as he tried to digest every bit of information the man had just told him. He might have thought the call was a practical joke, except his son didn't kid around in that way, and the mention of Kyle Wilson offset any possibility of kidding around.

Despite being almost all the way across the country, Lancaster had heard news about the Wilson family being massacred in an issue of *USA Today*. He seldom stayed in hotels, opting to sleep in his own truck, which meant news came from the radio or newspapers.

Wanting to learn more about the new development in his life, Lancaster briskly walked into the convenience store center, swiped up every different kind of newspaper available, and set them on the counter.

He had even picked a few outdated papers, hoping the cashier didn't make a big deal about selling issues they were supposed to send back. Giving the stack a quirky look, she said nothing, selling him the entire bundle.

Leaving the store, Lancaster became aware of profuse sweat soaking into his shirt, while droplets covered his neck. He jumped into the cab of his truck, moved to a safe location, and began skimming the newspapers for any news out of New York.

Within ten valuable minutes he learned that the Wilson triple homicide, and the murders of five hunters, were suspected as linked homicides. In a *New York Times,* he found information about the killer, along with a recent photograph.

"Eric Toomey," he muttered the name, just to make certain he wasn't dreaming.

This man had called him, obviously holding a grudge because of what happened to Kyle Wilson. Lancaster barely remembered the boy, since he worked on the road so often. His son and Kyle hardly ever played together, because visitation rights only brought his son to him on weekends during those years.

What happened to Kyle was a complete accident. Lancaster recalled the boy's father being broken up about the incident. He was a strict disciplinarian, but he cared about his son's well-being. Lancaster attended the funeral, recalling how Frank Wilson was on the verge of tears several times.

But who was Eric Toomey?

Searching the archives of his memory, the trucker tried to remember anyone who might have frequented the Wilson farm at the time. Bob Hagen's death linked together with the triple homicide, meaning the connection probably extended to himself and other neighbors.

When his phone rang beside him, Lancaster mentally chastised himself for not already being on the road, heading toward his son. A look down revealed the 716 area code from the Erie County area, though the phone number wasn't familiar.

Deciding it might be Toomey, he answered it.

"Hello?"

"Mr. Lancaster?"

"Yes," the trucker replied hesitantly.

"I'm Deputy Jeff Rawlings with the Erie County Sheriff's Department. Sir, we've been desperately trying to reach you since yesterday."

Lancaster's first thought was that they wanted to tell him his son was missing.

"We have reason to believe you may be in grave danger, sir. What's your location?"

"I'm out-of-state on a delivery," Lancaster answered, assuming they knew his occupation.

"Sheriff Paul Gaffney and our lead investigator, Terry Levine, are interested in speaking with you the second you reach New York."

"It may be a day or two," Lancaster lied, trying to buy time.

"Sir, this is an urgent matter."

Lancaster heard the deputy speak with someone in the background, wondering if this wasn't a trap of some sort. At this point, he didn't know who to trust, or what might be real.

A moment later, a different voice came over the phone.

"Mr. Lancaster, this is Terry Levine with the New York State Police. I'm part of a task force investigating the murders of your former neighbors."

"Oh?"

"It's important that I speak with you, but I understand you're on the road?"

"I'm on my way back, bringing some nitrogen to Syracuse."

"Much as I hate to do it this way, I'm going to break some news to you, because you may be in grave danger once you return to New York. I have reason to believe a man named Eric Toomey may want to kill you, based on your past relationship with Frank Wilson."

Lancaster said nothing. His concerns, along with the validity of the first call, had all been confirmed.

"Mr. Lancaster, I need to meet with you as soon as you reach the state line."

"Okay," Lancaster said, though he didn't mean the words.

"Where are you right now?"

"Missouri," Lancaster lied without hesitation.

The state trooper said nothing for a moment.

"I'm giving you my cell phone number, because I want you to call me the minute you reach the state line."

Lancaster pretended to take down the number, but he really didn't, mainly because he didn't want to break the deal with Toomey.

"Okay," he said slowly, now feeling like he was sentenced to death, his last living wish to save his son. "Thanks for the heads up."

"You're welcome, sir. Just be sure to call me, with everything you know, when you reach New York."

Lancaster hung up the phone, trying to decipher the last statement made by the trooper. He decided his deceit was good enough for him to reach Toomey, wherever the meeting place might be. Keeping his eyes on the road, he glanced at his phone every so often, waiting for Toomey to call back.

∗   ∗   ∗   ∗

"He lied to me," Terry told Gaffney, who looked at him with the same curiosity as someone viewing a lunatic.

Terry had since spoken with Lancaster's employers, after finding check stubs at the man's residence with Hardegen, which didn't endear him with the sheriff. He wasn't going to lie to Gaffney, but avoiding the truth didn't feel any better.

He still wasn't sure if Gaffney was upset with him for dragging Hardegen into their breaking and entering search, or irritated that the deputy went along with the plan so easily.

"How do you know? The man was probably in shock."

"His employers said he contacted them this morning from Indiana, meaning he's closer to home than he's telling me. And the man didn't ask any questions when I told him why I was calling. Most people would demand to know what's going on."

Doug Everett from the Onondaga Sheriff's Department had reported back from the junior Lancaster's house that no one appeared to be home, despite a rig parked to the side of the driveway.

Terry's mind raced, wondering why the trucker would lie to him after being told his life might be in immediate danger. Only one reason seemed plausible, unless the man lived a completely carefree lifestyle.

"Did the deputy see anything unusual at the residence?" he asked Gaffney, since Everett had reported directly to him from Onondaga County.

"He said the garage door frame had some minimal damage, but it was in place and locked. He figured the owner locked himself out at some point and had to break it."

"And that didn't seem odd to you?"

"No. I trust any deputy to give me honest assessments. If he said the place was secure, it was secure, Terry."

Gaffney looked irritated.

"What are you not telling me?"

"I think Toomey got the son before Everett checked the property, and I think he may have contacted Lancaster before we did."

"Why?"

"Because he's impatient, and he knows we're closing in. He wants to finish his plan before we catch up. With his face all over the news, he needed leverage against Lancaster."

Gaffney appeared surprised, then convinced, dismissing any earlier resentment toward the investigator.

"We've got to find Lancaster."

"We need Murphy to do it. Hopefully he can track him through the cell phone."

Nodding, the sheriff took up his cell phone to personally call the agent.

"I want to look at the son's property," Terry said. "Toomey probably needs him alive, but maybe we can find something that'll help. And just maybe he's confident enough to hide there."

"I'll go with you."

"Sure you don't want a warrant or something?"

"I guess this falls into one of those gray areas," Gaffney said with a grin. "Where you do a greater good by doing something wrong."

"Yeah. I know a little something about that."

Gaffney turned his attention to the phone, speaking with Murphy a moment later. The call took less than a minute, leaving the sheriff pleased with the results.

"He said they can track him as long as the phone is on. Right now he's working with the phone carrier, but he's working on getting the Bureau's tracking device brought to him."

Terry doubted Lancaster could afford to turn the phone off, because he expected to hear from Toomey or the authorities.

So long as the phone remained powered, Murphy could track the signal with the Bureau's equipment. The state police had two such machines capable of tracking cell phone signals, but one was currently dedicated to a case in Albany, while the other sat across the state under repair.

Terry felt confident they could locate Lancaster, but stopping Toomey from harming him was the real trick.

Gaffney grabbed the briefcase he had brought from a nearby table, swiping up some loose notes. He looked down at his uniform, scowling, as Terry led the way toward the front door.

"What's the matter?"

"I wore this in case we had a press conference. Wish I would have brought a change of clothes with me."

Considering it was late afternoon, and there were no pressing leads, Terry didn't feel rushed to examine the younger Lancaster's house. It wasn't exactly a few minutes to Syracuse from Buffalo, but he didn't want to linger too long, in case the task force caught wind of a new lead.

"We've got time if you want to change."

"My house is practically on the way, if you don't mind. And I've got an idea to get us to Lancaster's house a little quicker."

Fifteen minutes later, Terry almost thought a stranger had emerged from the room where Gaffney went to change. He had made small talk with the sheriff's wife until Gaffney returned, wearing blue jeans and a fairly casual long-sleeve shirt. He threw on a black leather jacket to shield him from the cold front sweeping through the state, then clipped his firearm along his hip.

"What's the matter?" Gaffney asked, noticing Terry's stare.

"I've just never seen you wear anything that required less than twelve buttons."

"Thanks, smart ass. Consider these my flight clothes, because we're taking the helicopter to save some time."

Terry had suspected as much, considering the call Gaffney placed before they left Buffalo.

Gaffney gave his wife a quick kiss, then they were out the door to the sheriff's car. Terry hated bumming rides from everyone, but they all knew the territory better than he did. Over ten years away from the county left him with more visual images than memorized roads. His borrowed car had remained at the Batavia barracks for the better part of the week.

"You don't see your wife much, do you?" Terry asked once they headed back to Buffalo to meet up with Jim Covington.

Gaffney phoned the captain before they left Buffalo to meet them at the landing zone. The timing seemed just about perfect, and the trip time was going to be shaved considerably.

"Nah," Gaffney answered. "I got her blessing before I ran for sheriff. Suzanne knew what she was getting into, but we still make it work."

"You're not that old to be a sheriff. When did you start working for the state?"

"I was one of the lucky few who got in young, back in the days when they usually made you test a few times before they accepted you."

Terry seemed to recall Hardegen mentioning the sheriff's age as 53, but he wasn't positive. He guessed it seemed pretty accurate.

"You happily married?" Gaffney asked as he passed a slower car.

Terry wasn't sure why the sheriff put the adjective before 'married' but figured it wasn't a loaded question. Only a handful of times had other cops asked him such a personal question before they were considered a friend. Perhaps the sheriff was about to give him the whole speech about letting Jesus into his life, or perhaps he had a different reason.

"Yeah. Sherri's put up with a lot of baggage from me, but she doesn't complain much. We moved twice after we married before I finally moved home. I went where the job wanted me to, and where I could take on the biggest cases, but it finally got to be too much."

"It happens. Bet she's not too happy with you right now."

"She blames Grant for bringing me here. She knows I didn't have a choice."

"You and I just missed working together in Batavia," Gaffney revealed. "I was working out of Rochester when you were here, then I made lieutenant and took the ride to Batavia after you went to the big city."

Taking the ride in trooper terminology meant going to another troop due to a promotion, or an opening in a specialty area. First assignments given after academy graduation were sometimes referred to the same way.

Terry thought of the small world his fellow troopers lived in. They were networked, sometimes meeting by random chance or at state police functions. For the most part they only knew their surrounding personnel and territories. His reputation followed him whenever he moved, because he had solved some harrowing cases. Troopers knew who he was, even if they didn't meet him personally.

Or at least they had back then.

Lamoureux was probably one of the few Batavia troopers who remembered Terry's legacy, and now he was paralyzed in a hospital bed for bringing it to the forefront.

"I take it you don't want me calling the Onondaga guys for any assistance," Gaffney said more than asked.

"That would be a correct assessment. Something tells me the property owner would give us his blessing right about now."

"Assuming he's still of this world," Gaffney muttered.

*   *   *   *

A short time later, Covington landed the helicopter in a clearing across the road from Lancaster's house. Still somewhat unaccustomed to protocol when exiting a chopper, Terry followed Gaffney's lead. Both carefully straddled a fence's wooden slats, then crossed the uneventful county road.

The sheriff immediately walked over to the rig parked beside the driveway, jotting any pertinent information in his notebook.

Considering no one in their group had confirmed the older Lancaster's employer, that they knew of, it seemed plausible he got his son hired into the same company. Terry waited for Gaffney to return before making his way toward the house's rear.

"Truck was secure," Gaffney commented. "And the front door looked intact when we pulled in."

"It would take a pretty stupid burglar or kidnapper to use the front door, particularly if he was lying in wait."

The garage entry door required very little persuasion before giving way at the junior Lancaster's house.

Terry stepped in first, taking a careful look around.

"Nice new truck," Gaffney commented, stepping around to get a look inside. "It doesn't have any plates."

He tried the doors, finding them locked, so he jotted down the vehicle identification number along the windshield.

Terry saw the sheriff's investigative intuition taking over. The man worked smoothly, working one side of the garage while Terry covered the other.

"Yuck," Terry muttered, finding a chair with several small pools of blood beneath it.

He also found tattered bits of flesh, before spying a board containing several bloody framing nails puncturing the narrow side. Nearby, the culprit remained attached to the air compressor that had assisted in the torture of a human being.

"There's fresh primer paint on the ground," Gaffney said a few seconds later, coming around the truck. "It's stinks to high heaven."

Terry held up the board for the sheriff to examine, a disgusted look crossing the man's face when he saw the blood and tissue remnants.

"Tell me that isn't what I think it is."

Terry nodded.

"We've got to check the house to make sure, Paul."

Gaffney bobbed his head, then followed Terry to the back door.

Both drew their firearms, though it seemed highly improbable they were going to need them.

"He probably has John's car, doesn't he?" Gaffney asked.

"A quick paint job, switch the plates, and who's going to know it was a cop's car?" Terry offered an explanation before giving the door a weak kick that sent it flying inward.

Between them, they cleared the house in less than a minute, finding bittersweet results.

"I've got to assume the kid's alive," Terry reasoned aloud as they stood in the kitchen. "Toomey has to make sure the father cooperates."

"Why bother torturing the kid?"

"We had a lot of trouble finding Senior, so I've got to assume Toomey got creative. Maybe he persuaded dad by letting him hear the son's screams. Maybe Lancaster held out and wouldn't give up his dad, or tried saying Toomey had the wrong guy. At this point, it doesn't matter. We *need* Murphy to track Lancaster wherever he's going right now. And we've got to get a team mobilized."

Gaffney looked at the phone receiver, then began searching atop the refrigerator and counter tops for something.

"If he was on the road a lot, wouldn't Junior have a cell phone?" the sheriff asked without looking up from his search.

"Probably."

Without another word, Terry began searching the other room for any documentation that might reveal his phone number, or carrier. Ten minutes passed with neither man finding a shred of evidence that pointed them in the right direction.

"Either he doesn't have one, or he throws his paperwork away," Gaffney deduced.

"And if he does have one, it's probably with the same provider his dad has. Most phone companies offer free calling for anyone who shares their service."

"Yeah. I'm aware. Murphy's already working with the phone company, so we'll have him check the records for Steve Junior."

Terry realized the need to fly back to the Buffalo area, because Lancaster was due to reach the state line virtually any moment. He wanted to check with Murphy, to see if any new developments had come the agent's way. If necessary, he would contact Lancaster directly to see if the trucker was willing to cooperate, despite any threats Toomey spoke against his son.

"Ready?" Gaffney asked.

"Yeah. How good are you at running a task force on the road?"

The sheriff responded with a grin.

"Been doing it most of my career."

"Good. I have an idea how to proceed, if you like it."

CHAPTER 41

▼

Terry's plan changed slightly when he spoke to Murphy over the phone. While flying back, Gaffney contacted Hardegen and members of the task force, getting them ready for action, whatever and wherever it might be.

Both the NYSP and Erie County Sheriff's Department SWAT teams were alerted and assembled. They were going into a hurry up and wait mode, which most of the members probably disliked.

Under normal circumstances, teams planned a raid to occupy their times, or carried out a fairly typical scenario they had rehearsed dozens, possibly hundreds of times before. This time they were being grouped together and readied for mobilization to whatever area Lancaster met with Toomey.

Immediately after landing, Terry and the sheriff were mobile again, taking Gaffney's car as a makeshift mobile command center.

"I'm way ahead of you," Murphy said when Terry phoned him, somewhat cheerfully.

"How's that?"

"Not only do we have his cell phone locked in, but I found his employer. I'm standing in their offices as we speak, watching a computer track his every move via satellite tracking system. He's about thirty miles away from the state line."

Terry had considered tractor trailers having tracking systems, but without Lancaster's new employer, they had no way to locate him that way.

"I'd like to talk to him, Greg. If he's willing to give me any kind of information, it'll save us from getting caught with our pants down."

"Have at it. Just don't give away what we know. If Toomey snags him, we may need to rely on the phone signal to follow them."

"I know. If he has a meeting spot, we could get the boys in position to take Toomey."

"Dead, preferably. Oh, that was my out-loud voice, wasn't it?"

Terry caught the joke, but decided not to comment.

"You going to be content standing around a trucking facility while we steal all the glory?"

"Of course. You know we FBI types prefer to avoid credit for anything, just letting the general public think the only thing we do is spy on them. You action heroes can have all the fun as far as I'm concerned. You're the ones who earned it."

Relieved that Murphy wasn't a stiff like some agents he had worked with, Terry respected the job the man had done. If the case ended well, he planned to give the Bureau as much credit as any other agency.

"We wouldn't be where we are without your input, Greg. Thanks a million for stepping up."

"Just nail Toomey, and put some heat on that trucker to cooperate, okay?"

"I'll certainly try. Thanks."

Terry shut his phone, severing the call.

Now seated in the passenger's seat of Gaffney's car, Terry watched buildings, signs, and bus stops slowly pass. They had nowhere particular to be at the moment.

"Any good word?" the sheriff asked.

"Murphy has a lock on Lancaster's position through the GPS on the man's truck."

"Great. We can't lose him, then."

"It only takes a quick bullet from Toomey to end it all."

Gaffney sighed heavily, realizing the situation still wasn't theirs to control.

"You have to call him."

"I'm about to. He's going to do whatever it takes to get his son back, so I've got to say the right things."

A few silent seconds passed between them.

"My son is getting married next spring," Gaffney said thoughtfully. "If it came down to it, I'd do anything to save him, including lay down my life."

Terry knew exactly what Gaffney meant, figuring Lancaster meant to see his son safe, even if it cost him his existence. Toomey was not to be trusted. Terry had yet to pinpoint the killer's stance on honesty and fairness, so he didn't want Lancaster walking into a trap that might kill him and his son.

"Don't rehearse it," Gaffney suggested. "Just tell him the truth, and don't let him walk in there alone."

"You're right," Terry said, lifting his phone and searching through the recent call list to find Lancaster's number.

He pushed the send button, hoping the man was willing to answer his phone.

*   *   *   *

Lancaster had already received word from Toomey that he wanted to meet in an old plaza parking lot. Somewhat unfamiliar with the Buffalo area, Lancaster felt odd asking a killer and kidnapper for directions. Toomey provided him with an address, which the trucker fed into his computerized navigation system.

He followed the directions from the electronic voice as they came, trying to devise a plan to save himself and his son. A holstered .38 remained under his seat at all times for protection, though he had never used it for more than target practice.

Toomey had warned him to come alone, unarmed, and without any tricks. Meeting in an abandoned parking lot sounded fairly safe, but Lancaster had no idea what to expect. Things were different when they weren't in the movies, because real lives were at stake. Calling the police seemed logical, but he felt certain Toomey would carry out his threat to kill his son, even as a final effort before death or capture.

A string of apartment buildings lined either side of the street he navigated, but he paid them little attention. He barely concentrated on the vehicles ahead of him, trying to plan how he wanted to handle Toomey. Not exactly a man to beg for anything, he had decided he would do what was required to keep his son alive.

When his phone rang from the cup holder beside him, he scooped it up, seeing the incoming number wasn't from a phone Toomey had used.

"Hello."

"Mr. Lancaster, this is Terry Levine with the New York State Police. Are you okay?"

"So far."

"I need you to listen to me very carefully, sir. Even though you've not been forthcoming, I know about your situation. Whatever Toomey has told you, don't trust him, don't believe him."

"What choice do I have? He's got Stevie."

"I know, and he's not giving your son back. He plans to kill you."

Lancaster already knew that, though he wondered how the police knew Toomey had his son. He wasn't going to simply walk up to Toomey and surrender himself without seeing his son freed first.

"If he sees any cops, he'll kill my boy."

"We can get there before he does. Or we can stop him when he leaves. Our job is not to endanger you or Steve."

"I know you mean well, but I can't risk it."

"Then at least keep your cell phone with you. That's all I ask."

"Why?"

"Because it may be the only thing that keeps you from being lost permanently."

Lancaster understood what he meant, realizing they were a step ahead of him. And Toomey.

If they knew to track his cell phone, then they were likely watching his truck's every movement.

"Okay," he agreed. "I'll keep my phone with me, but I don't want to see any of you at the meeting spot."

"He's made contact with you?"

"Yes."

"Sir, my concern is for your safety at this point. Do you know for a fact your son is still alive?"

The question pained Lancaster, because he had no recent confirmation. His son's agonized screams provided proof during the first phone call, but Lancaster hadn't thought to ask the second time. Seeing his son in person and getting to the meeting spot, seemed more important, overriding his common sense.

"I have to assume he's still alive."

"I'm begging you to reconsider meeting him under his terms, Mr. Lancaster. Toomey's not well, and there's no telling what he'll do once you meet him."

"That's a chance I have to take, isn't it?"

Lancaster shut down his phone before the trooper could reason further with him. He also felt emotionally drained, on the verge of breaking down, which he didn't want revealed in a conversation with a stranger.

Staring ahead, he focused on the task at hand, knowing he had help on the way, whether he wanted it or not.

Toomey wanted him at the parking lot by six, but rush hour traffic and a reported stalled car had reduced incoming traffic to one lane. Lancaster merged left, praying any delay wouldn't incur Toomey's wrath.

＊　　　＊　　　＊　　　＊

Hardegen seemed rejuvenated and eager when Terry and Gaffney picked him up at the task force command center. Now in constant contact with Murphy, Terry let Gaffney drive as he relayed directions from the FBI agent. Drawing closer to the trucker's location, he realized a need to maintain a safe distance from Lancaster.

All three men were dressed for action, wearing body armor and casual attire. Gaffney drove, while Hardegen sat quietly in the back, shotgun in tow, awaiting further orders.

The SWAT teams were also mobile, taking alternate routes in case of traffic troubles. Considering they had no idea exactly where they were heading, it seemed more important that they cover different areas of Buffalo so at least one team could reach Lancaster quickly. Megan had teamed with two other troopers in another car, providing additional backup.

"He's stuck in traffic," Murphy reported, "still heading northwest off the thruway."

Of course he was heading northwest, Terry thought, considering he had barely gotten into city limits.

"Any ideas where he's going?"

"Not really," Murphy answered. "There are all kinds of isolated areas in town, or he might have him head north out of Buffalo to evade us."

"Toomey might be crazy, but he's not stupid. Call me back when you get some action?"

"Sure."

As soon as Terry set down the phone, all eyes looked his way.

"Lancaster isn't moving," he reported. "Traffic jam."

Like everyone around him, Terry wasn't happy about chasing Lancaster through the city, but they were relying on him to track Toomey. Forcing the man to cooperate wasn't an option, and reasoning with him hadn't worked, leaving Terry their current option.

"What if he has a deadline?" Hardegen asked.

"Hard telling," Terry answered. "I think Toomey wants him badly enough to relocate the meeting, which would make our job a lot tougher."

Terry looked to Gaffney, who turned left to avoid the upcoming traffic jam from the opposite direction of Lancaster.

"You know the city as well as anyone. Where would you call a meeting?"

"Assuming I wanted solitude, like your boy probably does, I'd pick an old warehouse, or maybe a school since the kids are out."

"Are there any around here?"

"Why do you assume the meeting spot is anywhere near here?"

"Because if Toomey didn't want it in Buffalo, he certainly wouldn't have made Lancaster go through thick traffic instead of staying on the freeway."

Terry suspected Toomey wasn't an expert on Buffalo, but he probably knew how to avoid traffic. Still, if he devised his current plan on the fly, he might have made crucial errors.

Carrying a hostage around couldn't ease the burden of planning, either.

"He certainly isn't going to shoot for downtown," Gaffney surmised. "The south end has some vacant areas."

The sheriff hesitated, a concerned look crossed his face as he stopped the car at a corner.

"That's just a guess on my part. If I'm wrong …"

Terry held up a foreboding hand.

"I trust your judgment, Paul. We're going to stop him."

Gaffney's confidence returned with his usual hardened look.

"Okay, then. Let's head to the south end."

CHAPTER 42

▼

When traffic let up, Lancaster's real adventure began.

Toomey called him once more, telling him to drive his truck to the Hartman Pier along Lake Erie. He gave brief directions, and another address for the guidance map.

"Why the change in location?" Lancaster asked.

"You m-might have called the police. We can't have visitors now, can we?"

The usual stoic calm of his voice had broken for the first time. Lancaster could tell he fought to keep from sounding bad, or stuttering, but this time he couldn't contain his secret.

"How do I know my son's alive?"

"Whenever you ask that, I have to hurt him. You really want to know?"

Lancaster debated the option only a second or two.

"Yes."

He heard a painful scream over the phone, unmistakably from his son.

"Happy?"

"No. I've done everything you asked. The cops aren't coming, and I'm going wherever you ask me to."

"Good. Then get to the harbor and await my instructions."

During the ten minute drive to the harbor, Lancaster debated whether or not he had made a mistake by not involving the police. It didn't seem to matter, because Toomey now had him changing locations and playing games.

Go to the location and see what happens, he thought.

When he found the pier, which looked as though it housed commercial shipments by boat and tractor trailer, he saw very little activity. A few boats were in the process of leaving while a few men dressed in work clothes milled about. Several trailers were backed to a warehouse on the grounds, but Lancaster didn't see obvious signs of his son or Toomey.

So he didn't look conspicuous, Lancaster parked his truck beside several stored trailers. He stepped out of the truck, lighting a cigarette to calm his nerves as his eyes darted around the parking lot. Dusk settled over the area, but several overhead lights kicked on to illuminate the dock area.

Taking a deep drag, Lancaster exhaled upward, seeing the smoke drift lazily against one of the parking lot lamps. The light hummed as the bulb slowly grew more intense, distracting him until his phone rang from inside the truck.

Flicking away his cigarette, he scrambled to answer it, fumbling it like a greased football momentarily until he managed to open it.

"Lancaster."

"Are you at the pier?" Toomey's unfriendly voice inquired.

"I'm here. Where the hell are you?"

"Keeping your son safe for you. Look around, Steve. You'll see a brown car with primer paint at the edge of the driveway. Behind the front left tire you'll find the keys. Get in and drive to the south end of town."

"No more games. I want my son back."

"And you'll be reunited when you get down here. I promise."

Lancaster felt angry and frustrated, yet he remained helpless to do anything except follow orders.

"Bring your phone with you," Toomey said. "Same rules apply. No weapons, no cops."

"You've got a deal. Just let my boy go when I get there."

"Just be sure you get here. I'll call you back with directions in five minutes."

Toomey ended the call, leaving Lancaster seconds to collect himself before he reached into the truck, grabbing his pistol from under the seat. He locked the truck behind him, making sure he had everything he wanted for the short trip.

Giving the car a quick inspection for booby-traps, he unlocked it with the keys and slid inside, carefully starting the engine. He half expected it to explode, which it did not, then found his way to a busy street going south.

Maintaining normal driving habits required every bit of composure within him, but Lancaster stayed within the speed limit and followed street lights and signs perfectly. Avoiding police encounters kept Toomey happy, and he had no idea whether or not the kidnapper might be spying on him.

For the first time, he suspected he might be on his own. If the police were tracking his truck, they were all about to swarm a harbor that would take up valuable time and put distance between them and him.

He worried that death was now inevitable for him, though he didn't care. Patting the gun beside him, Lancaster prepared to do whatever might be required of him to save his offspring.

✳   ✳   ✳   ✳

"The truck has stopped," Murphy reported over the phone when Terry answered. "He's been in the same place for few minutes."

"Where?"

"Looks like Hartman Pier where they pack and ship cement."

Terry looked to Gaffney.

"You know Hartman Pier?"

"Of course," the sheriff answered, looking for the next turn that would put them facing the right direction.

Rethinking a moment, Terry contemplated the worst case scenario, which meant finding Lancaster murdered at the pier. More than likely, Toomey had forced him into the car, buying time to carry out a much more elaborate plan elsewhere.

"What about Lancaster's phone signal?" he asked Murphy.

"Why? We've got the truck."

"Call it professional curiosity."

"I still don't have our tracking device here. I'll have to get back with the phone guys. Be back with you in a minute."

"I'm not going anywhere."

Since Murphy set his phone down, Terry simply waited.

"What's that about?" Gaffney asked.

"I don't think Toomey is stupid enough to stay in one spot too long."

Gaffney pulled into the first available parking lot, putting the car in park before looking to Terry for further answers.

"What's your plan?"

"Send the SWAT guys to check out the rig," Terry suggested.

Hardegen lurched forward, itching for action, to catch every word of their conversation. He reminded Terry of his children when the family took a trip somewhere interesting.

Murphy returned to the line a few seconds later.

"He's on the move," the agent said with a tone that stated he was impressed at Terry's intuition.

"Which way?"

"He's still in town, heading south."

"You were right," Terry said aside to the sheriff. "He's heading toward the south end."

Gaffney gave a quick nod, then got the car moving in the correct direction along a primary street that Terry couldn't readily identify.

"He's still moving," Murphy said, not relaying information because he likely had a play-by-play coming to him through another phone line.

Terry felt adrenaline course through him, his stomach tightening like someone wringing a washcloth.

"We're beside Delaware Park," Terry told the agent. "How close are we?"

"Couldn't tell you. I'm a step behind with the phone company, because they can't pinpoint anything more than main roads. Somewhere around Cedar and William, I think. He's heading southeast, but mainly south."

"He just crossed William, heading south," Terry repeated for Gaffney.

"Got it."

"What?" Murphy asked over the line, raising his voice.

"I was relaying your message to Gaffney."

"Nah," Murphy said in a dismissive manner. "Sorry, Terry. That wasn't meant for you. My brain can't handle all this information at once."

Deciding to give the agent some space, Terry simply watched where Gaffney took them, waiting for the next change in direction. He wished he hadn't depended on the agent to ask for phone tracing equipment that still hadn't arrived. With his agencies devices tied up, however, he had little choice.

Bad timing and a conflict of priorities had kept them from keeping closer tabs on Lancaster. Now the entire operation felt like a disaster, spiraling out of control as they chased a distraught father across the city. Terry wanted to save the man from his own mistakes, not trusting the police, and believing Toomey.

If his current assessment about Toomey proved correct, he had time to save both Lancasters, even if they missed the next meeting spot. Toomey wasn't the type to simply shoot or stab someone and flee a scene.

No, he wanted a more fitting end for what he considered revenge. Considering Lancaster was probably the last close friend of Frank Wilson left alive, he might even want the chance to prove his point, or clarify some details.

Terry wondered how many of the memories haunting Toomey were fact, or figments of his imagination.

*   *   *   *

Lancaster finally received orders from Toomey to park near the guard shack at an abandoned factory on Buffalo's south end.

Without the benefit of a computerized map, he had more trouble finding it than he had the docks, but when the factory came into view, Lancaster knew he had arrived. He pulled through open mesh fence gates, finding the guard shack almost immediately.

Stepping out from the car, the trucker looked inside where his gun was hidden beneath the driver's seat. He wondered if he needed to grab it now, or forever live with regret. His cell phone remained at his side, now his one clinging hope to survival if he left the firearm behind.

He cupped his chin, then nervously rubbed his palm up and down against his cheek, glancing between the vacant lot and the car. Unable to wait, he peered inside the old guard shack, spying cobwebs and a chair covered with a thin layer of dust. Beyond the windows inside, the view was hazy, like looking through aquarium glass.

"About ready?" a voice asked behind him, causing him to jump as he spun around to find Toomey staring through him.

Lancaster quickly assessed the stare as a lion stalking his prey, determining its weaknesses and trophy value. Presented with a pair of handcuffs before he could evaluate Toomey, he simply stared at them, wanting answers.

"My son."

"He's safe. Put them on, behind you."

Lancaster hesitated, but Toomey produced a gun to ensure his cooperation. He didn't care if he lived or not, but the trucker wanted to make certain Toomey hadn't damaged his one bargaining chip.

Complying, Lancaster secured the cuffs behind his back, then gave an unblinking stare toward Toomey.

"My son," he said more firmly.

Without a word, Toomey walked to the driver's side door, pulled the keys from the ignition, then placed one of the keys into the trunk's lock when he returned. Lancaster looked downward to the trunk, then to Toomey, wondering if it could be so obvious. Had his son been locked in the trunk the entire time? And if so, why hadn't he made one single noise?

Toomey popped the trunk a few seconds later, but as Lancaster cautiously looked inside, he felt a shove from behind. He put up resistance, now knowing the trunk held nothing except police equipment, and the force barely got his torso over the trunk lip.

What he realized too late, however, was that Toomey didn't intend to stuff him inside the trunk, but rather set him up for a different method of subduing him. As Lancaster tried to fight his way away from the trunk, the lid slammed down on his head once, stunning him. Only half conscious, he continued to pull back from the car, but another downward thrust from the trunk ended his struggle.

CHAPTER 43

▼

By the time Gaffney pulled into the old factory's parking lot, the cell phone signal had been stationary nearly ten minutes. Heavy traffic tied them up a few times, badly enough that Gaffney's lights and siren were useless because there was nowhere else for vehicles to go.

Terry kept his grave concerns to himself, though he envisioned at least two corpses lying somewhere in the lot, or dragged into one of the nearby buildings. When the sheriff's car pulled into the lot, he saw no bodies, and no blood trails, relieving him somewhat.

Unfortunately the factory site appeared to be several large pole barns connected to more sturdy entrance sections made from tempered glass and steel. Gaffney had explained the buildings were constructed quickly for the various tasks the factory performed before closing. Like many subsidiary parts manufacturers, the company fell on hard times between import competition and the economy.

Nothing needed to be said as Gaffney put the car in park. All three doors opened simultaneously as the three men began checking buildings independent of one another to save time. Terry still had Murphy on his phone, though the agent hadn't asked anything once he confirmed they were extremely close to the signal.

"Can I call you back?" Terry asked as he drew near what looked like a secured building.

"Sure," Murphy answered.

Clipping his phone to his belt, Terry drew his firearm as he placed his back against the door, peeking inside its small window without placing much of his body in harm's way. Though he couldn't see if it was safe inside, lives were at stake, and he wasn't waiting for another team to back them up.

He slid in front of the door and mule-kicked it inward, finding it gave far too easily. Once inside, he kept himself to one side of the room, finding a few of the projection windows smashed, their pieces lying on the floor. It took a moment for his eyes to adjust to the darkness within the building, because the utilities were long since disconnected.

At least outside the three police officers had some lighting from the street, along with the purple haze of setting sun. In his hurry, Terry hadn't thought to ask Gaffney for any kind of portable lighting, and he never carried a flashlight as an investigator. Car trunks were meant to tote such things.

After a few seconds he stepped forward, spotting a crumpled pile in the opposite corner of the small room he had entered. He stepped over to it, then carefully touched it, discovering a soft texture that felt like cloth.

Picking it up, he examined the green towel as several objects fell from its folds, crashing against the concrete floor. He set the towel aside, examining the three cell phones lying atop the floor, knowing exactly what they were.

"Shit."

Terry quickly holstered his weapon, then used the towel as a collection device for all three phones. He scampered toward the door, finding Hardegen already in motion toward one of the other buildings where Gaffney flagged him from the doorway.

"Oh, no," Terry muttered, suspecting his worst case scenario had come true.

He followed the bobbing beam of Gaffney's flashlight into the building beyond the guard shack, nearly bumping into Hardegen as they reached an object in the middle of the second room. Gaffney rolled over a body, revealing the younger Lancaster, arms bound, mouth gagged, as his eyes darted between the police officers above him.

Removing the duct tape from Lancaster's mouth as carefully as possible, Gaffney examined him for wounds as he tried to remove the ropes around his wrists.

"Where'd he go?" Terry asked Lancaster, both for information and to break the trance overtaking the young man.

"I don't know," Lancaster answered, still stunned. "He dumped me off here and went outside a few minutes later."

"What was he driving?" Gaffney asked, causing Hardegen to wince.

"Brown car he customized with primer. Looked like a cop car."

Gaffney stood up, his look dismal.

"We've got to update the guys. Can you get Murphy back?"

"I can, but our problems run deeper than before," Terry stated, opening the towel to reveal the three cell phones.

"Ah, shit."

"That's what *I* said, but I have an idea where's he's going."

"Where?"

"Back to the only home he knows at the old factory."

Gaffney didn't appear satisfied with the answer.

"Would he really risk it?"

"If he thinks this is the last hurrah, he might."

"I can mobilize my people that way."

"No. I'll call if I need the SWAT teams. I want your people looking for John's car in case I'm wrong."

Gaffney nodded, stepping aside with Terry.

"The kid's not in any condition to travel, so I'll stay with him until medics arrive."

Terry knew the sheriff was itching to help them find Toomey, because he suspected the investigator's hunch was correct. A look at Lancaster's leg revealed blood and tattered strips of flesh around his jeans. Hardegen had helped the young man apply pressure, keeping him reassured and calm the entire time.

"Take my car, and take John," Gaffney insisted. "I'll get one of my deputies to give me a ride. Let me know if you're right, and I can be up there lickety-split."

"Will do."

Terry directed his attention toward Lancaster.

"Why do you think he let you live?"

"He promised my dad. That's all I can think of."

Terry felt perplexed. Toomey had murdered everyone associated with his victims before.

"That help?" Gaffney asked.

"No. Thanks for the car, Paul."

Hardegen stood, already understanding his role as the sheriff handed him the keys.

"Be careful, kid."

"Always, sheriff. Thanks."

"You two can hug later," Terry said. "We've got a killer to stop."

Hardegen smirked, giving the keys a playful toss as they headed for the sheriff's car. He contained his excitement, but Terry could tell the deputy was revved up about the thrill of the chase.

Luckily he had time enough to prepare Hardegen for what they might encounter. He only hoped the SWAT teams didn't show up and ruin his opportunity to subtly stop Toomey.

CHAPTER 44

▼

Lancaster awoke with a headache worse than any hangover or fistfight had ever provided him. He heard the distinctive clinks of handcuff chains tugging against one another behind him, refusing to let him rub the growing bump atop his head.

He had also experienced handcuffs after one particular bar fight in his younger days.

His vision blurred when he tried to sit up to survey the area around him. Managing to sit upright, Lancaster found his legs bound with rope. A rope looped around the handcuffs kept him bound to nearby heavy machinery, like a dog leashed in the backyard.

Lighting trickled in from the large windows along every side of what appeared to be an abandoned factory. Thick dust covered the length of the floor, some of it still falling like miniature raindrops through the visible spectrum provided by the windows.

Except for several large machines, leftover from the company's departure, Lancaster was able to see from one end to the other. At least the length of a football field, and almost twice as wide, the building offered minimal protection from the chilly early evening air. Several small chutes and filtering devices hung from the open ceiling above, which gave the place a gymnasium feel.

Old offices lined one wall, along a second level, accessible by a flight of steps. Everything appeared untouched for years. Looking down at his pants, he saw gray film covering the sides from the bonded dust particles. Where he had been lying a moment earlier looked like someone had come and done a snow angel of sorts on the floor dust.

Getting out of the predicament without help looked hopeless. He had no tools, much less a handcuff key, and he wasn't near anything useful. Even the machine keeping him in place was large, blunt on all ends, and useless. The thought of firing it up quickly died when he found it unplugged from a locking ceiling outlet.

"Damn it."

Silence filled the air around him, but he wondered if he was in the same place where Toomey had slammed the trunk against his head. Surely the police had caught up to his cell phone's signal, and perhaps captured or shot the killer in the process.

"Help!" he decided to yell out. "I'm in here!"

No movement.

No sound.

No change.

For his trouble, Lancaster's head ached like someone had rung a bell directly over him.

In the movies, people dislocated their thumbs to get out of cuffs. Lancaster wasn't certain how that worked, or if he could stomach such pain. Of course he could, he decided.

His life depended on it.

First, he attempted to swing his hands around toward his feet to slip his bound hands in front of him. He caught the chain on one of his cowboy boot heels, but managed to slip it around, finding himself fiercely constricted by his restraints and his unyielding blue jeans. With his hands caught around his feet, he decided he didn't care if the crotch ripped at this point.

With one forceful yank forward, he brought his hands to his waistline, not harming his jeans one bit. He hopped and stepped awkwardly until he gained his footing, deciding to see if the machine offered any kind of assistance. While he didn't see anything useful on the outer edges, he moved inward, seeing several rusted blades still suspended in air. They looked ominous, like weapons of death frozen in time, waiting for someone to push the DVD play button to release their fury.

Considering they rested around the same level as his shoulders, Lancaster knew he couldn't muster enough force to even nick the cuff chains. He found a piece of scrap wire on the work area, snatching it up with his right hand, immediately setting to work on undoing one of the locks.

One time while eating breakfast outside of Phoenix he overheard a conversation between two rather seedy looking individuals about how easy it was to manipulate the locks of handcuffs with sturdy wires.

As he inserted the wire into the keyhole, Lancaster heard footsteps approach from the opposite end of the factory. Already knowing it was Toomey, he seated himself on the floor as though he hadn't heard, secretly working the lock with the wire.

When he finally looked up, he found Toomey holding a rather large survival knife. Silhouetted by the dim lights behind him, the man looked even more menacing as a shadow.

"The time is near," Toomey said, straightforward enough that he might be reporting to a commanding officer.

"Kid, there's no reason to do this."

Toomey knelt down before him, toying dangerously with the knife.

"And there's no reason why you had to let Kyle Wilson die. But you did."

"It was an accident. Why would you think anyone had anything to do with that?"

"Because his father hated him."

Lancaster felt stunned. He was talking to a brick wall that could talk back.

"What do you want from *me*?"

"I want you to know that Kyle didn't deserve to die. Y-You could have stopped his father from killing him, as much as you were at their f-farm. Why didn't you?"

He felt incapable of fathoming the complex levels of such a statement, mainly because it was untrue at its central argument. Lancaster had spent time around the Wilsons when he lived near them, but Frank Wilson was no monster, and the man certainly wouldn't have plotted to murder his own son.

Frank exhibited tough love and farm punishment, but he cared about the boy, even bragging about him sometimes.

"You're wrong," Lancaster said plainly. "Kyle was playing in the field that day. His father was away."

Something fell into place for Lancaster as he realized the true identity of the young man before him.

"You were that neighbor kid," he said slowly. "Where were *you* the day he died?"

"You s-shut up."

Lancaster suspected he was already marked for death, so he wanted to know the truth. If Toomey was mentally disturbed, perhaps unclear about the events of the day in question, he might reconsider his stance.

"Were you and Kyle playing by the junkyard that day? Even though Frank told you two not to?"

Toomey appeared enraged by the statement, his nostrils flaring. Being a cynical smart ass by nature, Lancaster decided to push the lad's buttons a bit harder.

"If I had been there, I would have stopped him from killing Kyle."

"Stopped who? Can you even picture it in your head?"

Lancaster treaded on dangerous ground, but he had little to lose at this point.

"You've killed eight people based on an assumption?" Lancaster asked, daring to sharpen his tone.

"You were the last conspirator," Toomey sneered.

"Conspirator? Now you think Kyle's death was planned? Get it right, kid."

Toomey turned away, cupping his temples as though tormented. Lancaster wondered if his plan might work, or if a knife might carve out his heart any second.

When Toomey turned around again, it was as though his resolve came from a conversation within his head that guaranteed him his assessment was correct.

"Frank Wilson killed his own son, and you let him do it. You and Bob Hagen knew about it, and you did nothing."

Clutching the knife, Toomey stepped toward the trucker ominously.

"Oh, shit."

✳   ✳   ✳   ✳

"Why didn't you want the SWAT team with us?" Hardegen questioned as he turned onto Sawmill Road.

"I didn't want them with us right away," Terry answered. "We might be able to wrap this up on our own, and I'm still not sure I'm right."

Hardegen pulled up to the front gate a few minutes later. Several strands of yellow police tape flapped in the breeze from each end of the gate. Someone had broken through the deserted police line, and though it might have been one of his colleagues, Terry had to know for certain.

"Let's stay out here," he told Hardegen.

Answering with little more than a nod, the deputy kept the car out of plain sight, then popped the trunk. Terry checked over his own firearm as Hardegen returned with a riot shotgun and several shells.

"We stay in visual contact at all times," Terry reiterated a statement he made while Hardegen drove them to the scene. "If you see anything, just signal me."

Hardegen nodded in compliance. He wasn't about to let Toomey jump him a second time, nor was he going to ignore orders from a more experienced officer. In Terry's estimation, the deputy was lucky to still be a participant on the task force.

And Lamoureux was lucky to be alive.

Within minutes the two officers, walking briskly on opposites sides of the street, had cleared the main drag of the former village. Each gave the deserted stores a quick glance, while looking down any alleys for new vehicles, or signs of life.

At the end of the street, Terry motioned for Hardegen to meet him around the back of the nearby church. Terry cleared his section, then they stepped inside the building for a quick search, which yielded no results.

"The school," Terry whispered, noticing some color leave the deputy's face. "Just follow my lead."

While he typically led the investigations that brought down the bad guys, Terry seldom conducted the arrests. He usually stepped aside and let a SWAT team do the work, or teamed with colleagues. Terry never considered himself the heroic or aggressive type, who had to be there to see closure.

He certainly remembered the procedures, but guys like Hardegen and Lamoureux thirsted for action, so he let them have the glory. Even they didn't pull off perfect busts every time, so he decided to take the bulk of the stress off Hardegen's shoulders by assuming command.

While somewhat uncomfortable taking the lead, Terry questioned the validity of his theory. He wanted to believe Toomey had nowhere else to go, but chances were if the man had thought ahead enough to abduct both Lancasters, he might have been resourceful enough to find another hiding place.

Terry peered through the hollow school windows before daring to step inside. Hardegen realized what he wanted, then checked the other windows, looking for any booby-traps or hazards. Terry saw him signal with a thumbs up before coming around the building.

Finding the police tape undisturbed around the crumbling school, Terry wondered if someone from the police department had simply come back to the scene. He navigated the stairs upward, as silently as possible, then pointed for Hardegen to look inside first. The deputy responded without hesitation, looking, then stepping onto the second floor.

"Nothing," he said just above a whisper, then stared down to the floor where he and Lamoureux had met with foul play.

"Come on," Terry insisted, not allowing the deputy time to wallow in the past.

A moment later they found themselves outside the school, with very little left to check, except for the large factory building in front of them. Terry now knew why the once flourishing town shut down suddenly, and mysteriously, some years prior.

Almost overnight the citizens, workers, and shop owners left the village without saying one word to anyone outside of their circle. A small stream on the opposite side of the factory had been used for waste dumping by factory management. Unfortunately, the waste ran down the stream, into a large pond that eventually contaminated the village's water supply.

The waste, examined by the federal government after an anonymous tip, was found to have various chemicals that proved highly dangerous to human beings and animals. Days later, the town was quarantined, then abandoned soon after. Though the factory ownership was ordered to pay fines, and cleanup costs, they escaped the penalties by filing bankruptcy and hiring a sleazy lawyer.

No one wanted to buy the land, now tied up in litigation, because of the costs involved with removing the contamination. So the government left the area fenced off from the rest of the world until the old village's fate was decided.

Terry stepped forward with Hardegen at his side, facing the building's narrow side, wanting to look down the sides of the building from the outside before entering. He signaled with a pointed finger for the deputy to check his side of the building. Hardegen moved to the corner, peered down his end, and found nothing, before signaling that fact to Terry.

Taking a look down his end, the investigator found a car parked near one of the side entrances, brown in color, with primer paint along select areas.

He motioned for Hardegen to quickly take his side, then pulled out his cell phone, finding Gaffney's name in the phone list with rehearsed quickness. Pushing the button, he waited only one ring before the sheriff answered.

"Gaffney."

"Paul, I was right. Bring the whole dog pound with you."

"You got it."

A disgusted scream came from inside the building, changing what little plan Terry had devised in an instant.

"Gotta go, Paul."

Terry clipped the phone to his belt, drawing his sidearm as Hardegen held the shotgun in a very ready position.

"Carefully," Terry warned him. "Take to that side wall, and I'll go this way. Don't do anything without me signaling you first."

Hardegen nodded, then both men entered the factory, having a long, dangerous walk ahead of them in near dark conditions.

CHAPTER 45

▼

Lancaster couldn't believe it when his captor unzipped his pants, then proceeded to urinate on him. He yelped once or twice when the warm shower splashed across his face, then dribbled down his body.

Toomey had used the knife as an intimidation tactic, temporarily setting it down to carry out this next phase in his plan.

"How does it feel?" he asked the trucker.

"I'll gladly return the favor if you want to know."

Toomey smacked him across the face for the insult.

"Kyle didn't think it was funny when he was shoved into that trash pit."

"Then why did you shove him in?"

Another blow across the face, this one harder.

Lancaster grunted, still trying to undo the locking mechanism with the machine wire as he fell to the ground, acting more injured than he actually felt. He heard the survival knife scrape the ground as Toomey scooped it up for whatever purpose he had in mind.

"It's time for you to pay," Toomey said with false assurance that his assessment was correct.

He wanted to end Lancaster's life before doubts crept into his thoughts again.

"You don't have to do this," the trucker said, trying to back away from the young man. "Kyle wouldn't want you to hurt anyone."

Toomey showed his teeth like a rabid dog.

"He didn't ask for you and his father to plan his murder."

"And we *didn't*. Where were you that day? Why was Kyle playing by himself?"

"Because you and his father didn't want me around."

"You were an orphan," Lancaster said, still backing away, his words flying nervously from his lips. "No one wanted you, because you were a bad influence."

Toomey toyed with the knife, giving a silent warning.

"You probably showed Kyle that pile of junk, didn't you?"

"There's no denying your sins."

"And there's no running from your past. Killing me won't change what you've done."

"No, but I'll feel better."

Toomey stepped forward, causing Lancaster to backpedal from him until the machine stopped his egress. Literally backed into a corner, he couldn't talk his way out of an assault, and his defensive tactics were limited by the bindings around his hands and feet.

As Toomey lifted the knife to swing downward, Lancaster kicked out, striking the younger man in the knee, knocking him over. Keeping Toomey at bay was his best defense, because he lacked the ability to grapple for the knife if it came loose.

A whiff of the urine reached his nostrils as Toomey stabbed at him again. Lancaster deflected the knife with decent timing and a swing of his bound hands, but Toomey immediately scrambled after him again.

Lancaster engaged him in a struggle that placed the knife directly between them, ready to split the flesh of whomever it took aim at first. By managing to clasp Toomey's hands, the trucker kept the knife away from him, but his leverage began to dwindle.

"Freeze!" he heard someone yell, causing Toomey to grip the knife and slide behind him, pressing the blade against his throat.

Lancaster saw two men emerge from the shadows of the long ends of the building, stepping into the weak centralized light. They held firearms, so he hoped they were police officers there on his behalf.

"Let him go, Toomey," the dark-haired man holding a semi-automatic said.

He wore a shirt, tie, and slacks, indicating his position. Lancaster recognized his voice as that of Investigator Terry Levine.

Toomey said nothing, simply pressing the blade against Lancaster's throat enough that it drew a thin line of blood. Now confronted with the choice of slitting his victim's throat and running for it, or simply attempting an escape ran through his mind. The difference meant the chance for a clean escape versus being shot in the back.

Instead of doing either, he stood up, pressing himself and the blade against Lancaster, dragging him back, away from the officers. He cut the leash, freeing Lancaster from the machine, though involving him in greater danger.

Both officers followed, cautiously keeping their distance, guns at ready positions.

"You can't get away," Terry said to Toomey. "Give up and make it easy on yourself."

Seconds passed, then what seemed like minutes, until Toomey drew Lancaster with him toward a back entrance. A regular door, already open, offered him an escape to the outdoors, and Lancaster knew the moment of truth was upon him.

"Shoot him," he requested of the officers.

"Stop, Toomey," Terry said sternly. "This is your last chance."

Lancaster felt the knife move from his throat altogether after the words. He suspected Toomey was ready to retreat, but turned his body in case a different kind of attack came. As he spun away, the knife plunged awkwardly, thrusting into his side, rather than lodging itself in his abdomen. He clutched the new wound as best he could, then fell to the floor as Toomey disappeared through the door.

"After him," Terry ordered Hardegen, who darted outside with the shotgun.

Terry knelt beside Lancaster.

"How bad is it?"

"Bad enough to hurt."

Terry removed his tie, bundling it into a makeshift bandage as he put pressure on the wound. He looked toward the back door with concern in his blue eyes.

"I hope he blows that mother fucker away," Lancaster said.

Instead of replying, Terry simply kept pressure on the wound with his left hand, staring at the door. His right hand remained poised to clutch his firearm at a second's notice.

*   *   *   *

Hardegen immediately regretted stepping outside alone, without a light source, the moment he did so. A full moon provided shadowy light, along with several working lamps inside the compound.

The sound of trickling water reached the deputy's ears as he stepped forward, crunching leaves as he did so. He stopped completely, listening for any sounds of Toomey moving.

Hearing nothing, he began to wonder if the man had set a trap for him. Possibly lying in wait for the deputy, Toomey needed only rid himself of one adversary to make a clean escape, or return inside to fulfil his twisted fantasy.

Hardegen wasn't letting that happen.

Seconds passed, then leaves crunched behind him. Whirling around, the deputy planned to use the shotgun as a clubbing weapon, but it missed a ducking target. Toomey rammed the knife upward, but the deputy caught the blade with the butt of his shotgun, dislodging both weapons from their hands.

Not wasting a second, the deputy lit into Toomey with two consecutive punches, bloodying the man's face. Refusing to give up, Toomey locked horns with Hardegen as the two wrestled one another to the ground, exchanging punches and kicks. Still grappling, the two rolled down the hill until Hardegen's back struck a tree.

He grunted in pain, throwing Toomey away from him. Going for his sidearm, Hardegen was stopped as Toomey realized his plan, then jumped on him knee-first. The deputy struck his face again, then attempted separation once more, but Toomey wasn't about to disappear until his terms were reached.

Hardegen managed to stand, throwing Toomey against a tree in the process. The ground felt slick to the deputy, mainly because grass and vegetation didn't seem to grow anywhere nearby. Trees stood simply out of habit, threatening to break apart at their roots if the two guests smashed into them hard enough.

Toomey snagged a nearby branch from the ground, lashing it across the deputy's face. It felt as solid as a fist, and though Hardegen dropped to his knees, he didn't lose consciousness. Toomey swung the thick wood again, but the deputy deflected it, tackling his adversary to the ground immediately.

Another branch struck Hardegen upside the head as he tried to pin the killer down to unleash more punishment. To go for his gun at the moment felt risky to the deputy. With the shotgun and knife up the hill, he simply had to chance hand-to-hand combat until the opportunity to use a weapon presented itself.

He couldn't count on Terry to help him, especially if Lancaster's wound was deep. Unwilling to let his personal feelings interfere with good judgment, Hardegen decided to end the skirmish sooner than later. He threw a punch that connected with Toomey's nose, then kicked him further down the hill.

Toomey tumbled end over end, stopping himself by clasping a small, deteriorated tree. He stood up, his head and eyes looking upward to meet the deputy's. Hardegen had already drawn his sidearm, though he couldn't find a good firing position, particularly down a slope.

Assuming a tripod position on his knee would likely send him tumbling downward because he couldn't find good footing on the slimy ground. The second Toomey saw him armed, he started backing down the hill, ready to run at any moment. Hardegen leaned against the tree for stability, but as he fired at the man's torso, the tree gave way and snapped, causing his shot to sail upward.

Toomey reacted with a heavy flinch in his left shoulder, then fell back, rolling down the hill uncontrollably until a splashing sound reached the deputy's ears. Despite barely being able to see, the deputy darted down the hill, between tree silhouettes, until he reached a small, but powerful stream that now carried Toomey toward an unknown destination.

Slowly, the deputy holstered his sidearm.

Hardegen stood still momentarily, catching his breath as he watched an object float downstream with the current. Though details were absent, he knew the stream had taken the killer to freedom, but he wondered what kind of damage the bullet inflicted on Toomey's body. In the darkness, Hardegen never saw where he hit the man, but he doubted the shot was fatal, despite striking him in the torso.

Still, Toomey never made a sound.

Not even a grunt of pain.

Hardegen finally turned, trudging up the hill to check on Terry and Lancaster.

Sirens echoed in the distance, letting him know Gaffney had indeed sent the task force brigade to assist. The officers probably expected to find a standoff of some sort, but they were going to be part of a search team.

When he reached the area where Toomey had flinched, the deputy knelt down, finding large blood droplets on the ground, glistening in the moonlight. He swiped some of the blood from a fallen leaf, examining it to make certain it was real.

He exhaled through his nose, then stood to complete the uphill journey.

CHAPTER 46

▼

Within an hour the ghost town of New Alden looked alive once more. All of its lights were turned on, while additional lighting from the SWAT vehicles and local fire department were used to help search for Toomey.

Lancaster was transported quickly, demanding a bath as soon as the gash along his stomach was mended. The medics informed Terry and Hardegen that the wound didn't look terribly deep, and the fact that the trucker was able to yell and cuss seemed to be a good sign.

He had asked to see his son, and Gaffney relayed the location of his son to the medics, so they could share the same medical center.

"Toomey almost finished it," Terry said, standing next to Hardegen just outside the factory.

Below them, divers braved the toxic pond that adjoined the running stream. Mammoth floodlights guided their every move, while several boats helped them fish the waters in the hopes of finding Toomey dead. Decontamination showers from the local Hazmat team awaited them when they completed their task.

"He might be out there, still ready to finish it," Hardegen said pessimistically.

"This whole town is up and running again because of him."

"I hope he has to look up from hell to see it."

Based on the deputy's description of what happened, Terry wasn't convinced Toomey had expired. Hardegen hadn't seemed very confident that his shot proved fatal.

"He wouldn't give us the satisfaction of seeing him washed up like a dead animal, would he?" the deputy asked no one in particular.

Terry said nothing to the comment, simply watching the divers fall back from the boats, into the water. Others occasionally surfaced to report they had found nothing below. Terry suspected the pond wasn't terribly deep, particularly since the factory had quit using it over a decade prior.

Its reach, however, took the fence line out much further than the rest of the town required. It still haunted Terry that a town could simply be abandoned and forgotten so easily, the buildings remaining as a living history of sorts. If not for carelessness and negligence, New Alden might have been on every freshly printed atlas, with its population and coordinates listed in the back.

"There is a real danger if he's alive," Terry commented, trying to avoid alarming the deputy.

"What?"

"Lancaster and his son will be protected until we know Toomey is caught or dead. If he *isn't* found, he may turn his attention to the person responsible for keeping him from his goal."

Hardegen said nothing, simply staring at the pond.

"You trying to scare me?"

"No. I'm giving you an honest assessment."

"I thought you determined he was a sociopath."

"He's complex, John, and diseased in the mind. Reality and fantasy are one and the same for him, and his take on anyone he encounters can be altered by almost any stimuli."

Hardegen continued to stare downward, as though hoping at any moment a diver might surface with a thumbs up signal.

"I can't live the rest of my life looking over my shoulder."

"Don't. But just be aware of the danger until he's caught. He won't come after me, because I'm unattainable, and I didn't shoot him. For all we know, he may put you in allegiance with Hagen, Wilson, and Lancaster."

Gaffney walked over to them. He had been fending off the media hounds for the better part of the last fifteen minutes. His experience allowed him to coordinate a full search of the grounds in case Toomey had escaped on foot. The town, the pond, and the surrounding woods were being meticulously searched by four different agencies.

"What's the good word?"

"Terry here was trying to cheer me up by saying Toomey will make an attempt on my life."

Gaffney put his hand on the deputy's shoulder.

"Son, I've learned to put a lot of stock in what Trooper Levine says, but there's still a chance we'll find him at the bottom of that pond."

"I don't think so," Hardegen said, honestly assessing the situation with fading hope.

The sheriff turned to Terry.

"This is supposed to be the part where we pat each other on the back and wish each other luck in the future."

"I wish it were that simple."

"I've talked to the hospital staff," Gaffney reported. "They're going to keep father and son together, and I'm going to assign someone to be with them at all times until this is sorted out."

"What about long-term protection?"

"I've considered that. We'll cross that bridge when we come to it."

Terry wasn't certain if the task force had a future or not. He had taken time to call Murphy and thank the agent for his help. With Toomey a potential fugitive, any kind of coalition was overkill, now that the facts were all public.

For the investigator, the case was over, whether he had a formal parting with the task force or not. He planned to head home in the morning, ready to see his wife and three children.

Before doing so, however, he planned to visit Lamoureux again. Terry found it somewhat ironic that his friend called him down for an expert opinion, then suffered the consequences of getting too close to his own target.

He considered asking Gaffney about his friend's condition, but the sheriff had been too busy to check.

"You heading home soon?" Gaffney asked.

"Probably in the morning. I've got a wife who's about ready to disown me."

Gaffney understood. Anyone in politics who still had a marriage knew the intricacies of making it work in public and private.

The sheriff drew Terry aside, intentionally away from Hardegen.

"Were you just kidding with him about Toomey coming after him?"

"I don't kid about something like that. If you hide Lancaster, which you should, it seems the next logical step."

"This is all assuming Toomey survives."

Terry methodically turned to look at the pond below them.

"I don't see your divers coming up with anything from a stagnant body of water."

Gaffney's hopes visually deflated.

Realistically, any search in non-flowing water should have produced almost immediate results, and he knew it.

"Why John? Why not one of us?"

"We were faces in the paper, or on the TV, Paul. He confronted John twice, and the first time he granted him mercy for some reason. I can't guarantee I'm right, but it's my hunch based on everything I've seen, and your next logical steps. Plus he stole John's wallet, so he has a personal connection, sick as that may sound."

Hardegen turned around from the pond.

"If you two are going to talk about me, please include me."

"You know what we're talking about, so just be ready to protect yourself."

"I can reassign him," Gaffney thought aloud.

"No," Terry said, much to the deputy's relief. "John is going to have to be ready to take care of himself. And you'll have to tell Jamie, maybe not in so many words, but you can't leave her in the dark."

Everyone stood silently a moment.

"If he's in the woods, we'll find him," Gaffney said with newfound confidence. "The dogs will sniff him out."

Terry didn't feel so reassured. Toomey had a head start, and if he managed to stop the bleeding, he wouldn't leave much of a trail. The highway wasn't far off, and there the killer could find a plethora of vehicles and escape routes.

"Just the same, if Toomey isn't found, I'd tell everyone involved in this thing to watch their backs," Terry said.

He hated to spread pessimism on what should have been grounds for celebration, but Toomey had proven to be far more resourceful and vengeful than any typical criminal. Nothing short of the man's death could provide closure for the investigator. He suspected Toomey, given the right defender, might evade true punishment through some kind of mental incompetency loophole.

With several loose ends to clean up before he left, Terry shook hands with the sheriff, then Hardegen.

"It's been a pleasure," Gaffney said.

"Likewise, Sheriff. I hope you find him."

He turned to Hardegen.

"Don't live stepping on eggshells, but be careful, John. Maybe they'll find him dead in the woods, and you won't have any worries."

"Maybe," Hardegen said doubtfully.

Terry felt terrible as he left the two men behind to pick up the pieces of the investigation. Even worse, Hardegen seemed downright distraught at the thought of Toomey targeting him or his family. Terry had an obligation to warn the deputy of what he considered a major threat. If anything happened to Hardegen without him saying one word of warning, he never could have lived with himself.

Despite mixed feelings of anxiety and the thrill of the chase lingering in the air, Terry envisioned himself being home in time to hug his three children after spending the day with his wife. He wondered if Sherri might take the day off work when he called her with the news.

But first he needed to visit an old friend.

After that, he planned to complete any necessary paperwork, speak with the barracks commander, then say some goodbyes.

He found Megan, who had been searching the town with the others, then asked her for a ride.

"Where to?" she asked.

"To see your boss."

She hadn't taken Lamoureux's assault very well, though she had visited him. Terry had several things he wanted to tell her, including a great deal of thanks for her assistance. She possessed the tools necessary to become a solid investigator, but she needed some encouragement that Lamoureux was sometimes too busy to give.

While the VCIT leader was a great investigator in his own right, he was admittedly not the greatest mentor to his people.

Do as I do, not as I say, seemed to be his motto, since he led by actions and not words.

As long as his people paid attention, Lamoureux's style made him a phenomenal teacher.

Terry climbed into the passenger seat of Megan's car, watching the floodlights and neglected buildings pass by. When the old department store window came into view, he spied the mannequins in their poses. He wondered if Toomey had identified with them in some way, perhaps even giving them identities to make up for the losses in his own life.

"We got some information," Megan said, keeping her eyes on the road.

"Oh?"

"Not that it much matters now, but the DNA recovered from the sheep's anus belonged to Frank Wilson, like we figured. It got lost in the shuffle with everything that's happened the past few days."

"I guess that means it wasn't *all* in his head."

"Does that make him any less guilty?"

"No," Terry said thoughtfully, "unless you count him not guilty by reason of insanity."

Folding his arms, Terry tried to put Eric Toomey out of his mind. The young man was no longer his problem, and if things went well, the forest animals might make a meal of him.

CHAPTER 47

▼

One Month Later

Hardegen couldn't believe almost a foot of snow had fallen in the past two days. Following a tradition started by his father, he changed out of his good clothes after Sunday church services before taking his truck out in search of a nice Christmas tree.

One of his neighbors allowed him to pick a tree on his property, because the man planted dozens of new trees every spring. Since no one in his family had acquired allergies, Hardegen kept buying or chopping down real trees. To him, artificial trees didn't compare, because they lacked a pleasant scent, and possessed no individual traits that made for good holiday memories.

It took nearly half an hour to choose the right tree in the cold and wind, with snow blowing in his face no matter which direction he turned. Using an axe, like his father before him, Hardegen chopped down a nice Balsam Fir that required a lengthy drag to the truck.

Within a few years he planned on bringing his son along, to start the tradition anew.

Luckily the snow made the task of dragging the tree fairly easy. He didn't get slowed in his steps, and the branches glided easily along the fluffy white substance.

He put his axe in the truck bed, then pulled the tree inside, careful not to snap too many of the branches, or fold them into damaging positions. The old truck was given to him by his father a few years prior. Though bulky and a gas hog, it did the job. Rust spots now resided in the tailgate, doors, and parts of the fenders.

Hardegen planned to drive the thing around his property until it fell apart. He wasn't supposed to use the county car, now repaired and freshly painted, for recreational use, though he occasionally did. This particular chore required a larger vehicle anyhow.

This was one of the few times he left Jamie and the kids during the past month when he wasn't at work. He had informed her of the danger in such a way that she wasn't paranoid every waking second of every day. In fact, she seemed much happier with him home more often.

Teaching her some basic self-defense and gun use made him feel better about the times he couldn't be home.

Toomey was never found after an extensive search of the pond and the grounds in and around New Alden. That didn't necessarily mean he was still alive, roaming the country or state in search of victims.

But it didn't mean he wasn't, either.

Hardegen peered around his truck, then inside the cab before opening the door. He exercised much more caution than before, no matter where he went, or how many people accompanied him.

Lamoureux began rehabilitation on his legs, regaining more of his mobility over the passing weeks. While he remained optimistic he would someday return to active duty, doctors provided a mixed bag of opinions.

Gaffney put a positive spin on Toomey's escape, involving the public whole-heartedly in the search for him. The sheriff provided every shred of possible infor-mation about the man, including photographs, his habits, and what types of places he might frequent.

If Toomey remained in New York and went anywhere near a public place, he was going to be reported. That fact alone lessened Hardegen's fears, but he also knew Toomey was no social butterfly.

Before the election, Gaffney ordered his deputies to patrol the New Alden area, just in case Toomey returned home. They checked the property at least once during every shift, and never alone per the sheriff's orders. Gaffney won the elec-tion in a landslide over a retired small town police chief.

For the most part, Hardegen's life felt normal again. He returned to work with the drug task force, though he thought about putting in for a road job, which allowed for freedom to check on his family more often.

Driving home through the thick snow, he discovered the old truck didn't clear away the windshield like his patrol car, but it stayed on the road with ease. County trucks didn't always plow the roads in a hurry, partly because there were too many back roads to handle at one time.

Luckily Hardegen didn't have far to drive.

He pulled into his driveway, and despite being late morning, it looked like dusk setting on his home. Several lights inside shone brightly through the falling snow as he pulled the truck into the driveway, which he had spent part of the morning shoveling before church.

Stepping out of the truck, he put down the tailgate, then dragged the tree toward the back porch, looking to the windows. He saw no sign of the kids, or Jamie, which made him uneasy. Though the kids were young, he expected his wife to bring them to the window for a surprise as big as a Christmas tree.

Leaving the tree just short of the back porch landing, he stepped up, finding prints in the snowdrifts that had blown onto the wood floor. Hardegen knew they were too fresh to be his own prints, and he doubted even his wife could leave such wide marks in the snow. He cautiously looked through the back window, finding none of his family within the kitchen or living room.

He quietly turned the doorknob, letting his mind think the worst as he had the past month. Terry Levine's words stuck with him like the copy of the Lord's Prayer posted above his bed on a porcelain plate. Stepping into the kitchen, he looked to the ground, then into the living room. Nothing appeared disturbed, including the door and frame behind him.

"Jamie?" he called.

No answer.

"I'm home."

With heightened senses he stepped trepidly toward the living room, fearing what he might see beyond the safety of his kitchen. When he made his way into the living room, the deputy's worst fear was realized.

Holding a knife to Jamie's throat, Toomey had an almost crazed look in his eyes that came from living outside of society, hiding in the shadows, for a month. Hardegen's eyes darted in search of the kids. Not finding them, he assumed they were safe, or his wife would be hysterical.

Ever since Terry Levine warned him, Hardegen had run scenarios through his mind of what might happen. At work, at home, with or without the kids around, involving Jamie or coworkers, or just him by himself, Hardegen had envisioned it all.

"We can talk this over," he said to Toomey. "You want *me*, so just let my wife go and we'll settle our differences."

Toomey flashed a smile, though it was far from sincere.

It looked more insane than anything Hardegen had ever laid eyes upon.

Over the past few months, the deputy had rehearsed several tactics with Jamie, including the very predicament they found themselves in at the moment. His right hand inched toward the gun tucked into his backside, where it had resided the past month whenever he wasn't on duty.

His bed covers and pillow had indentations from the gun's usual spot while he slept.

"Your aim was a bit off," Toomey said, his eyes glancing toward his left shoulder, exactly where he flinched when the bullet ripped through his flesh.

"Just tell me what you want," Hardegen said, genuinely nervous about the knife to Jamie's throat.

Rehearsing for a hostage situation hadn't prepared him for the real thing, despite his police training.

"I want to ram this knife between your ribs until you tell me where to find Lancaster."

Hardegen couldn't fake his way out of the situation with an absurd answer, so his mind raced for the appropriate response.

"I'll do whatever you want. Just let my wife go."

Toomey replied by pressing the blade even closer to Jamie's throat. She held up well, her eyes waiting for a signal from her husband.

Hardegen simply needed an opening. Talking to Toomey might create the slightest release of tension against his wife's jugular. Jamie knew what to do if Hardegen signaled her, and she trusted him implicitly.

Hardegen's right hand rested near his hip, ready to draw the gun when the moment came.

"I can write down his location," Hardegen said, knowing Toomey didn't plan on leaving any witnesses at this point.

If he indeed had a chance to kill Lancaster, he wasn't going to risk anyone ruining the surprise by contacting the authorities. No matter what, Hardegen had to stop him here and now.

"Bring him here," Toomey insisted, surprising the deputy. "I kill him, and all of you can live."

Hardegen still didn't believe him, but he reached for his cellular phone on the counter.

"I have to get the number from my dispatchers," he said, watching Toomey's grip on the knife loosen as his knuckles moved from their numbed, set position.

Jamie sensed it too, dropping down as she protected her throat with raised hands, kicking Toomey in the shin as he prepared to slash down upon her. Hardegen had already drawn the gun, firing two shots directly into the killer's chest when his wife fell clear.

Toomey dropped limply to the floor as Hardegen rushed to his wife's side.

"Are you hurt?" he asked.

"No."

"The kids?"

"They're in back. He didn't touch them."

Hardegen stood over the body of Toomey. The man's eyes remained half-open, as though surprised his plan fell apart so easily, struggling to live long enough to see it through. The two bullets entered his heart, making certain he didn't live long enough to contemplate death, much less deal it out.

He wanted to say something witty, but appropriate words escaped Hardegen. Taking the cordless phone from the wall, he dialed 911, then sat on the floor with his wife, wrapping his free arm around her. Drawing her close, he kissed her forehead before the dispatcher picked up the phone.

At last the ordeal had closure, and he had Terry Levine's insight to thank for his family remaining safe.

Jamie remained strong, not crying or even talking, as though she had prepared herself for such a situation, like her husband. Hardegen wanted to check on the kids, but they weren't crying, so he stayed with his wife as dispatchers answered his call.

He felt awkward, calling in an emergency call rather than responding to one.

A dispatcher answered the phone as Jamie stood to check on the children. Spilling information to a familiar dispatcher faster than she probably wanted to receive it, Hardegen stared out the window at the falling snow. During his narration, the deputy decided to make more time for the things that mattered in life.

Waves of relief fell over him because his family could celebrate the holiday season without a sense of dread looming over them. He wondered if Gaffney might expedite a request for him to return to road duty when he requested it.

After he received the news of Toomey's death, the sheriff would probably honor any request within reason. Hardegen grinned to himself, planning to make a trip to Buffalo the next morning.

Only after spending some much needed time with his family to make amends.

978-0-595-47040-2
0-595-47040-8

CPSIA information can be obtained at www.ICGtesting.com
Printed in the USA

267021BV00002B/29/A